A BETTER
MAN

A Novel

LAURA MERCHANT

A BETTER MAN

Quantity sales and special discounts are available on quantity purchases by corporations, associations, and others. For details, contact the publisher at the address above.

Orders by U.S. trade bookstores and wholesalers. Email info@ BeyondPublishing.net

The Beyond Publishing Speakers Bureau can bring authors to your live event. For more information or to book an event contact the Beyond Publishing Speakers Bureau speak@BeyondPublishing.net

The Author can be reached directly at BeyondPublishing.net

Manufactured and printed in the United States of America distributed globally by BeyondPublishing.net

BEYOND
PUBLISHING

New York | Los Angeles | London | Sydney

ISBN Hardcover: 978-1-63792-601-7
ISBN Softcover: 978-1-63792-598-0

Dedicated to my students,
who make me better each and every day.

ACKNOWLEDGMENTS

Clark Ackerman

Chance & Jessie Adams

Michael & Mark Alger

Jasmine Ajamian

Anonymous

Ryan Baker

Nizar & Munira Bhulani

Clint & Aryn Calhoun

Jerry & Diane Cassel

Jerry & Nancy Cecco

Matthew & Kelli Chadwick

Francesca Cisneros

Brandon Cooley

Melinda Cotton

Christopher & Lauren Crites

Morgan Davis

Traci Duff

Jared Duncan

Adam & Leah Dyer

Debbie Eller

Elaine Erback

Rachel Gallegos

Dr. Bennett & Diane Gardner

Lauren Gill

Jersey & Taylor Goldman

Madyson Greenwood

Rusty Harding

Greg Harris

Michelle Hendrickson

Ann Henkels

Eddy & Melody Herring

Brian Hoffman

Quita Hughes

Jake & Kim Jackson

Joyce Jackson

Christopher Johnson

Cody & Lashenda Justice

Stan & Mary Carol Kelly

Fayzan & Kiran Keshwani

Chase & Jennifer Kimbrough

Eddy & Denise Kimbrough

Stephen Lester

Lesli Lord

Levi & Lynsee Mahan

Jason McCollough

Holly Martin

Diana Mays

Stephen Meador

John & Devonna Menard

West Meyers

Larry Miller

Anthony & Lori Montiel

Alex Mundo

Trish Myers

Kim Oliver

Tammy Partanen Palomino

Christopher Parrish

Cylinda Pearce

Chris & Amanda Phillips

Greg & Michelle Potts

Michael Riggs

Stephan Roberts

Ryan Roodenburg

Allan Schroeder

Royce & Janice Shields

Dr. Beatriz & Mr. Joshua Springer

James & DeeDee Stenstrom

Tom & Sheri Taylor

Ellie Trotter

Jason Valleau

Julie Vicars

Katelyn Walker

Abby Weeden

Greg & Magean Whaley

David Willie

PROLOGUE

October 1880

"Please, I didn't do this!"

A young inmate stood wringing his hands in the crude frontier jailhouse. Like all the buildings in town, the jail lacked sophistication and structural integrity. Upon his arrest, the teenager thought the modest property to be condemned and that, at any moment, it would be swept away with the wind. The singular cell wasn't much of a holding area, more like a box standing six by eight feet, constructed from rigid walls, precast steel, and a dirt-covered floor. The boy bent his knees to alleviate his legs, which were numb from prolonged standing. God only knew what had been on that floor. He didn't even have a chair or a wooden bench to sit down on. Still, he was relieved to be in an actual building and not tied to a tree or confined in some hole in the ground underneath the jailer's house. The boy had heard of such things and knew the stories of prisoners being treated like animals.

He wiped beads of sweat from his troubled brow. Yes, the boy was worried, but it was also humid. The sun had set hours ago, and the sticky-wet Texas heat now adequately filled the space. He would've given anything for a cool breeze to whisper through the tiny, barred window above his head!

What was the point of that window?

To air out the room or to deflate any person's hope of escape?

He had cooperated with the Sheriff and spent hours patiently waiting for answers, trying to understand how anyone could believe *he* was to blame for the foreman's death. The boy had never been convicted of a crime before. He'd never been in *any* kind of trouble with the law.

Surely this was a mistake!

"I know everyone must say that, but you have to believe me!"

The short, middle-aged boulder of a man responsible for the boy's incarceration rocked in his desk chair. Miraculously, the furniture hadn't given way beneath the Sheriff's massive weight. "Son, a man is dead, and a lot of people are angry."

"I know, but I didn't—it wasn't me!"

"That may be, but you might still swing for it."

The boy searched his inner arsenal, shielding his fear and selecting wisdom instead. There were rules to these proceedings. He would respectfully remind the Sheriff of that.

"What about a trial? Don't I get one?"

"You got a lawyer?"

"No, sir."

"You got the money to get a lawyer?"

"No, sir," the boy replied again.

He didn't need a lawyer. He was innocent!

"Well, how much money *do* you have?"

An opportunity presented itself. The boy knew of the corruption that often occurred between those with financial stability and those in positions of power. Everything had a price.

"I don't have any money," he lamented.

The truth was that while he had taken any and all work available, the boy was unable to acquire affordable lodging. For weeks, he resolved to sleep outside or squat in unattended barns overnight. He had no plan for how he'd survive the winter, choosing to take each day with stride.

He would have been thankful for the jail's shelter if he weren't taken into custody.

"Then I don't know what to tell you," the Sheriff said indifferently.

The boy closely examined his cell door. All that stood between him and freedom was man-made metal, a couple of hinges, and a keyhole. How a simple construction could rob a man of his liberty seemed immoral. He wrapped his fingers around the iron bars that encircled him and pressed, ensuring they wouldn't close in, as he was beginning to suspect. He took a deep breath. He wouldn't yell or beg; he'd look the Sheriff in the eye and talk to him like a man—the way his father taught him.

"I could pay you—*later*. I'd be in your debt."

The Sheriff leaned across the desk, his pudgy midsection protruding below the wooden drawers. He clicked his tongue.

"Are you attempting to bribe an officer of the law?"

With a sigh, the boy pressed his head against the cell door.

"No, sir. You made it sound like you'd take a bribe."

The Sheriff jumped from his seat and crossed to face the inmate, offended. Sweaty droplets sprinkled the floor with each hefty step. He retrieved a handkerchief and wiped the top of his bald head, sweeping down to catch any remaining dribble from his layered chins. "I take my job very seriously, kid. Part of my job is to observe. You're twisting my words around, and that's just the kind of manipulative, corrupt behavior one expects from a guilty party. I'm sure Judge Jenkins would agree once he finds out—if it comes to that."

The boy's brave face broke.

"But you can't do that! It isn't right!"

The official provided a near-toothless grin. "Take a look at the badge. It says, 'Sheriff,' which means I can do whatever I want."

The boy backed away from the bars and crouched in the corner, unable to wrap his mind around the injustice. He always believed that others would be good to him if he were good to others. He had obliged the Sheriff and respected his authority.

It's not fair.

The boy didn't know how he would ever convince someone of his innocence. He only knew that he didn't want to die. The wheels in his mind spun with fast and furious fear until he finally fell asleep.

It was still dark outside when the boy began to stir. He had the eerie feeling that he was being watched, and indeed he was. Two men stood on the other side of his cell. They were both dressed impeccably and while he knew it hardly mattered, the boy suddenly became aware of his own filthy, tattered attire. He quickly dusted himself off and rose to formally greet his visitors.

"Are you my lawyer?" he asked.

"No, son, I'm your savior. My name is Vernon Ashley. This is my nephew, Julian."

The boy stuck his hand through the bars to offer a handshake, which neither guest accepted. "Hello. I'm—"

"—We know who you are," Vernon stated.

"You *do*?"

"The entire town's talking about you," Vernon continued. "The way you threatened that man and then murdered him in such a grizzly fashion! *Very messy.*"

"I didn't! I mean, he was my boss, and I *threatened* him, but I didn't *kill* him!"

"We know," said Julian.

"*How?*"

"We've been watching you for a while." Vernon's voice echoed a preacher's, strong and bold. The veins along his temples would bulge and throb with each deliberate articulation. The forty-something savior was clean-shaven, with a full head of ivory-white hair and violet-blue eyes. His build suggested he was an average man—forgettable, even—in every way one could imagine, but his voice would either influence you or haunt you if you listened. He stared the boy down as if he were about to consume him.

"He's fat," mocked Julian.

"It's *muscle* from all that manual labor," Vernon replied. "And *you* could afford to build some!"

Julian frowned. "He doesn't look anything like me."

"He's the closest we've seen, and I imagine the closest we'll find."

The boy was unsure of what the duo meant by their quarreling or why the way he looked was so important to them.

"How old are you, son?" inquired Vernon.

"I just turned eighteen."

"Eighteen? *Uncle!*"

Julian was twenty and had already surpassed his adolescent transformation. A leading man towering at six feet with physical attributes serving as evidence of virility and strong genes, Julian held broad shoulders and a lean, athletic physique. The inmate shared the same mild skin tone as Julian and the same dark, shiny hair, which emphasized his facial features: the same thick eyebrows, the same straight-edged nose with a well-proportioned tip that was neither too large nor too small, the same blue, almond-shaped eyes, and the same full, symmetrical lips.

The most significant difference between them was that the inmate appeared juvenile, fresh-faced, and pure. Innocent. He was still an emerging adult, a skipper navigating the waters of self-discovery. Julian's face was more finely developed, displaying a rough yet magnetic beauty. He was experienced, confident, and understood how the world worked. Julian's gaze would slice you in half, and you could sharpen a knife on his cheekbones.

"He might be a few years younger, Julian, but as you both mature, that will even out, I think," Vernon offered.

"You *think?*"

"We can make it work!"

The boy quickly took inventory of his surroundings. Something—no, *someone*—was missing. "Where's the Sheriff?"

"Oh, we thought he could use a little break, so we gave it to him."

With a shit-eating grin, Julian stepped aside to reveal the Sheriff, who was bloodied, bound, and gagged, struggling in the corner behind them. The boy then noticed that the prison-house's main door had been blocked, barricaded from the inside. No one was entering or exiting without its removal.

"Have you got a sweetheart?" asked Vernon.

The boy cleared his throat in an attempt to remain calm. "No, sir."

"Of course not," Julian scoffed.

The inmate's brows furrowed in response.

"What about family?" Vernon continued.

The boy lowered his head. "I—I did, but not anymore."

"No parents?"

"They passed. My brother and I came here about six weeks back to find work, but now it's just me."

Julian snickered, "Tragic."

The boy bit his tongue and clenched his fists. It had been some time since he'd been in a brawl, and although he was younger, he was certain he could show Julian *tragedy* if he ever got out of that cell. Vernon began to pace in front of him.

"No job, no family, and no sweetheart… That's not much of a life if you ask me. Now you're here, and you're wanted for murder. You're in a pretty bad way, son."

"I know," said the boy.

Vernon shook his head and sighed. "You'll swing, for sure."

The boy once again clung to the steel bars. "No! C-can you help me? Please!"

"That depends," Vernon replied. "Can you help me?"

"I can try. What do you need?"

"I have a job vacancy that needs to be filled. You'd start immediately."

"What exactly would I be doing?" asked the boy, searching for clarity.

Smiling, Vernon answered, "You'd be an apprentice…of sorts."

The boy considered the offer. "That doesn't sound so bad…"

"He's like a monkey in a cage, Uncle." While Julian refrained from contributing to Vernon's sales pitch, he couldn't help but point out another person's misfortune.

"I don't understand," the boy said, looking to Vernon for guidance.

"I bet he can't even read," Julian sneered.

The boy pounded his fist against the cell walls. "I can read…a little!"

Vernon raised his hand to calm the boy, whose anger towards Julian was beginning to bubble. "That can be taught, Julian. I'm telling you, *this* is the one."

Julian shook his head in disbelief.

"Did you ever mock your parents when you were younger?" asked Vernon.

"No, sir! Never!" The boy remembered that if he had spoken disrespectfully to his elders, he would've been forced to fetch his own switch and wouldn't have sat for a week.

"What about your friends?" Vernon asked again.

"I don't reckon they'd be my friends if I mocked them."

"*In jest!*" huffed Vernon. "Did you ever mock them *in jest*?"

The boy was surprised at Vernon's faltering patience.

"Maybe once or twice, but they always knew I was only fooling about. Why?"

Vernon pointed at Julian. "Can you mock *him*?"

The boy's brow beetled. "Is this a trick?"

Julian sighed. "It's hopeless, Uncle. He's just wasting our time."

"Quiet, Julian. We're almost done here."

Even if the person had it coming, the boy was raised better than to produce such rude, immature behavior. "I don't even know him. Why would I mock him?"

Vernon leaned in, "Because I'm asking you to. Go on and give us your best impersonation."

Julian shrugged at the boy, who turned to face him. "You have my permission," he said.

The boy hesitated with newfound anxiety. He'd never been asked to do such a strange thing. If they didn't care for his interpretation, he could not protect himself within his cell.

"He can't do it, Uncle. He's pathetic."

"Pathetic," the boy parroted with an accurate tone and inflection.

Julian's head snapped toward the cell door. "What did you just call me?"

"What did you just call me?"

Mocking Julian proved to be entertaining to the boy after all. He would continue to mirror Julian's commentary with oral precision and a bit of physical flair.

"You must think you're pretty smart, don't you?" growled Julian.

"Don't you?"

"Uncle, this is crazy. Make him stop!"

"Make him stop!"

"I've seen enough," Vernon intervened with a smile. "That'll do just fine. Come, let's get you out of this cell."

The boy relished his deliverance as Vernon opened the cell door with the Sheriff's keys. "Oh, thank you!"

He boy swiftly searched the Sheriff's desk drawers for his personal effects while Vernon and Julian cleared the doorway. He possessed little, but the boy didn't wish to leave those belongings behind. Once he acquired them, he raced to his newfound friends, grateful for what they had done for him.

"There's just one thing I need before we go," Vernon said, stopping at the door.

"What's that?" the boy asked.

Vernon placed an old but well-polished revolver in the boy's hand. "I need you to shoot the sheriff."

"What?"

"The Sheriff. Shoot him."

"Dead. Shoot him *dead*," Julian added.

The boy held the heavy weapon and considered the cost of taking another man's life in exchange for his own. "I—I don't think I can do that, sir."

Vernon chewed his cheek. "Why not?"

"He's an innocent man!"

"*Innocent?*" Vernon stretched out an arm to point at their victim. All he needed was a Bible and a pulpit. "This sleazy, gluttonous, piss-poor excuse for a lawman would sell you to the highest bidder. He's a piece of shit! I doubt anyone would miss him."

Vernon had a point, but as he watched the Sheriff moan and cry for mercy, the boy felt conflicted.

"A man like that has no right to any position of authority," lectured Vernon.

"That doesn't mean he has no right to live! I *won't* do it!"

"He's abused his power and deserves what's coming to him."

Still, the boy was adamant. *"No!"*

"Shoot him or join him." Julian had his own sidearm pointed at the boy's head, who winced at the click of the hammer being pulled. He knew Julian wouldn't hesitate to end his life if he didn't do as they asked. The boy stared down at the small yet destructive object in his hand. It felt good to have that kind of power, though he hated to admit it.

"You *do* know how to use a gun?" Vernon probed.

"Yes, sir."

Julian lowered his weapon and restored it to neutral.

"I bet he's only shot chickens."

In one swift movement, the boy grabbed Julian by the front of his shirt and flung him over the Sheriff's desk, scattering supplies in the process. His experience with heavy lifting made Julian an easy paperweight, and it delighted the boy to hear the impact knock the wind out of him. "You don't shoot a chicken; you wring its neck! And that's exactly what I'm going to do to you if you don't shut up!"

Unknowingly, the boy had positioned the barrel right beneath Julian's rib cage.

In the face of death, Julian laughed. "Ooh-hoo-hoo! This is going to be *fun*!"

Vernon's voice chimed in with equal enthusiasm. "Yes! That's the spirit!"

The boy briefly considered apologizing, but they *wanted* him to behave badly. They forced his hand. He stepped away from the Sheriff's desk. This wasn't an exodus; this was extortion.

Vernon crossed to him, patting the boy's shoulder and slowly turning him to face the Sheriff. It had been so long since the boy had heard anyone express faith in him.

"You're the one," said Vernon. "We can't do this without you. Think of it as enlightenment. Rebirth. A chance to start over and be a completely different person. Your misfortune, your heartache—you can leave all that behind and start a brand-new life. It can only get better from here."

The boy's hands shook. He had already pulled back the hammer, and his finger sat readily on the trigger.

There would be no going back now.

He took aim and fired.

CHAPTER ONE

September 1898

"Now, whatever you do, don't stare!"

Ranger Everett Lawrence attempted to conceal his nervous excitement, for they were standing in a piece of North Texas history. Windhaven Hall served as a refugee house during the American Civil War for those fleeing the Union Army and remained a prime example of antebellum architecture. Standing on three acres of land, the two-story Greek Revival cottage made from brick, cypress, and pine invited historical romantics such as Everett to bask in the glory of its elaborate metal trim, scalloped shingles, and wraparound porch. The white exterior made the entire establishment look like an overpriced wedding cake. Its first occupants used additional land to labor cotton and crop production remotely. Though it hadn't been physically damaged during the war, those original owners fell deep into debt. They were forced to sell the home to a wealthy northeastern businessman named Samuel McNamara, where he and his family had taken residence for thirty years. It was the city of Rosewood's only "claim to fame," though many citizens looked at the house as a reminder of what was lost. Everett hoped it wouldn't be converted to a private school, as was becoming the trend with similar establishments.

"Why would I stare?" he asked.

"Because you're you and because her face is a little off-putting."

"You've mentioned that twice already. How bad can it be?"

"It's *bad*, alright?"

Everett's superior, Texas Ranger Horace Whatley, removed his broad-brimmed hat and overviewed the library of Windhaven Hall, where they'd been waiting for nearly an hour. He stared repeatedly at the same four corners of the English Aesthetic themed den, and in those fifty-two-and-a-half minutes, nothing had changed. The same globe, knick-knacks, paintings, rolling ladders, bookshelves, and robust furniture filled the space with warm anticipation for their hostess. Whatley huffed. Not only was it improper, but it was also disrespectful to waste his time. He understood that the girl had been through an ordeal and that the affluent generally had no sense of urgency, but he was beginning to lose his patience.

"I don't understand why it matters," Everett mused. He'd seen his fair share of male and female victims traumatized by the physical and emotional damage criminals inflicted. While facing such atrocities was unfortunate and initially difficult to stomach, Everett knew that was just part of the job.

"It doesn't," Whatley said flatly. "I'm merely suggesting that you prepare yourself and be professional."

Ranger Whatley tapped at his temples to signify Everett's eyeglasses. Everett was mildly near-sighted and had worn corrective lenses for years. The blue steel-wired frames with tortoiseshell temple-pads sat friendlily along the bridge of his nose, which was regal and narrowed to a point.

"How do you expect me to question her if I can't see her?"

Whatley crossed his arms, annoyed at the thought of anyone else taking the lead in the investigation. He was a skilled horseman and an established full-time professional lawman with almost twenty-six years of experience under his belt. It would be a cold day in Hell before he'd play "second fiddle" to some new recruit.

"I've been dispatching outlaws and freeloading hobo sonsabitches since before you learned to take aim when you piss, and I ain't never seen any kind of serious lawman wear spectacles. So, take 'em off!"

"Yes, sir." Ranger Everett indulged his colleague, rubbing at the indention they left behind. He placed the accessory into a pill-shaped case and slid them into the pocket of his dress coat. His caramel-colored eyes blinked repetitively, attempting to adjust to the now fuzzy surroundings.

"And another thing—*I* will be asking the questions, not you."

Whatley barked orders with the vocal integrity of a Siberian Husky, though his pretenses suggested alternative breeding. The soul behind those big blue eyes was all hound.

"Yes, sir," Everett nodded, wishing he could bat away the myopia. Even with Whatley standing so close, the ranger's face appeared as a blurry peach canvas. He could faintly make out the grey-white horseshoe mustache that perfectly matched Whatley's eyebrows and his coif of tight-knit curls.

"And stop squinting! You look like you're trying to take a shit."

"I'm sorry!" Everett pleaded. "It's just—I can't see!"

"You don't need to see. You need to shut your mouth and listen. You might learn something."

Ranger Everett plopped on a balloon-back tufted settee and ran his fingers over the solid walnut carvings, letting his sense of touch illustrate. The finish was simple yet beautiful, and the cocoa-brown velvet lightened when he pushed the dense fabric forward.

"It's a nice place," he said, giving the sofa another stripe.

"What part of 'shut your mouth and listen' did you not understand?"

Everett sighed. "It doesn't make sense that someone like her from a place like this would get mixed up with those fellas."

"He took her, Everett," said Ranger Whatley as he glanced at his pocket watch for the umpteenth time.

"I know that!"

"Those Disciple bastards kept her hostage, and it's a miracle she's still alive. We've been trying to catch Julian Crisp for over a decade. The man is a ghost! Miss McNamara spent the better part of a month with him, and I want to know every goddamned detail."

Ranger Everett was already fidgeting in his pocket for his glasses. He felt naked without them.

"Miss McNamara hardly mentioned Crisp when she talked to the sheriff," said Everett. "Most of her story was about this 'Alden Aubrey' character."

Whatley rolled his eyes. "You don't buy that duplicate theory, do you?"

It had been widely debated by law enforcement officials all over the state that Julian Crisp was a twin.

"No—I'm not sure. Texas is a big state, and some of these timelines of sightings, bank heists, and murders don't make any sense. The way they're all spread out—it's not possible."

"Psh!"

Everett shifted. "So, what do *you* think?"

"I think we've had our dicks in our hands all these years. Crisp has always been one step ahead, but not anymore. This girl is the key to answering all of our questions. Besides, I've asked some of the usual suspects we've got locked up about any 'Alden Aubrey,' and no one has ever heard of him."

Ennis, known largely as a center for trade and cotton farming, was the closest commercial town with prison inmates available for questioning. Rosewood was still largely frontier despite their best efforts to become cosmopolitan. Technological innovations such as telegraphs, trains, and gas lights all established connections with the neighboring cities of Midlothian and Waxahachie. Yet, the stories from every settlement in Ellis County regarding Julian Crisp and the gang of outlaws known as the Disciples were riddled with holes of ambiguity, rumors, and miscommunication.

"I've also questioned some folks around Fort Worth and got the same sort of answers," Whatley concluded.

Everett folded his hands, tapping his thumbs together. "She seemed very certain in her statement, sir."

"She's a woman," grumbled Whatley.

An upper-class woman like Rebecca McNamara was viewed as a living doll, dressed in only the most resplendent of fashions and meant to display charm and chastity. She would never work conventionally but was destined to sacrifice herself daily, sympathizing with the needs of others—especially her husband—and to serve the family. Later in life, she might pursue higher education or philanthropy, using the money she willed from her late spouse as she saw fit. Everett wondered how, then, with the abnormalities Whatley mentioned twice afore, Rebecca wasn't placed in isolation from an early age. Perhaps Mister McNamara shared his notion that those with physical differences *did* have a place in society. While his own vision was lacking, Everett believed that everyone looked the same in God's eyes.

"You think she's lying?" he asked.

"I think she's confused."

"*Do you?*"

A pleasant feminine aura filled the room as Rebecca McNamara closed the French doors behind her. She hadn't been introduced, which was customary, and surprised the officers. Everett quickly stood and removed his hat, smoothing his ginger-brown hair and straining to get her in focus. She stood slightly below average in height and possessed a petite, subtle frame that could easily suggest *girl*. Only the way she carried herself with poised etiquette and grace confirmed to the lawman that she was indeed *woman*. And not just any woman, a *lady*.

"I apologize for my tardiness, gentlemen. *Are you quite alright?*"

Ranger Whatley had quickly transitioned from exasperated to enthused at first sight of the witness, but upon seeing Everett's embarrassing attempts to view Miss McNamara, let out another frustrated sigh.

"Oh, for the love of—just put on your spectacles!"

Everett awkwardly fumbled through his jacket for the remedy, dropping them in the process. The three quickly hovered over the floor to retrieve them. While it wasn't the norm for a lady to exert herself in such a manner, Rebecca was the one to place the frames into Everett's hands. He quickly put them on.

Rebecca McNamara's soft, doe-like emerald eyes scanned across the library walls while Ranger Whatley gave his standard protocol greeting. Just two weeks prior, she was given a similar address from the Sheriff in Grady before questioning. She assumed it would only be a matter of time before she received a visit from a U.S. Marshall, though her present company ensured it wouldn't come to that.

"Do you enjoy fiction, Miss McNamara?" asked Ranger Whatley.

"I'm an avid reader if that is what you're asking."

The trio transitioned back to the sitting area for the interview. Everett had been warned, but he couldn't hide his quiet shock. Like a flourished signature, deep, faded scars swiped the right side of Rebecca McNamara's fair, heart-shaped face, beginning at the nostril and curling up the cheekbone. A second scar caught just outside her eyelid as if to accentuate the feature with wings. The third scar embedded deeply into her jawline up and through her side profile adjacent to one beautifully arched eyebrow, parting only to swirl sideways to a full upper lip. These were not recent injuries. These were congenital disabilities or possibly the result of a childhood accident.

Still, she's lovely.

With cinnamon hair and a spicy-sweet disposition, Rebecca didn't appear to be thwarted or traumatized by her experience with

Julian Crisp and his Disciples other than her left arm being secured in a sling. She would not express any emotional pain or physical discomfort or require sympathy for her injury. On the contrary, there was a hopeful, helpful calm to her voice, warm, eloquent, and fully present.

Did she have ulterior motives?

Everett's training taught him to suspect such behavior.

"Are you writing any of this down?" Whatley barked again.

Alert once more, Everett felt anxiously around his person for the notebook he had left on the oval marble coffee table before him. Rebecca smiled. She was making him nervous, and this pleased her. A month before, *she* would have been the one to act so nervously. She had been somewhat afraid of men, with good reason.

But she wasn't afraid anymore.

CHAPTER TWO

August 1898

The French doors leading into the library at Windhaven Hall swung wide open.

"It's a smart match."

"In what way? He's almost twice my age!"

Rebecca McNamara's Irish ancestry was beginning to show through her fiery temper. Yes, she was older, but being older differed from being an old maid. She still had time; she could marry later in life. She had the right to choose. Samuel McNamara huffed and closed the library doors to avoid interruption. He prepared for an emotional reaction to the news. He would soothe her, talk some sense into her, make her understand. He knew such an announcement would cause an upset, but what better time to broadcast his daughter's engagement than the annual Rosewood Ball?

"Let me remind you that you have also passed your time at Cotillion."

"You should have told me. This is humiliating!" Rebecca promptly placed a wine glass on the nearby table to smooth out her lavender tea gown, whose lush fabric became rumpled in their cross-exchange down the corridor. She had embarrassed him, but he embarrassed her first. Rebecca fumed at her father's tuxedo.

Why was men's attire so manageable and women's so wildly restrictive?

Why did it seem as though most things were easier for men?

She tugged down at her sleeves, fluffing the pillowed tops. Everything felt so tight! The elaborate dress fell loosely from a high waistline, draping her closely corseted figure with plenty of ruffles, mesh inserts, and mother-of-pearl buttons, skimming the floor in white lace and black satin ribbon. At the beginning of the evening, Rebecca heard a female guest commenting on her ensemble, saying it made Rebecca look like a *petit four*. Truly a shade meant for spring, Rebecca insisted on the color because it was the perfect accessory to her mother's silver brooch, which she wore often with pride. The flower-shaped pendant had a single pearl in the middle, reminding Rebecca to always seek wisdom through experience as well as from the elements around her. Her hair was swept up into soft garnet waves to treat her neck to the cool of the day, but it, along with her collar, was turning blotchy in her frustrated state. Samuel also attempted to compose himself.

"What, the fact that it's happening with *him* or that I had to do it for you?"

Her father's words cut deep. With the McNamara name and fortune attached to her, Rebecca believed she would have had more beaus than she knew what to do with if she were prettier. She didn't want to marry Nicholas Guillroy III or anyone like him, for that matter. He was loud, greasy, and would talk your ear off if his mouth weren't full of *étouffée*. Rebecca had enjoyed her visit to Louisiana, with its history, rich culture, and celebrations—even the swampy parts—but she had no wish to move there.

"The fact that it's happening at all! And you could have at least given me options!"

Samuel crossed his arms, sternly staring down as both father and businessman. "Where are your other suitors? Can you produce them?"

Rebecca mirrored him to demonstrate how ridiculous he appeared. Samuel was plump, with rosy cheeks and a jolly personality. If his hair weren't the same shade of crimson as Rebecca's, he would have been the spitting image of Kris Kringle. Icicles formed along his temples and jawline, the result of stress and inevitable aging. But Rebecca could never see her father as *older*, no matter how he looked.

That would mean *she* was older, and she didn't *feel* older.

"That isn't fair."

"What isn't fair is that I have to have this conversation right now when I should be speaking to my financial supporters. We will discuss this later."

Samuel wet his whistle with a sip of wine, spilling a bit in the process. He was already flustered, and merlot on the bib of his crisp white shirt would most certainly leave a stain. Rebecca relieved the goblet from her father, placing it beside her own, and attempted to blot the error with his handkerchief. They both huffed in anger, with faces frowning and flickering sweat. Neither had meant to make a scene. *They were the hosts of the evening! How foolish they must have appeared!* Each time they would argue, Rebecca felt the gnaw of guilt. She knew what her father could have done to her as a child. Babies with physical defects, however minimal, were often discarded to sanitoriums or asylums, where they would most likely be malnourished, abused terribly, and eventually replaced or forgotten. She understood that sacrifices were made and appreciated everything Samuel had done for her. Everything *except* for this.

"Is that what this is about?" she asked. "Your plans to run for public office?"

"No, I only meant—"

Rebecca whipped the handkerchief back at her father. "—Well done, Daddy. A high-profile wedding with you as the 'doting father' and your disfigured daughter as the 'blushing bride-to-be' would most certainly tug at voters' heartstrings."

Samuel hid his remorse and followed Rebecca deeper into the bookroom. The publicity would come at just the right time to make him favorable over the more established competition.

"Rebecca, do you have to be so melodramatic? Is it not enough for you to stand out the way you do already?"

"I'm sorry if I embarrass you. You always told me I was just like everyone else."

Samuel McNamara looked upon his daughter, the product of a limited amount of trained medical professionals in the South after the war and a defective pair of obstetric forceps. He accused the physician of malpractice due to the failure to deliver Rebecca using reasonable care, but the damage was done. Before passing from Puerperal fever, the late Mrs. McNamara made Samuel promise not to send the child away. Within three days of becoming a father, he was grieving the loss of a wife and tasked with raising a child who would require more from him than he could give. For years, he indulged Rebecca, supporting her thirst for knowledge through elite schooling, private tutors, and extended education. There were trips abroad, consultations with specialists, and spa sessions to possibly correct her condition. These gestures were enacted to keep well on his promise, not necessarily to push Rebecca away. Perhaps he *had* made mistakes. Perhaps there *was* a strain on the relationship. He may not have fully understood her, but he did know her. Rebecca was a firecracker and a free spirit, traits that reminded him of her mother and their plans for her life. He once made plans for himself as well but now lived with the regret of lost opportunities. He wouldn't live forever. *This was his time.* Samuel was aware of the Grangers and the Women's Christian Temperance Movement's effect on the country and the possible influence such a crusade could have on Rebecca's already liberal mindset. While he personally believed some practices could evolve, any radical behavior or activism from the family could hurt his own political endeavors.

No, it was time for Rebecca to take on the role as a keeper of family values. She would be a wife and a mother, continuing with tradition, ensuring her security and well-being. Why could she not understand that this was the best he could do?

Samuel took his daughter by the hands and shared his blue-green eyes with her in a look of sincerity. "I know what you're wanting. And it's a wonderful, beautiful thing to desire. It's just not realistic for—"

"—People like me. Is that what you were going to say?"

Rebecca turned from him. She hadn't meant to sound ungrateful or show disrespect, only to stress that his actions limited her. An arranged marriage would eliminate her opportunities to experience a world on the brink of change. Rebecca buried her nose in books all her life with the belief that if she kept studying, she would find herself. She only appeared youthful because Samuel kept her sheltered. She was twenty-eight years old and had yet to know adventure. *This was her time.* Armed with intelligence, drive, and wit, Rebecca planned to travel and turn her experiences into literature as something real that she could touch and always remember—something she could later use to connect with others. As a socialite, her success in the world hung heavily on its willingness to see past her unsightly features. As an author, she could be free from the pretentious, provincial world around her, leaving her mark where she saw fit.

Why did her father have such little faith?

The room continued to flood with the things Rebecca and her father couldn't say to each other. The pair spent hours together in this place during her childhood, letting the words of others speak for them. A love for the narrative seemed to be their only common bond. It was the one area in which Rebecca could reach her father. For this reason, she believed the library to be a wonderland and that literary matter was the only thing that mattered.

"Have you read this?"

He had selected Leo Tolstoy's *Anna Karenina* from a stack of books nestled neatly on a nearby shelf. Rebecca ran her fingers along the book's spine tenderly, in reverence. For so long, the written word was her only escape, her only solace.

"Yes. It's one of my favorites."

"I picked it up a few years back. I found it to be a bit racy, myself."

She returned the book to its place. "Passion isn't racy, Daddy. It's a part of life."

Samuel exclaimed, "Yes, life! This is your chance to finally have a life! A brand-new life! Think about your future. It can only get better from here."

Rebecca hated the notion that she would forever depend on a man, first as a daughter and then as a wife. While she had never been in love before, she was certain that indifference at the very thought of her future husband was a bad omen. Her romantic sensibilities weren't grounded in reality but rather in the visions of what love could be, of what it often was in her books: a concoction of ecstasy, confusion, hunger, and pain. So much pain. Heartache seemed glorious, like falling onto one's sword. She wanted it to *burn*. That was how one knew it meant something. If she was expected to spend the rest of her days with a man, he had better possess the same reckless ideation. Though it might make her destined for heartbreak, she could at least say she lived.

"I think I would rather die."

The incline in Mister McNamara's blood pressure peaking, "I can't talk to you when you're like this. You're behaving like a child, and I have neither the time nor the energy for it."

"Pity."

Samuel sighed. Why his daughter enjoyed challenging him was a mystery! Realizing his hands were empty, he circled the entryway, retracing his steps. "I had a glass of wine when I came in, did I not?"

"It's next to mine," Rebecca fussed, still firmly planted in her spot.

He shook his head. "I don't see yours, either. I must have left it downstairs."

Rebecca's father paused long enough to wave a cautionary finger at her from a distance, a gesture he often used to signify his seriousness. "He's waiting for you."

"Let him wait!"

Samuel said nothing, allowing the doors to slam in response behind him. Rebecca searched the entryway for her own wine glass, pausing to study herself in the reflection of the great grandfather clock. As she imagined being dressed all in white, she wished for the ability to stop time. She held no pride in the possibility of being a bride.

A shadow flickered in the background.

Rebecca turned.

"Is someone there?"

Silence.

Rebecca took a moment to consider that Windhaven Hall was old and most likely haunted. Once certain she was alone, Rebecca exited the library.

CHAPTER THREE

Windhaven Hall's elongated drawing room doubled as a ballroom and was lit and richly decorated for the evening's activities. Crowded footsteps tickled the hardwood floors with vibrations in-time to accompany a waltz that played in the background. Rebecca's kind, bright green eyes danced across the droves of people below her at the top of the stairwell, all communing in festive fellowship. Would that she could join them with sincere authenticity! Rebecca wondered why she even bothered going to the trouble of looking the part of hostess, for no one ever spoke to her directly. She was accustomed to attending parties without a chaperone present or the convenience of an escort. This was understandable. What dangers could possibly exist for a minger like her? And who would want to steal her away, anyhow? As far as Rebecca was concerned, *alone* didn't have to be a shameful word. She had no reason to hold her head down.

A looking glass in the corner caught Rebecca's sightline, reminding her of the cause for those initial reclusive tendencies. She touched the scars nestled on her cheek, no longer weary of their presence, only the shock others would impose upon her when they saw them. Her markings would be considered honorable if she were a wounded veteran. Instead, they continually served her hefty doses of humility. They never went with any outfit but were always part of the ensemble. They never asked to come along but would always serve as her uninvited guests.

Rebecca sighed. At least she wouldn't have to succumb to the standards of beauty that weighed so heavily on most women in society. Beauty would never be expected of her because it could never be achieved.

Nicholas Guillroy III may have been a catch in his youth, but Rebecca wanted nothing more than to throw the Cajun bluegill back into the waters he came from. With a staunch belly, light skin, and a poorly constructed black toupee, the fifty-two-year-old nobleman always seemed up to something.

"Laissez les bons temps rouler!"

Many of Nicholas's expressions were half-French and half-English, blended with a surly Southern drawl. Occasionally, he would deliver statements to heavily imply a laissez-faire lifestyle, yet implications were the best he could produce. He was all talk and had a reputation for being insufferable. Rebecca attempted to avoid Nicholas as she descended the steps, but the musings of other guests who viewed her blemishes for the first time provided an unwanted spotlight.

"I was worried you might have tried to elope without me!"

Rebecca stopped. *Wine. She would require wine to have this conversation.*

Nicholas supplied her with a glass of liquid courage as he poured over Mrs. McNamara's vast oil painting beyond the foot of the stairs.

"You look like her," he commented. "You're not as pretty, but you look like her."

"Thank you, Mr. Guillroy."

Rebecca didn't need to inspect the picture, for it was embroidered on her mind and branded on her heart. She *did* look like her mother, with the same eyes, hair, smile, and coloring. There was only one major design flaw. Rebecca always wondered if her father placed the portrait there out of respect for his late wife or to silence any possible inquiries from houseguests regarding her whereabouts. They would tell him

Rebecca needed a mother, to which he would simply reply that Rebecca needed many things.

"I was thinking October," pondered Nicholas.

"For what?"

"Our nuptials, of course!"

Rebecca turned on her heel away from him. "That is nowhere near enough time to plan a wedding."She would demand a lengthy engagement. She would fake an illness. She would join a nunnery.

Nicholas followed, his body somehow enforcing the laws of inertia. Rebecca bounced as she ran into everyone and everything surrounding her while the masses seemed to part for him.

"What's there to plan? I've got all you need back home. It'll be a Fais do-do!"

Rebecca slipped through a small crowd of visitors huddled in the main doorway, planning her escape onto the front lawn where she could disappear into a sea of guests. "Mr. Guillroy, I—"

"—Call me *Nicholas*," he said, following her onto the wraparound porch. It was a pleasant evening, yet most of the guests had huddled inside.

Rebecca pressed onward to the garden.

"Nicholas, I mean no offense by this, but I don't love you—"

"—Who said anything about love? This is business, my dear. I wish to leave behind a legacy."

Rebecca paused amongst scaffolded shrubbery and waist-high rosebushes. Her haven was so close! "You have three children already."

Nicholas Guillroy III was a widower, but the remainder of his family unit was well-established. "Daughters," he said. "I'm confident you'll give me a son."

"I—I'm barren," Rebecca lied, raising her glass to swallow any discomfort.

Nicholas slid a short, thick arm through her own to form a pairing. "Now, let's not start this accord on a foundation of dishonesty. I play cards with several of your doctors, each of whom has given you a clean bill of health, albeit an abraded one."

Rebecca discarded her empty goblet on a vacant bench nearby. Her father had sold her as though she were nothing more than a breeding horse. And Nicholas did his homework on her, inquiring before making any commitments. She wouldn't enter the garden; he led her far away from her flowery fortress back to forced civilization. Nicholas turned to tenderly pat her cheek with a pristinely manicured hand. If Rebecca were a small child, he might have pinched it instead.

"I am beyond thrilled that *this* is not genetic."

They walked at a leisurely pace now. Rebecca watched as a mosquito crawled across her fiancé's shoulder and fought the urge to smack at it, hoping Nicholas would be later inconvenienced by a pustule.

"My estate is much larger, but you'll adjust. You will be the lady of the manor, and you'll want for nothing. There's plenty of servants around to tend to your every need. They know their place, too."

"The war is over, Nicholas."

"So they say! Don't worry; I've never struck a colored folk that didn't deserve it."

Rebecca then wished she *had* slapped him. "Why are you telling me this?"

"I want to make sure you're prepared for our life together. You need to understand my expectations so that you can always keep me pleased." Leaning inward, "You *do* want to please me, don't you?"

Rebecca discreetly unlinked their arms. They were approaching the front of the house, and she would not be seen in public alongside him.

"No," she said. "And I won't marry you."

Nicholas huffed, appearing more annoyed than heartbroken. "C'est con. But you will, my darling. Do you know how much money your father paid me to take you off his hands?"

"It's called a dowry!"

"On top of that."

Rebecca's insides cried out while Nicholas locked his honey-colored gaze with her own. "Don't look so surprised. He practically begged me."

Rebecca opened her mouth as a scream interrupted from the very sky above them. *Or was that a real scream? Not from her.*

The pair jumped at the chaos spilling onto the lawn, separated by a frenzy of fashionable guests, pushing towards the nearest exit as gunshots echoed in the distance. Mister McNamara had hired private security for such a mishap, yet those men were nowhere to be found. Though Rebecca was taught as a young woman never to run, the instinct to survive far outweighed the instinct to conform.

"Hey, you come back here!" Nicholas called as he reached out for Rebecca in vain.

Clusters of brave men fought against the flow of those struggling to leave Windhaven Hall. Most had checked their firearms at the door and foolishly argued over which gun they would use for defense.

Did it matter?

Horses and buggies rocked with urgency to leave the grounds as drivers frantically labored to unhitch the steeds from their posts. It was anarchy! Rebecca knew of a shortcut around the front lawn and made a mad dash through the lawless traffic to locate her father. Together, they would find safety.

"Have you seen my father?" Rebecca clamored to those whizzing past her.

Few bothered to listen, and even fewer produced an answer.

"Samuel McNamara! Have you seen him?"

"He's over on the pavilion!" a passerby hollered.

Rebecca hiked up her skirts to sprint to the property's edge, where several more luxurious carriages were parked. She crouched behind a line of stagecoaches to take inventory of the pavilion's timber frame. The nearby gazebo was unoccupied and appeared recently deserted from a distance, with evidence of broken wine glasses scattered over the shiny finished wood foundation.

Clouds of smoke clung creepily to the late-August air, a byproduct of those still wishing to take matters into their own hands near the front of the estate. It seemed quieter now. *Too quiet.*

Suddenly, Rebecca was lifted from her hiding spot.

"Let go of me!"

She didn't know how Nicholas had discovered her so easily. He must have guessed that she would go looking for her father. Rebecca wagered that she couldn't have moved as hastily as she believed through the panicked masses if *Nicholas* could catch up with her. He briskly led them to a cashew-yellow Abbott-Downing Concord Coach made from sturdy basswood braced with iron fittings and black leather coverings for the front and back boots. While suitable for four passengers, the horse-drawn transport usually housed a trio of riders to accommodate Mister Guillroy's puffy physique, with a driver up front and two travelers stored within.

"Get in there and stay!" he wheezed. "We can hide until they leave."

Rebecca tumbled into a cushy compact of upholstered seats with Nicholas climbing in behind her. "What is happening?"

"Some outlaws crashed the party and started shooting up the place!"

"*No!*"

The gunshots sounded like they were drawing nearer, and the passenger compartment was closing in by the minute. Rebecca hated tight spaces.

"I have to find my father," she beckoned, unable to climb over Nicholas and his mountain of body fat.

Elbows and kneecaps buckled as the two wrestled inside the transport. Rebecca quickly lost the battle, with Nicholas proving stronger than he appeared. Suddenly, their carriage lurched at a dangerous speed along the unpaved road away from Windhaven Hall. Neither had heard anyone board the Driver's Box.

"We're *moving*!" Rebecca announced.

"Keep your voice down!" shushed Nicholas.

A leather curtain flapped violently against the stagecoach window in disrepair. One of them had pulled it down too hard to gain a foothold during the scuffle. Rebecca couldn't see where they were going or who might be leading them away from Windhaven Hall, but they were traveling at a hazardous momentum.

"Open the door!" she cried.

"What?"

"We have to jump!"

Nicholas's sweaty cranium bobbed side-to-side. He would lose his toupee before too long. "If we jump out, they'll see us!"

"They'll see us either way, Nicholas! At least we'll have a chance to escape!"

A dip in the earth made the stagecoach bounce as Rebecca finished her sentence, causing her voice to wobble blaringly. The turbulence took her tummy away, and she clutched at Nicholas for stability. It was a miracle that they hadn't tipped over or damaged a wheel! The carriage then came to an abrupt halt. She must have been too loud. Whoever was leading the buggy must have heard them. Nicholas and Rebecca strained to hold their breath and listen as several bodies inspected the cart.

One on top, one in the driver seat, and possibly another draped along the side.

Then, without warning or formal introduction, the stagecoach door opened.

CHAPTER FOUR

"Get out."

A divergent desperado waved his shiny sidearm to signal Nicholas and Rebecca to their exit. The bandit stood tall with a firmly defined upper body and a lean physique. His chestnut brown hair was much too long and seemed unkept under his hat but remained in accordance with his beard, which protruded from underneath the cloth covering his face. A gust of wind waved his scent in her direction, an earthy musk laced with coffee, liquor, and something sweet. *Peppermint?* Upon closer inspection, Rebecca noticed the shadowy bags under his cheerless eyes. This man was unwell.

"Hey, it's you," he said.

Rebecca's eyebrows squished together.

This man appeared to recognize her.

But how? And from where?

"You're a little out of season, don't you think?" the cowboy grinned beyond his face covering. Rebecca's dress reminded him of Homestead Purple Verbenas, which *flourished* in the spring and endured the summer heat but were usually *planted* in the fall. He wondered if she, too, had a lemony, floral scent.

"Do you know this man?" asked Nicholas.

Rebecca shook her head. "I've never seen him before in my life!"

But the outlaw continued as though he were amongst friends while casually suggesting their cooperation. "Money, jewelry, and any other valuables you've got, we'll gladly take them off your hands."

A much larger criminal then held a potato sack before Nicholas and Rebecca. At the same time, the first outlaw moved into the stagecoach to begin looting, but not before pointing to Rebecca with great interest.

"¿Alguna vez has visto algo así?" he asked the large man.

Rebecca meant to learn Spanish during her formal education but was distracted by a visually appetizing Latin instructor in her youth. He was older and had an air of ambiguity about him that first gave her impure thoughts. The Romantic Languages were similar and related, but not enough for Rebecca to comprehend fully. Still, even without a translation, she could tell that the leader's Spanish was choppy, and he struggled to conjugate the verbs accurately.

Is he drunk?

"No, nunca," the brawny bandit flatly replied before returning his attention to the job at hand, presenting the bounty bag once more.

Nicholas shed his worldly possessions: a gold pocket watch, a silver flask, and a gold signet ring with a ruby that he wore on his little finger. His bulging coin purse dampened most of each contribution's clinking sounds, but that didn't stop Nicholas from throwing each item into the potato sack with disgruntled cynicism.

"It's the same routine with these delinquents. They're savages, uneducated, and incapable of change."

"We're not the ones that need to change," the bulky robber growled.

Rebecca removed her pearl earrings in frightened desperation.

Once they had their belongings, what would these criminals do to them?

The original offender hopped down from the carriage with a bottle of rum that Nicholas kept aside for rough and tedious journeys, as the long trek from Louisiana to Texas proved uncomfortable for the old man. This violation seemed to provoke Nicholas more than any of the other stolen items.

"Aller se faire foutre!" Nicholas spat in frustration, enraged by the events unfolding and his own elderly state that prohibited him from having any significant defense against his assailants.

"Ooh, we've got ourselves an aristocrat!" said the premier bandit, pulling down his face mop to take a hearty swig of the molasses-colored spirit. "I'd respond, but my French is about as good as my Spanish. I *do* know foul language when I hear it, though. You should be ashamed talking that way in front of a lady."

Rebecca watched as he took a much greater mouthful, straining to see his face.

The hulk-sized henchman wrung the potato sack into a small knot and called out into the distance. "How's it coming with those horses?"

The third member of their company, a spritely fellow, quickly loosened the harnesses from the four steeds that brought them to their location. Rebecca couldn't see him clearly under the cloak of the evening sky, but his vowels and nasality—especially with the rise in his voice towards the end of a sentence, suggested he was foreign.

"¡Solo un minuto!"

"Well, hurry it up, will you?"

A rum-filled fragrance bowed in front of Rebecca.

"I'll be taking that silver brooch if you please."

It was once again that mysterious, thin man with sad grey eyes and a face hidden by a tan bandanna. Rebecca clutched the accessory. She had forgotten to place it in the bag, not that she would have wanted to. Perhaps the lead bandit would show her mercy.

"No, please. This belonged to my mother," Rebecca pleaded.

"And she had good taste!"

The autumn moonlight cast a veil over all of their faces. Even Nicholas, who was nodding at Rebecca, urging her cooperation, appeared monstrous. The thin man politely held out his hand, which had nubby nails and callouses along his skilled, slender fingertips. "If you don't give it to me, I'll have to take it by force."

Rebecca hesitated. Everything else could be replaced. Fighting back tears, she begrudgingly removed the flowery ornament and placed it in the robber's hand.

"Much obliged," he winked, tucking the trinket in his breast pocket.

"Coward!" Rebecca seethed as angry tears streamed down her face.

The bandit laughed. "You don't know how right you are!"

Rebecca shook her head.

How could a person be so playful and carefree during such a shameful act?

"I know you!" Nicholas exclaimed. "You're Julian Crisp! You're a thief and a murderer, and—"

"—Is *that* what you know?"

The shady character folded his arms across his broad chest, clutching the bottle in his hand. Rebecca remembered the "Wanted" posters at the post office and various other locations all over Rosewood—all over Texas! Julian Crisp was infamous!

Nicholas continued. "You're a wicked man. You've done despicable things."

"Then you'd better stay away," replied Julian. "You'd better stay *far,* far away…"

The thin man known as Julian Crisp hoisted his trousers, which seemed loose and sagged along his waistline. He took a final look at the victims before nodding to his well-built accomplice, whose clothes fit perfectly.

"Yep, I reckon that completes our transaction."

"Are you going to kill us now?" asked Rebecca as she watched Julian lift the bottle to his lips again.

"I could, but I won't," he answered, his speech slurring. "Lay down on the ground and count to seventy-five. Better yet, make it an even eighty."

The pair obeyed Julian's commands, dropping to their knees and falling flat on their fronts. Nicholas proved buoyant even outside of water, bobbing on his belly in protest as the thieves turned to walk away.

"Putain de merde!"

The pair stopped in their tracks to chastise the Frenchman. Julian turned.

"Now, what did I say about swearing in front of the lady?"

Nicholas fumbled along his right shin for the secret holster that concealed his Remington Model 95 Double Derringer with the nickel-plated finish and a lucent pearl handle. He lifted his arm and aimed at Julian Crisp, who stood close enough to wound mortally.

Rebecca gasped. "Nicholas, no!"

"Fils de pute!"

Julian's weapon sat on his right hip in an obvious alliance with his shooting hand, which was still holding the bottle of rum. He retrieved a weapon from the holster of the partner on his left, who had yet to react, and took Nicholas down with one ferocious blast. Rebecca watched her fiancé's body fall to the ground like a damaged kite, and the breath of life left him soon after. She wasn't sure if she had screamed, but at the sight of his blood spraying her face and chest, Rebecca let out a piercing cry.

Julian Crisp returned to his prey, tossing the mouse gun to the large man and squatting to study the damsel in distress. The sounds of her whimpering sobs made his stomach lurch. Or maybe it was the rum. He hadn't wanted to upset Rebecca any more than he wanted to kill Nicholas.

He was just doing his job.

"I tried to be reasonable, but some people don't know how to leave well-enough alone." Rebecca trembled as Julian slowly lifted her chin, exposing the peppered blood spatter. "I'm afraid I've ruined your pretty party dress," he said. "You should take it off."

"What?" Rebecca managed through a horrified whisper.

"Yeah, *what*?"

The larger outlaw tossed the bounty sack over his hefty shoulder.

This wasn't part of the plan.

Rebecca tilted her head, realizing Julian looked different from his picture in the moonlight. Feeling her studying him, Julian carefully stood.

"I think—yeah, I think—"

"—You think *what*?" Julian's accomplice was neither impressed nor amused at what he knew his employer was suggesting.

"We'll take her with us," decided Julian.

"That's a bad idea, Boss."

"I disagree. It's a *great* idea, possibly the *best* idea I've had in a long time."

The large man gritted his teeth in an attempt to hide his disapproval. "Are you out of your mind? You've had a lot to drink. Maybe you should slow down."

"Maybe you should mind your business!" Julian hissed. "Why don't you go see about the horses?"

"This will end badly," the large man warned under his breath. Rather than argue with Julian and waste more time, he did as his superior requested.

Giving a satisfied smile, Julian examined his newfound conquest. "Take off your dress," he said, rubbing his nose with his forearm before pulling off the bandana entirely.

"No," she said.

"Take off your dress, *please*." He was playful again, with his arms gesturing in a jovial display that rivaled a court jester.

"No!" Rebecca responded this time with strength.

"It's too heavy to make a quick getaway. Now, come on! Don't make me point my gun at you."

Knowing he would, Rebecca struggled to stand, defeated by fear, with knees that wouldn't cooperate. She knew there were too many buttons and ruffles to complete his request in a timely manner. Moreover, she believed her hands would betray her.

"Do you require assistance? Because I'd be happy to provide you with—"

"—No! That's not necessary."

But basic motor skills seemed futile for Rebecca under the pressure of Julian Crisp watching her undress as she stood in a pool of her escort's blood. The outlaw had summoned the lead ropes from his other associate, who finally wrangled one horse for each man. After giving the spare horse a hearty smack on the rear, sending it off into the wild, Julian approached Rebecca as she struggled in a lavender loofah of fabric.

"I don't have all night!" he said.

Julian placed the rum bottle under his arm and held the horse reins in his mouth while he stepped behind Rebecca to rip the soiled garment in three heavy stretches.

Rebecca froze. She couldn't scream, she couldn't fight, and she couldn't even weep for what was happening to her. The ground was soon littered with iridescent buttons, which reminded Julian of knocked-out teeth. Rebecca battled for short, quick breaths as the shock of a cool autumn breeze welcomed her delicate skin beneath sheer undergarments. She assumed the worst would follow, but Julian returned to her front and presented her with the rum bottle.

"Hold this," he demanded.

His hands were shaking, too.

Rebecca nodded, allowing both palms to circle the glass container. It was something to see, smell, touch, and listen to as the liquid inside sloshed back and forth. She focused on those things, grounding herself rather than watching as the slim leather straps looped around her wrists.

Once finished, Julian reclaimed the bottle. "Thank you."

As Julian led her away, Rebecca took one last look at Nicholas Guillroy III. Suddenly, married life on the bayou and bearing his children didn't seem like such a cruel, cruel fate. She missed her father and regretted how she had treated him in the library of Windhaven Hall.

Windhaven Hall.

She would never see her lovely home again.

At this revelation, Rebecca dropped to her knees, surprising Julian mid-swig. He lifted her with his free arm back to her feet, which continued to drag with each step. They wobbled, but Julian steadied them both against his horse, holding Rebecca firmly enough to whisper in her ear.

"If you scream, I'll give you a reason to scream."

Rebecca hadn't thought to scream out until that moment. Julian's hand clamped over her mouth as she bucked in one last act of resistance.

"I knew that was going to happen," he said. "Rog, would you do the honors?"

Julian spun Rebecca to face the hefty gentleman, *Rog,* who was now beside his own horse. Rog pulled out his revolver, gripping it by the barrel while Julian and the smaller outlaw observed. His plump, big-knuckled hand reared overhead, with the heavy grip raised like a hammer. "I'm real sorry, Miss."

As the large man brought the hammer down, everything went black.

CHAPTER FIVE

Rebecca flopped and bounced like a ragdoll on the back of the heavier bandit's horse, which he had thrown her over, a tagged deer, ready to be fleshed, salted, and tanned. *How long had they been riding?* She would bleat to express her discomfort but feared they might hit her again. Her head throbbed to the downbeat of the horses' steady rhythm. Hooves and earth blurred beneath her as she fought to ignore the staunch scent of the steed's undercarriage while the caravan continued into the night.

Lengthy branches reached from looming trees to form a cocoon-like covering over a path to the circular driveway in front of a grand property appropriately named "Sanctuary." A pre-war palace, the homestead was the perfect hideaway, easily defendable, surrounded by healthy farmland, woods, and ideal terrain for rainy seasons. Secluded and hidden by nature, it seemed another world within itself, lost in a forgotten time without conflict and the interconnected issues of politics, land, and lawlessness. Seemingly recent conventional repairs were visible along the balcony, roof, and outside steps. It appeared that efforts were made in vain to uphold the overgrown shrubbery that enveloped the porch. The fading estate echoed with memories of its former glory. No longer the pristine, virginal white of its early life, the house possessed a creamy, pearl-like sheen as though naturally preserved by the elements.

Upon reaching their destination, the thin man Nicholas had classified as Julian Crisp awkwardly dismounted and stumbled to the side of the house, mumbling about needing to relieve himself.

"How drunk would you say he is?" asked the scrappy thief beside Rebecca, exiting his steed. It was apparent that Nicholas's rum and possibly the contents of his silver flask had influenced the outlaw. Rog, the bulkier bandit, sighed.

"It's not the worst I've seen him, but it's close."

"I didn't think a person could get drunk that quickly."

Rog fussed like a protective older brother. "He gets drunk quickly because he drinks too much too quickly! He doesn't eat anything, either. I keep telling him he's too damn skinny!"

"You said he ate today," declared the other outlaw, his accent now more prominent.

"That was *yesterday*, damn it! It was *your* turn to watch him!"

"Mierda."

Rog then eased Rebecca off his horse and restored her to the upright position while his smaller accomplice retrieved the evening's take, pausing to address Rebecca directly.

"Perdoname, señorita. We're not accustomed to having female guests. My name is Miguel Manuel Serrano. You may call me 'Manny.'"

Manny Serrano personified a stick of dynamite with the promise of explosive energy. He was not as abridged as Rebecca first imagined, standing taller than she and holding a slim-built frame. His dark complexion was cozy and smooth, a cup of *café con leche* garnished by mocha eyes, artfully messy black curls, and a mustache shaved in the middle. His burgundy shirt, leather gauntlets, and black waistcoat starkly contrasted Rebecca's blindingly white garments under the evening sky.

"I'm Roger," said the heftier criminal.

Jacob Roger Mercer wasn't looking for a fight. He need not look, for he carried the fight with him. Men like Roger were continuously challenged to brawls and displays of brute strength due to their physical blueprints. If the fight were fair, Roger would win. And if it weren't, Roger would most likely win anyway. His mahogany hair tapered a bit, falling freely about his rounded face. Like Julian's, Roger's hair was much too long, offering a playful flip at the nape of the neck. Occasionally, one would catch him brushing it back with his fingers or the palm of his hand. Rebecca wondered if he truly needed a haircut or preferred it that way. There were slivers of silver in his bushy beard, his equally bushy eyebrows, and the sideburns that framed his face. His eyes were the clearest cerulean blue and held the deepest kindness within them. But it was his voice that provided the most comfort to Rebecca. Low, husky, and resonant, its warmth could stay with you like a hot cup of tea traveling down your throat on a cold, rainy day, spreading throughout the body before finally settling. Even his mutterings modulated enough to ease her worried mind as he removed his bulky brown jacket and placed it around her. It was significantly oversized, but Rebecca relished how it surrounded her in its embrace that smelled of sandalwood.

"We ain't kin or nothing like that," he said, referring to his accomplice.

Rebecca smiled at Roger's need to state the obvious as Manny moved closer.

"Sorry about...before..." he continued, gesturing to Rebecca's head with a shrug.

Leaning in, Manny stepped forward. "Listen, we are not bad men, but—"

"—Don't lie to her," Roger frowned.

"You're right. Okay, Miss—what is your name?"

Rebecca was both astonished and flattered by their modest greetings. Then again, almost anything was better than getting hit over the head with the butt of a revolver.

"I'm Rebecca McNamara."

Manny courteously shook her still-bound hands. "Well, Miss McNamara, we *are* bad men, but if you do what you're told, this will all be over soon."

"Who's there?" a booming voice leaped from the porch.
"It's us," replied Roger.

Rebecca strained to see the pillar-sized man who seemed to equally labor to identify her.

"Who's that with you? Is that a *girl*? *Did you bring home a girl, Roger?*"

Roger sighed again. He knew this would happen. "She's not mine; she's—"

The pillar shifted. "—Don't tell me it was *Aubrey*!"

"He's as full as a tick, and there was no stopping him."

"Ooh, he's in trouble now!" teased the stranger at the entrance before quickly moving into the house. His haughty laugh came with the delight of a child prepared to tattle on a sibling. Roger relieved the bounty bag from Manny's shoulder while steadying Rebecca with the other arm.

"Would you go check on him?" he asked. "I've got this."

Manny nodded, leaving Rebecca alone with Roger, who struggled to prepare a warning. He sat the bounty down and tenderly took Rebecca's soft face in his hands.

"Miss Rebecca, a man inside this house looks an awful lot like the man who took you tonight. You'll be tempted to beg him for your life, but if you know what's good for you, you'll keep your mouth shut. Do you understand?"

Rebecca said nothing.

"Do you understand?"

Rebecca opened her mouth to speak but again said nothing.

Roger smiled. "Good girl."

The main entrance stood like a highly decorated soldier, with considerably sized columns towering alongside a detailed lunette above the crimson-colored door. Ornamental ironwork framed a sweeping staircase in the grand foyer, and large, evenly spaced windows made room for the moonlight's proud presence. Intricately designed fixtures, high ceilings, and rich wooden floors flooded the entire space, which seemed to go on for miles. Obvious cosmetic issues of peeling paint and crumbled marble were evident, but the home had good bones and appeared structurally sound. Other than the door, there was little color in the house. Rebecca attempted to imagine bold, billowing curtains, embellished tapestries, rugs, and other furniture. Practicality told her the men had no need for frivolous décor and thus kept the area a blank canvas, but the bare fortress seemed more like a mausoleum, purposefully cold yet hauntingly beautiful.

Five criminals greeted them at the grand stairwell. There was no need for introductions; Rebecca could identify each of the Disciples from their images or written descriptions in the newspaper. Stories of these men, most of whom were close to her own age, and their nasty reputations were legendary.

The first man in the doorway was Edwin Riley, the embodiment of a fine-tipped pen. Outlining his equally proportioned frame were dark grey trousers, a midnight blue vest, and a light blue shirt. He removed his hat upon Rebecca's arrival, revealing patches of hickory cleverly combed over. Edwin was plagued by premature baldness from years of wearing boiler hats that were too tight for his pointed head, something others teased him about in his youth and was now always kept covered.

Reuben Jackson could have passed for a relative of Booker T. Washington, a prominent leader in the African-American community. He was a strapping man with broad shoulders, brown eyes, and short, neat black hair that swirled in smooth waves of ebony, appearing soft to the touch. Rueben seemed good-humored and carried himself like a gentleman in his white buttoned shirt, grey trousers, and tan boots to match his braces. He gave Rebecca an earnest nod of respect.

The robust Phillip Thompson was caddy-cornered in the foyer. Rumor was he was mute because his tongue was cut out, though Rebecca dared not inquire about his mysterious vow of silence. His muscular, lightened terracotta skin suggested a mixed ethnicity of Caucasian and Apache descent. Sharp, ink-colored eyes were bookended to a prominent nose shelved over cheekbones, perfectly parallel to his free-flowing hair and corresponding outfit.

"You see, Julian? I told you he was a liability! Not only did he fail to follow your orders, but he has compromised this whole operation by bringing in an outsider!"

Leviticus Bohannon was the post keeping watch at the main entrance. He towered nearly seven feet tall, holding sturdy shoulders and a muscular frame, with only Roger standing as a worthy opponent. In another life, Levi would have been a prize-fighter or a strongman. His attire was as grim as Death, dressed in only the darkest fabrics, from his neckerchief to his boots. He didn't personify gloom or darkness, though, but rather the absence of light. His gait began with a broad chest and clenched fists, and even the Earth trembled at his footsteps. He was surprisingly well-groomed, with a clearly defined part in his jet-black hair and minimal stubble across his sharply sculpted face. Based on appearances alone, Levi was physically flawless, down to the dimple in his chin. Rebecca might have found him irresistible if not for the wickedly empty look in his eyes, a piercing, icy blue. No, Rebecca disliked how Levi looked at her, up and down, with equal amounts of desire and disgust. She knew then that he would hurt her if he had the chance.

Rebecca gasped at the last Disciple, convinced she was seeing double.

The stories must be true.

*Julian Crisp **did** use a duplicate.*

"What outsider?" the clone inquired.

Levi pointed. *"Her!"*

The *real* Julian Crisp respectfully buttoned the black vest over his black shirt as he crept down the main staircase, a slightly more accurate depiction of the images Rebecca had seen in town. With each calculated step, the ebony stripes along his navy pants elongated his legs. It was understandable how one would confuse him with the thin man, for except for grooming and attire, the men were clear reflections of each other. A perfect yin and yang. They held the same height, weight, coloring, physique, stance, space, and temperament. The only major difference Rebecca could notice was the thin man's gaunt and disheveled appearance. Julian Crisp's chestnut hair was parted to the right with a clear transition into a well-kept beard. If Julian was the prince, the thin man must be the pauper. Rebecca expected Julian to study her face and comment on her scars, but he brushed right past her to confront the inebriated outlaw who had since stumbled in through the doorway.

"Alden?"

"Mm-hmm?"

Julian gestured in her direction. "Is this a bluff, or do you mean it for real play?"

Rebecca turned to Roger. "So, he's—the man who took me—he's *not*—who is he?"

Roger pulled her closer to him. *"Shh."* If he could keep Rebecca quiet, Julian might spare her. Manny fought to keep his colleague upright as the gang leader continued interrogating the thin man.

"Hey," Julian snapped his fingers in the thin man's face. "Alden! Alden Aubrey, are you *drunk*?"

Alden attempted to steady himself without Manny's assistance. "A little bit." He cleared his throat and smoothed his hair, struggling to keep balance and refrain from giggling. Nothing was more challenging than pretending to be sober when even *he* knew he was wasted.

"I—I just wanted a souvenir," Alden stammered.

Edwin and Rueben suppressed their amusement at the open act of defiance, while Phillip and Levi shared Julian's exasperation at Alden's intentional lack of respect.

"A person is not a party favor," growled Julian.

Alden raised a pointed hand, "That depends entirely on the type of party. Am I right, fellas?"

It was anyone's guess if Alden would then vex or vomit. He fainted instead. The guffaws of Edwin and Reuben escaped into the foyer, bouncing off the walls and mocking Julian even more.

Levi set his jaw. "You need to punish him."

"Oh, I will," swore Julian. "Phillip, take this buffoon to his room."

They watched as Phillip lifted Alden from the floor with little difficulty. Levi let Phillip pass him on the stairwell before joining the rest of the crew below.

"Edwin, get your squirrelly ass out of here! You too, Reuben!"

Levi's orders went without objection, the chain of command evident. Julian directed his attention to Roger and Manny. He was Simon Legree, Professor Moriarty, and Iago, all wrapped up into one marvelous villain. Rebecca knew that without great villains, there could be no great heroes. Such was the literary norm. *So, where was he?*

Where was her hero now when she needed him most?

CHAPTER SIX

"We've been telling you for *months* that Alden is not well."

Roger kept himself planted as Julian descended to the bottom of the stairs. Levi continued to lean against the opposite banister. Manny carefully moved Rebecca into a nearby corner.

Out of sight, out of mind.

"Why are you coddling him, Roger?" Levi called out.

"I'm not coddling anyone! He never got a chance to mourn Vernon properly—"

"—He had as much time as the rest of us."

"Then there was the incident at Newberry..."

"Oh, please!"

"You weren't there, Levi!"

"No, but if I were, I wouldn't still be belly-aching about it!"

Roger ran a hand through his hair. He would gladly surrender his shooting hand in exchange for Levi's permanent silence. Julian snickered. It was always enjoyable to listen to the two men argue.

"So, should we commit him? That'd be one way to end all this." Julian turned to Roger. "What makes you the expert, anyway?"

Taking a deep breath, Roger shared his haunted history. "My daddy was sick like this for a long time—*Manny, you know the story*—my momma and I never understood. He slept all day and couldn't remember drinking or beating on us."

Julian waved a hand in dismissal. "Alden's no drunk."

"I didn't say he was."

"He'll get better in time, Roger."

"He might, but if you push him… I saw what my daddy did. I'm the one that found him."

The image would forever be charred into Roger's memory. Rather than scream, the nine-year-old soiled himself. Mrs. Mercer scolded her son for his mess before stumbling upon the gruesome scene. In all the years that followed and even in the men he later killed, Roger had yet to see that much blood.

Levi shook his head. "It won't come to that."

"I've stopped Alden from taking his own life on *two* separate occasions, now."

Roger raised two fingers as his voice trembled with urgency. Manny stepped forward. "I found him in the barn loft last week with a shotgun. It took over an hour to talk him down."

Julian's head snapped to Manny. *"And I'm just now hearing about this?"*

Manny was notoriously slow to anger, operating just below boiling point. Vernon used him more as an expert assassin than an everyday assailant. When *Manny* raised his voice, you knew he meant business.

"We've been telling you, Julian! You don't listen!"

Rebecca couldn't cover her ears due to her bondage. She was unbothered by the yelling; her father often yelled about the state of the economy or crime rate and its possible effect on Rosewood's future success. She simply couldn't bear to hear another word about the man who had taken her. *If he was so careless with his own life, what did Alden Aubrey have in store for her?*

"If Alden's no longer man enough for this job, Julian, I say you do him a favor. Shit, I'll do it."

Levi's voluntary effort didn't sit well with Roger, who charged at the strongman in response. "So you could take his place? I bet you'd like that. But you don't exactly fit the profile, do you, big fella?"

"I fit just fine," purred Levi.

Do it, Roger. Take a swing. See what happens.

Julian yawned. Someday, one of them would kill the other. He hollered out to them but didn't care enough to physically intervene. "Alden never had a problem keeping up with me before," he shrugged.

Roger cracked his neck to relieve the tightened muscles. "You ask too much of him."

"Do I?" Despite Julian's smaller stature, Roger knew he would find a knife in his belly if he spoke out of turn again. "Oh, I see. You think I've *abused* him in some way. Let's explore that, shall we?"

Manny crossed his arms and began to rock on his heels, knowing a toxic work environment when he saw one. It was the reason he left Mexico. That, and he accidentally maimed a co-worker. His actions were justified but left him with few options for employment. Manny served as a Disciple for six of the seven years since crossing the border. He hoped for change upon relocating yet found neither honesty nor reason in his new position. Alden was the one endangering himself each week, not Julian. Julian had remained within the safe walls of Sanctuary for many months now.

"Maybe he just wanted a girl!" blurted Manny. He hadn't meant to draw focus onto Rebecca, but he had to say *something* to break the tension.

"Do you think he wanted *that* one?" Julian pointed at Rebecca, still not taking the time to formally address her or introduce himself. "*That* is nothing more than a distraction. If what you and Roger say about Alden is true, then the last thing he needs is to be distracted!"

Uncle Vernon taught Julian and the Disciples that women were—at best—distractions. Distractions agitate emotions, pull attention, and prohibit men from doing their best work. You could do what you needed to with them while in town or on a job, but you were *not* to bring them to Sanctuary.

Standing down, Roger carefully reasoned, "You know, distractions aren't always a bad thing."

"Name one *good* distraction."

Julian was distracted by a woman once. *Once, never again.* Amelia was dead now. Social hierarchy prevented them from having a happily ever after. There were too many rich, tyrannical fathers in the world and even more obedient daughters who were too naïve to know they were being duped. And if they were that *stupid*, they had no business being with him.

Manny looked to Rebecca and shook his head at Roger, who knew this was a trick. It would be unwise to paint her or *any* woman in a redeeming light. Such a comment might set Julian off.

Then again, Julian didn't need a reason to slit a woman's throat.

"I thought as much," Julian sneered, as back-pedaling proved difficult for Roger. "If Alden knows the rules, why would he purposely disobey them?"

"He's an idiot," Roger quickly replied, hating to shove his friend under the carriage like that. He hoped the remark would subside the outlaw's agitation. Julian scratched his bearded chin.

It's time for a shave.

"Do you think I'm happy about Alden's deteriorated mental state?" he asked.

Roger gave a submissive sigh. "No, Julian."

"But y'all blame me for it!" spat Julian. "The only thing I'm guilty of is asking Alden to do his job."

Rebecca recalled a fable she read about a farmer and an especially gifted goose during her youth. The animal would provide one golden egg to its owner each day. A singular golden egg was enough to support the farmer for a lifetime, but he soon became greedy and demanded the bird produce *two* precious prizes daily. The creature explained that it couldn't be done, and when it failed, the farmer killed it. One selfish, short-sided action destroyed the promise of a prosperous future.

Alden was a golden goose.

Levi laughed. "He's a fool, Julian. I bet he thinks you'll kill him if he makes you mad enough."

Roger bowed his head. Levi had taken the words right out of his mouth. He planned to spin them so that Julian might appear noble in front of the other Disciples for showing mercy, but Levi's delivery suggested he'd look like an ass if he lost his temper. Julian would lose all credibility.

Alden would be a martyr.

And he couldn't have that.

Julian shifted, now expressing his deep concern. "Alden is my *brother*! He's *precious* to me!"

"Julian, we're not saying you did anything," argued Manny. "We're saying he needs rest."

"A vacation?" Julian scoffed, moving to the stairwell. "This isn't a luxury resort."

"Take some of the pressure off, just for a while, it'll be easier..." reasoned Roger.

But Julian continued his ascent. Like Manny, Julian deemed it unnecessary to shout. Anything that needed shouting could be just as damning in a whisper. He wouldn't overreact. He would control himself. Only, his frustration was increasing along with his volume. Roger, now on his tail, Julian worked to set at least a stair or two above him to match noses.

"I gave him an easy job!" Julian claimed. "He was supposed to do reconnaissance at that ball and lift a few trinkets to sell. Instead, he brought home a hostage, which is attention we don't need!"

"What do you want us to do, Julian?" barked Roger. "Do you want us to take her back right now? 'Cause we can do that. *Or* we can use Alden's little mistake to make some money!" Roger was recommending a ransom, which could be lucrative if executed correctly.

"I say we put a bag over her head and take turns."

Levi's proposition was the first comment they had openly made about her deformity. Manny stepped back toward Rebecca, filling as much space between her and Levi as he could. Julian seemed amused by the suggestion, though not enough to encourage it. His concentration remained on the nearest Disciple. "A ransom will do nothing but bring attention our way, Roger. We can't risk it."

"So, we take her *out* of the way. We'll go to South. We can negotiate the terms and arrange the trade-off far from here. Julian, you're a businessman. You know how this works."

Still stuck on the bag idea, Levi gave his unwelcomed input. "We have other irons in the fire at the moment. Let's just kill her and deal with Alden in the morning."

Julian's eyes darted past the stairwell to Rebecca. *You're nothing special. Why would Aubrey want you?* "I don't have the energy for a ransom. Killing her would be simpler and much more entertaining."

Roger persisted. "If you kill her, you might as well dig two graves."

The gang leader's head zipped back at Roger. "Is that a threat?"

"No! Just—hear me out! I'm not sure what Alden is capable of, nor are any of you. There's a reason he brought her here. Let's see where it goes."

Rebecca felt four sets of eyes fall upon her. Her face flushed in horror, and she again became aware of her visible vulnerability.

"Take her to his room," said Julian, following Roger's last appeal. "No one else is to touch her until Alden does what he brought her here to do. You got that, Bohannon?"

Levi chewed his cheek. "Yeah, I got it."

Roger crossed his arms, with watchful eyes locked onto Julian, "So, you don't want her?"

Julian headed back up the stairs. "God, no! Just looking at her makes my stomach turn." He pointed to Levi, who promptly joined him. "And *you* with the bag! What on God's green earth is wrong with you? We used to be a civilized outfit. I bet Uncle Vernon is rolling in his grave!"

When the pair were out of sight, Manny helped the hostage to her feet.

"Why did you offer me to him?" Rebecca cried out to Roger.

"To make sure you don't get any surprises," he answered.

Roger soon led her down a hallway of bedrooms on the second floor while Manny trailed close behind them. Rebecca, who had lost her shoes during the voyage, tearfully dragged her bare feet in an attempt to delay the inevitable.

"No, please!"

Roger might as well have been putting a cat in a bathtub, for he practically plunged her through the doorway. "Julian could have snuffed you right there! I bought you a night! What more do you want?"

"To go home!" She clutched at Roger's collar. "Why can't I stay with you? Or Manny?"

"Because we're not the ones who took you!"

"You helped."

The outlaw sighed and brushed a palm through his hair.

How could she not understand?

"If someone wakes up and you're *not* in this room, there will be trouble."

"For all of us!" added Manny.

The bedroom was a standard eleven-by-twelve-foot space, exceptionally dark, with two of the three windows—those facing east—covered by wooden planks. *Mister Aubrey must not care for the morning sun.* Rebecca scanned the area. A dresser, nightstand, chair, and a four-post bed, each made from oak. These were things she could see and smell. She felt the chilly hardwood baseboards under her feet. She heard her own heavy breathing in contrast to Alden's sleepy sighs.

"Look at him. I bet he won't even know you're here," said Roger as he removed her woven handcuffs. Under normal circumstances, Roger might have laughed at his colleague sprawled on his belly in an open-mouthed drunken snooze with one boot hanging freely from his foot. "And I hate to tell you this, but I have to lock you in."

"No!"

"Listen to me! I know Alden; he won't hurt you!"

"How can you be so sure? You all talked about him like he was crazy!"

Roger seized Rebecca by the shoulders, his blue eyes pouring fiery protection for his friend. "He's *not* crazy, alright? He's just very, *very* sick!"

The intensity in Roger's voice stifled Rebecca's sobs. Manny hung his head.

"He's *sick*?" she sniffled. "Like…a cold?"

"Yeah, like a mighty bad cold," said Roger.

Nervously, Rebecca bit her lip. "What if you're wrong?"

"If I'm wrong—if he acts out in any way, I'll deal with him, myself. You have my word." Two plump thumbs brushed the tears from Rebecca's cheeks. "I'm real sorry, Miss Rebecca; Manny and me—we have to go now."

As Alden's bedroom door closed and clicked behind her, Rebecca rushed to hide beside the dresser, dropped to her knees, and cried herself to sleep.

CHAPTER SEVEN

Shoot him or join him.

He's like a monkey in a cage.

You'll swing, for sure.

Alden Aubrey opened his eyes. He was sickly, sore, and sweating. With a yawn, he starfished on the bed, his appendages slightly reaching over all four sides, save for the headboard, which made his crown curl inward. Battling dry-heaving gulps and gasps for breath, Alden transitioned to his side. He wasn't alone. There was a girl.

Oh, Christ. It was real.

Snippets of drunken moments filled with gunshots, tears, and trampling horse hooves from the night before replayed in his mind.

Maybe you should slow down...

Is that what you know?

We'll take her with us.

Coward!

And she had good taste!

Are you out of your mind?

If you scream, I'll give you a reason to scream.

Strongly opposing the sun pouring in from his window, Alden rubbed at his eyes, wishing he could blink himself out of the bedroom back into the darkness. He rolled onto his stomach with instant regret, for the room seemed to continue to roll without him. He steadied himself on the mattress. *Are those scars?* He didn't remember a girl with scars. There had been a girl. He *vaguely* remembered a girl, but not a girl with scars. It took a few seconds for the image to settle. His mouth was dry, and his tongue filmy. Alden wondered if the girl saw him stick his head out the window in the early morning to vomit.

She had.

"Did I do that to you?" he asked, circling his finger around his right profile.

Rebecca shook her head and shuttered at the thought that Alden could mistake her scars for his actions.

"Did I do anything to you?"

Rebecca glared at him. *How could he not remember? Had he been that intoxicated?* He was cold and cruel to her, yet cautious and controlled enough not to get sloppy during her capture. He led the group of outlaws back to camp with poise and precision…until he passed out.

"Well?"

He was still shirtless on his belly, resting a full, bushy-bearded head on his forearms. Alden could feel Rebecca's eyes studying his shoulders and triceps, which carried pink and white marks from heavy burns and the faded, discolored pigmentation of healed skin that traveled to the middle of his back.

"There was a fire," he explained. "I know you weren't there for that." Alden narrowed his eyes. There *might* have been scars. He simply paid no attention to them. "Can you not speak?" he barked, causing Rebecca to jump slightly.

"You robbed me," she shook. "You tied me up. You shot my— you killed someone. You tore my dress and brought me here." Her voice warbled as she spoke. Those events leading to and following the robbery were blurry as they happened but were quickly taking shape, sharpening in her memory. She would never forget.

"And that was it?"

Wasn't that enough?

"Yes," Rebecca answered.

"No one tried to…*abuse* you in any way?"

He meant *rape* but was too much of a gentleman to say it. He hated the word as much as he hated the act. Based solely on her general appearance, Alden assumed she was un-plucked before their meeting. As Rebecca recoiled in discomfort, Alden felt his stomach turn. *Please say no.*

Rebecca shook her head, "No."

"Good," he sighed.

Alden peeled himself from the bed and staggered to pick up the garments strewn across a nearby chair, discarded at some point in the middle of the night. Each movement felt like a marathon, with every mile showing him a new memory from the previous evening. He moaned and groaned with heavy footsteps in a hungover stupor, reminding himself to have a long talk with that horse when he got the chance. He either needed to ride more gently or stop drinking—and he had no plans to stop drinking. Rather than wear a full union suit, Alden opted for a two-piece set that kept him cooler in the summer months. He selected a wrinkly, inside-out, charcoal grey shirt for his outer layer. It was clean enough and smelled acceptable, so it would suffice. He reached inward to adjust the sleeves.

Rebecca's eyes followed Alden on his journey. When he exited the bed, Alden pulled up his britches at the opportune moment, leaving just enough mystery. She had never seen a man's bare chest before, and Alden possessed a symmetry that she didn't. There were deep lines and curves that rippled along his torso into a hidden valley and finely developed arms with the perfect amount of muscle. Broad yet thin, he tapered to a "V" in his midsection, with a tiny patch of hair dancing toward his waistline. The scaring on his back and shoulders reminded her of a painted landscape or mountainside.

He's beautiful.

"Do you see something you like, princess?"

Rebecca averted her eyes, embarrassed that he caught her watching him dress. Alden chuckled in amusement.

"You're lucky I'm not modest." He proceeded to tuck his shirt into his trousers, adjusting appropriately. He then looked over Rebecca's attire: a white chemise, white lace bloomers, and a white straight-seamed corset trimmed with pale blue ribbon. His eyes lingered a bit too long for Rebecca, who wrapped her arms around her body, focusing on the most important areas to conceal, for Roger's coat was on the floor, having been used for bedding.

"I take it *you* are, though." Alden grinned as he fumbled through the nearby dresser and tossed her a cornflower blue button-up with a bib front. It was one of the nicer articles of clothing he owned, saved for special occasions, but there was no need for her to know that.

"The best I can do. It's clean and should cover up most of what you've got."

He was right. While slightly fitted, the shirt was long enough on Rebecca to camouflage her womanly charms. She'd have worn anything to cover her undergarments in a house of questionable men. "Thank you, Mr. Aubrey," she said gratefully.

Alden straightened. He had planned on sneaking her out the same way he believed he snuck her in. Though there was no evidence of it happening before, Alden figured at least *one* of the other Disciples had secretly brought home a girl. But she knew his name, which meant she knew about Julian. The realization washed over him that he and his new roommate were in a lot of trouble.

Shit.

Rebecca bravely stepped forward. "My name is—"

"—Don't." Alden held his hand up to stop her. "Don't tell me anything about you. It's better this way."

Rebecca frowned. "Then why did you bring me here?"

Alden rested his hands on his hips, frustrated yet majestic. "I don't know."

"I don't believe you," she fussed, crossing her arms, raising her chin at an answer that was simply not good enough. He could do better. He would explain himself, and he would do so immediately.

"Then don't believe me!" Alden's apathy was partnered with equal amounts of anxiety. He had made mistakes, but this topped the cake. There was a knock at the door. The key turned, and Edwin poked his pointy head into the room.

"Any Romans or Sabine women here?" he quipped.

Rebecca understood the reference. In the mid-8th century, Rome had so few female inhabitants that the men of Rome abducted virgins from the neighboring area of Sabine to obtain wives and establish families. It was contested that their motivation for the abduction was purely based on populating the city, that no direct sexual assault had occurred, and that these women lived honorably with their new husbands, sharing both property and civil rights. Given that Rebecca wasn't alive at the time of the event, she had no way of knowing the truth. She suspected it was a mixture of the two and decided she did *not* appreciate Edwin's joke.

"You're funny," Alden replied half-heartedly.

"Julian wants to see you."

"I'm sure he does."

"*Now.* He wants you to bring the girl, too."

Alden huffed and gestured to Rebecca. "Fine. But will you do me a favor and see about finding this one some pants?" Giving her another scan, "Mine won't fit."

Edwin scratched his temple. "Pants? On a *woman*?"

"What, Edwin? You got some dresses hidden away that you're willing to share?"

"No!"

"Then find her some pants!"

"Do you think she'll need them?" Edwin's eyebrow twitched with sinister intent. With Rebecca wearing such little clothing, her soft, untouched body was so easily accessible. *I bet she smells like wildflowers.*

"I say she needs them." Alden's voice dropped to a growl that Rebecca hadn't heard before—not even during her abduction. It was commanding, dangerously low, and territorial. Any second, he might howl.

Edwin's eyebrow immediately returned to its normal shape in a respectful response. "I'll check Simon's room. He's built like a young lady, and it's not as though he'll be needing them anytime soon."

"What do you mean?" Alden yawned and stretched, arching his back with quiet pops and crackles.

"Didn't you hear?" asked Edwin. "That ignoramus went and got himself arrested near Pearson Pointe."

Alden yawned again and rubbed his nose with the heel of his hand. "Stupid kid."

Simon, who had never been arrested, was no doubt sitting in a jail cell. Alden knew what that was like; he would always remember that fear, that anxiety.

Maybe Judge Jenkins would've shown me mercy.

It happened eighteen years ago, yet Alden could still see the steel bars and dirt-covered floor. He wondered if the accommodations at Pearson Pointe were similar to what he experienced. Alden's guilty eyes looked over the prisoner wearing his cornflower blue shirt. Though he hated the idea of being locked up, at that moment, Alden Aubrey wished to trade places with Simon Whitaker more than anything.

CHAPTER EIGHT

Alden escorted Rebecca down the stairwell with a forced shuffle, audibly clicking his tongue to create enough moisture to combat the dry mouth. His initial response to Rebecca's presence was fueled by adrenaline and surprise, which were beginning to abandon him. The effects of alcohol from the night before hadn't worn off completely, either. Knowing that Julian would expect him to function soberly, Alden stopped Rebecca at the drawing room door, urging her to proceed cautiously.

"Okay, look at me."

He was listless, with blue, bloodshot eyes squinting at the difficulty of forming a sentence. If he closed them for long enough, maybe he could transcribe the words written on his brain.

"You don't talk to him, alright?" he advised. "Don't even look at him."

Roger had warned Rebecca not to directly address Julian. Now, Alden was giving her the same warning. "What if he talks to me?"

Alden shook his head.

A hiccup.

No, a sour burp.

"He won't. Julian thinks women are beneath him."

"How do you know he won't talk to me?"

"He *won't*. Especially not with the way you look..." Alden then sighed. He chose the words as delicately as possible, but they failed to stick the landing. Rebecca studied Alden, convinced he couldn't be the same man from the night before.

"I saw him last night. He doesn't seem to be that great of a threat," she lied.

"Thoughts like that will get you killed."

His forefinger was positioned directly between her eyes, the most precision Alden had shown her to date. Rebecca took a deep breath through her mouth.

One cannot reason with a drunk man.

Even one that was trying to help.

"I'm not afraid of him," she pledged. "Or you."

An impressed smile spread across his lips. "If you say so."

Rebecca waited for further explanation, yet Alden withdrew, only turning to face her again before touching the door handle.

"When we go in there, *not a word*, do you understand?"

She nodded, and the pair entered the drawing room. Meeting there made sense, as such areas were customarily suited for receiving visitors. However, once they cleared the threshold and the barren walls revealed an absence of showcased artistic expression, Rebecca felt she wouldn't be met with hospitality and refreshments.

"Jesus Christ on a cracker!" Julian was leaning against an inactive fireplace. "Alden, are you *that* hungover, or are you still drunk?"

"As you like," Alden shrugged.

"If Uncle Vernon were here—"

"—Well, he's not."

In depositing Rebecca beside a tall window, Alden felt a wash of embarrassment. There was no furniture to lead her to, only an assortment of crates and barrels stacked in a corner.

"I'll ignore your blatant disrespect because we have a lady in our presence." Julian gestured to Rebecca, but his focus remained fixed on his associate.

"You shaved," noted Alden.

"This morning. You will, too. I'm tired of us looking like vagrants."

Rebecca took inventory of the change in Julian's appearance. He was still clearly the alpha, classically handsome with definitive features hidden behind those now-absent whiskers, strong and razor-sharp along skin so smooth it would suggest that not even water could wet it. Not that it required much maintenance. Faces like Julian's were written about, filling one's daydreams with sighs and swoons, but were rarely ever *real*.

Alden crossed his arms. "Yes, because a *beard* is all that's keeping us from sophistication…" He gave Rebecca a slight once-over, noticing how the morning sun shot prisms of white over her shoulders, cascading onto the floor with righteous integrity. An angel who carried the light with her.

No, the difference is clear.

"Speaking of," began Julian. "Did you even think about what kind of people might be at that party last night?"

"Rich people."

Alden had a smart-aleck answer for everything, something he picked up from years of running with other clever men, though he was raised to behave differently. This, along with a mischievous grin, was merely a defense.

Julian pointed at Rebecca. "Do you have any idea who *this* is? She's not the comeliest thing, but she is well-known. She's Samuel McNamara's daughter."

"Who?"

"Some wealthy businessman from Vermont. Rueben did a job a while back… I've heard the name. He owns a freight yard in Jefferson and some other businesses on the east coast... I don't know all the details, but I know he's well-to-do. I believe he also has political aspirations, am I right?"

Rebecca looked to Alden and then again at Julian, who waited for her affirmative.

"You may answer me," he said.

Rebecca nodded.

Julian smiled. "See? There's value to her, after all—more than just a pretty face. Edwin went into town early this morning. He claims word's already gotten out about her disappearance."

Unmoved, Alden scratched his chin. "And?"

"And I can't believe you thought to bring her *here*. You know the rules."

Rebecca frowned. She didn't appreciate either of their tones, and the tension between the two men made her even more uneasy. Alden leaned against the wall, kicking a leg out before bringing it back in to casually cross at the ankles.

"You're not angry, are you, Julian? 'Cause if I made you angry, I don't think I could live with myself."

"I'm not angry."

But Alden knew it was a lie. Having Rebecca at Sanctuary jeopardized every bit of anonymity the gang worked years to establish. She knew their surroundings and, more importantly, their secret.

"You're not?"

"No, not at all."

Julian's comments had an almost musical quality, varying pitch and smoothly stitched with sarcasm. *Was his calm, collected demeanor a charade for her sake or part of his everyday persona?* The way he carried himself seemed to suggest the latter but still left Rebecca perplexed. *How could someone be both so nimble and so snake-like?* He circled the room, slithering with his chest puffed, a predator about to strike its prey. Alden kept his distance, remaining as solitarily planted as an oak.

"So...?"

"I'm concerned," Julian replied. "Roger told me about your latest spells of melancholy." He took a dramatic pause to give Alden a look of pity. Rebecca had seen that look many times before. Usually, it was a way to make those around her feel better about themselves. Alden fought his shame by shifting away from them and diverting his attention to the peeling paint on a nearby wall.

"Did he, now?"

Chalky white swirls curled under the tiny bits of nail left on Alden's fingers before tumbling to the floor. Julian circled back to the fireplace, retrieved a small box from the mantle, and rolled a cigarette along the ledge. *His* hands were steady and showed no signs of the stress-induced nail-biting that Alden possessed.

"It takes a strong man to admit when he's weak. Do you feel strong, Alden?"

Alden adjusted a bit and glared at the instigator. He knew what Julian was doing. There was a time he could whip Julian with minimal effort, but Alden wasn't that brawny young man anymore. His clothes sagged from weight loss, and he lacked the physical stamina to brawl. Still, his shoulders held a broad frame that made all the difference when straightened. Slanted sunlight broke through the window, casting much-needed color over his face. He cracked his knuckles.

"I'm fit as a fiddle."

Julian laughed. "Yeah, you look it."

Alden set his jaw. "I'm tired. There's a difference."

"I see." Julian put the finishing touches on his project before placing it on his lips. "You know, Roger had the brilliant idea to hold her for ransom. She could be here a while." He struck a match and flashed a smile at Rebecca as he took a long drag.

*Maybe I **do** need a distraction.*

"Wonderful," Alden managed through gritted teeth, still facing away from them.

"She can help you *rest*…or whatever you need. Once we have the—"

"—My father will not pay a ransom."

Both men turned to acknowledge her interruption. Alden let out a sigh. Julian smiled and advanced toward her. Alden's statement about Julian's misogynistic views proved true in how Julian's eyes looked not at her but *through* her. He floated to the place she stood. Once there, Julian paused momentarily to stroke Rebecca's head tenderly as though she were a pet. Smoke swirls lingered between them as he delicately took her hand and held it in his own.

"And why is that, my dear?"

"He thinks criminals like you are scum."

"*Criminals*? I prefer to be called 'opportunists.' We're merely doing our best to make a living here."

Rebecca looked past Julian to find Alden, whose coloring matched the peeling wall and appeared both crestfallen and furious. He shook his head and mouthed, *"No."*

"Your daddy's got a lot of money, more than enough to share." Julian jerked Rebecca's hand to reclaim her attention. "Why do you think your father wouldn't pay a ransom, Miss McNamara? Does he not believe his only daughter to be worth at least a small sum?"

Rebecca took a deep breath through her nose, forgetting about the smoke around her, and coughed. "He thinks it's—cowardly—to take something that's not yours—and—"

"—He thinks it's *cowardly*?"

Rebecca swore she heard Alden swear under his breath. Julian slowly turned Rebecca's palm upwards. He removed the cigarette from his mouth with his left hand and held her wrist with his right, letting it linger a few centimeters over. His fingers tightened as she tried to pull away.

"I think men like your father are cowardly! *They* are the scum!"

Julian hadn't raised his voice, but his speech sliced through the air with the precision of a scythe. He returned the cigarette to his lips before returning to Rebecca's palm. Bits of ash flickered with each movement, singeing everything it touched in one last moment of heated glory.

"Julian, don't!" Alden called out.

Yet Julian continued. "Men like your father make it hard for people like me to have any kind of life! They hide behind their fancy titles in expensive clothes and warm, comfy houses, and they think that extravagance means they're safe and they've got it all figured out. They say people like me are what's wrong with this country. They pass judgment on us while enjoying luxuries most folks will never know. The truth is that people like me are necessary to give people like your father—people like *you*—the feeling that they have something to lose. I *hate* men like your father!"

"That's enough, Julian!"

Julian freed Rebecca's hand. "For your sake, I hope you're wrong."

And with that, he shoved her into the wall.

Oof! Rather than argue, Rebecca remained in a clump on the floor. It seemed beneath Julian was the only place she would be safe.

"This is *your* mistake and, therefore, *your* responsibility," fumed Julian.

"I know," said Alden, having made grand strides to meet him. "I understand."

"Do you?" Julian cocked his head to study his duplicate. "Do you have any idea what you've done? And after you swore things would be different… I guess some things don't change, do they?"

When Alden gave no reply, Julian's arm extended to catch Rebecca by the hair, maintaining the standoff as he relished her soft cries of discomfort.

"Yes, you're in for a good time, sweetheart. We're going to have some *fun* with you!" He then turned to Alden. "The others are waiting. Why don't you just do it now? Go ahead, I'll help hold her down."

Instinctually, Rebecca clawed at Julian's grasp as her strands of strawberry were picked from the source.

"Ooh, she's got some fight in her, Alden! Are you sure you're up for it?"

Alden seethed, growling once more. "Get out of my sight."

With a shrug, Julian released Rebecca and took another drag. "Fine. You and I will finish this discussion later."

"Can't wait."

"Put some coffee in you, Aubrey, and for God's sake, get yourself cleaned up!"

The drawing room door closed behind them, yet it took a while for Julian's arrogant air to clear out. Alden rubbed his face in his hands. He could have handled himself differently. If only his head would stop pounding! Sobriety seemed so close, the alcohol burning out of his system with anger.

"I told you not to say anything!"

"Well, you weren't helping," she argued. "You just stood there and let him antagonize you."

Alden lowered himself to her level, sallow and visibly shaken from frustration. "I'll speak slowly so you can fully understand because I'm only going to say this once: *I don't care what happens to you. You're nothing to me. You're stolen goods.* Now, I've been somewhat gentlemanly and contributed to your wardrobe out of the goodness of my heart, but if you test me, I'll let the wolves have you. Savvy?"

Rebecca had been so brave up until that point. Most other women would be inconsolable under such circumstances, alternating between shrieks and fainting spells. Blinking away tears, she quietly nodded.

Alden lessened. "Are you hurt? Do you need me to carry you?"

"No."

"Alright, then. Let's go."

CHAPTER NINE

Levi Bohannon was a barber who also dabbled in medicine before turning to a life of crime. This explained his sharp, well-groomed appearance and his knack for tidying things. It was his responsibility to recreate whatever look Julian decided to sport. And Julian's style was ever-evolving as he attempted to keep up with modern trends without being too flashy. Alden watched Levi prepare a lathery mixture with a shaving brush, vigorously whisking away the soap puck inside a ceramic dish within the parlor, which had better light and more space to perform the procedure.

"Was it you or Julian who romanced that squaw after we did the job in Durham?" inquired Levi. "Gangly looking thing, but she sure had a pretty mouth..."

Having learned many secrets from behind the chair over the years, Levi spoke softly so the small audience across the room consisting of Manny, Rebecca, and Roger wouldn't hear him. He cared nothing for Manny and never truly trusted Roger. Yet, if uninterrupted, Levi could use his gift of gab to assuage Alden into telling him more about his most recent misstep.

Alden squinted and grimly prepared to bid his beard farewell. It was too bright and too early to reminisce about that poor girl and what they did to her people. In one of the few instances Alden and Julian teamed up with Levi, they pretended to be twin brothers rather than the same man. The tiny group of indigenous folks should have killed the three men for stumbling into their territory after they fled from a score gone sour, but instead chose to tend to Julian's injuries and provide each with food and a place to rest. That was when the brief love affair started.

"It was Julian," Alden bleakly replied. "Her name was Aponi, and you shouldn't speak ill of the dead."

Slowly, an assembly line of tools graced a side table. "I'll speak how I want to speak," Levi snarled, placing the instruments into a perfectly straight line. "Interesting people, those Injuns. Eating berries and shit...living off the land claiming the *white man* is to blame for all their problems..."

"You try having everything you've ever loved taken from you, Levi."

"Says the man who has made a living by taking things that aren't his!" Levi shook his head and clicked his tongue. *Hypocrite.* "How did I know you'd take their side?"

Their side. Levi had no shame. Alden snuck a glance at Rebecca, who sat sandwiched between Roger and Manny by the door. She was still bound but was at least wearing pants—though they didn't fit as well as he'd hoped, bunching and sagging in all the wrong places.

Levi's right. I'm no better.

Alden remained silent in his reminiscing. He was captivated by the customs of those different from him and eager to learn more. Aponi's people were open and wise in ways that surpassed his own understanding, having been more resourceful, never wasteful, and appreciative of the greater beauty in all things beyond their surface level. A marvelous little world so easily destroyed by the corrupt trio. Alden attempted to give them a sense of honor as he struck each victim down, but Levi and Julian were downright ruthless. Aponi wasn't gangly, only young, probably *too* young to be with any of them. Not that age ever stopped Julian, who preferred girls with fresh-faced features. Her name meant *butterfly*, yet she was never allowed to fully transform. Alden had to look away when Julian finished her last. Julian never kept loose ends.

Levi turned to face the sunlight, positioning a hand mirror upwards to examine an unruly nose hair, catching Rebecca's reflection behind him. He tugged at the bothersome sprout and sniffed. "Could you not have taken a pretty one? Christ, neither one of you has decent taste in women. We're in our prime and could have our pick." He subtly gestured to Rebecca. "Is that honestly what you prefer?"

"To each his own," said Alden. He didn't have to explain himself to Levi. The only person who deserved an explanation for Rebecca's capture was Rebecca, who caught notice of the two men eyeballing her: one disgusting and the other distraught. Levi's lips spread into an eerie smile.

"That girl looks at you with an almost carnal fascination, Alden."

Alden's eyes lowered as Rebecca looked away. "She's afraid of me."

"I would be, too." Levi took a moment to check his inventory for anything else he might need for Alden's makeover. He could change Alden's appearance all day long, but it would never change the fact that Alden was lesser. With inferiority on his mind, Levi snickered. "You know they squirm when you force them."

Alden fought back a flinch. The only way to detract foul men like Levi was to double-down. If Alden had a nickel for every time he'd said something equally offensive so that Levi would leave him alone, he wouldn't need to steal from people.

"Some of us don't have to use force," Alden quipped.

"Oh, you're planning on seducing her! *Nice.*"

Alden shrugged. "Yeah, why not? It might be fun."

"Well, of course, it'll be fun. It's always *fun*. Only, you know..." Levi theatrically slashed his hand across his face to signify Rebecca's disfigurement.

Over actor.

"I don't think it's that bad, really," said Alden.

Crossing thick arms over his brawny chest, Levi searched for reason. Alden was something of a conundrum as of late. "Really?"

"*Really*," said Alden, nodding simply. "And don't even think about trying to get there before me. I took her. She's mine."

Levi swallowed. A seduction, however trivial, would take time. While he hated waiting, Levi hated most that Alden had access to something off limits to him. *Stingy bastard.* He pulled out a chair. "Sit down, Charlatan."

Rebecca watched as Levi snipped, clipped, and styled Alden's hair, using each tool with great precision before returning it to the leather barber roll. She always believed that only women could be primped in such a manner. Roger emptied a pebble from his boot while Manny feigned disgust at his foot odor.

"Hey, Levi. When you're done with Alden, Manny's got a few teeth you can pull. We all know how much you enjoy hurting people."

Manny took a playful slap across Rebecca at the instigator. Rebecca raised her arms to shield herself from their childish scuffle. Levi gave a sickening grin as he proceeded to remove Alden's beard.

*He **did** enjoy hurting people.*

"You don't get the urge to slit throats anymore, do you?" asked Manny.

Levi beamed. "All the time."

"That's why he stopped being a barber," Roger whispered to Rebecca. "He kept killing people."

"Y'all don't give him any ideas," Alden fussed behind a face full of froth.

"Nah," cooed Levi. "We wouldn't want to make a mess of my masterpiece, would we?" But Levi didn't sound convincing. In fact, he *had* imagined killing Alden many times. It would be easy, especially now, as Alden sat so vulnerably with his neck exposed. The Pharyngeal veins throbbing, begging to be dissected. Yet, Levi resisted because he knew how valuable Alden was to Julian and the group's success. If that ever changed, he had a plan. There would be pain. There would be blood.

"Which do you enjoy more, Levi: pain or blood?"

Levi's grin morphed from strange to sinister at Roger's mockful query in a way that would have made the Cheshire Cat uncomfortable.

"Blood," he sizzled. "I like the way it spurts."

The heckling continued; still, Levi's focus never left his project. He moved swiftly and steadily through the makeover as if performing surgery. When the last reminisce of suds were wiped away, the oils and tonics applied, and all the tools returned to their rightful home, Levi placed the mirror in Alden's hand.

"There. Now you're almost as pretty as me," he said, stepping away to admire his craftsmanship. "*Almost.*"

With a sigh, Alden sat upright to examine his new look. "Just like Julian," he remarked, returning the mirror to Levi.

"That's the point, ain't it?"

Alden forced a convincing smile, yet there was disappointment in his eyes. Vernon was right; with every passing year, as he transitioned into manhood, Alden took more and more resemblance to Julian. He didn't just look similar to their leader; when groomed this way, he was a carbon copy. And he *hated* it. Alden stood to brush off any stray hairs, hoping he could also shake off his uneasiness.

Now that the forest around Alden's face had been cleared, Rebecca could finally get a keen look at her captor. Like Julian, Alden's face was smooth and perfectly symmetrical, with a sharp jaw, a strong chin, a long, thin nose, and clearly defined cheekbones. His dark brows remained furrowed, but they were often used as a means of expression—more so than with Julian. Rebecca was certain she had seen Alden crook an eyebrow once or twice in conversation. His lips were thin but had just enough pucker to bite. His eyes would have been beautiful in any shade, but Alden's, in their bountiful blue, were by far his best feature. Julian was an attractive man by definition, but an evil in his gaze proved repulsive and took away from his physical attributes. Alden was different. He was...actually...*dashing*.

Alden caught Rebecca looking at him. Their eyes locked in on each other with mutually awkward interest. It only lasted a moment, but the encounter was enough to splash both their faces with color.

Julian entered, and it was as though the room had become water-based, for the two men's reflections bounced off one another. "There he is!" Though Julian was pleased, it was more of a declaration of relief than happiness. Julian moved forward and placed his hand on Alden's shoulder. "Come, we must continue our chat."

"What about her?" asked Alden, motioning to Rebecca with lingering eyes, quietly torn. He knew he was being summoned but was unsure of if or where his responsibilities of accommodating Rebecca might conflict. There were elements—details of her capture and their plans for her—that she didn't need to know. Additionally, he had no wish to be embarrassed in front of her again.

"She can stay with me," chimed Levi.

Rebecca shuddered at the thought of being alone with Levi, who licked his lips and gave a wicked wink that made her skin crawl.

"Roger, you and Manny will tend to our guest," Julian ordered.

With that, the pair took their leave, all the while in perfect synchronization with the other. Their gait, the way their arms would sit relaxed at their sides as they walked, and even their weight distribution was parallel.

Extraordinary.

"Creepy, isn't it?"

Rebecca nodded at Roger as he slowly rose to escort her out of the parlor, with Manny leading the way.

CHAPTER TEN

Roger, Manny, and Rebecca watched Alden and Julian transform into tiny dots traveling down a hill beyond the house's back entrance. Slowly, Rebecca began piecing together the framework of their association. She couldn't help but marvel at their success, for highly organized crime seemed only plausible in storybooks. The Disciples were both pirates of the prairie and modern Merry Men, though, in her opinion, Julian Crisp was the furthest thing from Robin Hood. And Alden…

Alden was something else entirely.

"So, Mr. Aubrey is the duplicate?"

"Yep," confirmed Roger, allowing the mid-morning sun to wash his face. He preferred the outdoors and would gladly be a man of the woods if he had the freedom to know another occupation.

"He pretends to be Mr. Crisp?"

"Only when we're on a job."

"And, with a duplicate in place, that ensures you all can perform different crimes in different places with hopes that no one will be able to pinpoint your whereabouts?"

Roger nodded. "It's also to evade capture, imprisonment, and execution, but I figure you knew that."

The original mission of the Disciples was to spread truth, the *ugly* truth. Man would continue to serve himself as he had always done, selfishly and by any means necessary. There was no justice in the world. Faith, honor, and love were disruptive elements that distracted man from acquiring what was rightfully his. Those who believed in the aforementioned establishments were foolish and deserved their losses. Ambition, power, and survival crafted a man's true purpose. If you could obtain it, it would remain yours until you could no longer sustain it. Hardly a "steal from the rich and give to the poor" mentality, this truth was frigid and unforgiving but proposed a realism that so many travelers searching for ideals like Manifest Destiny needed to learn. Somehow, their views seemed justified.

Sanctuary served as a haven for these men to decompress and replenish whatever they lacked. Most had an adequate amount of downtime between scheduled jobs, with Alden being the only exception. Manny heard Julian refer to Alden as his "workhorse" on more than one occasion. Out of compassion, respect, and because Alden had saved his life several times before, Manny often volunteered to assist him.

"Do you always come here when you've finished a job?" asked Rebecca.

Manny shook his head. "Not always."

There were safehouses, brothels, and other hideaways for one to visit to lay low after a heist. It was nothing to share a small percentage of the take with a bystander who would give them a horse in exchange or a lawman who would turn their head the other way. Everyone had a price. The men were well versed in backroads or secret routes they could take to avoid civilization. They knew how to acquire provisions and make them last. Eventually, the heat would die down so they could come home.

"Are there really twelve of you like the newspapers say—like the real disciples?" she asked.

"There *were*."

Manny proceeded to recap a brief history of the gang members:

Over the years, the Disciples recruited many men, with their numbers never exceeding a dozen—an unintentional coincidence, with the understanding that once taken into the fold, you were a Discipline for life. A new participant would be selected in the unfortunate event of a member's death. They didn't have to make replacements often, nor had there been any recent replacements, for Alden and Julian's ruse kept authorities baffled about who ran with whom and where.

Outside of the octet residing at Sanctuary, there was the absentee Vernon Ashley, the Disciples' patriarch, who passed the year prior. The group believed Vernon's passing resulted from poor diet and alcohol abuse, but Julian suspected dysentery or cholera were to blame and insisted Levi school them all in healthier practices.

Simon Whitaker, the youngest Disciple, had been missing for over a week. Edwin claimed Simon was detained in a town south of their current whereabouts, though neither Roger nor Manny knew it to be true.

The Dewey brothers—William "Bill" and Sydney—hadn't been seen for many months. Julian sent them out on assignment near the Mexican border, and they weren't heard from since.

"I think they're dead," Roger hypothesized. "I think Julian had them followed and, uh, disposed of them."

Rebecca's palm moved to her mouth. "Why would he do that to his own men?"

"Because they wanted out. And because Julian can." Roger shrugged, having considered accompanying the Deweys on their last assignment. He secretly shared their sentiments and wanted out himself, but now he would never know what happened.

"They should have run," Manny said.

"Do you think that would have made things easier? Julian would've—"

"—I know."

Roger sighed deeply, then smiled as if he had just remembered something amusing. "Remember Robert Anne?"

"Robert *Dan*! You *pendejos* treated him like garbage!"

Rebecca loved how Manny's accent would passionately flourish when frustrated. Robert Daniel Tooley was a skilled looter who ran with the group until he was mysteriously gunned down outside San Antonio. Teased for his predominantly feminine features, *Robert Dan* quickly became *Robert Anne*. He was replaced by Levi, who seemed all too available to fill the team's void.

"*I* didn't treat him badly! He made me laugh! The others gave him that nickname," Roger defended. "I would prefer to still have Robert around. I liked having him here a Hell-of-a-lot more than I do Levi."

"Do you remember Connor?" Manny asked.

"The Irish fella? I never knew him that well. Poor guy."

Manny crossed himself in respect. "We didn't know he couldn't swim..."

There was a story there, but Rebecca chose to end the reminiscing with her own redirection. "I have another question."

"Just one?" Roger chuckled and ran a hand through his hair. After Alden's makeover and with a woman in attendance, he wished *he* were more presentable. "Truth be told, we shouldn't have said anything. We've told you enough to incriminate us ten times over."

"Do you think anyone would believe me?"

"Is that your question?"

"*Roger...*"

Roger gave an easy sigh. "Go ahead."

Rebecca studied the two tiny dots in the distance; identical figures she could only guess were determining her fate. "What happens if Mr. Crisp is killed?"

Roger and Manny looked at each other in mutual skepticism.

"That won't happen," said Roger.

Manny agreed, "Men like Julian will outlive us all."

"How do you mean?"

"He's lazy," said Manny, shaking his head. "Alden does all the dirty work now that Vernon's gone. If anyone is going out, it's him."

Rebecca looked downward in conflicted compassion for Alden. If anything were to die, she hoped it would be their agenda, their selfishness, and wicked ways. The injustice all seemed to stem from Julian, whose power as a puppet master was crafted both by circumstance and his own instinctive tendencies.

Did that mean Alden was merely a puppet?

"If Mr. Crisp *were* to die," she pondered, "by accident or illness, does that mean Mr. Aubrey becomes your leader?"

"Alden doesn't want to lead this group!" Manny exclaimed.

"I don't understand."

"Forget it," Roger ceased. There were too many moving parts and too many missing pieces for her to understand. Most of the time, it was beyond his own understanding.

"Then what is it for?" she posed. "Why settle for such a fruitless existence?"

"Fruitless?" questioned Manny.

Roger's massive arms stretched out to highlight the open wilderness before them. "You're looking at it! And the thrill of it all, I guess."

Rebecca began dry-washing her hands, as none of it made much sense. Men with their games and their guns combined with a deeply rooted drive to be masters of their own vocation, no matter the cost.

Where was their sense of pride? Where were their hearts?

"Not for you?" Manny was incredibly receptive and observant. He could feel her disproval of their life's choices.

She softened. "This is hardly a way to make a living, Manny."

Roger blew wind through his lips, making a popping sound with his cheeks before letting them deflate, a practice used to suppress any urges to needlessly snap at an individual. "With all due respect, Miss Rebecca, you don't know the first thing about making a living."

"A man's got to eat," Manny added. "We do what it takes to survive."

"Nevertheless," Rebecca continued, dumbstruck. "I can't wrap my mind around why any of you would commit to this lifestyle."

Manny shrugged. "Alden didn't choose—"

"—That ain't our story to tell!"

Manny was silenced so sharply by Roger's words and elbow that he squeaked in surprise, leaving Rebecca puzzled and eager to learn more.

"I'm sorry?"

Silence.

Manny's eyes darted to Roger, ensuring he wasn't poised to strike him again.

"Alden is indebted to Julian," he said quickly.

"Manny!"

Manny's arms bent around his midsection: protective, ready to block any more blows from Roger. "If she knew the truth, Roger, she might feel differently about him."

"I don't feel anything about him," Rebecca said sternly.

"*It ain't our story to tell!*" scolded Roger.

"What if she's meant to help him somehow?" Manny whispered, leaning inward. "What if that's why he took her?"

Roger rolled up his sleeves. Manny was treading on dangerous ground. Alden would have a fit if he knew anything about his past had been shared with an outsider—especially *her*. "The only way *anyone* can help Alden is to ensure he doesn't get caught or killed."

Rebecca listened as the two men cryptically argued, wondering what they were not saying. "Would someone please explain?"

Roger surrendered. Manny's heart was in the right place, but he had no right to introduce Rebecca to Alden's secrets. After what Alden had done, Roger doubted she would sympathize with him.

Manny turned to Rebecca. "You think you're trapped? At least you have your identity. Alden es…*el sombreador.*"

Rebecca paused for clarification. "What's that?"

Manny studied the two dots in the distance and shook his head at the knowledge that one mattered more than the other.

"A shadow."

CHAPTER ELEVEN

Blues, oranges, and purples fused in scattered skies across the Sanctuary horizon. Summer had been abnormally mild, with heavy winds and showers stealing the sunshine's throne. Seasonal hailstorms damaged some of the property, and Alden suspected that more rain was to come; he could smell it. Gentle breezes passed by to propose Alden take shelter. An oak tree nodded in agreement while providing a canopy for him and his commander, who requested his audience most certainly to scold him.

"I'm assuming you brought her here because you needed a woman so badly; you just couldn't wait."

"I don't *need* a woman, Julian. I haven't touched her. It wasn't like that."

"Tell me then. What was it like?"

As with Vernon, Julian loved being the boss and thrived on controlling those around him. Alden dusted off the remaining hair trimmings from his neck. He would have to get used to it being this length. "It happened so fast... I was drunk."

He was still processing the events of the night before, attempting to determine what was real and what was a heightened sense of reality. As flashes of the evening strobed in his mind, Alden understood that he had made a grave error in abducting Rebecca, and there was little he could do to change it.

"If you wanted female companionship," began Julian. "Those arrangements could've been made for you."

"Yes, because there are always *so* many options for me..."

When Alden wasn't working, Julian made sure to keep him hidden. He was limited before under Vernon's leadership, but Alden's current superior clipped his wings and prohibited him from stepping outside Sanctuary unless he was on the job.

Julian shifted his weight. "Now, that just sounds ungrateful. Do you need to be reminded of what was done for you?"

"No, Julian. I've been reminded every day for eighteen years."

They had promised Alden freedom, but what they gave him was nothing short of a loan, a hefty sum to be repaid. Anytime Alden showed defiance or disagreed with Julian, he was ungrateful. Whenever he would point out an injustice or mention unfair treatment in the house, he was ungrateful. Had Alden known he would be working off the debt for the rest of his life, he might have chosen differently all those years ago in the jailhouse, which was set ablaze that very night.

"I don't like it when we bicker," cooed Julian. "You're my brother, Alden. I don't want to fight with you."

"Sure."

"We're a handsome man. There's no need for you to go wading in the ugly pond."

An honorable woman wouldn't be caught dead in the company of a Disciple. Alden knew the selection of female partners that was readily available to him: painted ladies that had no business referring to themselves as such. True, they were physically appealing and gave him what he needed, but pushing the external aside, they made him feel cheap. Any man could have *those* women. Alden appreciated that Rebecca was different, seeing her as a variety and an upgrade.

"Are you honestly that shallow?"

"Yes, I am," said Julian. "And proud of it. As my counterpart, you should be, too." Pride might as well have been Julian's middle name. He analyzed his protégé in disgusted disproval. "Look at you. You look like Hell. It's no wonder you've lowered your standards. What happened to you?"

"*You know what happened.*" Alden's words were haunting. He need not elaborate; Julian knew to what he was referring.

"Why are we still talking about that? It's done, Alden. It's over. You don't see Roger and Manny pulling this kind of horseshit. Not that I would allow it."

"*You weren't there.*"

Healing was a process for Roger, Manny, and Alden, with whom the latter struggled the most. Julian couldn't comprehend what plagued his men. To him, it was a job; their affliction was nothing more than an occupational hazard. As such, they shouldn't be given special treatment. "Put yourself in my place."

"I usually do," murmured Alden.

"You know how it looks when I show favoritism."

"When have you *ever* favored me?"

"I favored you last night, believe it. And I'm showing you favor now."

Alden stared ahead. The only reason why he had any clout was because Julian couldn't perform his duties without him. Julian knew that as well as he did. Alden's happiness mattered, but only just. Julian shifted. "You were Uncle Vernon's favorite. You know you were. Don't deny it."

"I wasn't going to," Alden replied.

Rather than wade in the lukewarm, and because they had cornered him, Alden chose early on to dive head first into the ice. Led by Uncle Vernon's example, he and Julian grew into men who communicated a particular chill. Each could take a life without a second thought, leaving it to chance or within the hands of someone ill-equipped to provide rescue. They would kill a man simply to see his light go out. Other times, they would feign mercy to their victim, permitting him to flee, only to later shoot said victim in the back. Vernon convinced Alden that he no longer needed forbearance, devotion, or moral integrity. After all, such attributes hadn't served him well in the past. And Alden agreed. If they wanted a villain, he'd show them a villain. This would put him in direct competition with Julian for who could be the most careless or callous. Together, though Vernon's favoritism was apparent, they made the old man proud, and Vernon soon became a substitute for the father Alden had lost. Because of this, Vernon's drawn out death felt comparable to watching his own loved ones pass. Alden tried not to think about his life before entering the fold, a life that was simpler and happier with family, but every now and then, such recollections paid him a surprise visit.

God, I miss them.

With a solemn sigh, Alden returned to the present. "Are we going through with this ransom? Are we planning any correspondence with her father?"

"Yeah," Julian shrugged. "We might as well make a profit off of your stupidity. We can supply a finger or something to send with a note tomorrow."

Alden shook his head. "I'm not taking any of her fingers."

Julian scoffed. "Oh, but you'll take *something else!* You are a walking, talking contradiction! Do you know that?"

Alden looked away, aware that his actions were paradoxical. Julian persisted.

"Are you going to fuck her, Alden? Or should I pass her off to the rest of the crew? That's only fair."

"It's not on my immediate agenda, but—"

"—But you're going to?"

Alden threw his hands in the air. "Yes, Julian! Alright? Until we're both cripple!"

"When?"

"Soon," decided Alden. "Tonight, I guess."

"Good. When you've had enough of her, give someone else a turn."

"*Fine.*"

Julian shielded his eyes from a gust of dirt-bagging wind with the back of his hand. "Next time you decide to steal something, make sure it spreads twelve ways." With that, he turned towards the house, choosing to leave with a snide remark as the last word.

Alden cleared his throat. "Wait."

Julian paused to return to his look-alike.

"Edwin was telling me something the other day—something he read about a scientist using markings from a person's fingertips to classify their identity. He said that they found no two person's marks were identical."

"Yes, he also told me," replied Julian.

"Don't you think that's something we should worry about?"

"Why, Alden?"

Alden could raise his voice, but he knew that Julian would only listen to him if he kept a calm tone. "Do you honestly believe that this—this *game* we keep playing, this *illusion*—will keep us from the law forever? I'm telling you, Julian, sooner or later, someone is going to figure it out that we're not the same man. Mark my words, they'll find a way!"

He tried, but Alden's voice elevated in both pitch and volume. Julian rolled his eyes. "And how do you suspect the law will come to this conclusion?"

Alden clapped the back of his neck with one hand, giving his shoulder a slight squeeze. "I don't know. If it's not these *prints*, they could find something in our hair or our blood...maybe even our teeth. People are making new discoveries about this sort of thing daily."

"You may have plans to donate those things to the authorities, Alden, but I don't."

"It's coming to an end, Julian."

Julian suddenly snapped forward, "It ends when I say it ends!"

Alden nodded. It was better to submit, even if he felt he might be right. Additionally, he'd followed orders for so long that Alden knew any resistance was moot. Julian stared at him, taking a wide stance, thrusting his broad chest into the open before crossing his arms.

"You're scared."

"You're not?"

"Nope. Not one bit."

It seemed that Julian was never afraid. He could talk his way out of anything, even though most of the time, it wasn't his neck on the line. Only, Alden had kept a secret from him. Depression shouldn't be taken lightly because it proved so contagious. The last thing Julian wanted was an epidemic in the house. He would have to ask the right questions and pay closer attention to his associate.

"Is there anything else you want to tell me?"

"No," Alden answered.

"Nothing else about your *melancholy*?"

"I'm good, Julian. I just needed—"

"—A *woman*? It's alright. You can say it. *You just needed a woman.*"

Alden had often been coached on what to say and how to deliver a statement. He was groomed and conditioned to avoid conflict with Julian, but compliance usually meant sacrifice. Giving an artificial smile, "I just needed a woman."

"So, go get her, cowboy," said Julian, playfully slapping Alden's backside. "You'll feel better afterward."

Rather than engage in such horseplay, Alden picked at his fingertips. The nails were bitten so far down that he could only pull at the surrounding cuticle to acquire something to chew. Tugging at the salted rubbery, he tore the cuticle, and soon, a tiny thread of red filled his digit's archway. The rambling man knew what his hands were capable of and how Rebecca would undoubtedly react when they touched her.

Maybe he could get drunk again and blackout.

But then, someone else might take her if that happened...

They would hurt her.

*Maybe he could get **her** drunk.*

No, that wouldn't do.

Julian sensed Alden's hesitation. "Where's that swagger, huh? Where's that charm and charisma that you used to have?"

Alden wiped the blood from his hand onto his trousers. "I know where it is. I know how to channel it."

Once, in his tours near Harrisburg, Alden saw a sword swallower in a traveling show. It was explained to him that the weapon wasn't very sharp and that the man wasn't really swallowing; rather, he had repressed the muscles needed to swallow to keep the passage from the mouth to the stomach open for the sword. Still, there was a danger of scraping or puncturing the man's insides. Alden later told Roger that the experience was the closest he could relate to in describing what it meant to be Julian. Every single performance felt both damaging and damning.

"So, channel it already because you're embarrassing us both!" Julian huffed impatiently. The gang leader then headed back up the hill towards the house, leaving Alden alone with his thoughts. The wind pushed hard against Alden, urging him to accept his role and step into character.

He could draw it out. He could keep Rebecca close to him at all times.

He would pretend.

No real harm would be done.

It would be like it never happened.

CHAPTER TWELVE

"We'll have to send something along with the ransom note."

Later that day, Rebecca was permitted to only sign her name at the end of the demand letter, which Julian penned. It was scribed more eloquently than she initially imagined, with the threat to end her life being passive-aggressive yet polite. Julian used words that her father would understand and spoke to him respectfully from a position of authority. He wouldn't appear cowardly, even in print.

Alden made a small effort to tidy his bedroom for their first night together, having never formally entertained a female guest in his own personal space, always sharing the bed with a woman in a hotel, brothel, or the occasional wagon. Rebecca watched from the floor as her captor fumbled around the area. She had already seen him steal, murder, swear, rile, faint, vomit, and cower. There was no need to put on airs now.

A drop of sweat slid down Alden's temple. The clock was ticking, and the pressure to consummate Rebecca's capture was evident. If he could make it appear as though the deed had been done, Alden could win them time and formulate a plan to get her home safely. He shook his head.

This is Hell.

I'm in Hell.

To Alden, assaulting a woman was nothing more than a feeble act to prove one's masculinity, and he didn't need that validation. Over the years, Alden knew scores of lovers of all ages, races, and creeds, with his lifestyle encouraging Casanova's behavior and associating him with more than enough companions to satiate his appetite. But honestly, Alden hadn't been hungry in a long time. To make matters worse, he now had to simulate false intimacy with *her*, a celibate. He searched inward. Was insinuating that a horrendous act occurred as wrong as performing the act itself?

Probably, but it has to be done.

This is wrong.

*This is **so** wrong.*

With a heavy hand, Alden snatched the side of her head and relieved from her a lock of hair using the folding knife from his satchel. He severed through it like rope without the least hint of tenderness. As expected, a small *ack* escaped her, but nothing more. He swiftly settled Rebecca back onto the wooden flooring, wishing she had reacted louder.

That might have helped sell it.

"I would've given that to you," said Rebecca, rubbing her scalp sorely.

Alden gave a convincing grin and placed the strand into his bag. "Yeah, but it was more fun to take it." He plopped down onto the bed, boots and all, with his hat over his eyes. Once concealed, Alden gave a discouraged sigh.

She's strong.

If only she were more tender headed instead of tender hearted!

Alden turned to place his hat on a nearby pillow. Should he simply tell Rebecca what she needed to do?

*How does one begin **that** conversation?*

He could scare her to the point of believability. Her reactions would have to be authentic with the other Disciples down the hall from them. Anything less would cause suspicion. Alden rose from the mattress to inspect his image in the mirror.

What kind of man does such a thing—the real thing?

Was it Narcissism? Hostility towards women? Or just self-gratification?

He stole a quick glance in her direction. This was a woman surrounded by cold-blooded killers—madmen that tortured and mutilated other men nearly unrecognizable in colors one's nightmare's nightmares couldn't paint, yet to his knowledge, Julian had never violated a woman. Sure, he may have gotten a little rough on occasion, but he never downright defiled any of them. Roger and Manny were above such heinous acts; Edwin's attention was mostly directed at Reuben (who had little interest in anyone), and if Phillip had any malicious intent, he never voiced it—not that he could. Levi was the one who would hurt Rebecca if given the opportunity, no doubt. Because she was there. Because she was a woman. Because he could.

Setting his jaw, Alden attempted to assemble the necessary attributes. Levi's attributes. *You do this all the time, Alden. You pretend. You get the job done.*

Yet, some things—even as criminals—were out of bounds. Despicable acts that would wrench your insides just considering them, knowing that they even existed. He knew of such acts and had even—

No, don't think about that right now.

Rebecca nervously pressed herself into the corner of the room, farthest from him, and watched Alden silently stare in the mirror for many minutes as if internally arguing with his reflection. She knew what that was like.

But wishing to look different never made it so.

Then, crooking his head slightly, Alden smiled. No Levi was necessary. No, he would toy with her, having channeled the charisma and charm Julian suggested, mixing in his own sensual instincts. He *had* to. Alden slid a shaky hand across the bed and walked towards Rebecca, his stride artistically arrogant as he crossed the room. When he gently stroked her cheek, Rebecca let out an audible gulp. He was close—*too close.*

"Shh…it's alright," he told her.

Alden turned to nuzzle the side of her face as his hand slipped down to her shoulder, settling on Rebecca's waist. Rebecca flinched as a reflex to push him away but found herself fondling a bicep in a mixture of instinct and intrigue. The hair on his forearm was soft with skin that bore a surprisingly smooth finish. Alden's eyes widened.

What are you doing?

Aren't you afraid of me?

No, Alden, she's calling your bluff.

He would have to up the ante.

Now they both shook, with Rebecca completely flattened against the wall as Alden's hand continued grazing her torso, searching. It would all be over if he could find what would trigger her.

No, not there.

Not there, either.

He leaned closer to breathe her in, her neck still smelling of soap and the slightest hint of rosewater. Rebecca sought to send her thoughts somewhere else, anywhere else that would take her away from the stranger's hands that traveled slowly up, up, up, and then down, down, down before lifting the tail of the shirt to —

"NO!"

There it is.

An instinctual refusal shrieked into Alden's ear, accompanied by frantic pushback, but he wouldn't be moved. Alden reared back slightly to feign surprise.

"No?"

"Please, no," Rebecca sniffled, pushing against him. "I can't—I'm not ready."

The pair had frozen, save for Rebecca's shivery tears. She tried to be brave, telling herself she could endure the inevitable, but none of Rebecca's books educated her on what to expect regarding *this*. Sure, she would eavesdrop on scandalously delicious party conversations from glowing, newly married women, but those accounts were of *making love,* not whatever Alden was planning. Indeed, her books hadn't informed Rebecca of how a man might misuse her body, nor did they prepare her for what could happen once the violation was complete.

Alden returned his face inward, his nose resting on hers with eyes closed earnestly, like a man speaking the gospel. Rebecca held her breath so as not to inhale his wicked whisperings. "I know you're not," he cooed.

I'm not, either.

Rebecca winced as he surprisingly raised his hands to wipe away her tears. She remained a pancake between Alden and the wall, with every movement bringing him closer than she wished.

"That's fine. I can wait," he whispered. At that, Alden turned on his heel and returned to the bed. "But make no mistake, I will have you."

Rebecca dropped down the wall into the floor, wrapping her arms around her knees and wiping away any evidence of her distress. She liked the floor; now, she considered it an ally. Thus would be her life with the Disciples, always retreating to the ground, confused by the inconsistent patterns of her current living arrangements, fueled by shock, queasy from adrenaline, and dread.

Alden also felt a sick swirl in his stomach. Now, she'd *really* be afraid of him. Though it was an idle threat, while seemingly reaffirming his position of power, Alden had also exploited her innocence for sport. It was a very *Julian* thing to do, yet Rebecca reacted exactly the way Alden hoped she would. He lessened.

I just hope it's enough.

Rebecca's hands shook as she covered herself with Roger's coat. She would never fall asleep now. While he hadn't forced himself on her, Alden made it clear that he planned to do so. Hours passed without another word spoken between them. Now exhausted, Rebecca stifled her sobs, determined to stay awake at all costs. Since their exchange, Alden never so much as looked at her, staring blankly at the ceiling and rising only to obtain a bottle of whiskey.

A window sat mere feet from Alden's bed, easily accessible. It was the same window Rebecca saw him retch out of earlier that morning. An impact from the second story would hurt, no doubt. She would most likely break an arm or leg, but it would be a small price to pay for freedom.

The bottle on the bedside table soon lost its volume, yet it was Alden who felt empty. He could have apologized or explained, but the damage was done. *Even if she knew the truth, she wouldn't understand.* Rebecca would cry herself to sleep—because of *him* and *his* actions— and he didn't feel like listening.

Rebecca watched as the container of liquor became more and more transparent. *Yes, let aged wheat and barley ferment you right to sleep, you sot.*

She would wait until Alden was passed out to exercise her plan of escape.

CHAPTER THIRTEEN

Rebecca was familiar with the floors of Windhaven Hall, knowing which boards or steps would squeak in her midnight adventures, first to the library and then into the garden. She rarely needed a candle or lantern; moonlight often illuminated her reading material on those journeys outside to reflect, pray, or childishly make a wish. Rebecca planned to use the night sky once more to find the main road, counting on stars fashioned into a gourd-shaped compass to lead her in the right direction. But the floors of Sanctuary held their own mystery with each suspenseful step. She would have to circle around Alden's bed as he slept to reach the window and escape.

Alden's breathing patterns occurred in threes: three seconds of inhalation, three seconds held, and three seconds of exhalation. Rebecca breathed as Alden did while she crouched beside the window pane. Given the previously disorganized state of the bedroom, she was surprised to find the pane wiped down, leaving no remnants of an upset stomach. Rebecca continued to control her respirations, standing mere inches from Alden in this position. Slowly, she lifted the window.

"What have I done?"

Horrified, Rebecca turned to face Alden, bringing her gaze to his level. Alden had not awoken; he remained on an unconscious plateau. His eyelids were secured, but the rest of his body seemed completely overpowered, and he began to thrash in distress while his face glistened, covered in sweat.

Or were those tears?

"NO—Please, God! I didn't..."

Rebecca listened to his nervous mumblings, which harbored intense fear and anxiety with the occasional yelp. Alden coughed and sputtered, kicking at the mattress with his arms reaching out—not for something, but for *someone*.

"*Let me go!*" Alden cried, still imprisoned in an alternate reality. He struck the pillows and arched his back several times as if fighting an invisible force. It seemed he, too, was trying to escape. But what could plague such a man so dreadfully?

*He's **not** crazy, alright? He's just very, very sick!*

Roger's words had encouraged her compassion, yet a part of Rebecca wanted to let Alden suffer in his own horrific hallucinations. Instinctually, she reached to comfort him but stopped herself. Alden's actions were unforgivable. He *deserved* it. She stepped back to observe, her thin shadow looming over his face.

A shadow.

Manny's commentary from that afternoon echoed: *Alden is indebted to Julian... You think you're trapped?... If she knew the truth, she might feel differently about him... At least you have your identity... A man's got to eat... Alden es el sombreador...*

Rebecca stood bewildered by Alden's lurid struggle until, eventually, a sympathetic tear slipped down her cheek. She remembered his sullen eyes and how sickly he always appeared. This was clearly the way Alden slept every night, if he even slept at all. It was no wonder he drank so heavily! Her captor was undoubtedly disturbed and possibly deranged. In any case, he was obviously unwell and in pain.

What did Julian do to you?

"No! Just kill me," he gulped, tossing and turning in haunted misery. "Please."

She hadn't meant to, but Rebecca's soft fingertips now rested in the palm of Alden's hand, which relaxed immediately. She lifted them away one by one as his fingers pulsed for their return. He was stabilizing, with shaky breaths turning first to heavy sighs and then easing once more into a full slumber.

Rebecca scolded herself, knowing she had missed her chance. She remained for several minutes, stuck between two possible timelines. If she returned to her floor pallet, Alden would never know her plan to jump out the window. If she resumed, there was a chance he might awaken and punish her. And what if one of the other Disciples saw her flee? She would need a way to defend herself.

On the dresser sat Rebecca's salvation in the form of a .45 Colt Single Action Army revolver. Rebecca held her breath and navigated the bedroom again to retrieve the weapon, finding it not as heavy as she thought. No one ever forgets their first time holding a gun. The shiny sidearm had an ivory handle, smooth to the touch. She ran her fingers over the silver hardware and speculated how many men had been left in its wake.

"Woman, you're about to be in a world of hurt."

Rebecca spun around to see Alden with an expressionless flash of lightning in his eyes that made him seem both unliving and undead. She never heard him exit the mattress. He stepped forward.

"I wonder if you even know how to use that thing…"

Clutching the revolver with both hands, Rebecca took several steps away from him and gestured to the barrel. "I know this side does the killing."

Despite her threat, it was clear to Alden that Rebecca had no clue how to handle a gun. "And what will you do when you've finished with me?" he asked, continuing his pursuit. "There's a lot of men out there. A lot of *bad* men. There aren't enough bullets in that gun to shoot them all."

"I will make do." Rebecca then realized she had foolishly backed herself into the corner as she had hours earlier.

"Then let's make sure that the first shot doesn't go to waste." Alden ceased, allowing the gun's hollow point to press directly into his tight torso. "Go on. Do it."

A shaky hand. A cunning *click*. As far as Rebecca knew, this revolver committed treason. Alden remained pokerfaced. His chilly blue eyes made no attempts to evade hers, which were full of wide-eyed horror. He hadn't flinched, blinked, or even taken a breath, but she swore she saw him grin.

"It works better with bullets."

Rebecca screamed, and in one hasty movement, Alden relieved her of the revolver, finishing with a full wind-up smack. The sharp, biting sensation spread across Rebecca's left cheekbone. She didn't remember Alden being left-handed. Rebecca checked for damage, having never been physically struck before and shocked by the searing pain. She screamed again, her confused, adrenaline-fueled emotions delaying any attempts to put space between them. Rebecca reached the bedroom door to find it locked just before Alden caught her by the waist.

"Do you really think I'm that stupid?!" he spat, throwing her away from the door. He tossed the gun aside and faced Rebecca with his hand poised to strike again.

Rebecca shuffled away slowly. *Too slowly.* Fixtures and furniture crashed to the floor as the force of his body brought hers to the ground, throwing her back with a giant *whoosh*. Glass and porcelain shattered. The wooden flooring also packed a punch. *Slam!* A warm, red glaze melted down the side of Rebecca's forehead due to her discord with the dresser.

"Do you have any idea who you're dealing with?"

Alden had her pinned to the floor, his shaky hands firmly wrapped around her neck. As he squeezed, Rebecca felt herself beginning to lose consciousness.

"You're no one…" she choked. "You're—*counterfeit.*"

The last thing Rebecca saw that night was Alden's sudden surrender, the possessive spirit fleeing, abandoning him in the darkness. As he became completely alert, Roger burst through the door.

"My God, Alden! What did you do?"

CHAPTER FOURTEEN

"Congratulations, you just gave a woman a beating! Maybe we can go into town and find you a few nuns or someone's old granny for you next."

Alden rocked ever so slowly on the side of the bed. Explaining himself would be difficult. What happened wasn't a deliberate or outright act of brutality. He merely hallucinated a threat. Still, Rebecca was hurt, and Roger scooped her up and out of the room before Alden could say anything. In all honesty, he scarcely remembered the encounter, with it feeling more of an out-of-body experience. Alden chose not to follow Roger but waited for his return.

This conversation was overdue.

Alden wrung his hands. "I didn't know it was her," he pledged. "I mean, I *saw* her, but it didn't register—I thought—"

"—You got sick again, didn't you?" Roger fumed. "You drank too much and forgot where you were."

"I thought I was somewhere else. I thought I was Julian." Alden's eyes darted left and right, scanning the room for memories or clues— anything that would help him understand the misinterpretation.

"That gives you the right to hit a woman? Because *he* would? I oughta pop you one!" Roger hadn't completely dismissed the idea of a physical reprimand. After all, he promised Rebecca that he would deal with Alden if he acted out. "Keeping them quiet on the job is one thing, Alden, but when they're defenseless—"

"—She pointed a gun at me!"

"I'm sorry! Has that never happened to you before?" mocked Roger. "Should we all pray for the Lord to grant you peace after such a traumatic experience?" He kept his hands on his hips, believing the scolding would be a sufficient form of discipline. Alden was hard enough on himself.

I'm not mad.

I'm just disappointed.

The lecture continued. "We take what needs taking, we help who needs helping, and we kill who needs killing, but we're not about *this*. You know my thoughts about *this* sort of thing!"

"Then maybe you should talk to Levi!"

"Why? Are you trying to be like him now? A stand-up guy, that one!"

Alden rubbed his face with his hands and shuddered at the remanence of the sickly-sweet coppery smell: Rebecca's blood. He had washed, but no amount of scrubbing would ever remove that stain. Levi's reputation proceeded him, and Alden knew of Roger's dysfunctional family history. Yes, he knew of the physical and emotional scars that Nelson Mercer left behind.

Please don't compare me to them…

There was no need to exert his dominance over Rebecca. She understood where she was and the kind of men she was with. And to her, he was the worst. He was a coward. He was nobody. He was counterfeit.

Was the booze completely to blame?

Either way, it was his doing.

Where was his self-control?

Alden nibbled on a peeling fingernail. His insides hurt, yet not in a place he could directly pinpoint. It was almost as if his body had chosen to shun him for performing an act so contrary to his upbringing. *Son, defend yourself against other men if necessary, but never put your hands on a woman.* Alden gulped at his father's words. They were clear, calm, and with the same noble direction as when he first heard them. In his youth, Alden could never wrap his mind around such behavior; as a Disciple, it was a regular occurrence. Alden never said anything when he was witness to it. Maybe that was worse.

Roger shook his head. "Every time you step out of line here lately, it gets harder and harder to help you."

"So, stop helping me!"

"Is that what you really want?"

Alden said nothing, keeping his face hidden from his friend.

"Why did you bring her here?" pressed Roger. "You know what could happen..."

Alden's insides twisted once more. Yes, he *did* know. A mumbled response echoed in his hands. "I don't want to say."

"What?"

You wouldn't understand.

"Would you speak up?"

I shouldn't have taken her.

Alden sat upright. "I wish it would have been loaded."

"No, you don't. Come on, now..."

"Julian thinks I brought her here to—" Alden stood. "He expects me to—"

Roger's face turned taut. "—Tell me you *didn't!*"

"No, Rog! I didn't, and I won't! You *know* I won't!"

Roger then made a difficult inquiry. "What about when someone else tries to?"

With another gulp, Alden bowed his head. "I don't know. I really don't." It was only a matter of time. It would be his fault. Even Edwin looked at her with suspicious intent. The two took a brief recess to consider their own limitations as outlaws, as men. Their internal moral compasses never seemed to mutually point due north about anything except protecting the fairer sex.

"I'm losing my mind," Alden wavered. "I don't know who I am anymore. I'm not sure that I ever really knew. I don't want to be like Julian but after all this time…and Newberry… Most days, I can't tell the difference."

"You just need to get some rest. Eating something wouldn't hurt, either."

Any other man might have dismissed Alden's behavior, called him names, or said he belonged in a mental institution, but Roger knew that what ailed his friend was the byproduct of fear, guilt, and pain.

"The nightmares—" Alden gasped, his eyes wide and flooded with horror. "They won't stop. It's like this every night. *Every. Night.* I'm so tired, Rog! And it's too late! I can't undo any of the things I've done."

"None of us can, so we have to try to improve every tomorrow," Roger sighed as he put both hands on his friend's shoulders, the words catching in his throat. He knew what sights and sounds haunted Alden's dreams. He and Manny were there with him in Newberry and had experienced them firsthand.

Alden sought Roger's hefty hands and desperately positioned them around his neck. Roger was strong enough to crush a windpipe with minimal effort. *It would be quick, and maybe it wouldn't hurt so bad.* "Would you do it?" he whispered.

"*What?*"

"Would you kill me, Rog?" Alden blinked back tears, standing firm in the unshakable belief that his death would solve everything. "Julian—he can't continue if I'm not here. Do it. *Please.* Roger, please. I won't even fight you."

"*Alden—*"

"—If I die, it can all end."

"Not for *her*," Roger calmly reasoned. "*You* have to protect her now."

The struggle for strangulation continued. Alden gritted his teeth, not wanting Roger to be right. "You could keep her safer than I could."

"You'd put that on me?"

After some time, Alden let Roger's hands drop. "No. No, of course not."

Roger sighed again, this time from relief. "I have nightmares about Newberry, too," he admitted.

At this, Alden returned to the edge of the bed. Newberry had also been his fault. Alden winced at the recollection and again at the sight of Rebecca's little corner, the farthest possible location from where he sat. He knew she hid from him because she was afraid. "Where is she?" he finally asked.

"She's with Manny. She'll be fine, Alden. She's a bit roughed up, but no permanent damage."

"Levi didn't try to—"

"—Nope. There was no need for him to see her. Manny got her fixed right up."

"Yeah?"

For the first time, there was hope in Alden's voice.

If Manny had tended to her, then maybe she wasn't that hurt after all.

"I think you scared her more than anything," offered Roger.

Alden nodded and considered the nearby window. "I bet she was trying to leave."

"Can you blame her?"

"No." If climbing out a window were all it took to escape Sanctuary, Alden would've done it years ago.

"It's probably best we kept her with Manny until morning," said Roger. "We'll reconvene before breakfast."

"Alright."

"Don't drink any more tonight, okay? If you need help sleeping, I brought a book for you." Roger tapped the Bible on Alden's nightstand, a family heirloom that Roger frequented for guidance in recent months. He found the text held stories of men not too terribly unlike himself. Sometimes, the stories made him feel worse about the things he'd done, but most of the time, it helped. Alden lifted his eyes to the Good Book and quickly turned away. Simply looking at the sacred text made him feel guilty. He was unworthy of its comfort but hoped it would perhaps provide him with some wisdom?

You have to protect her now.

Alden ran his fingers along his bottom teeth. "Roger?"

"Yeah?"

"Do you think we are what we do?"

Roger stopped in the doorway. It was a question that haunted him most days, too. *Burglary, robbery, kidnapping, obstruction of justice, arson, murder...*

All immoral, wicked, and evil acts...

Unforgivable.

"I sure hope not."

CHAPTER FIFTEEN

The next morning, Rebecca found herself positioned among a line of men stationed at the breakfast table. Roger, Manny, Edwin, and Phillip sat while Rueben busily served the crew. Alden sat across from Rebecca but hadn't addressed her. She was noticeably unkempt and now sported a cut along her hairline and a slight welt on her left cheek. Alden's stomach sank.

I'm a monster.

Between bites, the other Disciples—those who weren't a part of the late-night drama—gave a side glance, first at her, then at Alden. Expressions ranged from surprise to indifference, yet their countenances maintained the practicality that matched their personal character traits. No words were said *about* Rebecca, necessarily, but there was definitely an understanding among the men.

Rebecca examined the cuisine, which consisted of a plate of bacon, eggs, and a slice of day-old bread. On her first morning at Sanctuary, she had no desire to eat, but as it was a new day, and with the alluring aroma charming her more and more, Rebecca found herself ravenous. She licked her lips as she scanned the dish before her, wondering where to begin. In all her literary findings, prisoners were held in dungeons with only scraps and water to sustain them.

This would be a feast for her fictional friends!

Alden bent his elbow and leaned onto the table, his bloodshot eyes faded, fully fatigued. "Well, we weren't about to let you go hungry."

Alden wasn't a morning person, especially not *that* morning. He had spent half the night queasy and wanted nothing more than to climb back into bed and sleep the day away. It was lazy, but that was how he would spend all his days if permitted. Nodding, Rebecca's doe eyes fluttered before lowering, ending their connection.

You pointed a gun at him, you fool. You're lucky he didn't break your neck.

Alden shifted to find Phillip, who slowly leaned in from his place at the table, crunching bacon, seemingly pleased. Alden's brows furrowed.

Do they honestly think I did it?

After providing a chin-up of acknowledgment, Alden looked away in disbelief.

They honestly think I did it.

"You should eat," Rueben fussed as he passed by, placing a plate in front of Alden. Rueben seemed equally grumpy this morning. While he had prepared the meal, it wasn't his job to serve anyone—not anymore— yet when service was required, the others always called on him.

The tin plate swiveled in adjustment to new gravity on the table's hard surface, carefully keeping its contents secure as it rotated. Flavorful smells wheeled towards Alden's nasal passages, which were unprepared and soon overstimulated. He turned his head and fought back an involuntary gag, which Reuben took as a critique of his cooking.

"You think you can do better?"

"I'm not hungry," Alden muttered.

Reuben huffed. "It's not a request; it's *orders*." Then, turning on his heel, Rueben mumbled something under his breath about being disrespectful before heading to his own seat. Alden surveyed the dish, already anticipating how sick he would later be. With shaking hands, Alden sighed and began breaking bread.

"Where's Julian?" Manny asked while searching visually from above his plate, for neither Levi nor Julian had entered the dining room.

"Probably forming some elaborate plan for world domination," Alden quipped.

Roger watched as Rebecca paused out of habit. She was a lady and, therefore, accustomed to more polite protocol at meals. He knew such gestures of gratitude in his youth but had carelessly forgotten them after leaving home.

Manners require no space in a suitcase.

He drummed his fingers self-consciously on the table. "We should say grace."

Manny nodded with enthusiasm while Alden shook his head at Roger's suggestion. "Seriously?"

"Why not?" Roger shrugged with adorable optimism.

Alden tugged at bread bits, much like a child, flattening the sponge-like squares with his thumbs. If he played with his food long enough, it might appear like he had eaten. "I killed a man two days ago, Rog. You say grace."

Manny and Roger each bowed their heads, and Rebecca followed instinctually, much to the chagrin of the rest of the diners, who mocked them but continued eating at a softer decibel. Perhaps there *was* something ingrained in the Disciples that recognized the importance of reverence for a higher power. Roger began with a voice that was deep and covered them all like a warm blanket.

"Gracious God, we have sinned against Thee, and are unworthy of Thy mercy; pardon our sins, and bless these mercies for our use, and help us to eat and drink to Thy glory, for Christ's sake. Amen."

"Amen," said Manny, who crossed himself in reverence.

The rest of the table would not comment on their brief meditation. For a moment, all that could be heard were the sounds of chewing and clinking utensils.

"Roger here believes he's going to help us all find salvation," Alden joked, hoping Rebecca might speak to them.

"If anything's worth finding, it's salvation." Roger's response was almost instinctual in what was a reoccurring conversation. "Lord knows we need it."

Saying nothing, Rebecca tore a piece of bread and slowly raised it to her lips. Even faintly opening her mouth proved painful.

"Is that any way to treat your guest?"

Levi tardily joined the group for breakfast and was undoubtedly referring to the newfound blemish on Rebecca's cheek. The way he smiled made her question whether his comment was out of concern or in jest. His hands settled on Rebecca's shoulders. Unsurprisingly, they made her feel more uneasy than anyone else's—especially when he began using them to massage around her collar. "My apologies, angel face. We raised Alden to have better manners."

At this, Alden rolled his eyes.

"Well, we did *try*," Levi added. "Perhaps he needs a lesson on how to treat a lady. If he doesn't take care of you, I'd be happy to provide my services."

Alden casually took a swig of coffee. "I know how to treat a lady."

"Do you? It's been so long, I reckon..." Levi's fingers trickled through her hair like spider legs. "I'm not sure if you can handle courting such a pretty little thing."

His haughty tone had a way of harassing everyone at the table, but it was Rebecca dropping her still-uneaten bread that broke the tension. Alden's bravado lessened out of embarrassment for Rebecca, whose color drained by the second.

"I can handle it," Alden simply replied.

Rebecca noticed the small lift of Alden's eyebrow as he faced Levi with a smile that revealed nothing but communicated everything in ways that only men knew how to decipher. A secret code of machismo. She couldn't tell if it was meant to appease Levi or make him leave her alone. Roger and Manny chose to continue chewing rather than chime in. Additionally, the less they had to interact with Levi, the better.

"Y'all have a good day," Levi sneered as he slithered away with lingering hands.

Rebecca tried to smooth her hair and clothing before picking up the bread once more. Levi had touched her, and that made her feel... *icky*.

"This might help you out a little," Roger recommended, sliding a fork to her.

Alden snapped his head to Roger. "Don't give her that!"

"Well, she's not gonna stick *me*!"

While the two men bickered, Rebecca slowly maneuvered to bring scoopfuls of eggs to her mouth. Like manna from Heaven, the warm, salty texture proved to be a gratifying source of nourishment.

"Perdoname, but may I ask, what happened to your face?"

Alden and Roger turned their attentions to Manny, who used his finger to slightly signify Rebecca's scars with little swishes. Alden flicked the bread bits back to his plate while Roger shifted in discomfort.

Manny shrugged. "What? Did I not word it correctly?"

"Geez, Manny," Roger moaned. "You can't just ask someone why they're disfigured. It's not polite."

"Since when are we polite?" Alden took a bite of bacon and chewed thoughtfully as Roger began explaining the correct protocol for social interactions.

Rebecca returned her fork to the table. "It's alright. Most people don't ask; they just stare. I know you're all wondering, though it's not very appropriate to discuss."

"You *do* realize who you're sitting with?"

Roger laughed at Manny's resolve. Alden squinted his eyes a bit, trying to solve the mystery himself. Never before had Rebecca held an audience of men, especially not with such captively undivided attention!

Should I feel embarrassed or excited?

Swirling her sentiments, she began, "My mother had difficulty bringing me into this world. The doctors believed that using a tool—an instrument to—to *assist*—would help…"

Manny was on the edge of his seat. "Did it?"

"No, not as much as they hoped. My mother—she—she passed shortly after I was born."

A pregnant pause fell over the table as the men shifted in confused discomfort. They knew little of women's matters—especially gynecology—so she need not say more. Rebecca's face fell. She always believed that sharing the story would desensitize her to the terror of her birth, but it never did.

"Does it hurt?" Manny's query seemed so innocent; it was almost endearing. Rebecca shook her head.

"Do you have a hard time showing your feelings?" Now that the floor had been opened for questioning, Roger struggled to ask his delicately.

"I had less control over my facial expressions when I was younger. I would sit in front of the mirror and practice talking or emoting for hours. It's not perfect, but it is much easier now."

Roger nodded, taking it all in. Rebecca then turned to Alden. Surely, he had a question, too. But Alden made no inquiries. He simply pushed his plate aside and excused himself from the table. Rebecca hung her head, prompting Roger to lightly nudge her with his elbow.

"Hey, that had nothing to do with you, alright?"

Giving a tiny smile, Rebecca knit her brow. "What was he like before?" she asked.

Roger slid Alden's plate to his own and piled on the leftovers.

No use for it to go to waste.

"How do you mean?"

"Manny told me last night that he used to be different."

"We all used to be different," Roger shrugged. "But there's no need to tell you about all that."

"Why? Did something happen?" Rebecca persisted. If she learned more about Alden, his secrets, and his inner workings, maybe she could develop a strategy to defend herself.

Roger stewed at Manny. "It's not as though talking about it would make it right."

"So, something *did* happen?" Rebecca inquired again.

Manny provided Roger with a guilty smile. He knew what Roger was thinking. Still, something *had* to be said to protect their friend. Manny's words wouldn't pardon what Alden did, but they might grant him a lighter sentence.

"I wonder," continued Rebecca. "Are you being so elusive because you're protecting Mr. Aubrey or because you're afraid I will think less of the two of you?"

Manny started and hesitated, "I don't understand the question."

"We all know there are some things you just don't do, right? Well, we've done those things, Miss Rebecca," Roger explained before giving a final huff on the matter. "And Alden—he's always been a better actor than an outlaw. That's all you need to know."

CHAPTER SIXTEEN

Alden attempted to steady his breathing as the knot in his throat thickened. His chest grew heavy, and beads of sweat collected along his collarbone. This was the *fourth* time he had gotten sick in front of Rebecca during the middle of the night, although on this occasion, whiskey wasn't to blame. He grimaced at the short, sharp spasms that traveled through his midsection. Having leaped abruptly from the warmth of the mattress, his body fighting the cramps and convulsions, Alden stuck his head outside the bedroom window. He would have been embarrassed if he weren't in so much pain. Alden clutched at the window panel with bent knees as he had numerous times before, but today, he didn't eat enough, so it was especially trying. He hadn't even drunk that much. This was all nerves. Finally, *relief* made its frothy, acidic entrance into the world.

"Are you alright?"

Rebecca's voice made Alden's very insides dip. He rested his hands on his knees to balance from the aftershock, finishing with a spit of embellishment before closing the window.

"Does it look like I'm alright?" Alden snapped as he went to the bureau. Rebecca watched him bring life to the lantern and take a swig of something with the name *Odol* emblazoned across the bottle, most likely an antiseptic. He swished and gargled for a few moments before expelling the contents into a tin bucket in the corner.

"Another bad dream?" she calmly assumed.

"Something like that," he mumbled. He *was* embarrassed now, as this had begun to happen more frequently, for with her arrival came *new* nightmares.

Alden attempted to make amends after the misunderstanding their first night together, apologizing even, but Rebecca could still never predict what each new evening with Alden might hold. She had yet to see him consume a full meal in her four days at Sanctuary, and while he *did* drink heavily—either liquor or strong black coffee, the cause of Alden's nausea seemed to stem from something impotable.

"Would you like to talk about it?" she asked.

"No."

Alden continued to swish and spit various substances until he was convinced the vomit's bitter taste had left him. He stopped to light a cigarette and crossed to Rebecca's side of the room. After wobbling a bit, he sat beside her against the wall, their shadows now dancing on the ceiling. The cool surface felt refreshing on his back, which had sweat through his shirt.

"This is looking much better," he noted, softly touching her bruised profile, grateful it hadn't swollen or turned as deeply purple as he believed it would. Rebecca flinched slightly and watched his expression fade, changing as though he might be sick again or simply realizing that she was still fearful of him.

Rebecca carefully examined her abductor in the lamplight, imagining how he might appear when happy and in good health. Alden was sincerely handsome but seemed to be wasting away, either by his own neglect or some sinister illness.

"Are you unwell?"

Hesitant, Alden confirmed, "Yes."

"Have you been sick for very long?"

"Six months, give or take." Alden had lost track of the time that had passed since Newberry. He was touched that she cared enough to ask; most people merely commented on his ghostly state, comparing him to Julian, which was how he was *supposed to look.*

"Is it terminal?" she inquired.

"God, I hope so," Alden said with a chuckle. Adding, "Don't worry, it's not communicable." He turned from the now-warmed wall to lower himself to the floor, his back delighting again at the cold surface but rebuking its construction.

She's slept here for days and never once requested a pillow or blanket.

*This woman of privilege hasn't asked for **anything**.*

"*Ugh!* This can't be comfortable!" Alden rolled onto his side, propping an elbow to lean on and taking a long drag through a now friendly smile. "You should come to bed with me. We'll ignore the gossip."

Rebecca waved at the smoke that traveled her direction, choosing to stare ahead, not knowing what to make of his offer or his sudden acknowledgment of infirmity.

"I've never shared a bed with a man," she said flatly.

"That's something we have in common." Alden waited for even a slight response to his attempt at humor, then slowly rose to face her, the cigarette still hanging casually from his lips. "Hey, look at me."

Rebecca obliged. With his cobalt eyes never looking as low as her neckline, Alden took in her face's smooth, subtle curves and how all of her features appeared as though they were tailor-made, placed there by God, Himself. He didn't terry on Rebecca's scars, but rather her eyes, which seemed so friendly yet frightened, greenery that contained specks of gold he had never noticed before. His gaze finally fell upon her lips. A puckering pink, they sweetly curved on one side due to her markings.

Alden wondered if she had ever been kissed.

"You're beautiful," he said. "Do you know that?"

Rebecca frowned in disbelief. She had been called many things, but *beautiful* was never one of them. *What was he up to?* Because the words upset her, she wouldn't formally accept his compliment.

"Thank you, Mr. Aubrey," she shook, "But I don't *feel* beautiful."

"Why? Because of this?" He faintly gestured to his own right profile. "Because you're here—with *me*?"

"It doesn't matter why."

Puzzled, Alden blew his smoke in the opposite direction. He never could understand why women picked themselves apart the way they did.

Every woman should feel beautiful in their own right.

"I think it does," he shrugged. "When was the last time you felt beautiful?"

"Why do you want to know?"

"Because I want to know!" Alden persisted.

Why were women like this?

Everything is encoded or protected by a wall of frustratingly feminine pride!

"I'm just—I'm trying to make conversation."

"Never, absolutely," she quickly revealed. "I've never felt beautiful." It was a surprising self-assessment, but Rebecca's delivery proved as committed as the flick of a wrist.

"Well, you *are*," he whispered. Rebecca's mane was secured only by a handful of brave pins. With his free hand, Alden reached for the lock of hair that fell and tucked it behind her ear. He was apparently exhausted and had opened up to her for some unknown reason. Instinctually, Rebecca backed away. Even if he *was* sick, she knew better than to play into his charms. She learned *that* her first evening with him.

"Why are you saying all of this? So I won't suspect what you're going to do?"

Alden yawned. "What I'm going to do…?"

"You know very well to what I'm referring."

Ah, that. Alden raised his cigarette to consider its length of ashes. He had forgotten about his idle threat. Teasing her that way was downright shameful. "Is that what you think I'm doing? Feeding you lies? Trying to butter you up?"

"Yes."

"You can relax. I'm not going to molest you." Alden decided he could take one more drag and gestured outward. "It's cold down here, and there's room on the bed; I thought we might enjoy each other's company." He slowly stood to extinguish his roll-up in a nearby ashtray, adding, "Look, all that talk before was just to scare you, that's all."

Rebecca sat astonished at this revelation, not knowing if she was annoyed or insulted. "Well, that wasn't very nice!"

"This may come as a shock, Miss—"

"—McNamara. *Rebecca,*" she chewed.

"Right. *I knew that.* This may shock you, Rebecca," he said, pausing to say her name for the first time. It felt soft on his lips and tasted like sweet red wine. "But I'm not a nice man."

Dumbfounded, Rebecca shook her head as if doing so would reconfigure her comprehension skills.

Why were men like this? So wishy-washy!

Did they believe it might merit them a sense of mystery?

And, if that were how he saw himself, could she trust Alden not to harm her?

"What kind of an outlaw are you?" she asked.

"Not a very good one anymore."

Alden's eyes fell to her face once again.

*How could she not think of herself as anything **but** beautiful?*

Rebecca turned away. She was used to being gawked at, but never for this long and certainly never with such deep sentiment. Most of the other Disciples looked at her with lust, yet Alden's gaze held an earnest longing that made her more uncomfortable. "If it's all the same to you, Mr. Aubrey, I'd like to request that you *not* stare at me."

"I'm not staring; I'm studying."

"What's the difference?"

"Intent."

His irregularity left Rebecca unsure whether she should be angry with Alden or afraid of him. "Whatever's ailing you, I hope you find yourself on the mend soon. That's no way to leave this world."

Alden gave a tiny smile, "Thank you."

"You *should* be at the end of a rope."

Like the native horned frog, Rebecca's eyes went red, shooting out an angry display of defense toward her captor. She believed such words would set him off, but instead, they noticeably pierced his heart. He had spoken sweetly to her, genuinely, but she dismissed him. Alden's eyes glazed over, detaching from any emotion. He pressed the back of a fist to his lips, knuckling down the nausea that resurfaced from either his cigarette or internal shock. First, she called him *counterfeit*, and now he deserved to hang from the neck until he was no longer living. He nodded in cheerless agreement. He *did* deserve such a fate.

"That's fair." Alden turned down the wick raiser nob of the lantern and quietly worked his way back to the mattress, settling close enough to the window to make another deposit if necessary. "You should start saving some of that bite, Becca. You might need it one of these days."

A feathered pillow landed inches from Rebecca's spot on the floor. She hugged the cushion, having taken such luxuries for granted. The unexpected kindness was soft and smelled like him.

"Mr. Aubrey?"

At this point, all offers had expired. Alden was closed for business.

"Go to sleep," he said.

He was tired of being sick.

He was tired of the way he felt.

Alden hadn't thought to hang himself.

Perhaps he would try it once Rebecca was gone.

CHAPTER SEVENTEEN

For one full week, Rebecca marked the passing of time by watching Sanctuary's daily operations from the bedroom window. Each Disciple had a series of tasks to be completed efficiently and effectively before the day's end: feeding the livestock, chopping wood, and repairing any damages to the property. These weren't your average criminals. Most came from broken, impoverished homes with rocky backgrounds, yet each had a trade and was a skilled survivalist. This organization and self-discipline rivaled military regimes, which explained their long-term success and evasion of the law.

Rueben was the group's cook, usually crafting dishes for whatever the more skilled hunters like Alden, Manny, or Julian could catch. Roger, Phillip, or Levi did most of the heavy lifting. Edwin and the absent Simon were the youngest and would run errands for the group, occasionally scouting for leads on the next job. Each man tended to their horse and performed the everyday task of washing and tidying their quarters. In the evenings, a different Disciple or Discipled Duo would take the night watch to protect their camp. Despite the low numbers, all remaining men held themselves accountable and picked up the slack where necessary, so the crew's working order could run like a well-oiled machine.

Rebecca made no attempts to escape again, nor had there been any other awkward exchanges with Alden since their fourth night together. In fact, there was little communication between them at all, save for the informative dialogue regarding mealtimes and regular trips to the outhouse. Nighttime seemed like the best time to visit, and though collectively they secretly wished to know more about the other, both were too afraid to ask. Furthermore, due to Mister McNamara's lack of correspondence, Rebecca was convinced her days at Sanctuary were numbered.

"What is Mr. Crisp planning for me if my father refuses to pay?"

A bold question, but a valid one. There was no reply to the ransom demands sent out on the second day. Rebecca knew they couldn't possibly spare her, for she knew too much, and because she was neither desirable to them nor skilled at seduction, the Disciples had no reason to keep her around. Alden stood at the window finishing a cigarette, allowing the smoke to escape into the light rain shower outside because he remembered that Rebecca disliked the smell.

"He'll kill you. Or he'll make me do it." His voice was soft and low, like a father who would tell a story at bedtime, filled with a somewhat comforting honesty, given the circumstances. After sharing his pillow with her, Rebecca decided she might have fancied Alden if he hadn't been the one to take her from her home.

"How long do I have?"

"A couple of days…maybe when the rain stops."

Rebecca audibly gulped. It wasn't her intention, but the rain ran on its own clock and had failed to inform her of any schedule. *Did the rain need to stop completely or simply dwindle to a drizzle? How was he going to do it? What would happen to her body? Would anyone ever know what happened to her?* Such questions stacked internally until the most important one toppled out. "Will it…*hurt*?"

Alden closed the window and rubbed at his temples, wishing to be rid of everything that ailed him: his throbbing head, sour insides, and inability to control the weather. "It depends on who does it."

He chose not to lie to her. She wouldn't fare well if Julian finished her off because Julian was Julian, not quite as bloodthirsty as Levi, but it would be gruesome and painful, just the same. Alden had a gut-wrenching feeling that the task would fall to him, and he knew he hadn't the stomach for it.

"I think I'd like for it to be you," said Rebecca somberly. "It's only fitting since you're the one who brought me here."

"If that's what you want."

"So?"

In all actuality, Alden never thought about it, but he decided to satisfy her inquiries. "I'll make it quick. It'll only hurt for a moment; then you won't feel anything."

"Because I'll be dead," Rebecca realized as she ran her now sweaty hands over her thighs down her knees, clasping them around her in one cuddled cocoon. She considered how quickly death came for Nicholas and shuddered at the thought of taking a bullet. If there was pain, he never showed it. "I should be crying. *Why can't I cry*?"

It was all so overwhelming, the thought of her life ending. Soon, a babbling dialogue flowed around Rebecca, who had never spoken so freely or restlessly. Little of what she had to say was directed at Alden, but that didn't stop him from listening wholeheartedly.

"I thought I might someday be a writer or even a librarian. Did you know that?"

Of course, he didn't.

She continued, "We could be reading the very same story, and even though the pictures in our minds—the way we imagine it—may be different, we're still transported to the same place. It's the *same* place, but it's different for different people. That's kind of magical, don't you find?"

She was rambling.

Alden heard less eloquent speeches from men facing their untimely demise. They had a wife and family at home waiting for them;

they would do things differently because they had *so* much to live for! Alden wouldn't look at Rebecca but remained stoic, choosing to let her speak and (hopefully) wear herself out. She was calm enough. There was no need to silence her, not that he had the right to do so. *Let it out. Let it all out.* Deep down, he was sympathetic; somehow, he understood exactly how she felt.

"There's a whole world inside them—books." Rebecca stopped only to shake her head at the injustice of her next thought. "There's a whole world out there, too. I had hoped I might see it someday."

A tumbler of whiskey lowered to her face. Alden sampled the spirit one last time before fully relinquishing it. Rebecca didn't notice him pour the drink or cross the room to bring it to her. From where she sat, his long legs made him appear like a stilt walker. The simple intimidation of size alone frightened her into compliance. Rebecca accepted the glass and grimaced as she sipped the dry liquor, which reminded her of astringent, leaving her mouth duller.

"Nuh-uh," he said. "Not like that. *All of it.*"

Alden stared down at her, expressionless, save for the same sad eyes that always seemed to look at her. Blue and bluer. Rebecca frowned at the warm, dark liquid, believing she had already finished the beverage, but the glass was still half-full.

"All at once?"

Nodding, he softly suggested, "It'll help you sleep."

Rebecca considered that she'd have plenty of time to sleep when she was dead, which relied heavily on the amount of precipitation occurring at that very moment. She wanted the drink to be poison. Hemlock or Nightshade was the least he could produce for her; that way, she wouldn't have to feel *anything*, even if *only for a moment*. Rebecca took a great breath and suffered through the brief burning sensation as the whiskey traveled down the glass into her throat. She fought the urge to gag or stick out her tongue as a syrupy warmth drizzled over.

"Attagirl," Alden whispered, slowly taking the empty glass as she let out a sigh of relaxation. It was the first time she had ever seen him fully smile. His teeth were like porcelain, perfectly straight and all accounted for. She wondered if they were even real. What amused Alden enough to show them to her remained a mystery.

Perhaps he's immune to poison.

Perhaps he's planning to smother me in my sleep.

"You could have left me there," Rebecca said plainly as the whiskey warmth spread. "By the carriage. After you shot Nicholas. I hadn't seen your faces. I didn't know your secrets. Admittedly, I'm the last person any man would choose for—" she shook her head. "So, I don't understand. You didn't bring me here for a ransom, Mr. Aubrey, and you didn't bring me here for recreation. *Why did you bring me here?*"

Another bold question but a valid one. When her tears came, they were heavier than anticipated. Commandeering sobs would soon shake Rebecca to her core. She clamped both hands over her mouth to suppress them.

Again, Alden was silent.

"*And you took my mother's brooch!*" Rebecca cried, suddenly feeling both heavy and light. "It was my favorite, and you took it! You didn't have to do that, but you did!"

Turning away, Alden clenched his jaw.

"I wish you would've left me alone," she concluded, burying her face into Roger's coat, wanting desperately for its arms to wrap around her in a warm embrace. "I wish I'd never met you."

The sullen stilt-walker had not lowered from his position on high, nor had he returned to face her. Rebecca couldn't see it, but Alden shed a tear of his own.

Quickly wiping his face, he admitted, "Me too."

CHAPTER EIGHTEEN

Rebecca yawned and rubbed her eyes. It was still dark outside, but the rain had stopped. A foreboding chill swept over her. *It was time. She was going to die.* When she gasped at this realization, a similar sound parroted back from across the room.

What was that?

Rebecca sat upright and listened. The echo was reminiscent of her father, whose deviated septum created an uneven airflow through the nostrils, resulting in atrocious wheezes when he dozed in the library. It always made her laugh. *But was Alden really snoring?* He never snored before.

No, this was more of a *gurgling* noise, almost like *choking.*

"Mr. Aubrey?" she whispered.

No response.

Rebecca, now concerned, crawled slowly toward the bed to inspect more closely. Alden's face was its usual deathly white, yet his eyes were open, and slow, erratic breaths escaped him. Rebecca tapped his shoulder.

"Mr. Aubrey?"

He *was* choking. A slight stream seeped from the corner of his mouth, which had begun to turn blue.

He's dying.

"Help!" cried Rebecca.

The first words to escape her lips brought no alarm.

She tried again.

A cry for help must be common for prisoners and, therefore, easily ignored.

"Roger!"

Every second seemed to drag, and it wasn't until Rebecca called out for a *third* time that there was movement outside the bedroom. The door was locked, but she remembered that Alden had the key. Rebecca quickly turned him on his side and searched his person. When the brass solution was acquired, the door swung wildly from the hinges as Roger barreled through.

"What happened? What did he do to himself?"

Rebecca stepped back to accept the lantern Roger had brought with him. "He's here. I don't know. I was sleeping. Are you going to help him?"

"Do I look like a doctor to you?"

Roger's voice resonated like kettle drums through the manor, calling for anyone and everyone in the house to assist while also attempting to revive his friend. Rebecca noticed the bedroom door stood wide open. Escape was feasible, yet she wouldn't run for her freedom.

Criminal or not, he can't die this way.

Rebecca felt a hard nudge from her spectator spot. It was Levi.

"Shit!"

Outlaws quickly filled the room, lanterns in hand, each commentating with deep concern. Reuben and Manny were the last to enter. Reuben picked up a small tumbler sitting on the dresser and gave a sniff of inspection.

"Whiskey, and something else…something nutty."

"Laudanum, I bet," said Levi. "It's got that smell to it."

"Wait, laudanum can't kill you, can it?" Manny's attempt to reason with the events unfolding was admirable, for everyone knew what had occurred. "Maybe he just wanted to sleep."

"Almost anything can kill you if you have too much of it," Edwin stated.

Rueben nodded, "He'll sleep indefinitely if we don't do something fast."

Manny shook his head at Reuben's remark. "But his eyes are open!"

"I'm fairly certain you can die with your eyes open, Manny!"

The men continued to argue, yet Roger said nothing. After each rushed to Alden's side and gave his quietly quaking body a few shakes, Roger knelt quickly at the foot of the bed.

He was praying.

"Hey, Reverend! Do you really think that's going to help?" taunted Levi.

"Well, it sure as shit ain't gonna hurt!"

Julian made his way into the bedroom. "What the Hell is going on here?! Some of us are trying to—" He pushed past the others, save for Roger, who planted himself firmly beside the bed. His eyes finally fell on Alden, the gurgling sounds prominent. None could say whether Alden was winning or losing the fight for his life. "Goddammit."

"I told you he wasn't well, Julian! I told you!"

"Not now, Roger!" Julian lessened. "I didn't know he had a problem."

Manny continued shaking his head in disbelief. "He doesn't— not with laudanum, anyway."

Roger huffed to hide emotion. "He probably wanted to make sure it was quiet when he went."

Some Disciples took a moment to consider their futures within the gang with Alden gone. None of their plans could be executed without him. Others were more interested in how it would feel to bury a friend, as friendships among criminals were scarce. Their leader took a slow, deep breath before giving his troops orders to vacate the area.

None questioned him, and most he didn't have to ask twice. Roger and Levi were the only men Julian permitted to stay. Once he took notice of Rebecca, Julian let out an exhausted chuckle.

"Miss McNamara, I forgot you were there. Roger, would you please escort our guest to my room?"

Rebecca trembled. With Alden unavailable, anyone in the house could claim her. *Not Julian.*

"My room's closer," offered Levi.

Suddenly, rooming with Julian seemed less frightening. She wished for Roger or Manny to request her company—even Rueben seemed a safe alternative, yet both Manny and Rueben had left the bedroom, and Roger would not be moved.

"If you think I'm leaving," he said. "You're sorely mistaken."

Julian's eyes widened at Roger's defiance, but Roger didn't so much as bat an eyelash. Levi snickered. Rebecca watched with bated breath, waiting for one of them to engage. "Fine, I'll deal with this." Julian pointed to Levi. "But *you* stay. Get him back on his feet. Ask around; I'm sure one of these idiots has some herbs or smelling salts hidden somewhere."

Levi looked at the patient and shook his head. "I don't think it's gonna be that simple, Boss..."

"Fix him, *now!*" barked Julian.

"What do you expect me to do?"

"Science, voodoo, divine intervention; I don't care how you do it, just do it!"

With that, Julian begrudgingly offered his arm to Rebecca, who accepted it out of habit and partial confusion.

Had Julian been schooled in matters of social etiquette?

If so, why was he generally hostile towards women?

The hallway was silent, save for the few whispers of those who conversed to hide their uneasiness.

"He'll be alright. Alden just wants attention."

"That's an awful thing to say!"

"Did you see the look on Julian's face?"

"Yep. There goes our meal ticket."

As they walked, and upon closer inspection, Rebecca noticed that Julian was aging less gracefully than Alden. *They couldn't possibly be twins.* If he were a painting, Julian would be a Monet, for he possessed a pleasing composition, yet it could only be seen from a certain vantage point. He *was* handsome, yes, but his skin had the quality of a worn-down saddle, with cracks and wrinkles just below the surface and deep lines around his eyes. Beautifully blue and not as fatigued as Alden's, Julian's eyes concealed that he was worse for wear, hardened, calcifying from the inside out, a crumbling consequence from years of toxic living. At this pace, he would soon disintegrate.

Is this what wickedness does to a man?

Julian's quarters were located in the master suite on the other side of the house, spacious, refined, and easily the most elegant. *This was a showroom!* There were fine oil paintings on the walls and posh brass fixtures. A lounger, a four-post bed covered in satin, and piles of pillows also took residence. Mountains of books were stacked at opposite corners, rivaling the phonograph positioned by the window. It seemed Julian had a wide selection of entertainment options at his disposal.

Either that, or he was bored out of his mind.

While Julian's escort was a treat compared to Alden's incessant grabbing, Rebecca discovered herself locked into the bedroom faster than she expected. Julian said not a word to her and remained absent for the rest of the night. Rebecca anxiously watched the door for any sign of activity or updates, fearing that her safety had been compromised and wondering if peppermint would ever smell the same.

CHAPTER NINETEEN

Morning poured in through the bedroom window, splashing Rebecca's eyes like a friendly fountain. She couldn't remember leaving Julian's chambers and returning to Alden's room, but there she was, lying in his bed beside him. Alden's sleepy eyes smiled as he stirred and brought her closer.

"See? Isn't this better? I told you you'd like it up here with me."

Rebecca resisted at first but froze once she noticed the cornflower blue shirt he was wearing. It suited him well, hugging all the places a shirt should hug a man. Rolled at the sleeves, exposing a hearty amount of arm hair, Rebecca let her fingers glide over the starched fabric. It *felt* real enough, though she had no memory of returning the garment to him, nor could she explain her attire: the lavender gown from the Rosewood Ball. Layers of ruffles crunched beneath her as she fought to comprehend the reality of her new surroundings. *None of this makes any sense.*

"Are we dead?" Rebecca whispered.

Still holding her, Alden shook his head and smiled. "You're beautiful. Do you know that?" He seemed fuller and possessed a healthy hue for once; there was even an ethereal glow to him.

Rebecca slowly lifted her hand to touch his face, which sustained a hope she hadn't seen before. "What happened to you?"

Alden raised an eyebrow to question her inquiry.

"I saw you," said Rebecca. "You were dying."

She knew Alden could not dismiss the events from the night before. Nothing could justify that swift of a recovery. Alden tilted his head, permitting Rebecca to reach him fully. He was warm and smooth, and the exchange felt safely intimate.

"I *was* dying, but you helped me."

"Por eso está ella aquí," a familiar voice theorized in the distance. Rebecca jumped at the interruption, which pulled her from Alden's magnetic gaze. It was Manny leaning against the nearby bureau with a glass of whiskey while Roger read his Bible in the corner. "Ella no sabe que él la necesita," he continued.

Roger looked up from his scriptures. "She'll find out soon enough."

Rebecca, dumbfounded, *"What?"* She sunk into the fluffy mattress as Alden adjusted into a full, gentle snuggle. Nothing about his touch seemed threatening. In fact, it was the most comfortable she'd been since arriving at Sanctuary.

"Podrías salvarlo."

"Manny, I don't speak Spanish," Rebecca fussed.

But Manny seemed to be speaking in the distance like he were behind an invisible wall. "Podrías amarlo."

Roger nodded. "She could if she wanted to."

Alden leaned in to loop a strand of strawberry hair behind Rebecca's ear.

"Do you want to?" he whispered softly.

Rebecca wondered why the affirmative seemed to almost leap from her lips. *This* Alden, whole and strong, was what he could be, what he was deep down, and what he had tried to show her the night he first told her she was beautiful. She eased deeper into his arms and the marshmallow bedding, marveling at how they could have found such a beautiful place together.

Manny smiled. "Ellos podrían amarse."

Roger nodded, and Alden seemed to swell at the idea.

"Only if she would have me," he sweetly replied. "Would you have me?"

Questions scattered the ceiling like stars in the night sky, with his shining brightest. Rebecca looked to Roger and Manny, who patiently waited for her response. Though she swooned at such a preview, Rebecca knew she shouldn't fall for what a man *could* be. Alden was what he was.

"This is a dream," Rebecca realized, somewhat disappointed.

Alden nestled his head on a nearby pillow. "Is it a bad dream?"

"No," she started. "But I'm confused."

"God is not the author of confusion, Miss Rebecca," Roger preached from a greater distance. The room had begun to stretch and thin out. Their faces were fading, save for Alden's, which remained just beyond Rebecca's fingertips.

"Ella no sabe…" Manny shook his head, letting the whiskey finish his sentiment.

Alden nodded. "You're right. She'll have to figure it out some other way."

Rebecca's eyes fluttered. "Figure out what?"

Alden leaned on his side. The glow was still there, but he was disappearing, too.

"I can't tell you, Becca. It's time to wake up."

"No, wait! Please!"

Alden playfully tapped her nose with his index finger. "Wake up."

Rebecca wriggled her nose and opened her eyes.

"Wake up! Wake up, little one!"

It was Julian.

"What? Where is—what happened to—"

Julian's fingertips silenced her, settling over Rebecca's lips. "— Women should only speak when spoken to. Although I might make an exception because you look so damn good in my bed." He was fully pressed against her, causing them to collapse into the otherwise comfortable mattress. "Believe it or not, you're the first woman to sleep here. Kinda makes me want to christen it."

Rebecca's mind whirled at the sudden change of bedfellows. One seemed noble, while the other was nasty. *Had they shared the night?*

"I thought I disgusted you," she argued.

Julian shifted, not smelling of peppermint at all but of smokey birch and patchouli. It was the amalgamation of power and control. "I'm sure I could tolerate it."

He continued to stroke her cheek with a velvet hand. Rebecca fought the urge to roll her eyes. Julian had *such* a way with women.

"Have you ever seen a painted glass window?" Julian asked, his thumb gliding over the various forkings of her scar. He, of course, was referring to stained glass, which frequented churches and cathedrals. "That's what this reminds me of… Alden was right: touching you feels *holy*."

Was?

Julian paused his creepy violation as if he had read her mind.

"He's alive. I have no clue *how*, but he's alive."

After Rebecca's sigh of relief, Julian swung his leg over, positioning himself directly on top in a seemingly jealous reaction. Rebecca braced herself against the fine maroon linens, which were much more luxurious than the modest quilt on Alden's bed. *How she wished she were there instead!* But Julian wasn't set out to further harass her; he merely wanted to investigate.

"You're *glad* he's alive," he noted matter-of-factly.

After a beat, Rebecca nodded. Julian's eyebrows knit in bewilderment.

"You could've left him and ran for your freedom, but you chose to alert us. Why?"

"It was the right thing to do."

Julian smiled, his body weight pressing down just enough to be intrusive. "Remarkable," he hummed as he withdrew.

Rebecca breathed a heftier sigh of relief and sat upright, grateful that her chastity was still intact. Julian crossed the room to acquire a cigarette before lounging on the edge of the bed.

"It would seem as though the Disciples are indebted to you, Miss McNamara." He passed the cigarette to Rebecca. "And I never forget a debt."

Rebecca's hand shook as she held the fire stick. She understood that Julian needed Alden up and about for the Disciples to continue their nefarious occupation. *Alive* could mean many things. *Was he coherent? Was he weaker than before? If not, why wasn't he there to bring her back to his bedroom?* Somehow, this felt like a business proposition. She had never smoked before but, wishing to appear confident and experienced, brought the item to her lips and inhaled as she'd seen many women do at social gatherings. Her lungs rejected the union, and Rebecca stifled several coughs.

Julian grinned and recovered his accessory. "I think I'll let you live a bit longer." He settled onto his back, blowing tiny halos up to the ceiling. "I'd take you for myself, but it would be wiser to give Alden something to look forward to. We'll have our fun once he's had enough."

Rebecca scraped her tongue along the roof of her mouth, wanting to be rid of the stale tobacco aftertaste and any reminisce of Julian's genetic material.

We'll have our fun once he's had enough.

Her stomach swirled in regret. She wanted Alden to live, but she should have saved herself.

"I'll take you to him," said Julian. "You'll see that his needs are met until he's fully recovered."

"I am not qualified to perform the duties of a nurse, Mr. Crisp."

Julian used his tongue to lodge the cigarette against his bottom teeth, causing it to flip playfully. The mannerism reminded her of Alden, though Rebecca was no longer certain of its origin.

In all the time that Alden studied Julian, how many of Alden's eccentricities did Julian steal for himself?

"You think I'm suggesting medicine. That's cute." Rolling onto his belly, Julian repositioned the smoke in his left hand while using his right hand to tickle Rebecca's ankles. "I could tell you. I could show you."

Rebecca rolled up into a tight coil and shook her head.

Julian slithered to her inch by inch and with a hypnotic blue gaze. Rebecca remembered how he almost branded her hand before. *Was he planning to try again?* Alden wasn't there to intervene. Julian's stare burned blindly and without mercy. He wanted to make sure he had her attention.

"If he dies, you die. Get it?"

Nodding, Rebecca looked away, fully understanding her assignment. She would serve as Alden's companion, keeping him inspired and satisfied. Any objections or failure to do so would result in her death.

Julian rose to extinguish his cigarette and offered an arm to her in a complete juxtaposition of his previous behavior. The hallway to Alden's room seemed much longer than before, and both Roger and Manny were nowhere in sight. The bedroom closed and locked behind her before Rebecca could inquire about their whereabouts. She was alone now, with *him*.

Rebecca had never seen a dead body, save for the brief encounter with Nicholas being fatally wounded. Slowly, she walked to Alden, who was so stagnant on the bed it was disturbing.

Had he died already?

She leaned in to examine. Alden's eyes were closed, and he was cold to the touch, but he was breathing.

"You can do this," she told herself.

Dream fragments replayed in Rebecca's mind, comparing the lively individual who smiled and held her sweetly to the chalky, comatose man before her.

He did have a lovely smile.

"What a strange dream." Accepting her challenge, Rebecca sat beside Alden, taking his hand in her own, and traced the crevasses of his palm with her fingertips.

What did it all mean?

And how could she possibly care for a man who cared so little for himself?

"I haven't the foggiest idea of what to do with you, Mr. Aubrey."

However, one thing was certain: she needed to learn Spanish.

CHAPTER TWENTY

"What's the matter? Are you too good to talk to a colored man?"

For days, Rebecca welcomed the visitations of Manny and Roger, along with the occasional Edwin or Rueben. It was late evening, and her dinner dishes had already been fetched, so when an unexpected guest entered the bedroom, Rebecca took great strides to put distance between them. This was the first time Rueben paid a solo social call since Alden fell ill. She meant no offense by staring; she knew what it felt like to be gawked at and judged by appearance. But she'd never been alone with a black man, so she *had* to study him. Melanin washed beautifully over Rueben's skin, smooth and sexy.

He wasn't ebony or obsidian.

Onyx.

"No, not at all! I was expecting Manny," she stuttered, unafraid yet still surprised by how physically appealing most of the Disciples were.

"Manny got called for the night watch since *this* one isn't currently working." Rueben grumpily motioned to a comatose Alden, not out of inconvenience but concern. "He said you wanted this." In his hand was a small leather roll taken from Levi's quarters. *A manicure kit!* Because it was the only thing Rebecca requested since her arrival, Rueben agreed with Manny that they should oblige her.

"Don't worry, I don't like Levi either," he said. "If he finds it missing, just tell him it was Edwin."

"Thank you, but it's not for me," she said, accepting the instruments. "Mr. Aubrey has new growth. I thought he might appreciate the gesture."

"You're not gonna...?" Reuben mimed a jugular attack with a sharp object, sticking out his tongue for dramatic effect.

"I suppose I *could*," shrugged Rebecca. "Though that would directly violate your employer's request."

"Which was?"

"To tend to Mr. Aubrey, see that his needs are met."

"I don't think trimming a hangnail is what Julian meant."

"What would you suggest?" challenged Rebecca.

Reuben put his hands on his hips and chewed his cheek. He wasn't going to *say it*. "You're doing a fine job," he mumbled. He then noted Alden's bare feet shining from beyond the covers. They were *clean*, and the basin on the nearby dresser showed recent use. "You washed his feet. That's—that's mighty decent of you."

Reuben turned to face the newly appointed nurse, realizing he'd underestimated her. Feet washing was considered a lowly service, even in Biblical times when practiced by enslaved people. He knew how degrading servitude could often be and how easily one was taken for granted. This action was more than hospitality; it was an act of humility from an unlikely source. If Alden knew, it would both warm and break his heart.

"Can I get *you* anything?" Reuben asked, touched by her compassion.

"A book would be lovely; *any* book."

Reuben frowned. "Julian keeps all the books locked in his room."

"He prohibits you from reading?"

"Well, not all of us *can* read that well, but I was improving there for a while." Alden tutored Reuben between assignments before Vernon's death and Rueben's demotion to the kitchen. Reuben knew his predecessor, a gregarious soul named Leroy, and there was nothing wrong with his cooking. Vernon was just old and worn, rotted from the inside out.

"I don't understand," said Rebecca. "Roger has his Bible."

"And *nobody* is going to take that away from him!"

"Why, then?"

Rueben hemmed and hawed, crossing his arms before recalling Julian's absurd logic. "We can't just be outlaws. That wouldn't be enough. Vernon wanted a smarter, different breed of criminal who couldn't get caught. He encouraged free-thinking and progress, but Julian likes to know what goes in our heads to guess what we might do. You know, just hearing that out loud makes it even more ridiculous. Alden says it's his way of finding footing as our leader, exploring what he can and can't control."

"That sounds like a dictatorship to me."

"Well, whatever it is, we still have our ways." Rueben then knelt near the foot of the bed, pressing down baseboards until one lifted slightly. "Don't tell anyone I showed you this," he instructed.

Each Disciple had a secret endeavor or hobby of some sort. Reuben was an aspiring inventor, a tinkerer who hated being in the kitchen, though he enjoyed experimenting with different pairings of food and drink. Vernon convinced him that he could be the next George Washington Carver. It was this flattery that persuaded Reuben to enter the fold. His idiosyncrasies were simple, but Alden was a multifaceted man, inexplicably complex. Rebecca set the nail kit aside to collect the stack of books Reuben presented: Keats, Frost, Blake, Yeats, Shakespeare; the list went on and on.

Her jaw dropped. "Mr. Aubrey enjoys poetry?"

"And short stories and historical essays," Rueben replied. "You wouldn't know it to look at him, but Alden's *deep*. For a while, he was all about those books on—what is it—knowledge of ideas and behaviors?"

Rebecca, giving a slight smile, answered, "Philosophy?"

"Yeah, that too. He's a sponge; he soaks up everything. And don't get him started on politics. He's pretty passionate about that, too. He's on my side as well as yours."

"My side?" she tilted. Rebecca could understand the support for racial uniformity, as she believed that all people, regardless of color, status, or creed, should be treated fairly and with kindness. *To what was Rueben referring?*

"Women."

Rebecca would have never believed suffrage mattered to someone who regularly broke the law. Rueben explained that Alden was provoked by discrimination towards those without a voice, having spent many late-night conversations on the topic. Alden recognized his privilege and agreed that the world desperately needed change.

"Has Julian come to see him today?" asked Rueben, already knowing the answer.

The only way Julian would care is if Alden died.

"No, only Roger," said Rebecca, eyeing her cotenant. "He came this morning with Mr. Bohannon to observe—well, *look*! He's doing it now! Come see for yourself."

Together, the pair watched Alden's hands flickering in deliberate patterns: thumb, middle, pinky, followed by all three creating a blocked formation in the right hand against a rocking pinky-thumb in the left, ending with cascading fingertips rolling up and down in sequential order. If the movement weren't so organized, Rebecca might have guessed he was having another nightmare or, worse, a seizure.

Rebecca fretted, "Mr. Bohannon says these are non-purposeful movements; they don't mean anything."

Rueben studied his friend more closely. Alden possessed a handspan large enough to stretch beyond an eight-key octave yet not so bulky as to struggle with closed hand positions that required fingers to be within a small space. His digits were flexible but not hypermobile, curved, and malleable.

"Do you know what *that* is?" Rueben determined with a pleased expression. "*That's a piano!* Whatcha playing, Aldy?"

Rebecca's eyes bloomed. "Mr. Aubrey is *musical?*"

"Oh, yeah! He plays a couple of instruments and has a fairly decent voice, too—though not as good as my own."

Rebecca had noticed an unpretentious upright piano in the foyer that first evening at Sanctuary but had yet to hear any music fill the halls of the seasoned estate. As was the tradition in her social class, Rebecca received a formal music education, studying privately with a tutor twice a week. A competent flutist in her youth, Rebecca was never convinced the flute was *her*. Samuel McNamara suggested the woodwind instrument to serve the prominent teardrop on her upper lip. Rebecca suspected it was, in reality, to cover as much of her face as possible. Given the option, she would have selected a more obscure instrument, perhaps the bassoon. Alden appeared to be the rugged, self-taught guitar-playing sort, suited for crooning around a campfire, picking or lazily strumming with a velvety-calloused hand. For all she knew, Alden tickled the ivories to escape his current reality. *But what sort of melodies would take him away?* She wanted to believe that Alden would shepherd carols during the holiday season or the occasional hymn with Roger. However, envisioning Disciples gathered around the instrument, drunkenly singing about restless vagabonds and loose women, seemed less of a stretch.

How many crass choruses did Alden know?

Surely, he was not the only Disciple who was musically inclined!

Had music, like so many things, been prohibited under Julian's reign?

"This is *good*," said Rueben. "This means something's still there, something worth saving."

The muted melody soon refrained, with Alden returning to a vegetative state. Rueben bowed his head. Great injustices had occurred to push his friend to this place. *We should've done more for him.*

"He used to be different, you know," Rueben began. "I wouldn't say he was *happy*, but he was *happier*. He got the job done. There was a very clear line between who Alden was and what he'd do. He had this way of separating himself from it all. He'd put it out of his mind, somehow. Or maybe he was ignoring it; I don't know. He never—anyway, all that changed at Newberry."

"Newberry?"

"It's a farm. *Was* a farm. Happened a few months back."

"What happened?"

Conflicted, Rueben tightened his mouth and lowered his eyebrows.

Dare he say?

Should she know about the fire that fueled Alden's nightmares?

Would she sympathize with her captor's undoing?

"We do bad things, but Alden did a *real* bad thing," Rueben revealed. "It wasn't *all* his fault." He paused to consider how drastically his ally had been altered. "Newberry was too much for him. It was like someone snuffed out the light inside. He thinks he's a lost cause. He's removed himself from everything entirely, but he's still in chains as long as he's here. You know, there's only so much a person can do when they're bound." Taking a beat to conceal emotion, "And that very clear line—it's gone."

Rebecca exhaled, not realizing she'd been holding her breath. "Do you think that's why he—?" *Overdosed? Overindulged?* What was the *polite* term for this action? What would be *appropriate*?

Nodding, Rueben raised a palm to stop her. This was a hard conversation to have. They could spend the entire day discussing a possible motive and never know the truth.

"Roger thinks so. Roger believes Alden wanted to end it all. Maybe he did. I have my own theory." Rebecca shifted her arms to form a better grip on the books, patiently waiting for Rueben to elaborate. "Honestly, I think it was a diversion."

"A *diversion*?"

Rueben shuffled. "Alden knew it was a mistake to bring you here. Maybe with our attention all on him, we'd forget about you. Maybe you could've gotten away."

"Any of you could have finished me off, especially if I ran."

"No one's done it yet," said the Disciple with a friendly wink. "And you don't have to worry about me."

"What about Mr. Aubrey?" considered Rebecca. "When he wakes up?"

If he wakes up.

Rueben shook his head. "I don't think Alden wants to hurt you."

"That doesn't mean he won't," she said, touching her bruised cheek. "He has before."

"That wasn't Alden. That was the man in chains." Rueben tapped the stack of books. "*This* is Alden. You don't know him like me, like Manny and Roger know him. If you did, I think you'd like him. Most people do."

Rueben then scanned Rebecca, face to foot and up again, before turning to his friend, giving a side-smile that produced a dimple she initially overlooked.

"But what do I know?" he shrugged. "I'm just the cook."

Rebecca paused to interpret Alden's dichotomy. He was deadly, vigorous, and deep; taciturn but spoke with passion when convicted; impulsive yet studious, artistic, and eager to learn.

Rueben again tapped the stack of books in her arms, bringing her back to the present. "Read those to him, *please*. 'Cause I can't. It'll keep him alert and remind him that he's not alone."

"Do you think he knows I'm here?"

"He's playing songs for you, ain't he?" At this, Rueben's expression grew into a full-faced grin. Rebecca mirrored in response.

To suggest that Alden was somehow serenading her beyond oblivion!

"I appreciate your help, Mr. Jackson," blushed Rebecca.

"Call me, *Rueben*."

Rebecca clutched at the hardcovers. Simply the smell of the wood-based paper mixed with a faint remanence of vanilla and other volatile organic compounds was enough to make her feel at home.

Home.

A criminal's bedroom was her home now.

"It's kinda nice having a woman here," decided Rueben, turning to exit.

"Oh, I'm not sure *my* efforts are making much of a difference."

Rueben stopped. "You're making a difference, trust me. I can see why Alden chose you."

The stack of books almost fell to the floor. Rebecca teetered.

Chose me?

"Are you suggesting that Mr. Aubrey specifically wanted *me*?"

Reuben beamed with mystery. "I have a theory about that, too."

Struggling to cradle the volumes, Rebecca stepped forward. "Rueben—"

Holding the door open, Rueben stuck his neck back into the room. "—I have to lock this now and head down to the kitchen. I'll be back for that kit after-while."

CHAPTER TWENTY-ONE

Three days had passed since Alden abused the laudanum. Rebecca knew she should have run when she had the chance, but rather than scold herself for not doing so, she chose to view Alden's incubation period as an extension of her own life. She wished to know the man Reuben described, the man from her dreams who felt so deeply and passionately for things, who had a song in his heart and was easily moved.

If only Alden would've mentioned his enthusiasm for poetry!

The rain hadn't let up for days, falling in heavy sheets outside the bedroom window. *If he dies, you die.* Rebecca attempted to obey Julian's commands, tending to Alden as best she could and entertaining him as she saw fit, but Julian's threat seemed to paint the walls. Rebecca looked at her patient with a heavy heart. Alden's eyelids were encircled with deep shades of purple and gray that lie dormant while he slept. Sporadic breaths traveled through his lungs, respirations running late for an appointment. The non-purposeful movements had stopped. His body decompressed. There was no music anymore. Rebecca felt helpless and was understandably afraid, yet she maintained the cheerful disposition Reuben recommended in the off-chance that Alden could hear her.

"How does a bit of the Bard sound today, Mr. Aubrey?" said Rebecca, as she opened a book to the passage Alden dog-eared: *Sonnet 71* in an edition of Shakespeare.

"No longer mourn for me when I am dead
Than you shall hear the surly, sullen bell
Give warning to the world that I am fled
From this vile world with vilest worms to dwell:
Nay, if you read this line, remember not
The hand that writ it, for I love you so,
That I, in your sweet thoughts, would be forgot,
If thinking on me then should make you woe..."

Rebecca's lip quivered. There was no need to remind her of Alden's possible fate.

"Perhaps another selection?"

She flipped through the pages to *Sonnet 47*, which was also bookmarked.

"Betwixt mine eye and heart, a league is took,
And each doth good turns now unto the other:
When that mine eye is famish'd for a look,
Or heart in love with sighs himself doth smother,
With my love's picture then my eye doth feast,
And to the painted banquet bids my heart;
Another time, mine eye is my heart's guest,
And in his thoughts of love doth share a part:
So, either by thy picture or my love,
Thy self away, art present still with me;
For thou not farther than my thoughts canst move,
And I am still with them, and they with thee;
Or, if they sleep, thy picture in my sight
Awakes my heart, to heart's and eyes' delight."

Rebecca was all too familiar with the war between the eyes and heart. She would witness a battle every time a man looked at her. The eye was meant to behold physical beauty and held a powerful influence within a man's core, causing him to respond genetically with either criticism or intrigue.

Interpretations of the poem considered how one might refer to a portrait or a mental image to access fond memories. Rebecca believed it was a call to examine one's own thoughts and, in her own residual analysis, a recommendation to love blindly. It wasn't William Shakespeare's most popular or successful sonnet, yet it never failed to strike an emotional chord with Rebecca, and she was pleased to know it had also touched Alden in some way.

"Shakespeare always stirs up my allergies," said Rebecca, now moved, as she closed the book and returned it to the secret place Reuben had shown her. She sniffled and retrieved another volume from Alden's hidden treasure trove.

Songs of Innocence and Experience by William Blake

Rebecca shook her head at another wounded page that Alden folded over, skimming to the section marked. Each motion to conceal his love of poetry must have been enacted hastily. "You really should take better care of your books, Mr. Aubrey. Even a ribbon would suffice."

William Blake's *"The Tyger"* was originally penned to illustrate man's duality, this piece focusing not on his purity but his more primal tendencies. Good versus Evil. Heaven and Hell. It served as a follow-up and a direct counterpoint to "The Lamb," also penned by Blake and bookmarked. Rebecca read the poem aloud, pausing to note the section Alden previously circled.

"When the stars threw down their spears
And water'd heaven with their tears:
Did he smile his work to see?
Did he who made the Lamb make thee?"

Something was written at the top of the page. Rebecca unfolded the corner.

James 1:8

Roger had returned his Bible to the bedroom that morning. Rebecca carefully fanned the pages of the New Testament until she found the source of Alden's transcription.

"He is a double-minded man, unstable in all his ways."

At this, Rebecca understood that Alden's illness hadn't been on a physical level, as she once believed, though it manifested in such forms. It wouldn't explain why he took her from Rosewood, but it would vindicate many of his other actions.

"What were you searching for, Mr. Aubrey?"

While it may have been justified, Rebecca knew she had misjudged him. Alden attempted to show her a different part of himself, a vulnerable part, but she was dismissive. She would have to work on recognizing such offerings. Rebecca closed the sacred text, her sleuthing serving as a reminder that some answers couldn't be found in a book. Nevertheless, she was thankful for the information.

"Manny believes you brought me here to help you. I *would* help if I knew what you needed."

She waited for a reply. Even if Alden *could* hear her, he hadn't shown any evidence of reception. It was impossible to know if he was healing or regressing during his varying states of consciousness.

"Please, help me to understand. I read to you, I sang to you, I held your hand—I've *washed* your hands and feet, I've talked to you, and you're still—I don't know, it's like you're under some sort of..."

Spell.

Rebecca knew how to break a spell, for all her books had provided the remedy. She laughed in modest embarrassment at the very concept, convinced it was his idea and mocking the obvious role reversal.

"I'm sure you know I've never done it before."

Alden remained sleeping and unshaken. She recalled how he once tucked her hair behind an ear while looking at her with such pain in his eyes. Those eyes had explored her carefully above a bandana the night of her capture and studied her during their evenings together with sincere interest and waves of empathy. Rebecca imagined his smile, which dazzled her upon its initial reveal. His top lip was cloaked somewhat before Levi removed all his facial hair. But it was present now, joined with a full bottom lip, and both appeared soft, pliant. She sat beside Alden on the bed, as he had often requested before his enchanted slumber. She slid her hand through the opening of Alden's shirt and let it rest over his heart, feeling it somehow fitting. The warm rhythm of his heartbeat resonated like Morse Code in crisp tendrils of dark chest hair that vibrated under her fingertips.

"Alright, Mr. Aubrey, but you are *not* to let it go to your head."

With gentle chastity and hope never to be forgotten, Rebecca gave Alden her most sincere affection. Alden continued in a dreamlike state without reciprocation or sign of resurrection. Rebecca sighed. *She failed.*

"I'm sorry."

Alden's hand grasped hers tightly, followed by a large upheaval in his chest.

"Tickles," he whispered.

Rebecca squeezed his hand in an excited response. "Mr. Aubrey, can you hear me?"

Alden licked his lips and attempted to form a sentence. Heavy eyelids fought for ascension. He mumbled back through broken speech in what sounded like a request for her to use his first name.

"Alden?" she complied.

He smiled and softly nodded.

"Can you open your eyes for me, Alden?"

He swallowed and licked his lips again as he fluttered feathery eyelashes in obedience. His eyes were a deeper blue than she remembered and seemed to rattle when they registered who she was. "You're still here."

"Yes, Mr. Au—Alden."

Alden closed his eyes, still holding her hand. "I need to talk to Roger."

"Yes," said Rebecca as she began to rise. Alden's grip remained.

"Not Julian. Roger first," his voice crackled.

"Of course."

With a happy heart and a greater appreciation for fairy tales, Rebecca moved to the bedroom door. It was still locked, but if she hollered loud enough, Roger would hear her. Alden was awake, which meant she was, for the moment, safe once again.

CHAPTER TWENTY-TWO

"Otra vez," instructed Manny. "Again."

"Buenas noches. Me llamo Rebecca."

"Mucho gusto, Rebecca. Mi nombre es Manny."

Alden radiated contentment from his post beside the bedroom window. Two days had passed since his awakening, and though his own conversations with Rebecca were merely the civil, informative interactions from before, he did enjoy hearing her express happiness within the walls of Sanctuary. To him, Rebecca was strong yet feminine, possessing a girlish wonder but carried herself like a lady. She was a dreamer, though not overly emotional, giving as much as she was given. Having once skimmed through Mary Wollstonecraft's *A Vindication of the Rights*, Alden wagered that Rebecca was just as progressive. Women like Rebecca would balance the scales of gender inequality—or at least pave the way. And yet, *she* had taken care of *him*. She could have left him to choke on his vomit but chose not to; she stayed. Alden knew Julian practically forced Rebecca to tend to his needs; for Roger, Manny, and Rueben each provided a summary of her bedside manner upon his revival, and there was no reason for such tenderness other than Rebecca being genuinely a *good* person.

"If Roger were here," Alden began, "along with Manny, you'd have the best Spanish education Sanctuary has to offer."

Roger held the night watch the evening prior and was catching up on sleep, leaving a noticeable hole in their entourage.

"Roger is fluent?" asked Rebecca.

"Sí," said Manny before pointing to Alden. "He would be, too, if he practiced."

Alden recalled first learning basic greetings from Manny in years past. He understood Spanish better than he could speak it and found it *did* come in handy more often than not, but Julian deemed bilingualism a useless skill.

"They should learn English," he'd say.

Alden extended his hands in playful surrender. "Lo siento."

"I don't want an apology," nagged Manny. "I want you to learn!"

Rebecca couldn't help but smile at the two men. Even while Manny chided him, she believed that most of the Disciples held Alden in high regard and were relieved he had survived. Julian seemed preoccupied, and Levi appeared indifferent during his recuperation period; yet, Alden's improvement alone restored the working order for the rest of Sanctuary, bringing it back to a state of normalcy.

"¿Quien es Alden?" asked Manny, noticing her watching Alden from the floor. Rebecca stumbled over recent vocabulary but maintained a studious confidence.

"Alden es…un bandido…"

"He is a bandit. That's correct."

Alden gave a self-deprecating laugh. "Could you teach her something *nice* to say? I'm right here." But Manny ignored him and encouraged Rebecca to continue.

"Alden es un…vaquero…"

"A cowboy! Si!"

"You're forgetting *guapo*…" added Alden.

"That's what I call him. A cowboy, that is."

"Inteligente…"

Rebecca giggled, suspecting Alden may have been a jokester in his youth.

I bet he stole a lot of hearts, too.

"Alden…es el hombre…"

"He is a man—the man—"

"—Last I checked," Alden said to himself.

Rebecca studied her roommate. It was a miracle that he was alive. Though still much too thin, Alden emitted better coloring and greater energy than before. His spirit was as unharvested gold, buttery yellow glimmering between rocky patches of silver and white. The multiplicitous metal would find its full value only when separated from wasteful leaverite. After his being so ill and close to death, the excavation seemed already underway. Considering this, Rebecca gave a balmy smile. Perhaps in time, she would see the man from her dreams. "Dreams," she whispered.

"Huh?"

Manny and Alden were both attentive now, with the latter deeply invested.

"He has bad dreams," she recovered. "How would you say that?"

Concerned, Manny turned to Alden. "¿Todavía tienes pesadillas?"

Alden said nothing, wondering if Rebecca had said what she meant to say.

"Alden, I asked you a question."

"Yes! I still have nightmares," fussed Alden. The admission embarrassed him. While he hadn't been ill in the middle of the night since emerging from his laudanum-induced slumber, there were dreams in *that* dark place, too—good and bad. He had splashed in puddles with his bare feet. He had played the piano only to find it suddenly mute and unresponsive to his touch. There were rays of sunshine that warmed his chest and a cool fountain that made his lips tremble when the water kissed them.

Indeed, there were far more realms and dimensions than religion or science would've led one to believe.

Rebecca turned over the parchment she was using to take notes. A bold, Texas-sized headline sprawled across the cheap paper in an audacious, jet-black typeface. Julian's sketch was sandwiched between the marvelous transcripts.

"A 'Wanted' poster!" she exclaimed, shaking her head. "Could you not have used something else?"

Manny shrugged. "We needed paper."

The poster reminded Rebecca that she was in the presence of a celebrity. Giving the advertisement another study, she compared the image to the man across from her. It was a close depiction but lacked the emotional gravity that made Alden memorable.

He's better in color.

"I saw a different one in the post office," she said. "That picture didn't look much like you, either."

Alden joined in on the class discussion. "I suppose that's a good thing, though it's always some mixture of the two of us. There's a sketch in El Paso that's fairly accurate. Can't go back there for a while…"

If ever.

Together, they read the posted description of the outrageously wicked Julian Crisp: *NOTORIOUS BADMAN WANTED DEAD OR ALIVE! COLD-BLOODED KILLER AND THIEF! REWARD $3,500!*

"This must be old," Manny remarked. "Your bounty is much more than that, now."

The disreputable Jesse James was worth a $10,000 bounty in Missouri before being assassinated by Robert Ford, a member of his own gang. Rebecca wondered how much the Texas government would pay for the entirety of the Disciples or if Alden had ever considered following in Ford's footsteps.

"*La Fantasma*," Alden pointed to the bottom of the bulletin at the text printed just below the picture. "That's what our neighbors to the south call Julian."

Rebecca mulled over the possible derivatives: *fantasy, phantasm, phantom...*

"The Ghost," Manny translated.

A ghost and a shadow. Rebecca considered Alden's role within the Disciples with newfound compassion. While a ghost could remain indefinitely, once a shadow was gone, it was gone.

"Women can be outlaws, too, you know," joked Manny.

"Really?" Rebecca beamed, suddenly intrigued by the thrill of infamy.

"¡Claro que si! Have you never heard of Belle Starr?"

Rebecca smiled, noting the similarities between herself and the well-to-do daughter of a Virginian businessman who once ran along with Jesse James and the Younger Brothers. "And what would be *my* bounty?" she mused. "You sent my father a ransom. How much was it?"

Alden and Manny looked at each other in equal discomfort. Something about Rebecca being at Sanctuary made them forget themselves. They, too, were wicked men, her captors, and she was leverage. Manny cleared his throat and proceeded to slink away towards the door. "¡Adios!"

"Thanks, Manny. You're a real pal," stewed Alden.

"Did I say something wrong?" Rebecca asked once the door was closed.

"No."

"I have a right to know what I'm worth."

"You asked what someone would *pay*, not what you're *worth*."

As Rebecca opened her mouth to question him, he held the poster upright and pointed to the bounty. "Do you believe I'm worth a measly $3,500?"

"That's a considerable amount of money," she said.

"Is it worth my life?"

Rebecca shook her head.

"Even though I'm a bad man?"

She nodded. Crimes aside, who was she to assign another person's value?

"So, what do you believe *you're* worth?" he asked.

Rebecca pursed her lips. "I've never thought about it before."

Alden turned, taking the poster with him to the bureau. He would dispose of it later. "Stretch your mind for a ridiculous number and add a dollar for every time you've felt offended, rejected, or forgotten. Then multiply it by the number of years you've felt that way and round it up. Once you've reached that number, then and only then should you begin to negotiate."

After a few moments of silence, Rebecca audibly pondered, "How bad does one have to be to earn a bounty?" Her question was meant to be somewhat adorable, but it struck a nerve upon delivery.

"My God, Becca! Do you find this amusing? Do you consider this fun?"

"No, Alden," she shuddered.

"I think you do!" He presented the 'Wanted' poster again, pointing to Julian's image, ashamed to resemble him even remotely. "Do you understand what *this* man has done? What he's capable of?" Alden pointed to himself and back to the image. "I am not proud of *this*! No one should *want* to be on a wanted poster, no matter how high the bounty!"

He then crumpled the paper in his right hand before forming it into a tighter ball with his left and cast it into the corner. Rubbing the back of his neck, Alden returned his attention to his roommate. He hadn't made Rebecca cry, but he was close. Having lessened, he gently brought Rebecca to her feet.

"I'm not angry with *you*, alright?" he lamented. "I'm sorry."

They faced each other as they had their first evening together, though now there was no agenda, no charm for Alden to channel, no loss of self or pretending with shaky hands. He was...*calm*, and his close proximity seemed no longer invasive or threatening to Rebecca. After all, she'd been even closer while he slept. Alden playfully tugged at the strand of hair that continuously fell into Rebecca's face.

"Cabello," he said, tucking it behind her ear.

Rebecca echoed his dictation.

Alden opened his mouth and signaled within. "Boca."

"Food?"

"Mouth," Alden grinned, pointing to his teeth. "Dientes." He then teasingly tapped her on the nose. "Nariz."

As in her dream, Rebecca bashfully swiped at his hand, which merited a slight chuckle in response. There was a conscientious man with a sense of humor peeking out from within her bandit, testing the waters, making sure it was safe for him to be himself. Slowly, Alden took her hand and brought it to his chest.

"Corazon."

Rebecca repeated the term, noting that his heartrate seemed as speedy as hers.

"Beso," whispered Alden before tilting his head to lean inward.

"Money?" Rebecca blurted.

Alden laughed and released her hand. "That's *Peso*," he replied, taking a step back. "Dinero."

"Dinero."

The error was embarrassing for Rebecca but not enough to remove her curiosity. She stepped forward. "What did the other word mean?"

Alden felt his chest tighten in heavy hunger, a first for him in quite some time.

"Close your eyes," he said softly.

Rebecca lowered her eyelids as warm peppermint moved closer. She soon felt his fingers lacing her hair while Alden cradled her head as though she were something precious, not fragile.

"Vaquero!"

The bedroom door rattled with urgency, a hyphen suspending any romantic moment they might have shared. An *almost* moment. The separation caused them both to wobble as they made an awkward return to reality. Manny felt a great rush of air greet him when the door opened.

"Yes?" huffed Alden.

"Ay, perdón!" Manny beseeched.

"What is it?"

Manny watched Rebecca quietly resign herself to the edge of the bed, settling what must have been a dizzy spell. Upon noticing the berry tint to Alden's cheeks, Manny read the room and realized he had interrupted *something*.

"Julian's asking for you," he said apologetically.

"Alright," Alden nodded with a tone that concealed his reluctance. "Manny, will you stay with her?"

She interjected, "No one needs—"

"—It's only until I get back," promised Alden.

But who knows how long that could be?

"He'll keep you company, won't you, Manny?" Alden's words suggested convenience, yet Manny knew this was an earnest request. With Alden absent and Roger sleeping off the night watch, Rebecca was fair game to anyone else in the house.

Manny beamed. "It would be my honor."

Alden exited the room without another look at Rebecca. Once the door was closed behind him, he exhaled deeply, taking the necessary moment needed to recover.

Manny drummed his fingers on his thighs while Rebecca mused on the mattress.

"Shall we continue our lesson?" he suggested, roosting alongside her.

"Yes, of course." However, Rebecca cared not for the vocabulary relating to household items or animals. There was only one word she wanted to learn. Quickly turning to Manny, she asked. "What is a *beso?*"

Manny gave a hearty chuckle and ran his thumb and forefinger over his mustache. "Where did you hear that word?"

When she couldn't successfully produce an answer, Manny laughed.

No wonder Alden looked so flustered!

"Are you sure you want me to tell you? I do not feel it is my place to show you."

"What do you mean?"

"A *beso*..." he began, noting how her intrigue seemed heavily coated with hope. "A *beso* is a kiss."

Rebecca's cheeks soon matched the color of her hair. "Oh," she said simply.

Manny then changed the conversation topic to that of the weather. *Esta lloviendo.* While he would later tell Roger, and they would undoubtedly rib him for it, Manny was delighted that Alden felt compelled to make such a brave advance. As for Rebecca...

She doesn't look upset, only mildly self-conscious.

Rebecca let the linguistic instruction pass through one ear and out the other, for she was too busy processing additional information. *A kiss.* Alden wanted to kiss *her* and would have if not for the interruption.

What would that have been like?

*Was it possible that he remembered her own **beso**?*

And most importantly...

Would he try again?

CHAPTER TWENTY-THREE

Later that evening, Roger entered the parlor to find Rueben, Edwin, and Phillip playing cards around a makeshift table. When Sanctuary was first discovered, blood-red tapestries and rugs framed the grand entertainment space, whose once snowy-white walls were now peeling in wintry protest. Vernon had since removed the frivolities, choosing only to let the majestic fireplace, rusted fixtures, and a few mismatched chairs garnish the area. If he concentrated hard enough, Roger could faintly make out the scent of expensive cigars and brandy, which seemed to be embedded into the walls along with pre-war memories and ghostly snippets of conversations from more civilized men.

"How nice of you to grace us with your presence! Did you enjoy sleeping all day?" Phillip smirked at Edwin's comment. It was mighty brave of anyone to pester Roger when he had just woken up. Roger rolled his shoulders back a few times, still adjusting to being vertical.

"I had the night watch," he said. "You know that."

Edwin shrugged, and Rueben lit a cigar. They all hated the night watch, as keeping odd hours could have an effect on them that was worse than a hangover. In time, a person would feel better after drinking too much, but inconsistent sleeping patterns drain a man to feeling he might never catch up. Julian remained paranoid that their hidden fortress would eventually be discovered. Yet, there was usually nothing to report, save for a few coyotes that would wander too close to the house or property damage from the rain. The assignment was generally as boring as it was futile.

"What's going on?" asked Roger.

Phillip put a finger over his lips, and Edwin waved at Roger to keep his voice down. Roger yawned, noticing that the trio of men weren't as actively engaged in their card game as they initially appeared. The parlor sat directly below Julian's bedroom; if you were quiet, one could sufficiently make out any spoken dialogue.

"What is it?" he asked again.

"*Shh!* We're listening," Edwin whispered.

"To what?"

Rueben playfully fanned out his cards before popping them back into a solitary stack in his hand. "Alden and Julian have been going at it for over an hour."

Roger's eyebrow lifted. "What are they arguing about?"

"Beats me."

Edwin took a swig of lukewarm coffee, wishing it were a beer. If Vernon were alive, they would all be free to go into town and enjoy a frothy beverage. But things were different now. "Oh, come on! You *know* what they're fighting over."

Phillip suddenly grabbed Edwin's cards for review and grunted at his own losing hand. He slapped the table in protest before granting his attention to a whittling stick in the corner. Even without vocalizing it, Phillip was a sore loser. Edwin leaned in toward Rueben and Roger, who took Phillip's vacant seat.

"Do you think if Alden gets to keep a girl, I could have one too?"

Since the game appeared to be over, Rueben overturned his cards. He would have won. "That depends, Edwin. Did you have any luck getting girls before?"

Edwin provided an obscene gesture in response. Roger chuckled. "Speaking of, where is she?"

"Upstairs with Manny," Rueben replied.

The parlor acoustics rivaled a concert hall. Though the sound was above them, each Disciple had a front-row seat to the apparent debate, with a pair of angry voices resonating overhead.

Edwin took another sip of bitter coffee, puckering in dismay. "It's not fair. Just because Alden looks like Julian doesn't mean he should have free reign!"

Rueben rocked in his chair, absentmindedly fashioning a house of cards. "You think Alden has free reign? That man has been in a testicle vice for the three years I've known him."

They each winced at the thought, for Rueben's diagnosis was correct. Everyone knew the job would always come first because the whole operation depended on Alden's willingness to cooperate. There had scarcely been any pushback from Alden before the Newberry Farm incident. Regardless of Alden's reasoning, taking Rebecca was a deliberate act of defiance.

Heavy footsteps continued to echo above them. Roger began to build his own carded construction, although his thick hands made steadying the cards difficult, and he couldn't seem to focus on anything other than the noise from on high.

"Has it gotten physical up there?"

"I couldn't say, but we heard some glass shatter before you got here," Rueben remarked. His house of cards had gained a fair amount of height but soon gave in to gravity. He took a moment to reconfigure the error of his design before starting again as booming voices bled through the baseboards.

"It's hard to tell who's talking," Edwin noted as he traced his finger along the rim of his cup.

"Shut your goddamned mouth!"

Roger sighed, knowing Alden's passionate timbre all too well. He shook his head. "Julian's not one to raise his voice."

"*You've lost your mind!*"

Rueben paused his project. "*That* was him."

Edwin attempted to aide Rueben in his assembly. "Maybe Alden doesn't want to keep the girl."

"He *should* want to," said Rueben, swatting Edwin's hand away. "She's nice."

"Since when does Alden deserve something *nice*?"

"Are you jealous, Edwin?"

"I'm not jealous! It's just not fair, like I said."

It wasn't that Edwin disliked Alden; he merely wanted equal treatment.

"Everyone deserves something nice in their lifetime," offered Rueben. "Even if it's only for a little while."

Rueben and Edwin resumed bickering over card houses and coffee while Phillip whittled away in the corner. Few things would phase Phillip, who had witnessed the horrors of sacred land being ripped away from his people. He may have elected to be a Disciple, but he would always be a tribe of one. Roger looked directly upward with growing concern, wondering if Manny had a better understanding of the argument from his location or if he should go to Julian's room to intervene.

"*You are way out of line!*"

The men all froze with their heads elevated as the crackling fire gave a burning underscore. After several seconds of silence, they resumed their activities. Remaining observant, Roger feigned an interest in the happenings around the table.

"Who do you think would win in a fight?" asked Edwin.

Reuben shrugged. "Well, Alden's still kinda sickly, and we all know Julian doesn't fight fair." He stacked a card vertically before opting for the horizontal position. "Now, *Levi* would snap them both in two."

"He's not with them, is he?" Roger inquired.

If Levi were upstairs, Roger would *absolutely* intervene.

"Nah, Levi left a couple of hours ago, just before Alden went in."

"Julian, please!"

A hush fell over the room.

"Please?" Edwin gave a low whistle. Such a word rarely came from members of the group to Julian and *never* from Alden.

"Whatever it is, Alden wants it bad enough to ask nicely," said Rueben sadly.

Shifting, Roger's face reddened. "That's not asking nicely; that's *begging*."

Rueben finished another level of his creation and wagged his head. "Poor guy can't catch a break,"

Roger stewed silently with clenched fists and rolled his shoulders. He believed Julian *would* kill Alden, either through abuse or his own hand, before the year's end. A man could only take so much. Alden seldom shared what would happen behind closed doors with Julian, but Roger and Manny both suspected a power struggle. Roger considered that with Levi gone, he could make easy work of their gang leader. At this point, he didn't need a reason. Rueben and Edwin would most likely stay out of his way, but if he chose to fight, Phillip could serve up some serious damage.

"Do you know what this reminds me of?" Edwin posed. He and Rueben were now collaborating on a ranch-style structure with stables. "Those meetings we used to have each week."

"Where we'd all get together?" said Rueben. "Yeah, that was always fun."

"I liked knowing what was happening with everybody and what the next job would be."

Rueben delicately slid a card on top of what he deemed was the outhouse. "Me too. You know, all this waiting keeps me on my toes, but, if I'm honest, it makes me kinda nervous."

Edwin lifted Rueben's newest contribution, believing the shape should be a silo, not an outhouse.

"Don't bend the cards!" snapped Rueben.

"I'm not!" Edwin argued as he placed the card down, plotting to fashion it to his liking once Reuben looked away. "And why are you nervous? Don't you like being told what to do?"

Rueben adamantly returned the card to its original position. Edwin may have appreciated the concept of order and discipline, but he would never understand what it meant to be *owned*. "No, I don't."

"Alright! Fine!"

The ceiling shook, causing the silo-shaped outhouse to crumble on the table along with the rest of the construction. Reuben threw his hands up in surrender.

There was no use trying to build anything in Sanctuary.

Edwin flung a fallen card that spun like an uninspired boomerang to Rueben's chest. "Ooh, Alden is madder than a wet hornet!" he beamed.

Rueben laughed at the King of Spades and retaliated. "I guess he didn't get what he wanted."

Roger shifted again in his chair. "We don't know that."

The childish behavior continued as cards flew through the air, landing on the table, sliding along the floor, and occasionally slipping into cups of coffee. Rueben wiped down a soiled two-of-hearts. "It's nice to hear Alden have some fervor again."

"And if you pull another stunt like that, Alden, I'll kill you myself!"

Edwin gave a smug smile and flicked one last card. "I told you he would get in trouble eventually."

Roger stood, having heard enough, and moved to exit the parlor.

"He keeps it locked, Rog," Rueben called.

"A locked door has never stopped me." Roger barreled up the grand stairwell, two at a time, noticing that Manny was down the hall, standing in the doorway to Alden's room with the door positioned just wide enough for him to slip through or promptly shut if needed. *He had been listening, as well.*

The door to Julian's room opened before Roger could test the handle. If it were possible to be pale and red-faced with anger, Alden was both. The sudden appearance of a friend startled them equally. Any view of Julian's bedroom quickly disappeared behind Alden once the entrance closed, but Roger was able to notice the glass on the floor that Rueben mentioned.

"Everything alright?" Roger queried.

Alden wiped the sweat from his brow with a shaky hand, his mind processing orders given on the other side of the door. Fresh blood laced his knuckles, serving as the reminder of a punched wall.

"Boss?" Roger slowly placed his hand on Alden's shoulder. His shirt was damp, suggesting that Alden may have overexerted himself. Alden's initial expression revealed nothing, but the touch of an ally brought him back to reality. Anxious eyes full of fear and sadness locked in with Roger. Alden's voice shook.

"She's leaving."

CHAPTER TWENTY-FOUR

As awkwardly as she arrived, Rebecca found herself ineptly preparing for departure. Seeing as she had nothing to take, Rebecca watched as Alden packed modestly before sharing their itinerary. For some strange reason, his walls had gone up once more, and he was all business. They were taking her to Grady, a neighboring town of Waco, much like Marlin, just along the Brazos River, sandwiched between Fort Worth and Austin. They, along with Roger and Manny, would join Levi at Pearson Pointe to acquire Simon en route. Rebecca had never heard of Grady but understood it was far out of the way. Her safe return would be executed once the ransom was paid at an undisclosed time near the train station. The Grady Train would bring her home. Their journey would be long and taxing, but he promised Rebecca protection if she cooperated.

"We shouldn't ride double," Alden told Roger as they crossed the front lawn. "Not without a pillion saddle, which we don't have."

"I don't understand why we don't have one. We *should* have one."

Manny nodded. "I agree."

Alden drummed his fingers on his thighs, his hands in desperate need of occupation, as they were generally accustomed to holding a cigarette first thing in the morning. He willed himself *not* to chew on the thumbnail that had grown to a healthier length. "We'll alternate and take turns walking. It won't hurt 'em if it's for a short time."

Roger's head bobbed. "Alright, but if anyone angers The Colonel—"

"—Who's The Colonel?" asked Rebecca.

With a proud and friendly smile, Roger gently took her arm. "Come and see."

Roger explained the threat of over-encumbering a horse as the quad traveled to the stables. Even if it could handle the load, there were always the risks of exhaustion, loss of control, and potential injury. If the horse didn't buck at the idea entirely, the rider's combined weight and distribution of such weight meant that the horse would be more likely to stumble, especially in rough terrain.

"*This* is The Colonel," Roger announced as he patted the Arabian stallion's broad forehead. A reddish-to-brown chestnut flowed over the animal's body from its short cannons to its wide yet condensed back. Rebecca was surprised that such a small breed could carry Roger's body weight. *That alone merited a salute!* The Colonel leaned into Roger's affections with soft, relaxed nostrils and a lip line that curled slightly downward.

Manny's horse, a Barb appropriately named *Rico*, had a refined honey roan coloring, with white hairs interspersed to form a "V" among the knee and hock. Rico began nickering the moment they entered the stables with happy anticipation as if to say, "Hola! Ven a mi, por favor!" Manny laughed and muttered something playful in Spanish while he went to the gate.

As a child, Rebecca took riding lessons but never saw horses as anything more than property or means of transportation. For Roger, Manny, and Alden, the animals might as well have been a part of the family. Unbiased companions who were reliable at "getting them out of tight spots," according to Manny, the horses were cared for because they took care of them.

"We don't have many things to call our own," Roger continued, reaching for a dandy brush. "We also don't have that many friends on account that so many people want us spitting blood or swinging..." His voice trailed, lost in the activity of grooming.

"Gambit!" Alden whistled, followed by a beckoning click in his cheek.

The American Quarter Horse had a bay-brown body with a black mane, tail, ear edges, and lower legs. Standing chest to chest and under the chin, Gambit's owner reached his arms around the steed's neck, giving simple strokes and low, hushed whispers. Rebecca watched as Alden stole away to have a quiet moment with his horse and take inventory of the animal's overall health.

What delicious secrets were locked away inside that wedge-shaped head?

"You want to give it a try?" Roger held out the brush.

Rebecca instinctually took a step back. "Oh, I don't clean animals." Realizing then how rude she must have sounded, "I only mean, he looks clean enough to me."

Roger snickered. "This isn't about cleaning. You could groom a horse all day, and they'd love it. This is about *communicating*. Here." He placed the tool in her hand. Rebecca hesitated.

"Don't be afraid," Manny kindly encouraged.

"I don't know how—"

But Roger directed her through each soft, sweeping stroke. The horse's body was delicate and warm, a fine suede, with each caress producing an earthly-rich, grainy fragrance. The Colonel sighed in relaxation as he adjusted to Rebecca's touch and subtly lipped the top of her head. Rebecca giggled with delighted uncertainty.

The noise took Alden away from his own horse. He turned to observe The Colonel nuzzling Rebecca as if he were about to return the service at any second. Rebecca's laughter fell sweet on Alden's ears but hung heavily on his heart. This was a precious occasion, as a woman's laughter wasn't common at Sanctuary. Additionally, it was the first time he had seen Rebecca fully smile. Simple and mildly crooked, hers proved to be quite contagious. Manny left Rico to join Roger and Rebecca, whose hair was now—courtesy of The Colonel's styling—in great disarray. Chuckles and commentary bubbled around them, another rare occurrence. Alden harbored his own grin along his horse's mane with a twinge of guilt and something else...*jealousy*? Roger was no threat, but Alden wished that he were the one to orchestrate the moment.

He wanted to make Rebecca smile.

Rueben carefully crossed the piles of hay and landmines left by the horses.

"What kind of idiot gets arrested for stealing a horse?" he quipped, handing Alden an assortment of wrapped vittles. Apples, bread, salted beef, a cheese wedge, and a small portion of penny candy.

Alden popped a lemon drop into his mouth and puckered at its sour salutation.

"Simon's fifteen, Rueben."

"Julian said he had half a mind to leave him there."

"He wouldn't do that." Alden gave the citrusy sweet a hearty suckle.

"You sure?"

"He didn't do it to me." Alden expected Rueben to leave after placing the items in Gambit's saddlebag, but Rueben joined him in grooming after allowing himself a tangy treat.

"I should be insulted that you're not asking me to go with you."

"It's not my call," said Alden while inspecting Gambit's hooves. Rueben's head popped up on the other side of the hefty creature. He had to look busy in the event Julian caught him standing around.

"Come on! Let me ride along. I could take Roger's place."

"Not this time, friend."

"Why not?" Rueben exclaimed and gestured to Roger, "I'm a faster draw than *that* fat fuck!"

"Hey!" Roger was slow to speak at times but had impeccable hearing. Alden waved him off before returning to the conversation. Poor Reuben hadn't been out of the house since Vernon died.

Alden leaned across the small of Gambit's back. "Look, I'd take you with us if I could, but Julian wants you to stay here."

"Yeah, so I can go on being his little house ni—"

"—Rueben, if you've got a problem, you need to take it up with Julian."

"I'm taking it up with *you*! I ain't seen any kind of action in God-knows-when!"

Alden crunched the candy in protest. It was difficult to argue with it in his mouth, anyway. "What do you want *me* to do? I've got orders to follow just like everybody else."

"Except for when you're pretending."

"So?"

"So, pretend right now!"

"In case you haven't noticed, I've got my hands full right now."

Rueben knew Alden was referring to Rebecca. *"Psh*, that's on you!"

"I know, Rueben! But I can't tell you how this will play out, and I don't particularly feel comfortable telling a grown man who is *no different* from me how to do his job. If it bothers you that much, just meet us in Grady. You don't need permission from me or anybody else."

Reuben smiled. This was what Rueben appreciated about Alden; he saw Rueben as an equal and always treated him fairly. Such conversations wouldn't happen with Julian, who showed little interest in him. Unlike Alden, Julian was a bit racist. There was never any willingness to meet in the middle with Rueben or allow him to show the others what he was truly capable of doing. Julian was his boss, but Alden was his friend.

Alden took a mighty swig from his flask and grimaced with regret as the whiskey hit his empty stomach. It was too early for liquor, but lemon was *not* his flavor.

He should have just had a cigarette.

Rueben frowned. Though Alden was alive, he still worried for his well-being. "If you keep drinking like that, you're gonna die."

Following a sigh, Alden sniffed and cleared his throat. "You'd think."

The pair then turned their attention to Rebecca, who was now fully acquainted with The Colonel. "Is she giving you any more trouble?"

Alden lowered his eyes, guilty. "She's no trouble. She's innocent. That's the rub." Returning the flask to his satchel, he shifted. "You know I didn't—I wouldn't have done that to her..."

"Yeah, Manny told me. I never really believed you had, anyway. Only Edwin and Phillip—"

"—It's fine."

With a laugh, Rueben swept the dandy brush over Gambit's hindquarters. "Alden, I know you're not the bastard you pretend to be." The dinner bell echoed from the front porch. It wasn't mealtime, merely a way for Julian to get Rueben to return to the house. His nostrils flared. "That lazy ass! The war ended, right?"

"It did."

"Then why the Hell has nothing changed?"

Alden accepted the brush from Rueben. "Change takes time."

"Yeah, I know that, too." Rueben turned to exit, stopping to add, "Give yourself some grace, will you? Some of us like having you around."

At this, Alden gave a half-nod shrug while Rueben walked away. The morning hours soon slipped past the travelers as they journeyed with only the horses, horizon, and humidity for entertainment.

"Manny, what is Mexico like?" asked Rebecca.

"It's like the sky: bright, bursting with color, and muy diversa!"

"Diverse," mouthed Roger.

"Rich in history and tradition," continued Manny. "Even the air is full of flavor!"

Horseback, Rebecca wrapped her arms around Manny's midsection. "It sounds wonderful."

Alden scoffed. "It's also got corruption, poverty, and violence, like anyplace else."

Manny gave an exasperated exhalation. "Vaquero, *this* is what's wrong with you! You're not kind to yourself, and it makes you grumpy a todos las demas."

"I'm kind to myself!"

"Bullshit," grunted Roger.

"¡Tan deprimido!" Manny argued. "You only see things in the way that is most disagreeable."

"That isn't true!" Alden insisted.

Manny continued. "It's a choice, you know. How can you be happy if you don't choose to push the unpleasant aside or fight to see past it? How will you ever know anything good or beautiful?"

Alden shrugged, "Beauty in things exists merely in the mind which contemplates them."

Rebecca's eyes grew greener at his reference. "You've read David Hume's essay!"

Giving a sideways look upward, "Does that surprise you?" he grinned.

"Considering what you boys do—" she blushed. "Hearing y'all talk like this makes you seem like decent men."

Alden laughed. "We ain't *decent*! If you knew what Manny could do to a fella with his knife, you'd change your mind real quick."

Manny's cut eyes at Alden in astonished betrayal. Rebecca looked at Manny and the knife in his gunbelt, remembering the blood of those horrifically murdered at the Rosewood Ball. She imagined him attacking anonymous figures as she recreated the scene in her mind. *Was her new friend capable of such brutality?*

Manny gave her a tight-lipped smile in response, then looked away, embarrassed by his former transgressions. Alden attempted to atone for having spoken out of turn.

"I should mention that Manny has renounced violence. It makes him a lousy outlaw, but we like him, so we keep him around."

Manny kept an about-face. "Who else would be willing to put up with you?"

As the silence settled, Rebecca turned to Alden. "And what about Roger?"

Roger veered to Alden, his bulky frame almost toppling over the horse beneath him. "Yeah, what about Roger, Alden?"

Not a question but a challenge. *Was it imprudent to discuss the gory details of one's misdeeds when living a life of crime, even amongst a colleague?* It was difficult for Rebecca to imagine Roger doing anything shameful or immoral.

Alden gave Roger a good-humored slap on the shoulder. "He may not be decent, but he's certainly the prettiest!"

"That's the *right* answer!" Roger said with a chuckle.

Even Manny laughed at this, and Roger resumed his usual stance. It was evident to Rebecca that the men accompanying her weren't proud of their life's work. Little did she know that this change of heart was only as recent as February.

"Do you think I'm decent, too, Becca?" Alden leaned in to pose the question. "That's if a man can be both decent *and* counterfeit."

He seemed worried that the others would disclose his sins as carelessly as he had theirs. The smooth timbre of his voice mixed with peppermint's slight scent almost made Rebecca lose her concentration. She looked away, unable to answer, revealing a stunning undamaged profile. Alden considered what she would look like if her complexion were fully intact, then decided he preferred her as she was.

Rebecca turned back to face him as though she could read his thoughts.

"I'm not sure."

"That's alright," he nodded. "I'm not sure most days, myself."

Alden shifted. Manny was right; he *was* depressed and grumpy, but he was working on himself. He was in repair. What none understood was that Rebecca's presence alone made him want to try a little harder. Yes, for her and the others, but mostly for himself. He stared ahead. Taking a hostage was a complicated business. He wished only to be kind to her, yet Alden had his reasons for holding back. Suppressing such sentiments proved incredibly painful.

And their journey had only begun.

CHAPTER TWENTY-FIVE

They stopped for the night, and not a moment too soon. Rebecca was already weary from their travels, though she understood they were far from Grady. While there would be no tent at this camp, each man offered an item from their bedrolls for her personal convenience. *How considerate for a group of felons!* She would stuff Roger's wool cover inside Manny's canvas outer to create a pillow and cover herself in Alden's woven yellow blanket. Her captor wandered off as the others got settled. He would be gone for several hours. *Something was on his mind.* Roger kindly explained that this was a regular occurrence, stating that Alden preferred solitude on most assignments.

Despite their hospitality, it was frightening; the thought of sleeping outdoors. These men had proven trustworthy while she slept at Sanctuary, but her chaperones were no longer the only threat present. What about strangers? Or the elements? Several insects and animals thrived under the cloak of darkness, their noisy remarks signaling that they were surely up to no good.

Ahooo.

Screech.

Hoo-hoo.

But what Rebecca found most terrifying was the *silence* so great that she believed it would swallow her whole. Her surroundings seemed to blend in with swirls of deep blues, shiny greys, and blacks covering what was once green. She fixated on the wicked treetops above her and considered the possibility of escape while the Disciples dozed. None of them took the night watch as they did at Sanctuary. There was no need; they were in the middle of nowhere, and Rebecca hadn't the slightest inkling of which direction might lead her to civilization. If she ran away and got lost, no one would lead her back to safety. If she found herself in danger, only nature would hear her scream.

Yes, staying put would be wisest.

Footsteps fell faintly in the distance, slowly growing in volume. Rebecca quickly closed her eyes and held her breath as Alden's spurs and steady stride moved overhead. He stopped, and Rebecca soon felt the sides of the daffodil blanket straighten over her extremities. Alden slowly turned to check on the others. Manny was curled in a tight little ball with his back in the opposite direction. Roger remained slightly upright against a nearby tree's trunk, his head hanging slightly diagonal to the rest of his body. If Roger was awake, it was just barely.

Crouching down, inspired to touch Rebecca but opting not to, Alden whispered, "Are you asleep?"

Sounds of the world around them contributed to the lunar symphony: branches rustled in the wind, a gentle neigh murmured from one of the horses, and even the dwindling fire provided underlying tonality. Alden watched as deep, heavy breaths filled her chest in great waves that would rise and fall with a hushed rhythm. Rebecca listened with sealed eyes as he struggled to form the words.

"I'm sorry," he gulped. "You need to know how sorry I am for all of it. You did nothing wrong. You didn't deserve this. *Do you hear me?* I'm a selfish man, and..." Alden never finished his heartrending apology, which traveled further than intended.

Roger feigned sleep while eavesdropping from his resting place. Though Alden hadn't disclosed such feelings with him, Roger knew of the *almost* affection that occurred before their leaving. Alden's actions affirmed that he cared much more for Rebecca than he was letting on.

That might be a problem.

Upon his exit, Rebecca slowly opened her eyes, wishing she would have opened them before, wondering how the exchange might have unfolded if she'd acted awake. Such thoughts would rob her of any sleep that night.

When morning came, and as they moved beyond their woodland wonderland, Manny noticed a change in the group's dynamic. Roger carefully watched Alden, who seemed a bit more chatty than usual.

"El Conejo," Alden pointed out as he guided his horse in front. Rebecca was riding Gambit aside, which gave Alden an excuse to look and talk to her without his interest being obvious.

"What's that?" she asked.

"*Rabbit*. See the white buds on the tips? They're bunny tails."

Rebecca smiled. Lush, whimsical waves of sapphire and tanzanite standing two-feet tall forever rolled along the hills before them. Wildflowers with fifty blooms on one stem and leaves green with white edges, channel-like and cradling droplets of rain in their hands; the blossom had many names: *Lupine, Buffalo Clover, Wolf Flower*. Summer was ending, and more *bluebonnets* would need to be planted to ensure their germination for spring, but there were still several patches of belligerent beauties holding on, longing to be admired just once more. Rebecca instinctively reached for her escort to dismount, her eyes never leaving the cobalt garden. Native American lore suggested the flower was a gift from the "Great Spirit." She felt no need to disturb such sacred vegetation, wanting only to behold their charm.

"Go on," said Alden. "We've got time. The horses need water, anyway."

As Rebecca scurried off, Alden looked on in amazement, slowly scanning the countryside to save the image in his mind. After months of nightmares, it was a dream to watch Rebecca move into a place where she felt free. His cornflower blue shirt helped her to float right through the rustic rivers of indigo.

This was where she belonged.

When she caught him staring, Alden leaned slightly in the other direction and pretended to study an area past her position. Roger and Manny returned, having filled their canteens with fresh water from the nearby stream. After carefully observing Alden from a distance, they had many questions.

"Do you still see that girl from Fairmont?" asked Roger, hoping for an easy segue to the *real* topic.

"Which one?" Alden removed the cap from his bottle. "Julian's got a few lovers tucked away."

"Curly blonde hair."

"*Which one?*" Alden bent his elbow while the other men struggled to put names with faces. Julian's lustful habits and the amount of time they spent traveling made it hard to keep track.

"Samantha?" Manny suggested.

Roger shook his head. "No, she's got a freckle on her lip."

Manny wiped the excess liquid from his mustache. "Annie."

"Annie!" Roger exclaimed so loudly that Rebecca's head perked up in observance.

"That ended a while ago," Alden replied. "She might even be married now."

"Really?" Roger countered. "You never said anything."

Alden shrugged. "She wasn't mine, so it didn't bother me. It didn't faze Julian much, either."

"You sure spent a lot of time with her," noted Manny.

Alden raised a guilty eyebrow. *Diddling* someone wasn't the same as *spending time* with them. He *liked* many of Julian's lovers and certainly enjoyed their company, but it wasn't as though *he* selected those girls. None of them were *his* to claim.

"Julian's got a reputation to uphold," Alden argued.

Being Julian Crisp *did* have its perks. When younger and inexperienced, Alden took advantage of every opportunity to learn his way around a bedroom. He could account for how he walked just a *little* taller and how the Disciples' inaugural group praised him after his first conquest. Such practices contradicted his upbringing, but abstinence and marriage were out of the question under Vernon's leadership. Alden and Julian's carefree, Lothario lifestyle was encouraged, and while *he* took precautions, Alden knew neither of them would ever be held accountable. It was exhilarating to key things up initially, but eventually, even the most satisfactory of lovers became predictable. Each tryst felt the same. Those romantic partners never sighed *his* name in the dark. They always wanted Julian.

Roger paused mid-swig. "You say that like women are exhausting."

"Women *are* exhausting!" Alden announced. "Why do you think I haven't taken a lover of my own?"

"Because they all expect you to be someone else," offered Manny before another savory gulp.

Alden nodded. "That, and I don't want to share."

Roger swished a bit, allowing the water to move through the parched nooks-and-crannies. He knew Julian and Alden had an understanding and respected the latter's stance on exclusivity. While it didn't excuse the philandering, making such a decision—even though it left him lonely and limited—was one of the few things Alden *could* control.

"How do you remember their names?" asked Manny, who once attempted to juggle two women but foolishly lost them both when he called one by the other's name.

"I don't know; it's like I can see their portraits in my mind."

Alden had a photographic memory, a useful skill for reading or preparing a heist. Admittedly, the information he found most memorable, most desirable, was the subtle nuances and the physical features other men might disregard, such as a freckle…

Or a scar.

"I honestly thought you fancied Annie," continued Roger.

"Annie was fun, but she wasn't what I wanted. They never are."

Alden's voice trailed as his eyes fell on Rebecca from a distance.

"That's a tall order, Alden," noted Roger.

"I didn't say I wanted *her.*"

Roger retreated. "I'm not saying you do, but we all want something, right?"

"What do *you* want, Rog?"

"I ain't decided."

Alden turned to his other associate. "What about you, Manny?"

"Peace," answered Manny.

"Just peace?"

"Just peace," Manny scratched his head. "And maybe a beer."

Alden's face lit up with laughter long enough for him to notice Rebecca's gaze. He considered sharing his smile but chose to ignore her. Smiles were a complicated means of communication. As he had minutes before, she looked away from him.

"What do you think she wants?" he posed.

Roger blew a raspberry, still amused by Manny's comment. "Search me. What does *any* woman want?"

The three men looked ahead, waiting for the other to contribute a possible answer, but the truth was none of them had any idea—guns and games they understood. Women were an entirely other concept.

"I bet no one's ever brought her flowers," Manny sadly commented.

Roger smiled. "We brought her some today.

"We sure did," said Alden. With this, he left his colleagues with nauseous anxiety. *Maybe it was the heat; maybe it was something else.* Roger followed.

"You alright, Boss?"

"Yeah."

"This whole *team* thing only works if you talk to me."

"I'll tell you when we get to Discovery."

"You don't want to tell me *now*?"

"No, I don't." Alden stopped. "Manny, would you mind collecting our flower girl?" He gave a cheek click to Gambit, who replied with a friendly whinny and trotted to him. Roger whistled at The Colonel while Manny moved down the hilly blue waterfall.

Rebecca sighed at the footsteps approaching, unready to leave that azure slice of Eden. Manny stepped gently at first, as not to crush the blossoms, but then shuffled to the side a bit before halting completely. He gave no warning as his knife suddenly came down in one swift movement near her head. She screamed.

They never warned her about the possibility of snakes circling within the wildflowers. Manny had the rattler impaled mere inches from where Rebecca sat, her having not noted the cautionary percussion it made before assuming the position to strike. If it weren't for Manny's intuition, quick-thinking, and accuracy, Rebecca would've surely been bitten.

Manny wiped the blood from his blade. "That was close!"

"Did you get a snake?" Roger called from The Colonel's side.

Rebecca recoiled at the scaly creature lying at her feet, belly exposed, its mouth open, and fangs protruding in one last expression of terror. Manny kicked the corpse away from them. "Yeah, we really should've told her about—*mmph!*"

Rebecca's lips crashed into Manny's with ecstatic gratitude. It was the only way she could think to reward his heroism. Kissing someone alert proved a completely different form of indulgence for Rebecca, for she could feel the rapid increase of his pulse and the sweat sliding down his temple, along with tiny puffs of air that traveled out of his nose onto the mustache that twitched in a surprised response. Rebecca's arms wrapped around his sturdy neck, committed to establishing contact. Manny's eyes widened. He was generally accustomed to being overlooked by the opposite gender and had never kissed a woman from such a high station. It felt like a baptism. Or knighting. His arms flailed about before finally stretching in surrender, unsure how or if he should reciprocate.

"Thank you!" Rebecca said breathlessly. Her gesture was nothing more than a heartfelt peck, yet as Manny left her embrace, he sensed that Rebecca withheld a great, fiery passion. Something wild and untold slumbered deep inside. Such heat would be too much for him to handle. But Alden?

Lord, help him.

Roger chuckled as Manny walked briskly yet awkwardly to Rico. Alden gave a partial smile in response. He wasn't surprised. Rebecca was one of those *buttoned-up women.* Steam engines: valves and pistons gaining momentum, poised to blow at any moment. The thought made his stomachache subside, only to be replaced with a wash of desire. He remembered how she responded to him with such curiosity their first evening together and how her eyes secretly studied his body each time he dressed. Having only known women of seasoned sexual expertise, Rebecca's untouched wonder created a whole new level of longing.

What would it be like?

To be the first one there...the first one to ever make her—

—No, Alden. You've done enough.

As it was Roger's turn to ride with Rebecca, Alden slowed his pace to join alongside Manny. "Well, how was it?"

Manny blushed. He didn't have stories of multiple conquests like most Disciples, as his shy, agreeable nature gave him the title of "friend," if anything. Rebecca's kiss would be a highlight for some time. "Wet," he finally answered.

Alden grinned, a part of him knowing that was the most elaborate detail Manny would provide, while a larger part wished *he* were the one to rescue her.

CHAPTER TWENTY-SIX

After supper, Manny left the campsite to meditate. Yes, he knew that in addition to Rebecca, somewhere, a furry little creature was thankful that the rattlesnake was dead, but he still felt guilty. He felt guilty every time he saw a deer mounted to a wall, every time he noticed a horse being mistreated, and even every time he ate an animal, which was seldom as of late. Who decided that *those* creatures should be destined for such an existence? Did their animal instincts provide them with any insight into their place in the world? If they *could* know their true purpose, would it change how they lived? Manny took a deep breath and listened to insects, birds, frogs, and other nocturnal transmissions. The signs of life were all around him, a life that existed not for the living—not for his benefit—but because it could exist and because it was created by a sentient universe. Who was he to *ever* take life away?

Something so wrong shouldn't be so easy.

Beyond the stillness, Alden contemplated his own mode of operation. Roger had left for a spell, so he and Rebecca were alone for the first time since leaving Sanctuary. He could've gone to sleep, not that he was tired. No, it was all too rewarding to have her sitting so close, wrapped in his yellow blanket, wearing his blue shirt.

Feels like Christmas.

"Did you enjoy yourself today?" he asked.

"You mean *before* the poisonous reptile?"

"Yes."

"I suppose," chided Rebecca. "You boys certainly keep things interesting."

Alden gave a slight smile. "What kind of hosts would we be if you weren't entertained?"

Rebecca crossed her arms. "Entertained or endangered?"

"Danger can be entertaining."

"Then, rest assured, Mr. Aubrey, you've been *very* accommodating."

Rebecca was angry, and rightfully so. Alden was the one to let her roam in the bluebonnets without giving the slightest warning. Though he put his best foot forward, it seemed nothing had changed. From the moment he came into her life, Alden kept Rebecca in a perpetual state of endangerment. *Damnit.*

He shifted. "I should've told you or walked you down there myself. My apologies. It slipped my mind."

"*Slipped your mind?!* I wonder if you even have one to call your own!"

"You were *happy*—" Alden began.

*For the first time with **me**, you were happy.*

He waved an observant finger, "There's that bite again! I was wondering where it went."

When Rebecca said nothing, Alden shook his head. He never had to try *this* hard with other women. Fortunately, Roger and Manny weren't around to witness his failure. He could continue to make small-talk. He could sit there with her in the awkward silence. Or he could talk to her, *really* talk to her the way he had before when they were alone in his bedroom when he took her face in his hands and nearly kissed her.

Jesus, Alden. You almost kissed her.

How would that have panned out?

His behavior wasn't in line with his beliefs—not by a long shot—and yet it was still easier to gloss over his emotions, make excuses, and simply pretend. Anonymity promised the comforts of home, while authenticity…that was unfamiliar territory. Alden retrieved a jug beside the meal prep area and removed its corky closure. Just the smell of its contents made his eyes water.

"What is *that*?" asked Rebecca, also catching a whiff.

"One of Rueben's concoctions," he replied.

"Is it safe for you to drink?"

"We'll find out!"

Rebecca frowned. "You're going to make yourself sick."

"No more than I already am."

"Well, you're going to make yourself *worse*."

With a grin, Alden raised a toast of solidarity. "Here's hoping!"

The mountain rye gave a smack hearty enough to leave a handprint, but Rebecca wasn't impressed. "Do you *want* to die?"

Alden sniffed and clapped back, "In a shoot-out or at the end of a rope, as you so kindly suggested?"

"I'm serious," she retorted as he drank again before wiping his mouth.

"What do you care?"

"I care."

Alden blinked in curious confusion, silent. *Could she mean it?*

"What about before when you—the laudanum—" inquired Rebecca. "Did you want to die then?"

Not one of the Disciples had asked him that question outright. It was always skirted around but never uttered, the one question he *needed* to be asked. What a shock for it to come from her! Rebecca watched the façade shift within him, a hidden bookshelf revealing the secret passageway to his heart. *There he is.*

"I wanted to disappear," he whispered, breaking a sweat from the adrenaline rush of honesty. Rebecca nodded. *Perhaps Rueben was right.* She gestured to the canister.

"Does this do that for you?"

"Sometimes."

Much to his bewilderment, Rebecca reached for the jug.

"It's strong," he cautioned. "You won't like it."

"It might be worth it."

Alden's smile grew. "Aren't you full of surprises! You want to disappear, too?"

"Only all of my life."

Rebecca could smell the pungent liquor long before it reached her lips. It reeked of medicinal oils, pine, and cadavers. She hesitated. As with the whiskey, Rebecca tossed back the swig of moonshine, which kicked like a mule and resulted in the most painful few minutes of her life. Coughing, sputtering, and teary-eyed, Rebecca retched as Alden's smile quickly turned into satisfied laughter.

"Not exactly red wine, is it?"

Rebecca understood that alcohol's effects on any given person were purely scientific: substances reacting to other substances within the human body. While she would nurse a glass of merlot on occasion, Rebecca usually practiced temperance. This experiment made her question anyone's appreciation for hard liquor...or chemistry.

"Stop laughing," she said hoarsely.

"I'll stop laughing when it's not funny anymore." Alden gave Rebecca a few comforting pats on the back, his shoulders still bouncing. Her nose was running, and she was flushed, but to him, Rebecca appeared positively radiant.

"Am I transparent yet?" she asked.

"On the contrary," he beamed, leaning closer. "I see you quite clearly."

"What did you do to her, Alden?"

Alden quickly put some distance between them. Roger returned to nab the spot on the other side of Rebecca, but not before relieving her of the bottle, which she was all too willing to hand over.

"Don't let him pester you none, Miss Rebecca. Alden hasn't always been able to hold his liquor. Not that he's that tolerant now. No, I remember the day we met…"

"Rog, she doesn't need to—"

But Roger continued, "—I was out on an early morning ride, and I see this skinny little fella walking down the side of the road, three sheets to the wind and naked as the day he was born, save for a pair of boots. To this day, I don't know what sort of trouble he'd gotten himself into…"

"Trouble is trouble, no matter the sort," replied Alden, his ears now reddening.

"He didn't ask for money or assistance into town," Roger chortled. "He simply asked if he could borrow my hat!"

Alden permitted a shrewd shrug. "It was a nice hat."

"I told him he could keep it. Then he wound up keeping me."

At this, Alden smiled, offering a second shrug that was more subdued in gracious matter-of-factness. "The Disciples needed a strongman, and I needed a friend."

The moonshine loosened their lips with sentimentality. A brotherhood existed between Alden, Roger, and Manny, with mutual respect rarely verbally acknowledged. They were groomed to believe that men didn't generally speak to each other in such regard and that Disciples shouldn't form any attachments or alliances that could overthrow the group.

Manny casually strolled toward them. "Que paso? What's going on over here?"

"Roger was telling how he came to join the Disciples," said Rebecca.

Manny settled on Alden's other side and gestured to him. "Did they mention how I won *this* one in a card game?"

Rebecca giggled. "Like a prize?"

"Mmm-hmm."

"It's the only time I've ever been caught," explained Alden, his eyes sparkling. "This fella near Galveston got the best of me and was all set on turning me in for the reward money. He decided to celebrate prematurely on the way into town. Manny was sitting at the table, Aces Full."

"A lucky hand," Manny modestly protested.

Roger clarified that a trio of aces with any pair could beat another Full House in a poker game. As part of his strategy, Manny would pretend he didn't understand the game, speaking broken English and losing the occasional round. Not only did Manny have three aces, but also a pair of kings to solidify his win.

It was an *extremely* lucky hand.

"Manny said he intended to hand me over to the authorities," said Alden. "And for a second, I believed he would."

"I still could," Manny replied. "Roger and I already agreed to split the bounty, fifty-fifty."

"Sixty-forty," corrected Roger.

Alden looked at his friend. It had been quite some time since he considered or even expressed gratitude for Manny's unexpected decision to spare him.

"You made a different call," he said. "Though, I don't know why."

"And you never will."

Alden nodded. Nothing more needed to be said. Loyalty was as rare as clean water in those parts but just as essential. The value of healthy, solid relationships with good people in a man's life is priceless. *He was blessed.*

Manny turned to Rebecca, "Tell us about your friends."

"I couldn't say that I have any."

As their expressions fell, Rebecca understood that she had dampened the mood. They didn't need to know about the absentee playdates or false friendships that were often forced and so hurtful. How while growing up, she never understood why *she* couldn't be the princess in those make-believe games until finally, the other children explained.

Princesses have to be pretty!

You're not pretty, Rebecca. Don't you know you're not pretty?

Her voice trailed, "I have acquaintances, folks that I greatly esteem…"

"They're just scars," stressed Alden. "Everyone's got them."

Alden then watched Rebecca's pride lessen into a look comparable to the very one he had given her, an image that genuinely mirrored that same fear of vulnerability.

"You're choosing not to see me as others see me."

"People see what they want to see," he argued.

"What do *you* see?"

For a moment, it was only the two of them, her question remaining suspended mid-air on a trapeze of possibilities, swaying with each passing second.

Back-and-forth.

Back-and-forth.

"It's late." Alden cleared his throat. "We should try to get some shut-eye."

Rebecca ran nervous fingers through a frizzy hairline, nodding in agreement with the rest of the concurring party. Now, she *really* wanted to disappear. Roger smoothed out a makeshift bedroll nearby, sighing past the awkward moment to wriggle in the contentment of its comfort.

Manny took the transition as an opportunity to remove his boots. Most cowboys slept with their boots *on*, but not him. When goodnight wishes had all been given and received, Alden took the jug with him in the direction of his own pallet. The moonshine slid smoothly to its final resting place on the ground. Alden tossed the empty container and watched as the earth drank in the puddle of spirits.

"What are you doing?" he asked himself, as though the physical act of speaking would invoke a response from the universe, any explanation as to how he could behave the way he did. Back near the other bedrolls, Roger propped himself up on an elbow.

"I'll be your friend, Miss Rebecca, if you'd have me."

Touched, Rebecca nodded. "I'd like that, Roger."

"Buenas noches, amiga," called Manny from his booted bedposts.

"Buenas noches, Manny."

CHAPTER TWENTY-SEVEN

It was only through traveling with the troublesome trio that Rebecca realized how little she knew about her home state. With cultures so distinct and even more diverse terrain, it was understandable how Texas had once been its own nation. Every stop felt like a different country! High plains, canyons, forested hills, and prairies stretched the horizon before her in various orientations of slope, scene, and surface water flow. Much like a transition from one chapter to the next, the view would plateau after a few miles, proving uneventful or monotonous, only to shift in landscape and wildlife, capturing her attention once more. There had been an armadillo, a coyote, a skunk from a distance, and a grand assortment of avifauna. Those evolving surroundings were a welcome distraction from the smell of fresh male sweat. Roger wore a glistening wreath along his temples, and Manny seemed to always have moisture along his upper lip while Alden donned a damp collar and the slightest ribbon down the small of his back. Each man secreted slightly beneath their arms, their musk encouraging her hormonal heart rate to climb. Sweat was supposed to be *dirty*, but none of them *smelled* dirty. Quite the opposite, when the wind blew, their pleasant pheromones dazzled her senses. Rebecca hoped *her* scent wasn't off-putting. The rosewater, her signature fragrance from the Rosewood Ball, had long since worn off, and with the weather varying between mighty storms and scorching temps, Rebecca was all too aware of her own need for maintenance. Despite knowing this, along with the certainty that the southern sun would freckle her, Rebecca never complained. This was better than any book, for *this* was an adventure. *This was living!*

Having made progress in their journey, Rebecca rode with the men in rotation many times. They each respected their horse's needs, paying close attention to their disposition and never overloading or riding too long. Depending on her guide's size and the landscape, Rebecca would ride side-saddle, in front, behind, or above whichever man decided to stretch his legs for a spell. Roger was so bulky Rebecca could scarcely wrap her arms around him, and Manny jostled just as much as she when saddled atop Rico. Yet, Alden maintained a steady balance of poise and athleticism when riding. Sitting straight and with his left hand holding the reins near his hip bone, Alden led his steed in smooth, confident movements as though they were one. Perhaps his center of gravity was better suited for the activity, resting low and settling perfectly along his belt buckle. Rebecca rarely needed to reposition herself when she rode with him, though Alden would always smirk when bumpy terrain forced her to grab on a little tighter. Soon, many of the miles were spent wrapped tightly around him.

You're doing this on purpose.

Rebecca's thoughts lingered back to their first morning together, remembering how his physique initially impressed her. Alden was thin, but there was muscle underneath that washboard torso.

"Do you want some?" he asked, leaning back slightly into her, relaxing the reins a bit to brush through his hair with his free hand. "It's sweet." He had bitten into a shiny red apple. Rebecca shook her head, but he gave it to her anyway.

"Becca, you need to eat something."

Rebecca couldn't help but smile at the gift that bore evidence of his ideal bite. She turned the apple over. That side was also bitten into in either an obnoxious act or one of flirtation. He watched her out of the corner of his eye, waiting to see if she would further contemplate eating after him. Rebecca elected for a coquettish response, making eye contact while sinking her teeth into the crunchy, sweet fruit and lightly dabbing the juicy dribble away with her thumb. This seemed to please him, though his eyes promptly left hers and returned to the road ahead as Roger adjacently joined with The Colonel.

"You see him?" asked Roger.

"Yeah, I see him."

"Who?" Manny inquired.

Alden gave a slight chin-up. "We've got a tail about 100 paces back."

Roger concurred, noting. "He's been following us for a while now."

They led their horses to a smooth, nonchalant halt and dismounted.

"Keep calm," said Alden. "Maybe he needs something. No need to get suspicious."

Roger gave a justified huff, his hand already resting on his holster. "I'm always suspicious."

Alden then eased Rebecca off of Gambit's back. "Stay put," he instructed before turning to strategize with his men. He should've seen it coming. Hands-free and with the Disciples momentarily indisposed, Rebecca could easily flee to the figure traveling in their direction. She wouldn't need to go to Grady or endure further days of the unknown. This stranger who followed them could have her back at Windhaven Hall in a fortnight. As she had the evening of the Rosewood Ball, Rebecca took off sprinting into the distance, discarding Alden's apple behind her.

"Shit!" Alden exclaimed.

"What d'ya want to do, Boss?"

"Well, we can't shoot her!"

Manny fought the urge to laugh. "Impulsive, that one."

Roger hid his own amusement. "Reminds me of someone else I know..."

Noticeably stirred, Alden adjusted the back of his shirt and rolled up his sleeves in preparation for retrieval. "When did I become the wet nurse? Can somebody tell me that?"

"You're the one that took her, Alden."

"Shut up, Manny!"

Her rescuer proved less stately than Rebecca hoped, with an air more akin to Phillip's, but seeing as she was a woman in distress, the roughrider came quickly to her aid. "You alright, Miss?"

"Help me, please!"

The stranger slowly dismounted. "Now, hold on—"

"—Sir, thank yew fur comin' to help my sweet bay-by sister. She's nawt right in the head." Alden was out of breath from the chase and spoke with a heavily exaggerated Southern accent, a yokel adding slight squeaks of inflection to suggest a lower level of intelligence.

"—Eleanor, it's Jimmy. Let's not be cross wit one anudder. I'm sawry I got a little frustrated witch-a. I prow-mise I won't raise my voice a-gin. Come owhn now, Eleanor. Let's leave this nice fella a-lone."

But Rebecca beseeched her champion. "That's not my name! These men are Disciples! They've taken me hostage! I'm Rebecca McNamara. You *have* to believe me!"

The stranger's overgrown eyebrows pinched in suspicion as he looked to Rebecca and then to Alden. "She's pretty adamant about who she is. I'm inclined to believe her."

"Why's that?" Alden asked.

"Because I know who *you* are, Julian Crisp."

Alden slowly lowered his eyelids, his spirit shifting to reveal Julian once they were opened. A screen of evil arrogance befell him with unholy lightning flashing within the green slivers of his sky-blue eyes. *"Well, why didn't you just say so?"*

Rebecca stood close to her ally. She witnessed Alden's impersonation of the Disciple leader during the stagecoach robbery, but his tipsy temperament took the edge off his performance. Sober now, though held at gunpoint, Alden was eerily calm and collected.

"Toss your weapons over yonder," said the foreigner. "Tell your men to do the same."

Alden unceremoniously pitched his firearm to the side, raising his hands in surrender, smiling all the while. "If that's what you want. Boys, do as he says."

Roger and Manny made their way to the showdown and steadily complied. Seceding from their weapons in standoffs was a regular occurrence.

"Alright, you've proven your point," Alden conceded. "Name your price."

Rebecca could feel Alden's determined gaze burning into her skin. The outsider shook his head, abandoning her as he moseyed over to the outlaw.

"I'm not interested in a barter."

"You sure?" Alden advocated. "A smart man like yourself must know the value of human life." He gestured to Rebecca and continued his approach, arms still lifted. "I value *her* life a great deal. If it means taking yours to get her back, so be it."

"Stop right there, or I'll shoot!" the stranger instructed.

"But I'm worth *so* much more alive!" Alden playfully argued. "Are you certain you want to put a bullet in me?"

The revolver clicked as the gunman's thumb pulled the hammer. Alden gave a forward bow, having stopped at the gentleman's warning but standing far from a forfeit.

Last chance.

Inexplicably, Alden began to spasm as though something had possessed him, clawing at his arched back and scratching at his shoulders, neck, and sides.

"Keep your hands where I can see them!" barked the rider.

"I would, but this tension has me itching something awful!"

"Stand still!"

"Relax!" Alden purred, working his left hand over the small of his back. "You've got our guns. This ain't even my shooting hand…"

Rebecca then caught eyes with Manny, noticing how the sides of his mouth had begun to curl. The size of a man need not matter in a fight; it was whoever could draw the fastest. A short breath leaped out of her chest as she soon understood her great oversight. "He's ambidextrous!"

The stranger turned his head. "What?"

And that was the last word he said. The bullet entered his right temple, bringing him to the ground with a clumsy flop and modest splatter. Alden had tucked the firearm into his trousers, resting just beneath the curve of his spine. Furious, he started towards her. Rebecca always assumed that a man's anger would be shown through flared nostrils, violent outbursts, and shades of red, but not Alden. No, his aggression was a scalding, searing white.

"You ran away," he fumed. "I *specifically* told you to stay put, and you ran away!"

Rebecca, clearly still in shock, "You killed him!"

"He was no doubt a bounty hunter! Who knows what he was after! He might have killed us all!"

"You don't know that!"

Alden snatched Rebecca by the forearm. He wanted to shake her, to make her understand. "Do you have any idea how much danger you just put us in? How much danger you put yourself in?"

Rebecca winced as Alden squeezed her chin.

"Look at me," he seethed. *"Look at me!"*

When she obliged, he relaxed his grip. "You're acting a fool! How well do you think you could fare out here alone, huh? I didn't *have* to kill that man, but it was either him or me. Do you *want* it to be me?"

Alden's eyes locked in on hers with a shaky hand still clutching her face as he leaned in to sternly whisper, "You're not to run unless I tell you. Do you understand? Say it." Rebecca pursed her lips, fighting back tears, not wanting him to be right about the hazards around them but knowing she was ill-equipped for survival on her own.

"*Say it.*"

Gulping, she submitted. "I'm not to run unless you tell me."

Alden then led a teary-eyed Rebecca to Manny and Roger as they retrieved their weapons, walking briskly past the deceased, whose confusion remained permanent in his glassy expression. *I never knew his name.*

Rebecca looked down in defeat as Roger brought her wrists together and bound them with rope. He worked quickly, saying nothing while ensuring the knots were secure enough to disprove future escapes. For him, this was business as usual. The whole ordeal had been a minor hiccup. For her, this was the most epic of failures and had cost a man his life.

Some friend!

As Roger attempted to heave her onto The Colonel once more, she resisted.

"Oh, come on—not *this* again!" he grumbled.

The Colonel's body held true like a brick wall as Rebecca shimmied across him, ensuring Roger would fail to get a firm hold. Manny stepped in to assist but was also unsuccessful. Rebecca bucked and stamped in protest. She didn't have to make this easy for them. She would wiggle and writhe. She'd get dirty. She would go limp. She'd bite if she had to! Alden soon began his advance. There was no way she could evade all three of them at once. Determined, Rebecca planted herself firmly into the ground.

"Promise me that you won't kill anyone else!"

At this, the Disciples burst into hearty chuckles and roaring laughter. "You're not in much of a place to be making demands, sweetheart," Alden stated.

"You need my cooperation," argued Rebecca. "You need me alive, or you won't get your money!"

Alden casually turned to his associates, still amused. "You know, I don't remember if we were told she *had* to be alive. Do you?" Roger and Manny shrugged their shoulders in agreement.

"How will you stop me from running again?" Rebecca questioned.

With a smirk, Alden replied, "A few ideas come to mind."

Roger stepped in. "Listen, these sorts of things follow us wherever we go—"

"—*Killing people?*" she protested. "There *has* to be another way!"

Alden was staring at her again. *No, not staring; studying.* The skilled swindler cocked his head. "Do you think it makes any difference to me whether or not I kill people?"

"Yes, I do," she dared. "I think it bothers you so much it makes you *sick*!"

Alden snarled. "Get on the horse, Becca."

"No."

Alden's voice dropped to the guttural growl he used with Edwin that first morning at Sanctuary. "Get on the horse, or I'll *tie* you to it like the cargo you are!"

"No!"

Before she knew it, Rebecca was hog-tied, gagged, and thrown over The Colonel's rear end. Lying flat on her belly, Rebecca winced as The Colonel's hooves thundered and clicked along the scenic countryside.

The view wasn't ideal, and watching the ground move at high speeds made her head feel fuzzy.

To be fair, Alden *did* warn her.

In his peripheral, Roger caught Alden observing his own view of Rebecca's backside with the tiniest side-smile, lost in a cheeky thought.

If she acts up again, I'll just turn her over my knee.

"Quit that," Roger chastised.

Alden gave an about-face. "What? I'm making sure she doesn't fall off. With the way *you* ride…"

Roger shook his head. "You can fancy her, Alden. We won't hold it against you."

The outlaw set his jaw. "The only thing I fancy is getting to Discovery."

CHAPTER TWENTY-EIGHT

There was little fanfare upon their late-night arrival to Discovery. In fact, they completely bypassed the hotel's main reception area, heading straight to the back stairwell up to a third-story guestroom. No explanation as to why Rebecca was bound was necessary to gain admission, nor was there any currency exchange between Alden and the busty matron at the side entrance. He merely smiled as he whispered in the woman's ear, giving a slight nod and completing the transaction with a gentle peck. Roger and Manny chose to find alternative lodging, though Rebecca didn't understand *why*. The newly renovated inn seemed a nice enough place. Though not the reputable establishments she frequented with her father in the past, Discovery's most popular boarding house certainly provided *some* hospitality.

Once the door had closed behind them, Rebecca was seated in the corner of the suite, which appeared much too fancy for Alden's taste. *Was this for her benefit?* Heavily furnished and highly decorative, it reminded her of Julian's quarters. Alden removed the fabric that silenced her, fashioning it around her neck, but the roommates said nothing for many minutes. Alden proceeded to clean his gun to pass the time, which made Rebecca's eyes swell in somber remembrance of the bounty hunter he had slain.

"Don't look at me like that," he frowned. "You know what you did."

Alden returned his attention to the poked cloth in his firearm, loosening the built-up carbon. "When you ran to that bounty hunter, we didn't have time to prepare an offense. Now, I don't care so much about myself, but I *do* care about Roger and Manny. I'm the one that took you; there's no reason for them to get arrested or killed because of my foolishness. I understand your instinct to flee, but… I don't want to hurt you, alright?"

"But you will."

He sat the shiny sidearm on a nearby table. "Let's look at this logically. You're a long way from home, Becca. You know as well as I do that it's dangerous out here. So, I'll make you deal: If you swear to cooperate and do *exactly* what I tell you *when* I tell you, you'll be protected, and no more men will needlessly lose their lives for the remainder of our journey. If you continue to be difficult or draw attention to yourself when we're close to any sort of law, the deal's off."

Rebecca processed his proposal. This was a fair offer, possibly the only one she would get. "Let's strike hands on it," she said, hoping it would prompt him to untie her. "That's what my father does with his business proceedings."

"Which is why *this* arrangement will remain an oral agreement."

Rebecca made sure to look Alden in the eye, something she knew mattered to a man. "You won't kill anyone?"

"Zero casualties," he promised.

Several seconds passed, with the pair locked in on one another, looking for any excuse not to trust. Rebecca needed to blink, but Alden hadn't moved. He was waiting for her affirmative. "Very well," she agreed.

"Good, then it's settled."

Alden stood and crossed to Rebecca before falling frozen, first by the knock at the door and then from a voice he recognized, a *feminine* voice beckoning the infamous Julian Crisp. "Oh, no," he moaned. "*Oh, no!*"

Rebecca looked to the door and then to Alden, who cringed with dread.

"Are you expecting someone?" she asked.

"I am truly, truly sorry about this."

With hesitation, he forced the gag back into Rebecca's mouth. Rebecca swore at him through muffled inconvenience. Alden anxiously smoothed the front of his shirt and turned to Rebecca one last time. "I apologized beforehand," he said. "Remember that."

When the door opened, a risqué tornado blew in with sloppy wet kisses and the famished caresses of body parts Rebecca never thought to touch—even while Alden was sleeping. Rebecca watched as Alden answered every advance from his female caller, unsure if he was responding instinctually or as someone else.

"Julian!"

"Hello, Alice."

"Minnie said she saw you come in through the back."

Rebecca studied their guest. Everything about Alice was appetizing: a generous serving of strawberry lips, chocolatey hair, and milky skin that smelled of vanilla. She was thin yet curvaceous enough to provide something to grab onto, with sapphires for eyes and bosoms that could catch anyone's attention. Despite never acting very bright, Alice Wolford *was* smart, a businesswoman who made well on her investments because she knew how to use her assets.

"Who's she?" Alice inquired of Rebecca through an impressive amount of rouge and lipstick.

Alden's eyes searched Rebecca for an answer. "She's my...sister."

"I didn't know you had a sister!" said Alice. "She doesn't look like you."

"Did I say sister? I meant *cousin*."

"Whatever you say, Julian… Only, why is she all tied up?"

Alden scratched his chin. "She's not well. In the head. I'm taking her to a sanitorium further south."

"That's mighty noble of you, Julian." Alice moved her hands to encircle Alden's midsection. *He seemed out of sorts. She'd set him straight.*

The soiled dove's eyes scanned Rebecca with surprising sympathy. "Poor thing. People like her will never know what it means to love someone or be loved back. Never kiss anyone or have another person's body fused with their own. Oh, I've missed you!"

After that, Alice's hands were much less discreet. Alden gave a heavy huff and cleared his throat. These were sounds that Rebecca had only heard animals make, never a man. He was completely twisted physically, but his expression seemed more conflicted than pained. Alice put her hands on her hips.

"What's wrong with you, Julian? You look ghastly."

Forcing a smile, "It's all that time I've spent missing you, darlin'."

"*Aww!* Well, next time, don't stay away so long!"

Alden struggled to downplay the rise of sexual tension. "Why don't you come back a little later, and we can have some privacy?"

Having heard this, Alice grinned and let her hands flow freely while she leaned into his reluctance. "Julian, we've had an audience before."

Alden waivered. "*We have? We have!*" Though not surprised, this would certainly be a first for him.

Alice turned her head to the side and examined Rebecca's countenance, which was silent in anything but comfort. "I wonder if she understands what's about to happen," she queried, biting Alden's bottom lip.

"*Ack*—I'm sure she has an idea," Alden lurched. He need not look at Rebecca; he could feel her emerald eyes upon him, watching in dismay. "Do you really think we should do this *now*?"

Alice rolled her eyes. "I thought you said you didn't want me to think."

"Is that what I said?"

"Mm-hmm! That's what you told me the last time you were here." Alice changed her stance to embody the rugged villain. "I don't pay you to think, Alice. I pay you to shut your mouth and take it!"

Her depiction of Julian was both accurate and believable. Alice then boldly positioned herself on the mattress. "So, are you gonna give it to me, or ain't you? I've got other customers, but I thought I'd let you go first."

How thoughtful. Alden deliberated over what Julian would do before concluding that he would undoubtedly service Alice if in the same situation. That meant he'd have to do it, too, though it wouldn't be quiet. Alice was *never* quiet during the act. Alden took a moment to consider the scars on his upper back and shoulders. She hadn't seen them and would surely have questions, especially when the *real* Julian returned. If he positioned himself correctly, they might go unnoticed.

"Oh, alright," he said, easing himself onto the bed.

Alice squealed with delight. Romancing Julian Crisp always held a bit of mystery. This time, Julian was solicitous to her, which meant he would be unruly the next time he paid a visit!

Shocked, embarrassed tears clung unhappily to the bandana fixed around Rebecca's face. Of all the terrors she experienced since her capture, Alice's words were the most traumatic. Rebecca always considered herself a noblewoman with a healthy yet appropriate sensual imagination, all things considered. Girls like Alice were inferior.

I'm not supposed to want to be her.

But she did. Rebecca envied Alice's confidence, her experience, her seductive prowess, and most of all, her beauty. She would never possess such features. Alice was right; she would most likely die alone.

She could even die before the week's end without knowing what it meant to love and be loved in return.

Rebecca sought to put the events unfolding before her out of her mind, yet closing her eyes only amplified the smacking sounds of kisses, heavy breathing, and the hasty shedding of clothing. She knew what the female body looked like, but Rebecca wasn't certain she was ready to see a naked man.

"Julian, what's wrong?" asked Alice impatiently.

Alden had pulled the bedcurtain. Now, all Rebecca could see was the strange formation of shadowy fornicators, who suddenly stopped before they even got started. "Nothing!" he said. "Why?"

"You've usually got more…*vigor.*"

"I've got *vigor*, I just—Give me a minute!"

Alice sighed heavily beyond the veil. "Don't tell me you don't *wanna?*"

"It's not that!" Alden stammered. *"Would you stop talking for a second?"*

Alice sighed again. "Maybe you'd rather have your cousin!"

"Maybe you're not as good at your job as you think!"

Rebecca heard a hard *crack* from behind the curtain. Alice then scurried out of the bedroom as quickly as she entered, garments in hand, insulted and irate with dissatisfaction. "And I thought you knew how to treat a lady, Julian Crisp!" she hollered.

"That's funny; I didn't realize I was *with* one!"

The door slammed in damning resentment. Alice Wolford wouldn't return to Julian's bedchamber that night or ever again. Alden let out a deep, exasperated groan. His body would punish him tomorrow. "Hold on," he lamented. "I'll be right there."

Rebecca couldn't discern why it took him so long to roll over and get dressed. Alden seemed to move slower and with more frigidity than in his hungover hobble that first morning at Sanctuary.

"Why are *you* crying?" he moaned after removing her salted suppressor.

"I'm frustrated!" Rebecca whimpered.

"Who isn't?!"

Alden sat on his laurels beside her. The sight nearly broke his heart. She was filthy, disheveled, and, like him, appeared exhausted. Shades of deep purple, green, and grey danced up her arms, evidence of his handiwork. *Alden, you know better than that.* Noting that Roger's knots were much too tight, he wondered if Rebecca had any feeling left in her hands at all. Alden sought after the folding knife from his nearby satchel. Rebecca's sobs bubbled over upon his return with it in hand.

"No, no, no!" he cooed. "It's for your wrists."

Alden severed the banded twists ever so gently until each dusty strand fell to the floor. Together, they watched the color slowly return to her hands as signs of life began to flow freely through her fingers once again. Rebecca smiled at Alden in appreciation and massaged her wrists. His shirt buttons had gone off-track in his haste to dress, exposing a clearly defined collarbone. She raised her hand…

And then, with gusto, she slapped him.

CHAPTER TWENTY-NINE

"What the—?

Rebecca's sudden change in character nearly knocked Alden off his heels.

"—That's for making me watch whatever that was!" she sizzled.

Shocked, Alden rubbed his cheek. *"You hit me!"*

"You hit me first!"

Alden settled. He might have gotten carried away with Alice. Admittedly, he and Julian would often try to one-up each other, leaving behind mementos or messages along bedposts noting naughty details and other less noble personal accounts that only men would brag about.

"You must engage in these excursions frequently," Rebecca fumed as she moved to put some space between them.

"Don't pass judgment on me, you shrew. Girls like Alice are… well, they aren't just for the types of fellas I run with," he spat, still sore. "I bet even your father has known his share of painted ladies."

"You take that back!"

"Sometimes they can be helpful in a pinch, but most of the time, they're just *fun*! But you wouldn't know anything about that kind of fun, would you?" Alden smirked. *"Would you,* Miss Rosewood Debutante, in her frilly purple gown? So refined! So educated! You know, I think that maybe what you need is a *different* kind of schooling."

He advanced in her direction.

Heel-toe, heel-toe.

Rebecca retreated. "You said you wouldn't!"

Alden shrugged, "I figure a man has the right to change his mind."

Yes, he *was* slowly chasing her around the bedroom, a mighty lion on the prowl. He was enjoying it, too, even walking on the bed to close in on her. If they were children, such behavior would be seen as entertaining, endearing even! Rebecca couldn't remember a boy ever chasing her around the schoolyard, but she was certain none had ever done so with such a strange expression on their face.

"Come on; I've seen how you look at me," he teased. "You might even like me a little."

"Not at all!" Rebecca fussed.

"Now, that hurts my feelings."

She ran to the opposite corner. "Don't touch me!"

He spread his arms. "You're all the way across the room! How could I touch you?"

"Well, you're making me uncomfortable and—"

"—*And?*"

"You're scaring me!"

Alden hopped down from a nearby piece of furniture, gaining much ground between them. "What are you scared of: that I'll touch you or that you'll *like* it?"

"If you come any closer—" she warned.

"—What are you going to do?"

"I'll scream!"

Alden presented a swaggery smile, "Do you think you'd be the first woman to scream behind closed doors because of me?"

Rebecca's eyes widened. *I know what he's suggesting.*

*At least, I **think** I do.*

"You are *foul!*" she exclaimed.

"And you're a prude!"

Her jaw couldn't fall any lower. In a moment of madness, Rebecca pulled at the buttons of Alden's cornflower blue shirt, fumbling over her bodice with nervous fabric and static fingers that wouldn't cooperate.

"Fine, Alden! Go on and have me since that's what you're set on doing!"

"Oh, stop! You're not worth the effort it would take!"

"It didn't sound to me like you had any effort to give!"

Alden brought a fist to his lips to cover any amusement. They both jumped at the loud *thud* that hammered a neighboring bedroom wall, followed by suggestive moans from a feminine voice and expletives from a familiar male voice.

"What was that?" Rebecca gasped, her heart still pounding.

"My guess? Levi."

The sensual overture continued to swell into their room with affirmation. Rebecca blinked wildly in confusion, her instincts to cover her ears failing.

"Is it supposed to be that raucous?"

Alden sucked in his lips in an attempt to be mature, which proved unsuccessful. *She's just as much fun as Alice, maybe even more.* "You want to try to beat them?"

"What? No!"

Alden flashed another flirtatious smile and extended his hand. *It was worth a try.* "Alright, then. Let's go out on the balcony."

"Do I have to?"

"We can stay if you'd prefer to continue sampling the musical stylings of Levi Bohannon. I can ignore it, but you won't like the way it ends."

As if he were the maestro, the wall continued to pulse at Alden's comment, louder and with more aggression. Whoever was with Levi on the other side of that wall sounded genuinely in pain!

A rush of cool Texas wind nipped at their faces as Alden and Rebecca met the outside world. The brothel's balcony proved deep enough for two people to comfortably visit, albeit without furniture. Wooden railings stood sturdy and high enough to lean on without feeling you might lose your balance. The evening sky was a clearly painted canvas of purples, blacks, and blues. Yet, the aerial view of Discovery's night-life was nothing to write home about: shops closing, horses neighing, drunken conversations, and a couple of men cat-calling to one of Alice's associates in the street.

Alden fished for a topic of conversation. *She's sure fun to rile up.* Had he been more cordial initially, perhaps Rebecca would have talked to him as she did Roger and Manny. He bounced his left leg anxiously. Maybe he *was* a little jealous. Rebecca appeared indifferent, saying nothing to her captor. *The horses. She'd liked the horses.*

"Gambit," he offered. "My horse—he's named after a chess move."

Rebecca stewed. She dared not look at him. As much as she hated to admit it, Alden was pleasing to the eye. Only, he'd been a brute and a pest since leaving Sanctuary. She decided she liked him better when he was dying. *This* Alden didn't warrant her affections or her attention, so she would give him neither, nor would she grant him the satisfaction of knowing that his very presence unsettled her in the most unusual way.

"I didn't think people like you knew how to play chess," she chided.

It was a cheap comment, but he deserved it.

Alden's head bobbed in amusement. *"People like me."*

After several minutes of awkward silence, Alden reached into his vest for what appeared to be a cigarette and positioned it between his lips. A gust of wind blew through the balcony's pocket, revealing a cool, fresh, and sharp aroma. Rebecca's eyes widened in disbelief.

The source of Alden's scent was a peppermint stick! The idea of a candy-eating cutthroat proved surprising and endearing to Rebecca, who couldn't help but gaze at Alden with curious intrigue.

"I don't have too many vices, but this is one of them." Alden swirled the treat in his mouth. "When I first joined the gang, I was always sick," he revealed. "The things I had to do or learn kept my stomach in knots. I'll spare you the details." He suckled for a moment. "It went away for a while, then it came back. It sounds silly, but this helps."

Rebecca wondered how many peppermint sticks it took to numb a stomach of such sinister sins. *Was Alden sickly now as they conversed, or was he merely enjoying his guilty pleasure?* "Why not see a doctor or take medicine?" she asked.

"I don't like taking medicine," he replied. "Or doctors."

A typical male response.

"It's my last one," he said. Before she could decline, Alden bit off a piece of the chalky straw and presented it to her.

Unbelievable.

Alden licked his fingertips before returning to his portion of the sweet. Rebecca felt obliged to accept his peace offering and politely nibbled on the striped stub. A strong minty flavor flooded her senses with soothing refreshment. His thoughtfulness was unexpected, which Rebecca believed was the best kind.

"Who do you think you would be if you weren't with the Disciples?" she posed.

"I think you mean *what*."

"I know what I asked."

Alden dug for pieces of compacted sugar in the crevasses of his back teeth with his tongue. "Why do you want to know?"

"Because I want to know!" Rebecca responded in a deliberate parody of his words from Sanctuary. "I'm just making conversation."

His leg began to bounce again, as this was the most honest

exchange Alden had shared with any woman in over a decade. "I was always fairly decent at woodwork. I'm good with my hands when they're steady. Maybe I would have been a cobbler like my father or a carpenter."

Rebecca crunched louder than anticipated. "A carpenter? How poetic!"

"I didn't name this team I run with."

"*Team*. Is that what you call it?"

"Well, it's not a *family*. Not unless you count Roger and Manny. It hasn't been for a long time."

Alden stopped to add to his statement but chose against it. She need not know about the division between the others. Sharing privileged intel with Rebecca was risky enough; he figured she already knew more than she should. His thoughts turned to her previous inquiry. Much time had passed since another person questioned what *he* wanted. He'd suppressed those desires for so long that, upon asking, vocalizing them proved difficult. Alden's eyes stared into the distance, lost in what might have been. The dreams were blurry and faded but still discernable if he focused hard enough.

"I could have had a shop in town, or maybe I would work the land. Definitely something outdoors…"

His voice trailed, detached from the present. That version of Alden was healthier and happier, with calloused hands, slices of grey along his temple, and a twinkle in his eye. He had a loving wife and children, Sunday dinners, and quiet evenings at home. He could grow old, something the *real* Alden deemed impossible, having already resolved that he'd most likely go out in a blaze of bullets.

Lightning flashed in the distance. Alden's eyes fluttered as he returned to his surroundings. "Truth be told, I'd do pretty much anything not to be doing this. As far as *who* I would be, I don't know that I would be that different. I figure I'd still be me, but I think I'd be *good*."

"Serve on the town committee?" joked Rebecca.

"Sure."

"Well, you still could."

"What, attend town council?" he chuckled. "I don't reckon they'd have me."

"You can still be good, Alden. It's a choice, like Manny said."

Alden, giving a defensive sneer, "You're wrong."

Rebecca frowned at this response. Alden then turned his upper body away from her, leaning a little too far over the railing for comfort. "You're hopelessly naïve to assume I could turn it all around just like that. Do you think I don't want to? You think I haven't tried?"

"*Have* you tried?"

Alden snapped upright. "Okay, Librarian! Who would you be if it weren't for your little predicament? You can't marry those books. They won't keep you warm at night. You could choose for yourself and be perfectly happy with how you ended up. You've had every advantage given to you, yet you act like you're limited."

"I *am* limited," argued Rebecca.

"You hold more cards than you think."

She retorted, "Look at me! Look at my face! It's not the same for you!"

"*It's exactly the same!*" he raved. "You try living with *this* face! You want to talk about being limited? I look in the mirror and see a liar and a fiend. And that's just Julian. Let's not consider *my* transgressions."

Rebecca shook her head. "I don't see him in you," she said simply.

As both shifted, they softened, equally shocked by her statement.

"You saw him today. You saw him that first night and the night I roughed you up a bit." Alden stumbled over the end of the sentence, still ashamed of his actions. His father would have had his hide if he knew Alden had ever hit a woman.

Sharpening her eyes to study him further, she said, "Do you know what I think?"

Tempted to chew, Alden brought his thumb to his mouth and positioned the nail over a canine. "No, but I bet you're going to tell me."

Gently, out of protective instinct, Rebecca brought his hand down in front of him and held it there. Alden looked at their connection, then back at her incredulously. This wasn't a woman who had what she thought was *Julian's* hand but his *own*. They were just fingers, just funny flesh, and yet Rebecca's hand was so soft, so different. Alden had forgotten how it felt and how very dainty a girl's hand appeared when placed within his own. He hadn't held a girl's hand like that—*not as himself*—in almost twenty years. Rebecca also relished in their union, remembering how happy he made her in Sanctuary by simply squeezing her hand when he awoke. Feeling the responsive warmth of Alden's hand was so much better than holding it while he slept. It was like magic, like breaking a spell. *Like a kiss.*

Drawing her in, Alden squeezed her hand once more. "Tell me," he whispered. Rebecca nervously shook at the golden opportunity. There he was, the man from her dreams, in the flesh, beaming at her, his heart light shining in her eyes. Alden smiled.

Those eyes. He could lose himself in those bright green eyes.

"Alden..."

"Tell me, Becca."

Realizing she knew little of mining or mercurial men, yet feeling the need to respond, Rebecca quickly answered, "I think—I *don't* think you're like Julian at all."

She watched the glimmer fade as Alden's smile fell, and he slowly released her hand. Whatever it was he wanted her to say, that wasn't it.

"I'm close enough," he reasoned with a sigh.

You should've kissed her when you had the chance.

As the refreshing treats left their palates and the rowdy sounds of the neighboring bedroom subsided, cooler winds drove them indoors.

More rain was on the way.

"You can have the bed," he told her.

"Are you sure?"

Keeping his distance, Alden positioned himself in a wooden chair facing away from her and propped his legs against the corner wall. "I'm sure."

Rebecca regretted her hasty statement and wished their conversation could have been about music or poetry. *You should've told him the truth.* She considered giving Alden the spot beside her. She tossed him a pillow instead.

CHAPTER THIRTY

It was joy unspeakable to awaken in an actual bed rather than on the cold, hard floor! Billows, as soft as meringue, enfolded Rebecca's body, granting both warmth and comfort. How wonderful it was to be back in Windhaven Hall! She wriggled under the blankets. *It was all a dream.* Sadly, the sounds of the outside world soon pulled her back to reality, to Discovery: birds chirping, horses trotting, strangers passing by, and the faint scent of leather and peppermint—*peppermint*?

Alden.

Rebecca quickly sat upright to find him facing the dresser. He appeared to be organizing something. She turned on her knees and leaned forward to investigate. There was soap, a sponge, a hairbrush, and oral hygiene products. Steam rose from hot water inside the basin. Beside it stood a tiny bottle of rose water.

He did all this for me?

Rebecca smiled, settling back into a sleeping position just before Alden turned to wake her. She felt his hand slide along hers onto her forearm before giving it a gentle squeeze. "Becca?"

She pretended to stir, batting her eyelashes before focusing on him. Alden looked tired, but his face was calm and kind.

"Mornin'," he said.

"Good morning."

Alden gestured to the dresser. "I realize you're accustomed to—well, finer things than this, but I—*we* thought that you'd feel more like yourself if you... Manny picked out the clothes."

Rebecca noticed a pale blue blouse with white buttons and a navy-blue skirt draped over a chair in the corner. *And shoes!* Though she had no clue how he determined her size, it would be a blessing not to walk on bare feet. Alden had mentioned that his father was a cobbler. *Perhaps that was it.* Rebecca felt that leaving behind Alden's cornflower blue shirt would be bittersweet, as it was the first thing he gave her. So much had happened since that first morning at Sanctuary.

"I'll step out to give you some privacy," he said. Alden had also cleaned himself up, sporting a new white shirt with thin grey stripes and a slate grey vest.

"A *gentleman*?" Rebecca blurted, though she hadn't meant to sound surprised.

Alden shrugged. "Despite my best efforts."

He excused himself from the room before she could fully thank him for his thoughtfulness. Upon peeling herself from the bed and seeing her reflection in the mirror, Rebecca understood why Alden made such a gesture—she was a *fright!* A banshee in the flesh! Rebecca quickly disrobed and made fast work of cleansing herself. Sweat, dirt, and blood began to vanish as the hot, soapy water worked its magic with each scrub. And it never felt better! Rebecca often longed to be the kind of woman who would wake up beautiful, but she knew she would always require *some* maintenance.

Once dressed, Rebecca gave the finishing touches to her hair, choosing to smooth ornery strands with rose water and a hairbrush before securing it with what little hairpins she had left. She looked in the mirror and let out a sigh of relief. Alden was right; she *did* feel more like herself.

Manny was the one to fetch her from the bedroom, knocking ever-so-sweetly before unlocking the door. He brought with him another gift: a two-bladed jack knife with an amber bone handle. It was similar to Alden's folding knife, only this dagger was smaller, measuring 3 5/8" when closed.

Presenting the weapon, Manny gave a careful directive, "When you stab a man, go deep, up, and twist. That's how you'll do the most damage. Between the ribs, under the arm, thigh, or even the neck—it doesn't matter where, but don't forget the twist."

Rebecca shook her head. *She would fight, but she could never stab a person!*

"Entiendeme, we may not always be close enough to protect you."

"I couldn't do that."

"If it's between your life and theirs, you'll do things you never thought possible."

"Does Alden know about this?" Rebecca asked before questioning herself as to why it mattered.

"He's the one who asked me to give it to you."

It mystified Rebecca that her captors would think to arm her, but as Manny led her downstairs to the street entrance, she considered that maybe Alden *did* have her best interest at heart. Or, so she thought.

"Poor you. What a waste."

For some unknown reason, they left her alone with Levi for a spell, promising they would return. The barbaric barber seemed to fit in perfectly with the townspeople busily milling about the streets of Discovery. He was so handsome that those who dared to look at Levi could only manage a glance. It was like looking at the sun with a vanity that made him glow even brighter. Passersby were so easily distracted by his radiance that none of them appeared to notice Rebecca. She averted her eyes. If this were polite society, Rebecca would have excused herself without a second thought. But she was far from nobility or the comfort of sophisticated pleasantries.

Levi dangerously eyed Rebecca's right profile. "You ever think about working on the other side to even it out?" Her mismatched scarring made his insides twitch, and the lack of balance was enough to get under his skin. He stretched a square-shaped hand to stroke her cheek, his thumbnail digging into the flesh deep enough to hurt. Rebecca's face went numb as though Levi's hands were fangs that possessed a paralyzing poison.

"What are you doing? Don't you have some baby birds to kill or something?"

As promised, Alden returned; his new brown Stetson tilted so low that Rebecca wondered how he could see clearly enough to walk. Roger and Manny stood aside, both wearing somber expressions.

"I'm being friendly," Levi swore while maintaining close proximity.

"Be *less* friendly, Levi."

Levi shifted, still carrying that ridiculous grin. Alden spoke softly and in a lower register so as to remain incognito. It was dangerous for them to be clumped together out in the open—especially during daylight.

"I've hitched the horses over yonder," he pointed. "Manny will take the lead, and Levi can—well, you know what to do."

After the group nodded at Alden's directive, Roger extended his arm to guide Rebecca as the entourage began to travel in formation. He appeared distraught and kept his mouth twisted in a tight grimace. She'd seen that look before, but it was always from Alden, never from him.

"Roger, are you alright?"

He didn't seem like his jolly self, and it was out of character for Roger not to wish her a good morning. "Manny and I got some bad news, that's all," he said, swallowing hard before speaking.

Rebecca patted his forearm tenderly. "I'm so sorry." She was positioned away from the street, blocking her from view or escape and simultaneously keeping Alden out of sight. Alden walked a few steps behind them while Levi tapered, enforcing full coverage of their crew. They believed this configuration would protect each of them.

But they were wrong.

After crossing a few side streets, Manny abruptly disconnected from the group, and Levi stopped in his tracks, spinning on his heel to enter a nearby shop. In the distance stood a rugged lawman who seemed all too interested in Rebecca's escort. Roger's chest started to rise and fall in hasty huffs of anxiety.

"Just keep walking, Rog," Alden instructed.

"I don't exactly *blend*, Boss."

Rebecca heard Roger swear heavily under his breath, another thing he rarely did. She promised Alden the night before not to draw attention to herself in the presence of the law. Even if it would provide her freedom, breaking that agreement would undoubtedly result in bloodshed, as the Disciples would never be taken alive.

And she didn't want Roger to die. *If there were only a way to make the suspecting onlooker turn his attention elsewhere.*

Thinking quick on her feet, Rebecca spun herself sideways and pulled Roger in by the lapel. His head was heavy, and his bushy beard tickled her face. Roger's earthy aroma reminded her of warm and cozy things, like cider on a chilly autumn evening. Somehow, Rebecca found his lips on the first try, utilizing a soft feminine pressure just long enough to make a smacking sound when she pulled away. The quality of the kiss wasn't much dissimilar to what she shared with Manny in the bluebonnets, only given Roger's pleased response, Rebecca believed her skills were improving.

Alden instinctively dropped to his knee when he saw Rebecca turn, blocking his face and pretending to scrape mud off the heel of his boot. He was ready to aim at the lawman if he approached them. Much to his surprise, Rebecca's interference worked. The deputy was now occupied with shielding an offended matron from the scandalous scene. *Well, I'll be damned.* They could still get a stern warning, possibly a citation, but with the townswoman's inconsolable behavior, the deputy wouldn't get the chance. Alden smiled.

"Sir, can I have my ball back?"

A canvas ball then nudged Alden's foot, urging him to lift his head. An engaging little boy, no older than nine or ten, called out to Alden from across the street with a host of friends standing by.

Alden's hands fumbled over the grapefruit-sized toy as the young man ventured into the middle of the road to meet him. Rebecca watched Alden struggle with the hand-off as though any exchange with a child was unbearable.

But why?

There were no further interruptions to delay the group from reaching the transport. Their brush with the law proved stressful, and only the growing distance between them and the city provided comfort. Discovery soon faded, leaving the quintet to their own devices for entertainment.

"There's blood on your shirt, Levi," noted Manny after a long spell of silence.

Levi tugged at his collar to examine the tiny stain. He smiled. "Mmm… *Alice.*"

Alden narrowed his eyes, feeling Rebecca's uneasiness as she settled behind him. From what he heard the night before, the pair simply participated in mutual fornication, albeit obnoxiously. "What did you do?"

His smile spreading, Levi answered. "After you sent her away, what *didn't* I do?"

Roger shook his head. Machismo was Levi's specialty. He would sodomize a sheep if it showed interest—and maybe even if it didn't. Alice was no different from any other fleece following Levi's lascivious lead. Alden raised an eyebrow to question Levi, but Roger intervened. "Don't encourage him."

Levi rolled his eyes, satisfied with his conquest but agitated that *Roger*, of all people, would judge him. "She got paid, Roger. What do you care?"

"I don't."

In a night of debauchery, Roger confessed to Levi that he once loved a girl much like Alice before joining the Disciples. *Tess.* Roger had known Tess as other men had known her and yet offered Tess a life without bawdy solicitation and soiled bedsheets. Tess proudly chose to keep her occupation, resolving that Roger would always possess the physical strength to take care of her but not the pocketbook. He had no formal education and held little potential outside of degrading manual labor, the same work his father had done. Roger saw no harm in honest work, but brawn and honesty were all he had to his name. It was devastating to learn that Tess preferred lending her body out to sweaty strangers rather than living with him. She would accept Roger's hard-earned wages but not his heart. As a Disciple, Roger was no more honorable than she was. Still, he would never again set foot in a brothel, guarding his heart and electing to live celibately before supporting the profession. He would also monitor his alcohol consumption.

Levi took a moment to revel in the knowledge that there was something he could use against Roger. Rather than antagonize him directly, Levi chose to do the next best thing. "Hey, Alden. I heard you pissed yourself back at Sanctuary while you were up in your room, convulsing and moaning like a whore. It's a good thing Reverend Roger was there to pray you through. What's next? You gonna walk on water?"

Alden's shoulders swelled, but after Rebecca's slender arms wrapped around him, he elected not to engage. Roger flashed a gregarious grin. "I wouldn't mock it, Levi. There's power in prayer."

"Power? That ain't power." Levi tapped the grip of the revolver, resting his hand on its holster. "*This* is the only power I believe in. The highest power!"

"That's fine," Roger purred. "You don't have to believe. I'll still pray for you."

"And just what do you pray for?"

"That you'll get consumption and die."

Manny snickered.

"Enough," Alden implored, resolved within himself yet still annoyed.

"Maybe you should turn them loose on each other," ribbed Rebecca.

Alden turned over his shoulder.

"I thought you said you didn't want any more fighting."

"I said I didn't want any more *killing*," she kindly corrected. "It might do them some good to get it out of their system."

"Trust me," Alden warned. "That's one fight you *don't* want to see."

Then again, they were a long way from Pearson Pointe. She might get her wish.

CHAPTER THIRTY-ONE

On the outskirts of Pearson Pointe, country clouds rolled back like a sacred scroll, revealing the pearlescent evening sky beneath them. Among the growing light of a campfire, Roger opened his family Bible—a bulky text that took up a great deal of his knapsack—and turned to the story of the murderous Saul. Saul (who later became Paul the Apostle) wasn't one of the original twelve disciples but was called to serve by the resurrected Jesus, Himself. As Roger began reading, Rebecca relished in her surroundings while subtle crackles and pops from the fire chimed in with spontaneous commentary, bringing them all together. Charming. Intimate. Other than this circle of warmth, there was nowhere else to be. Only Alden had chosen to keep his distance.

Though the fire was months ago, the scars on his back and shoulders seemed to gravitate toward heat instinctually, seemingly summoned by nature. It would start with the sweaty reminder that *everything* burns. Those smoky lips that first touched his skin made his eyes water in initial panic, and that pain—the unholy, all-encompassing agony that pulled sounds deep from his belly—was just as traumatic. He would never forget the way fire tasted, oily and bitter. Even in its aftermath, Alden continued to feel the chilly burn that would later haunt his dreams.

Would it always hurt this way?

"A Bible study, huh?" Levi jeered. "I didn't realize I was riding with a bunch of missionaries."

"Just a little light reading, Levi. You should join us," suggested Manny.

Roger added sheepishly, "And afterward, I'll baptize you in the creek."

"No, thanks. I prefer to keep my sins out on display where everyone can see 'em," Levi scoffed as his sights fell on Rebecca. Julian specifically instructed Levi to keep his hands to himself until Alden had her, but two whole weeks had passed since her capture, and Levi was losing his patience. No woman was worth waiting *that* long. *What made her so special?* To him, Rebecca was no more anatomically different than any other woman, so there was no reason for him to be denied physical gratification simply because Alden had suddenly chosen chivalry. Levi shifted his weight as a tiny grunt escaped him. *Why hadn't he taken her yet?* Alden was as silver-tongued as Julian and could charm the britches off of a novice. Levi shook his head. If the so-called *seduction* was taking any shape at all, it was unbeknownst to him. His original plan was to take Rebecca while Alden was incapacitated; only Roger had stayed close to serve as the dutiful watchdog.

But Roger wasn't the only one surveilling him now.

Though not actively involved in the fellowship, Alden watched Levi watch Rebecca. With his eyes giving a protective glow, Alden repeatedly opened and spun the cylinder of his revolver. *Pop. Whirl. Click. Pop. Whirl. Click.* By doing this, a gunman could find that everything inside the weapon was in working order; it was ready for use. Levi soon caught on to the unspoken warning and, whistling tauntingly, left the area.

Rebecca, who failed to notice the exchange, threw her head back in laughter at something Manny said. Alden returned the revolver to its holster, his eyes dimming slightly into a warm look of wonder. In a way, they were both on the same path, wanting to be seen for their true selves, wanting to *be* their true selves. His physical desire was one thing, but what Alden longed for most was to really *know* Rebecca and be near her beautiful soul. Knowing *about* Rebecca wouldn't be enough. No, to gain such knowledge meant he would have to step outside what was comfortable or easy. Alden took a deep breath and moved to the inner circle of the bonfire, where Rebecca just-so-happened to have available space for him. Roger smiled at the new addition and continued reading from the ninth chapter of Acts.

"And Saul yet breathing out threatenings and slaughter against the disciples of the Lord went unto the high priest and desired of him letters to Damascus to the synagogues, that if he found any of this way, whether they were men or women, he might bring them bound unto Jerusalem. And as he journeyed, he came near Damascus: and suddenly, there shined round about him a light from heaven: And he fell to the earth and heard a voice saying unto him, 'Saul, Saul, why persecutest thou me?' And he said, 'Who art thou, Lord?' And the Lord said, 'I am Jesus whom thou persecutest: it is hard for thee to kick against the pricks.' And he, trembling and astonished, said, 'Lord, what wilt thou have me to do?' And the Lord said unto him, 'Arise, and go into the city, and it shall be told thee what thou must do.' And the men which journeyed with him stood speechless, hearing a voice but seeing no man. And Saul arose from the earth; and when his eyes were opened, he saw no man: but they led him by the hand and brought him into Damascus. And he was three days without sight, and neither did eat nor drink."

As she listened, Rebecca revisited the balcony conversation with Alden in Discovery. *He could change if he really wanted to; they all could.* She considered other Biblical parables and their characters. Abraham was old, David committed adultery, and Lazarus had died. The ability for humanity to turn over a new leaf was one of God's greatest gifts. *What made these men any different?*

Roger often referred to Saul's conversion as a reminder of the grace he so desperately needed, one that could find him, uplift him, and protect him. Manny enjoyed it because he believed he, like Saul, was in a transitional phase. Alden yearned for something more profound, something meaningful and greater than himself. If anything were to save him—to redirect his life—it would have to be divine.

"And immediately there fell from his eyes as it had been scales, and he received sight forthwith, and arose, and was baptized. And when he had received meat, he was strengthened. Then was Saul certain days with the disciples which were at Damascus. And straightway, he preached Christ in the synagogues, that he is the Son of God."

Roger closed the Good Book. "Now *that* is redemption."

The others nodded in reverent agreement.

"I bet it was loud when God spoke," said Manny. "Like thunder!"

Roger leaned back. "See, I imagine it to be more of a whisper..."

"I think I'd like it if the Lord spoke to me," Alden softly admitted.

"Maybe you should try to speak to Him," offered Rebecca.

Alden gave a slight smile in response. The option was always there, for God was never absent or indisposed. *But why would a higher power listen to him?* The amber hues of heat brought color to his face, and soon, he and Rebecca felt a different kind of warmth. If they had been alone, he might have reached for her hand. She might have let him.

"I think I'd like that, too, though it would certainly depend on what God had to say," Manny shrugged. "And I don't want to be blinded. Who *would*?"

Though they knew what he meant, Manny's insight and an adorably positive outlook always made the group chuckle. Rebecca took the momentary shift in topic to pose a question.

"What is Newberry?"

The encampment dynamic suddenly distorted. Manny sighed and shook his head at Roger, who sniffed before clearing his throat.

Alden remained frozen, triggered to ice by the very word, barely able to form a response. "How do you know about that?"

Rebecca shrugged. "It's just something I—"

"—Who told you?" Alden trembled.

"Boss..." warned Roger.

"No one," she stammered. "I mean, I don't remember—"

"—Well, you had to have heard something from someone, or else you wouldn't have asked." Manny's words were infused with heavy suspicion. He and Roger had been sworn to secrecy, and Alden would have *never* shared such damning intel.

"Who told you?"

Alden had no recollection of standing, yet both Roger and Manny rose to meet him; Manny, with a patient hand placed gently on Alden's shoulder, and Roger stretched across Rebecca in the event their leader forgot himself for a *second* time.

Behind his broken blues, Alden relived the trauma, sweating, shuddering yet not blinking, hypnotized by horror. Roger and Manny strained to catch his focus, only to see themselves in Alden's ocular reflections and recoil at their own misdeeds. Together, the men and campfire snaps performed in a quartet of heavy, anxious breaths for several seconds until Alden regained his composure.

"It's a farm," he finally revealed.

Manny gulped. "You don't have to say anything."

"No, I—I can talk about it."

With a shudder, Alden slowly returned to a seated position, never losing that shattered stare as the others followed suit. He couldn't bring himself to face Rebecca, but he could answer her question.

"There was a job, and I—"

"—*We*," Roger interjected, also trembling.

"*I* missed a detail," Alden corrected. "It ended badly."

Rebecca leaned along Alden's profile to meet him square-on, yet he continued to look straight ahead. "Someone got hurt?"

Alden nodded. A *real* man wouldn't weep, but he could feel his masculine conviction slipping away. Manny stared into the fire, his countenance pained.

"I think Julian knew what would happen," he said.

"I agree," added Roger.

Following Vernon's death, Roger and Manny discussed a transfer of authority. They pitched the idea to several of the men in Sanctuary, who were equally skeptical about Julian's direction. Alden would be a fair leader, perhaps even disbanding the group, splitting the earnings, and releasing them to live the remainder of their lives peacefully. At that time, the Disciples were firmly united, high in numbers, and strong in morale. Levi and Phillip were the only real defenses against an uprising. Several of the men said they were willing to take them on; they merely needed to convince Alden, who was unaware of any covert plot. A hostile takeover seemed plausible until the events of the Newberry Farm. Shortly after Simon was brought into the fold, the Dewey brothers went missing, and all talk of a mutiny ceased. Like Manny, Roger believed that Julian had caught wind of their plans and orchestrated the job in Newberry with the intent to kill Alden, which would free him of any convictions. Rather than destroy his decoy, Julian broke him along with any hope of emancipation. Manny assured Roger that even if Julian did suspect their rebellion, Newberry would have happened regardless, but Roger still felt they should have warned their friend.

Alden shook his head. "Julian's not that cruel."

"You sure about that, Vaquero?"

"That must have been awful for you," said Rebecca. "I never meant to pry."

Saying nothing, Alden left the campfire's flames to talk amongst themselves.

"Should someone go after him?" Rebecca asked.

Roger crossed his arms. "Absolutely not. It's best to leave him alone."

"Don't ask any more questions about Newberry," Manny sighed. "*Please.*"

Rebecca nodded. Though not scolded, she felt she had wronged them somehow. Manny stared into the fire more intently. "We need to try harder to help him."

"What do you think I've been trying to do?" barked Roger. "That's all I've been doing for the last six months! It's about time he learned to help himself!"

Memories of Newberry haunted Roger, too. Though he hadn't been burned, Roger witnessed the tragedy. He had watched his friend writhe in agony, hearing the sounds Alden made when he and Manny had to peel off his clothes to tend the wounds. As with his father's death, Roger would never forget those cries or the smell of fabric taking flesh with it once removed. Seeing those he cared for suffering was his idea of Hell.

Manny continued to focus on the flames before him. One tiny spark created that fire. One tiny spark caused the catastrophe in Newberry that broke his friend's spirit. The others mocked Manny for his choice to avoid conflict, but he would fight again when those dry bones of Alden's came back to life.

All Alden needs is a spark.

Rebecca looked off into the direction of darkness Alden had entered. While she wouldn't follow, she hated for him to be alone and that her inquiry caused him pain.

Somewhere within the wilderness, Alden dropped to his knees. His task was too difficult, the burden too heavy, and he knew the cup would be too bitter when he drank from it. There was a choice to make.

Alden thought he understood what suffering meant, but every potential outcome seemed more than he could handle.

"Lord, you know I'm not a praying man, but I don't know what to do. Please, help me find a way…"

That night, face-down in the earth, Alden Aubrey appealed to the higher powers with all his might, begging that the proverbial cup might pass from him.

CHAPTER THIRTY-TWO

Hidden away in a blink-and-you'll-miss-it little development sat Pearson Pointe. What started as a ranching community in 1838 once held great promise after establishing a post office and a few small businesses before the war. Now, all that remained were the reminisces of a migrant worker's camp and a small but surprisingly secure jailhouse, of which only the locals, lawmen, and lawless knew where to locate. Just behind this holding area, nestled along a botanical library, stood Alden and Rebecca. Under any other circumstances, its natural aesthetic would have been moving, romantic even, as the sun scaled over a bushy green canopy. But while the environment gave off a fragrance more pleasing than anything in a bottle, it proved vastly ineffective at subduing Rebecca's allergies.

"Could you try to sneeze a little louder?" teased Alden. "We want to make sure everyone knows we're coming."

"Why do we have to be out here around all this... shrubbery? *A-choo!*"

Alden shook his head. There was something endearing about a woman complaining that he never realized he missed until that exact moment. Alden took no pleasure in disparaging women or trivializing their concerns; he merely found Rebecca's fussing humorous. A grown woman, whose hemming and hawing reminded him of a little girl, both aggravating and adorable.

"We're out here because you and I have unfortunate faces."

Rebecca sniffled and turned to Alden with a somewhat bruised expression. He would have to work on his phrasing because although she acted like such comments never bothered her, he was completely convinced they did. Alden pulled his head to the side to release a gentle crack. "I didn't mean that the way it sounded."

"No one ever does."

Making a second attempt, "Listen, I'm a wanted man with a face that will—"

"—Fetch a price?"

"Yes," said Alden. "And *your* face—people would remember seeing you here. Your face is…memorable."

"*Memorable,* he says!" Rebecca gave a cynical smile.

"No, really—it *is* memorable!" Alden turned Rebecca to face him directly, using his gently placed hands on her shoulders to pivot. There was almost a full-foot height difference between them and, though he hadn't tried it, he was certain his chin could rest perfectly on the top of her head without bending if he pulled her close enough. Chaste and youthful, Rebecca's beauty was simple and unrefined, but it was there. A fair complexion complemented her subtlety balanced features as though even the slightest change might disturb them. Alden's eyes once again reviewed the delicate curves of Rebecca's face and the roses that had begun to blossom on her cheeks. The mouth so busy nagging him moments before stayed fixed in a puzzled pucker. Her scars, though he knew they were there, seemed camouflaged somehow. "Like, your mouth…" he started. "When you smile—the way it hooks—it's crooked."

Rebecca's smile faded. It was simply *wrong* to dissect one's imperfections only to point them out so directly. She could find physical flaws in him, too…though it would take some time.

"Don't get upset," he cooed. "It's charming, really."

"My crooked mouth is *charming*?"

"It's memorable—like I said!"

Rebecca deflated against a giant green thicket, the color of which gave such a verdant background against her that her eyes flashed fluorescent when she finally looked up at him. But Alden had also turned away, thinning his mouth, brooding in discontent. After several minutes of silence, his countenance fell both vacant and seriously focused, pained even. Alden gave a heavy sigh.

"I know it won't make much of a difference, but—" His hands were once again on her shoulders, moving up to her neck and knitting themselves into her hair. Feeling this behavior somehow familiar, Rebecca submitted to the pressure of his body leading them into the wall of bushes, prickly and poking behind her.

Had the temperature suddenly increased? It seemed much, much warmer now.

"—Are you trying to kiss me?" Rebecca stammered. He hadn't asked permission. She wasn't ready for it. She wasn't even sure she wanted it.

Alden would have been able to withhold his amusement if Rebecca's delivery hadn't been so deadpanned. He shuffled and returned his hands to her shoulders, resting his chin on the top of her head with a fit as perfect as the one he imagined.

"No," he chortled quietly. "I was, uh—*reaching for this.*" He stretched overhead to produce a sweetly scented, bell-shaped flower, white and drying to yellow with a tube-like stem in the middle. Realizing he was still heavily invading her personal space, Alden took a few steps back before using his thumbnail to pinch the bottom tip of the bloom and pull out the stamen. Rebecca watched as he licked the nectar off the stem, delighted at its tastiness. "Don't tell me you've never had one?" Alden posed, reaching for the honeysuckle vine a second time. "That's right, I forgot. You're *fancy.*"

"I'm not *fancy*; I just don't eat flowers," Rebecca fussed.

"You don't eat the flower, you—" He swallowed a chuckle. "Open your mouth."

Rebecca shook her head defiantly, remembering the moonshine he once served her. *This was surely a trick!* He would only laugh at her again. In fact, Alden's flirtatious expression proved he was already there.

"Why not?" he asked, suckling the runaway juices from his thumb.

"Isn't it dangerous?"

"Dangerous? Do you think I'd purposely put you in danger?"

Her green eyes growing, "My captor? Put me in danger? *Never!*"

Alden reeled. "It's *honeysuckle*. How could honeysuckle be dangerous?"

"I don't know! *You're* the one who said danger was entertaining!"

"Becca, open your mouth," Alden gently ordered as he reached again for the vine. "I swear, I'm *not* going to kiss you," he pledged. "Although, you kissed Manny and Roger—if you call *that* kissing. And you did that in broad daylight, too! There's a word for women who do that."

Rebecca's eyes sharpened.

"Which you are *not*," he quickly recovered. "If I wanted to kiss you, I'd do it."

Rebecca thought back to Discovery and then to their Spanish lesson that rainy afternoon. *Beso.* Alden was just as close now, just as warm and eager to teach her something new. He had toyed with her before but always showed restraint. She wasn't sure she believed him.

"Come on; this is a good one." Alden prepared another honeysuckle stem, which dripped with gooey nectar. She hesitated, then tilted her head to accept his offering. It was the taste of summer, better than it smelled, not too bitter or too sweet. *Delicious.* Rebecca's face lit up, which prompted a similar response from Alden.

"It's nice, right?"

She nodded.

The pair enjoyed several more of Mother Nature's treats, their fingers sticky from the hidden sweets, shedding blossoms like the promise of autumn. A leaf strayed off the vine to tickle Rebecca's shoulder. No, *not* a leaf; a *honeybee*. Rebecca stiffened, holding her breath as the fuzzy insect bumbled across a shoulder to her collarbone. She had never been stung by a bee before, but after seeing a young schoolmate endure the pain, she decided it was one experience she would rather live without. The assailant left its stinger behind, a jagged knife with a swollen red welt in its wake. One would have thought the child lost an arm, the way he hollered!

"Don't be scared," Alden advised, noticing her bumbling beau. "I promise, he's more afraid of you. After all, you're in his territory."

"Not by choice," chewed Rebecca.

"Aw, let him explore a little bit." Alden followed closely with his eyes. "And try not to sneeze," he added. The furry critter circled back, crawling on teeny tiny legs to its original landing spot and settling there. Lively vibrations nuzzled near Rebecca's neck and into her ear. Her instinct was to swat it away, but that would surely result in another injury to suffer until they reached Grady.

"Do I have permission to come closer and assist?" asked Alden. "Remember, I'm *not* going to kiss you."

When Rebecca said nothing, Alden leaned inward once more. Soft air flew from his lips as he politely blew the well-mannered insect away as though to respectfully suggest alternative territories to explore. Rather than be shooed, the honeybee rode the air current off Rebecca's shoulder to a nearby flower, thus continuing its busywork. Though not exactly an act of heroism, Rebecca beamed at her bee charmer, who was anything but present, choosing to focus on the foliage around him.

"My brother and I got stung all the time when we were kids.

Stupid. It hurt like Hell. He always asked for the ones way up top or out of reach, convinced they tasted different. They didn't, but I'd get them for him anyway. A pain in my ass. So precocious, too. I swear he'd stir up a whole hive of those rascals just to see what would happen."

How precious it is for the mind to pocket a memory only for it to peek out at exactly the right moment. Alden remembered being young and mischievous yet innocent, the way only little boys knew how to be, long before bloodshed and bounties. A time when he was championed by a younger sibling who never asked Alden to prove himself, wanting only to accompany him on the next adventure.

"Where is he now?" asked Rebecca.

"He died a long time ago," Alden revealed, wondering what his little brother would think of his current occupation.

"I'm so sorry," she said. "What was his name?"

"Benjamin. I haven't spoken about him in years..." His voice trailed, the memory fading into the fog of things forgotten. "I don't know what made me want to all of the sudden..."

The afternoon proved the most sensual and sacred experience that Rebecca ever shared with another human being. She was certain that Alden was *not* like Julian, for the further Alden got away from Sanctuary, the less hardened he would behave. And these escapes, these *almost moments* full of unspoken attractions, made all things new. Life seemed richly full of storybook beauty in those places, and he had been the one to show her that there were such things. Rebecca was sympathetic to Alden, his loss, the things unknown about him, and the memories still locked away in his mind.

Contently high on honey, Rebecca reached for Alden's stubbled cheek, allowing her fingertips to skim past his earlobes before settling behind his neck as she pulled his face to her own. Though she had kissed him once before, Rebecca knew that *this* kiss would be different. *And it was!* Warm, sugary rain drizzled overhead in buzzworthy droplets as two sets of lips mutually stole a breath and bared their souls. Alden closed his eyes, instinctually responding to her kiss, then graciously accompanying it, gently demonstrating exactly how it was supposed to be. Slow and exploratory, an earnest attempt was made to be respectful at first, but soon, the kiss grew immensely deep and hungry, prompting an invitation for something more.

Then, suddenly, it ended.

"Don't do that!" Alden scolded, pushing himself away, visibly frustrated and pointing his finger at Rebecca as though she were a naughty child. More than anything, he was scolding himself. *This was dangerous.* This was what Vernon had meant about women being distractions. If something went wrong or there were any missteps, he might have to flee or aid the group. He needed to be more careful.

Rebecca was met with waves of confused, embarrassed rejection. Manny and Roger hadn't pushed her away. She hadn't said anything distasteful to Alden or groped him inappropriately as Alice had in Discovery. Perhaps she misread him, or she was bad at it. Perhaps he didn't like kissing her at all.

Alden held a shaky hand over his mouth, wanting to both wipe her away *and* soak her in as Rebecca's kiss continued to spread like a mouth tattoo, bursting over his cheeks and biting through the tips of his teeth. He fell flushed with parted lips that beckoned for a return to sweetness.

Why was honey so much better when it came from her?

A fiery flash went off in the distance. In her bold efforts, Rebecca forgot that a jailbreak was underway, yet the Disciples mentioned nothing about an explosion! A light mist of startled bees scattered away on the gust of wind, leaves, and dust that blasted in the surge. Rebecca felt one hand stifle her scream while another drew her in by the waist. Alden completely cocooned himself around her, poised to take the impact from any debris. The burst of energy was almost enough to knock them both over, but they bent and did not break. She screamed a handful or more times, along with a string of other townspeople reacting in the wake of the detonation. Out of instinct, Rebecca clawed at Alden's hand for vocal release, a kettle ready to whistle. And yet he held her close to him, tightly, calmly whispering in her ear. "It's alright. You're alright."

Soon, the sky softened, leaving an eerie quiet in the aftermath. Smoke and earth continued rumbling around her, and Rebecca was convinced she had lost her hearing ability. Feeling faint, she allowed herself to weaken in his embrace, the back of her head resting on his shoulder. Alden's hand slowly lifted from her face, but he wouldn't fully release her, not until he knew she could stand on her own.

"It's okay," he promised. "I've got you."

And for the first time, she believed him.

CHAPTER THIRTY-THREE

Simon Whitaker was a petty thief from Canton, a city located about forty miles southeast of Tyler. An orphan with a cherub face that could play to the hearts of men and women. Bold, scrappy, and pimpled, Simon held the potential to be as dashing as the rest of the Disciples once his transition into manhood was complete. Simon's frame rivaled Rebecca's, except for his plucky shoulders, smaller hips, and a trouser bulge. He modeled floppy hair the color of wheat with chinned stowaways to match. His curious brown eyes watched her closely beyond the campfire, holding little judgment, for Simon had yet to know a woman. Rebecca's chest tightened with shame, knowing men like her father failed Simon somehow. Youth wouldn't protect Simon from harsh punishment when he was caught. And he'd already been caught once. Seeing as Simon was still a young man, there *must* be an alternative to incarceration or death. Rebecca considered his possible background. No boy from a *loving* home would choose such a life.

"Have you ever been in love, Levi?" Simon hadn't stopped grilling Levi about his past since leaving Pearson Pointe, but this was the first truly interesting prompt he presented since they'd set up camp for the night.

Roger groaned in protest from the opposite side of the fire. Levi's presence alone made him irritable, so it was best to put some distance between them.

"I loved my mother," Levi said plainly.

Rebecca shifted. It was strange to envision a man like Levi ever having a mother, receiving parental guidance, or even being vulnerable enough to require another individual's care. Rebecca imagined a frail, grey woman with bags under her eyes and an embarrassing amount of exhaustion towards her unruly child who would consistently sprout unpredictable chaos, much like a weed in the garden.

Then again, perhaps she was as cold and beautiful as he. Perhaps Levi was an adorable child with manipulative eyes and a face that would get away with murder.

"I loved my wife, too," he added.

Manny tilted his head to the side, much like a confused puppy. "I didn't know you were married."

"You never asked."

The idea of Levi participating in holy matrimony seemed even more improbable. There was the whole matter of monogamy to consider, and, to Rebecca, vile men like Levi would burst into flames if they even crossed a church's threshold. Nevertheless, she considered that Satan knew the Bible well enough to quote scripture and would often do so to destroy faith, so it was feasible that Levi could be immune to sacred ground.

But what sort of woman would agree to marry a man like Levi?

"Moira Gayle," he said. "We were kids when she hitched her wagon to mine. Long, raven hair with eyes too big for her face. Skinny little thing, God rest her soul."

"She passed?" Manny hung on to Levi's every word. His chocolate eyes were wide, unblinking, and full of hope that this peek into Levi's history would make the brute seem human or at least a bit easier to tolerate. *Where did you meet? What was her favorite flower? Was she as sociable as you, or did she have a gentler disposition?*

Additionally, if *Levi* could find love, did that mean he could, too?

"Yep."

And that was all Levi said. The group offered a compassionate silence to the convict. For all they knew, this *Moira Gayle* was the love of his life, taken tragically from him much too soon. Could her passing be the catalyst for Levi's twisted, troubled soul? Rebecca watched as the corners of Levi's mouth twisted upward while he scanned his memories in an expression not bittersweet, just bitter. She wished he were lying about ever having a spouse, but Rebecca had an unsettling feeling that the truth was far grizzlier. "You killed her," she realized.

Levi gasped in a caricature's display of offense, his hand clutching the left side of his chest. "How...*dare you*! That's a horrible thing to say! Moira Gayle was my bride! What makes you think I had anything to do with her passing?"

Rebecca fumed in disgust. "You're smiling."

Levi forced a solemn expression. It was undoubtedly the same face he'd made at Moira Gayle's funeral to feign innocence. He removed the twig he used as a toothpick from his mouth, holding it between his thumb and forefinger to make a point.

"Moira Gayle was a terribly clumsy woman who unfortunately took a nasty spill down the stairs."

"But that won't kill a person, will it?" Simon asked blindly, missing Levi's underlying message.

"If you land on your neck, it will." Levi pressed his thumb to break the toothpick with a subtle *crack* that made everyone jump. "It sounded just like that."

Roger shook his head, a typical response to most of Levi's personal accounts. Simon provided a small laugh of approval while Manny deflated, wondering why he even bothered. Alden rubbed his face in an attempt to wipe away any evidence of repulsion. They all knew the truth about Levi, but there was still a part of each of them that hoped for a different outcome.

Levi turned to Simon's unfinished plate. "Are you going to eat that?"

Simon offered his dinner to Levi, who immediately began gobbling its remains. Alden rose to his feet and brushed the dirt off the back of his trousers, not caring so much about being dirty, simply choosing to distract his hands from squeezing Levi's throat. It seemed criminal to dispose of someone who loved and trusted him. And then to joke about it with such a lack of respect? *Shameless.*

"Well, that answers *that* question," determined Alden.

"What's that?" Levi posed mid-chew.

"The only thing Levi loves is himself."

The group chuckled, joining in on the jest. Even Levi accepted this roasting with humility. "At least I have good taste."

Levi sat the empty plate at his feet and turned to face Rebecca, whose mouth remained agape and trembling. His wife had been plain but more beautiful than her. Rebecca mentally pictured Moira Gayle's unfortunate demise, and the snap of Levi's toothpick added an unexpected layer of reality to his story.

"I promise you; she didn't feel it," Levi whispered, scooting closer before reaching up to restore her jaw to its original state. "You'd better close that. You might catch something."

And then the tears came, free-falling down Rebecca's cheeks in a cathartic kamikaze. Levi beamed, knowing he had both frightened and embarrassed her. His hands delayed leaving her face.

"How about that? You're almost pretty when you cry."

"Alright, that's enough torture for one evening." Alden tenderly took Rebecca's forearm and lifted her away from her spot. He didn't like the idea of Levi putting his hands on her.

"That's not torture," Levi stated. "Not even close."

"Well, it's torturing me! Shit!"

Roger's exasperation came with a warning, for there was only so much of Levi he could stomach in one sitting. He then let out a bellowing sigh and returned to a more comfortable position.

Rebecca was all too ready to go with Alden, but Levi's iron grip snatched her other arm. She often imagined two men fighting for her like the ingénues in her novels, but this was neither exciting nor flattering. Levi pulled her closer to him.

"How come everyone except me has gotten a turn with her?"

Alden slowly towed back in response. "We're not taking *turns*; she's riding with us in rotation for the sake of the horses."

The tug-of-war continued. Levi bared his teeth in a predatory smile. His plans for Rebecca were abominable. "Well, I'd like to be considered for a *ride in rotation*…for the sake of the horses."

Rebecca saw the rough way Levi handled his horse. He'd thump and smack the steed's head with no regard for its health or well-being, and when the animal would resist, Levi hit even harder. She wanted nothing more than to see him ejected while riding, take a nasty spill, and land on his own neck.

"We've talked about this," Alden said firmly. "It's not going to happen."

Levi's countenance mirrored an impatient little boy who might throw a temper tantrum to get his way, only it seemed more genuinely self-deprecating. Rebecca half-expected to see his bottom lip form a Fauntleroy pout. *This was how he won over Moira Gayle.* "Why not?" he puckered. "What's wrong with *me*?"

Rebecca gritted her teeth. "Ask your wife!"

Despite his superficial charm and charisma, Levi's dormant narcissism would erupt in a full-swinging backhand. Rebecca's right profile whinnied. Roger sat upright, recognizing the *whack* from his childhood. He despised that sound and was on his feet before Levi's hand could fully rotate. Simon moved as Manny stepped in to deescalate.

"Let Alden handle this."

Alden knew what was coming but wasn't fast enough to block Levi's heavy blow. After carefully helping Rebecca upright as she dropped from the impact, Alden came forward to confront Levi with his folding knife flexed and poised to puncture.

"If you touch her again, I'll gut you like a fish!"

"Sure, okay…" Levi chuckled. Alden's blade was sharp but easily malleable.

Alden, his anger silent, "I mean it."

"Killing a woman is no different than killing a kid or a crook or anyone else out there," Levi sang to Rebecca before turning to Alden. "But of course, you already know that." Smiling, he picked and sucked between his teeth with his tongue. "Hypocrite."

Though they weren't engaged in physical contact, Alden and Levi were on edge. Alden stood down. Levi puffed and turned to Simon, who responded with an equally affirmative act of unanimity. Together, they left the group to smoke. Alden put the knife away and turned to Roger, who was tending to Rebecca. Levi's blow hadn't broken the skin, but her face would show evidence of another man's misconduct. At this, Alden rubbed between the bridges of his brows.

"Why did you say that?" he groaned.

"Somebody needed to stand up to him!"

Roger had already prepared a rebuttal, but Rebecca took the words right out of his mouth.

"That's Levi!" argued Alden. "That's just how he is!"

Rebecca cradled her cheek, shocked that he could defend such a bully.

"How you put up with him…"

Alden paced back and forth, unable to apologize for his gender because he was just as guilty. "What do you want me to do? Do you want me to shoot him?"

"I'll do it," Roger offered.

"He's part of our crew," Alden reasoned. "Besides, we all know it's gonna take a lot more than a bullet to shut him up."

Manny shrugged. "We could try a muzzle."

Roger roared with laughter. "Now *that* I would pay to see!"

CHAPTER THIRTY-FOUR

Rebecca tossed and turned, fidgety, flustered by the afternoon's events, and disappointed that Alden had failed to even comment on the matter.

Why did you kiss him? He obviously hated it. He probably gets kissed all the time. He probably prefers kisses from girls like Alice. And why wouldn't he!

Such thoughts made her heart plummet deep in her stomach, its pulse pulling focus from her throbbing face. She wagered that at least her cheeks would match now. *Roughhouse Rouge.* Rebecca struggled to find a restful position, for the earth was lumpy and couldn't be fashioned into a pillow as with their other campsites.

"Are you cold?" Alden whispered. He was stationed closest to her, with Roger and Manny dozing nearby, keeping them separate from Levi and Simon, who slumbered heavily in the distance.

"I'm uncomfortable."

Alden slid over to her, having also been restless. "Come here."

Rebecca submitted. Having never laid beside Alden before, Rebecca found him easy to burrow into; she could effortlessly nestle her head on his shoulder. Not too big, not too small. He was just right. A mockingbird gave an audacious performance in the neighboring tree, startling Rebecca but failing to get any response from her bedfellow. "If I didn't know any better, I'd say you enjoyed sleeping outdoors."

"Oh, it's not so bad," he replied. "Look at where we are! Look at that night sky! There's not a house in existence with a ceiling that compares to this."

It was true. An extraordinarily vast starfield covered them with a rump-roast moon cooking close by, an observant mother hen with her millions upon millions of chicks. Rebecca noticed suspicious clouds framing her peripheral. "And if it rains?"

Alden smiled. "If it rains, I imagine we'll get wet."

They remained there, lost in a powerful silence for several minutes, heat and heartbeats rising. Remembering the conversation topic from their latest mealtime, Alden nervously posed the question.

"Did you love him?"

"Who?"

"The man you were with. The man I shot."

"Nicholas? No." Rebecca felt convicted. She had yet to mourn her dead fiancé, with over a week passing since she even *thought* of him. She wondered if anyone found his body and feared that wild animals had gotten to him first. "My father," she followed with a sigh. "He arranged the match."

Alden nodded. He understood how the world worked and how men of high authority would use their daughters as collateral, investments, and pawns to exploit for individual gain. Rebecca would inherit nothing, for the man she married would be granted everything entitled to her. *It wasn't right.*

She raised a curious chin. "Have you ever been in love?"

"You've seen the company I keep, and there's the small matter of stability."

"Does that mean you haven't?"

"You don't want to hear my sad stories, Becca."

"So, tell me a happy one."

Alden let out a long exhalation, then paused to scratch his cheek, forgetting that he no longer had a beard. He liked having a beard; it made shaving one less thing to worry about. Additionally, his facial hair was much fuller than Julian's, a fact that always seemed to aggravate his superior.

"Well?" Rebecca pressed.

"I'm thinking."

Alden's head filled with flashes of forgotten pastimes. Echoes of laughter, running barefoot in the grass, climbing tall trees, catching frogs by the creek, and a gentle humming in the distance. His mother. She had red hair, too. Curlier than Rebecca's but just as soft. He stretched himself, wishing he could remember all the words she would sing to him—a hauntingly sweet and repetitive melody.

Close your eyes, O love of my heart,
My everything and my love.
Close your eyes, O love of my heart,
And you'll get a present tomorrow...

"I had a happy childhood," he said finally. "I didn't realize how little we had growing up because we never talked about what we didn't have. We had gratitude. We had each other. Me, Benjamin, and my folks—I don't know how they did it, but we were always clean, and we were always fed." He struggled with the images in his mind. It had been so long since he'd seen their faces. Alden was built like his father but had his mother's eyes. *God, I miss her!* She made everything beautiful. "Momma went first, and I swear Daddy died of a broken heart. He loved her so much."

"That doesn't sound happy, Alden."

"You don't have my memories," he smiled, savoring the bittersweet recollections. He couldn't fully describe them, but Rebecca would see fragments of Alden's nostalgia in his expressions.

She envied him, believing that parents often took the example they set for their children for granted. Alden may have never known love, but at least he had seen it. He recognized it. He could point his finger at it and say, "That's what I want." Rebecca couldn't say the same. Samuel McNamara never courted another woman and rarely spoke of his late wife. Rebecca often inquired about her mother, but the conversations would quickly sour. Her father would grimace and excuse himself from the room. Perhaps it was too painful. Perhaps it was easier to forget.

Rebecca shrugged into Alden's shoulder and stared at the stardust canopy above them. No one had ever held her that way before, only embracing her slightly and never for as long as she needed. It felt like a promise. Her eyes glanced sidelong. Alden was studying her again. He shifted his weight, and a long, warm, open expression of tenderness followed. Within an instant, Rebecca was back in the honeysuckle. She closed her eyes and let his mouth roll over hers while he cradled her head, keeping it from the earth beneath them. He could show her love or something like it.

"Now we're even," he said, followed by a final peck.

What?!

"You are so grossly immature," she growled.

"You started something at Pearson Pointe," he smiled through a minty whisper. "I've been waiting for a chance to play my turn."

She gulped, still gaining her composure. "I didn't realize it was a game."

"Well, it's over now." Alden settled on his side, letting her head dip slightly, relieved in knowing he had won. Admittedly, she got him sufficiently hot and bothered in the honeysuckle, and this was payback. Rebecca fumed. What wasn't already pulsating from injury felt like it was on fire. Her entire body had gone limp all the way to her toes, which curled up instinctually, and she'd pulled shards of grass out of the ground in her arousal. Embarrassed, Rebecca brushed earth-filled hands over her skirt.

"You—you no good…philanderer!" she spat. "You should be ashamed of yourself!"

"*Me?*" defended Alden. "If memory serves, you kissed me first!"

Rebecca continued to boil, yet Alden swam deeper into the simmering waters of vulnerability. "Why'd you do it, anyway?" he queried. "Why did you kiss me?"

"You were…so sad."

Her response might as well have been a slap to the face.

"Ah, you felt sorry for me," he chuckled. "Thanks, but I don't need any handouts. And shame on *you*. You, of all people, should know how unkind that is."

"No, that's not what I—"

"—What, then?" Alden turned to face her once more. "You didn't kiss Roger or Manny like that. No one kisses like *that* unless they want something. So what do you want? Do you want me to turn you loose?"

The night sky settled on Alden, making him a living picture. An animated black and white portrait. The same image she'd seen on the wanted posters and headlining newspapers. Rebecca stared into blue-grey eyes that were no longer troubled but burning brightly, eagerly awaiting her response.

"Would you?"

"Why? So your father can hand you off to another man you don't love?"

Rebecca shook her head. "What do you expect me to do?"

"You could fight it," he shrugged. "Tell your father that isn't what you want. Use some of that bite; I know you've got it in you."

Rebecca's bottom lip tightened. *How dare he!* Alden had no idea how much she struggled to communicate those strong objections to her father.

"I don't see *you* fighting to be your own person," she challenged. "I doubt you even know what you want."

"I didn't choose this," he protested, his victory now reduced.

"Oh, I'm sure! You were *forced* into it, I gather? You were perfectly innocent before. Fate just happened to come along one day and point a gun to your head."

A modest laugh escaped Alden's chest. "That's exactly what they did."

He would never forget the sound of that hammer pulling back. When he wasn't tormented by Newberry, that *click* would equally haunt his dreams. "I wasn't that much older than Simon," he shared. "At least he had a choice. They did other things that you can't imagine. They beat me…tortured me…tied me to a tree for days…like a dog."

He could tell her about the pit Vernon left him in to slim him down because Julian building muscle would have been "too difficult." The hole wasn't necessary. If Alden agreed to cooperate and be a Disciple, his training would be much easier to tolerate. Each time they took him out, he would deny them. So, they beat him and put him back in the ground. He could tell her how he was alone to stare at muddy walls in his own filth, not knowing when the next piece of bread or canteen of water would come. They wouldn't let him die. *That* would have been a waste. No, but they would let him believe he'd die there.

"Winter came early that year," he stated matter-of-factly. The blue had escaped his eyes completely. They were now a blank, lifeless grey. His gaze locked in with hers, fiercely frozen and filled with shame. "Would you like to know how many days it took for me to comply—to break me?"

Rebecca's lips quivered as she pictured Alden as a young man enduring such cruelties. She said nothing, only managing a slight refusal.

"Forty-eight."

Rebecca gasped.

"How feeble I must look to you," he continued. "I fought. I lost. But I'm alive. If you call this living. And as for what I want…" With a somber smile inspired by some secret, heartbreaking irony, Alden moved to carefully brush away a tear that was clinging to her cheekbone. "It doesn't matter because I can't have it."

Rebecca pulled away and upright, moving to stand. Alden caught her hand. "You're upset."

"Yes. No. I don't know."

It was too horrific for her to imagine and much too heavy for her to understand. This was long before Roger and Manny joined the fold. Did they know what Alden endured to fulfill Vernon's villainous vision? Alden probably would have said or done anything to survive after that, even epitomize Julian Crisp. *After such trauma, anyone would have nightmares.* Rueben once stated that Alden could separate himself from his horrendous acts. Those words made sense now. Alden was practically a prisoner before, and, in a way, he still was. *No wonder he tried to escape through music, poetry, booze, and women!* Escapism could be smart if practiced wisely.

"Stay, Becca," pressed Alden, bringing her closer. "I've frightened you, and I'm sorry. It was wrong of me to—I shouldn't have said anything. Please, stay."

"Why? Because of your story? I'd be lying if I said I didn't pity you, now."

Moonlight beamed through the shadows from overhead trees, creating an almost halo-like effect around Alden's skull. He was first ornery and then so intense, but his eyes smiled peace.

"That's fine. Only, stay 'cause I'm asking you to…and 'cause maybe you want to?"

Rebecca weighed out the importance of pride if no one were there to judge her. *What would it mean?* If she laid beside Alden now, would he always expect it from her?

"If you're seeking what you had in Discovery—"

"—I could have had it in Discovery," he replied. "That's not what I'm after here."

She liked how she felt in his arms, so she returned to them, scooting close yet reserved while resting on his shoulder. Alden acknowledged the twilight that at the moment twinkled like a wink from the universe, as he, too, relished in what it meant to be held. This wasn't romance, passion, or heat. This was *intimacy*, and it was just what he needed. Alden would wait until Rebecca fell asleep to remove his arm, as he did on countless occasions with nighttime companions. She was the first woman he shared a bed with and had not bedded. He considered that Rebecca wouldn't have returned to him if she didn't trust him in some small fashion. Not many knew of his painful past. Maybe now she would understand.

Maybe now she could forgive him.

CHAPTER THIRTY-FIVE

Alden's left hand drummed over his sidearm's ivory handle as he watched the sunrise the next morning. He could ride all over Texas, but there was still so much land to be explored. Verdant waves stretched out for as far as his eyes could reach. *This* was the future. Someday, the vast space would belong to someone who would claim it and create something new and meaningful. Perhaps a schoolhouse or a small business. A homestead would fit there nicely, too. He believed he only knew how to tear things down, but somehow, the idea of building something no longer seemed impossible.

That was how the other half lived, and they didn't need guns to make it happen.

He could do it, too.

"We're restless today," Rebecca noticed as she joined him.

"No need for concern." He gestured to his holster. "She's just feeling a bit neglected from lack of use."

"*She*? Like a scorned lover?"

"*Hell hath no fury.*"

They laughed. Alden was unruffled, his coloring fully returned, and his stride seemed almost jovial. There was much to be jolly about, for he recognized something had shifted within him. When the travelers broke bread at breakfast, he had an appetite. When he ate and drank, his body hadn't rejected those provisions. He slept soundly the night before; he could relax, and his body didn't echo with discomfort when he inhaled.

Alden was *healing*.

"I suppose an apology is in order for my behavior last night," he said. "I shouldn't play games with you."

Alden never got the chance to court a woman the way *he* wanted to, but Rebecca seemed to take his trial-and-error bullshit in stride without being a doormat.

"You *could* apologize if you were really sorry. *Are you sorry, Alden?*" Rebecca's words were flat, but a smile hid behind her own well-rested eyes. She noticed the way his pupils dilated when he looked at her and suspected that hers did the same. Alden had teased her, chased her around a bedroom, and been flirtatiously cantankerous since the moment they met. This was all new for her, too, yet she matched him tit-for-tat.

"For kissing you?" His warm grin spreading, "Not even a little."

*Yes, he **did** have feelings for her, but surely that was no crime.*

Manny sat beside Roger along the base of a nearby red oak tree, ensuring the blankets of branches would shield them from the morning sun.

"Are you watching this?"

"I'm watching." Roger crossed his arms and leaned gently back against the tree trunk. The coy smiles, the body language, and the overall changes in Alden's behavior may have been discreet enough to throw off the others, but not them. Neither ever saw him behave in such a manner. They had watched Alden interact with women while on the job, which was his only chance to socialize with the opposite sex. Romancing women as Julian Crisp was all about control, a domineering performance. *This* Alden seemed more genuine, playful, and carefree.

"She's good for him," Manny noted in Spanish. "They're good for each other."

Roger continued the conversation in Manny's native tongue, which neither Levi nor Simon understood.

"That may be, but he needs to be careful. He's not going to be able to finish this, and if he does, we're going to have a whole new set of problems when we get back to Sanctuary."

"If he ever goes back to Sanctuary."

"One of us should step in," Roger suggested.

"Do you really want to take this away from them?"

In the distance, Alden and Rebecca leaned against the remains of a wooden split-rail fence. It remained unclear what the luscious land around them was once used for, as it had been reclaimed righteously by nature. Alden was telling a story, to which Rebecca hung tightly onto every word. Manny sighed heavily as Rebecca's laughter fluttered in the distance. She, too, seemed beyond their help.

"It appears we are far past an intervention, Roger."

Roger clasped his hands together, settling his elbows on his knees before lowering his head. In their combined years of knowing him, Alden hadn't taken anything for himself. He sampled death and destruction but never tasted the flavors of life. They both knew that Alden believed his time as a Disciple was ending. Manny proposed a respectful acceptance of Alden's choices and prepared for his departure. Of course, Roger wanted more for his friend, but he also wanted his friend to live.

"This will kill him."

"I know," said Manny.

Still, it's better to die happy than live miserable.

Roger sighed. "If Levi suspects…"

"Let's make sure he doesn't."

Manny patted his friend's shoulder and stood to seek a new vantage point near Simon. They would protect Alden by discouraging any suspicions Simon or Levi might have. However, Simon paid no attention to the parties in question, choosing to carve his initials into a neighboring oak tree.

Alden walked Rebecca through the steps of loading a single-action revolver, pointing out that although there were six cartridges, one should only load five. He shared a somewhat comical account of a former foe who ignored such safety precautions and shot himself in the foot. *Amateur.*

"Do you want to learn?" asked Alden.

"To do what, exactly?"

"To shoot."

With a laugh, she refused. "No, thank you."

"Oh, come on. It'll be fun." Alden believed the best gifts were those of experience. He would never give Rebecca diamonds or the elegant trinkets she deserved, but he could supply her with a memory and a skill she might use at a later time.

Rebecca cast her mind back to their first night together. It seemed like a lifetime ago; their circumstances and understandings had changed, and they were now both different people. She was glad she hadn't harmed him.

"If I knew how to use a gun, Mr. Aubrey, you wouldn't be here right now."

"If you knew how to use a gun, Miss McNamara, *you* wouldn't be *here* right now," Alden pointed out. He then handed over the heavy hardware, which suddenly appeared much larger to them both in her hands.

"Why not teach me how to fight with my fists?" she asked.

"We can do that, too. One thing at a time."

Rebecca slid her fingers over the smooth steel. It looked so different in the daylight. "I *can* defend myself, you know. I'm not completely helpless."

"Taking Levi's backhand is not a defense. You should know how to fight back."

Batting her eyelashes, "Against scoundrels like you?"

"Exactly."

She permitted Alden to lead her tenderly by the waist toward an open field behind them to safely prepare her shot. Through careful instruction on grip, aim, and alignment, Rebecca understood the confidence and security a weapon could provide and the high regard one should possess for such power.

"This is hardly target practice, but you'll at least have a feel for the kickback."

Her eyes widened. "Kickback?"

"You'll see. Now, don't put your finger on the trigger until you're ready to shoot." Remembering this, Alden winced at how his own trigger-finger first betrayed him all those years ago in the jailhouse. He recovered and reminded Rebecca not to flinch, taking several steps back and occasionally leaning over to check her stance.

"Becca, you have to open your eyes."

"They *are* open!"

"No, they're not." Alden returned to her side, amused. "Hold onto the sound of my voice. Open your eyes! Good. Take a deep breath. Let it out slowly. Now, pull the trigger."

Despite his direction, Rebecca anticipated the kickback, jerking the trigger, flexing, and pushing her arms against the recoil, causing the muzzle to dip. If there had been a target, she'd have hit low. She would need more dry practice, but the *crack* from the charge, along with the knowledge that *she* produced it, was exhilarating.

"What the Hell is this?" Levi barked as he marched up the hill. He had either been relieving himself or pleasuring himself because his pants were only partially buttoned. At the sight of Rebecca holding a firearm, Levi gawked at Alden.

"*Are you out of your mind?* Since when do we give weapons to hostages?"

Alden retrieved the handgun. "I was right here, and she wasn't going to shoot any of us, were you?"

Though Rebecca shook her head, Alden knew she would have taken a shot at Levi if given the opportunity. *Heck, anyone would.* She seemed to read his mind because when Alden's eyes met hers, she looked away, feigning innocence. Alden covered his growing smile and returned his weapon to its holster.

"We're in the middle of nowhere," Roger offered from his roost. "There's not a town for miles. Let them have their fun."

"This isn't *fun*, Roger. This is a job that *some of us* need to take more seriously." Levi leaned in to give Alden a hard shove. "I can think of something else you could do with her that would save a couple of bullets."

"Christ, is that *all* you think about?" Simon remarked.

Levi turned to face Simon. "No. Sometimes I think about food."

Levi forgot how strong Alden could be when healthier. Alden, who stumbled back a few steps, used Simon's distraction as a chance to retaliate by throwing his entire body into Levi's lower half, knocking the wind out of him. Levi went down like a severed tree trunk, hard and heavy, but not without taking Alden with him.

"Alright!" applauded Simon. "It's about time we saw some action!"

Rebecca floundered away from the altercation to Manny, whose eyes were fixed on the two men brawling and whose hand rested on his revolver. She then noticed Roger's attention was split between the fight and Simon, who remained a mere spectator. Roger moved quickly from the oak tree and stood two feet from the quarrel.

While Alden benefited from giving the first blow, Levi soon wrestled his way to an advantage. He pinned Alden to the ground, levying his weight with one hand clutching Alden's neck while the other arm swung repeatedly. Every few swings, there was a loud *thwack*, establishing contact. Levi's arm might as well have been a Greek column because Alden's attempts to break its lock proved futile. Levi was laboriously limestone, made of marble, muscle, and madness. Alden blocked all of the punches he could with his forearms, but his lungs were being crushed, pressed by Levi's massive weight.

"I can't breathe!" Alden whispered, for a whisper was all he could produce. He tasted blood and felt himself losing consciousness. His fingers lobbied for the lonely hardware at his side. A shot was fired.

"That's enough!" Roger exclaimed with his firearm still hanging in the air.

Levi shifted away from Alden, who rolled to his side, coughing, wheezing, and gasping for air. Levi stood, straightening himself, feeling compelled to kick Alden but, finding Roger watching so closely, resisted. Roger lowered his weapon. Levi huffed, puffed, and blew angry breaths with each step, spitting and pausing only to look down at Alden, who continued recovering.

"That's the last time you put your hands on me, you little shit!"

Simon hailed his hero, "I had your back, Levi!"

"I don't need your help!" Levi snapped.

Alden sat upright, sporting a small cut below his right eye and a bloody nose. He rubbed his lower jawline, gathering enough air and energy to speak. "You need *me*." His voice squeaked with adolescent integrity as his lungs continued adjusting to inflation. He wiped the blood from his nose.

"Me...Julian... I'm the closest thing...you need *me* to finish this job. I'm still the leader here."

Levi smoothed his hair as a means of self-soothing. His appearance was hardly disheveled, and while his face showed no signs of damage, his pride was wavering. "Then maybe you should start acting like it!"

Rebecca, who had frozen during the fight, felt something warm spread across her palm. Manny held her hand, or maybe she reached for his out of fear. Whatever happened, she was relieved. Rebecca looked at Manny for comfort, but his expression hadn't changed. His eyes were locked onto Levi, and his other hand sat readily on his firearm. A stoic Roger finally captured Manny's attention, not with words, but with a look. When Roger shook his head, Manny stood down, finally noticing Rebecca. With a nod, he released her hand.

Levi started back down the hill with Simon taking the rear. Alden's retaliation was indeed a surprise, and if there was one thing Levi Bohannon hated, it was surprises.

CHAPTER THIRTY-SIX

The rest of the day proved uneventful, with Levi stationed at the opposite side of their newest campsite come sundown. For Alden, nighttime couldn't get there soon enough! The night was where he and Rebecca could be themselves, where they were free to talk without interruption about any topic they wished. He could reach for her, knowing she would be there; he could hold her close enough to whisper in her ear and tell her all about his past while lacing her fingers with his own.

They were friends, he told himself.

Friends could share secrets and lay in a field together under the stars.

Friends might even hold hands on occasion.

Besides, holding hands with Rebecca would be far less dangerous than a kiss.

Oh, but the thought of kissing her again…

Wanting, Alden squeezed her hand.

There had been a girl, the *singular* sweetheart of Alden's formative years, *Mary Lou*. It was silly and awkward at sixteen, but he held her hand just the same and unapologetically stole a kiss when permitted. After his mother died, Mary Lou was there, her presence alone restoring some of the missing femininity in his life. Alden soon understood that nothing in the world would compare to the love of a woman. He may not have *loved* Mary Lou, but he liked her well enough. He might have asked Mary Lou's father for his blessing if his own father wouldn't have fallen ill. After that, responsibilities changed, and Alden had little time for romantic endeavors. Mary Lou was heartbroken yet moved on fairly quickly, marrying just a few months later to that freckled boy who lived one town over... *Franklin? Or was it Frederick?* By then, Alden had buried both his parents and was set to leave San Augustine with his brother. They could have gone to Louisiana, but Benjamin wanted to stay in Texas, so they traveled west to Nacogdoches. That was where Alden laid him to rest.

It was where Vernon found him.

Rebecca remained moved by Alden's stories. Sure, she was more cultured, but he had more life experience and would share those hidden parts of himself so sincerely, as though they were all he could give. His words were heartfelt and delivered with such passion, far better than any volume she might have picked up on her own!

Alden stroked her face, remembering a book he read about the centuries-old Japanese art form, *Kintsugi*. Often used for repairing broken ceramics, artisans would use lavish materials such as lacquer and gold pigment to bring the shattered pieces back together. Her scars were *Kintsugi*, adding to what was already beautiful. And *Kintsugi* is what she was to him, precious matter restoring his ruined self, filling in all the obscure spaces. The informative text stated that mending was the hardest part.

No, the hardest part would be living without her.

"I like talking to you," he confessed. "Though I'm afraid neither of us will get any sleep."

Rebecca shook her head, "I don't mind catching up on lost conversation. And you slept enough before."

Returning his hand to hers, "I just realized that I never thanked you for taking care of me."

"It was nothing, though I didn't have much choice," Rebecca offered.

"You chose," said Alden. "You chose goodness when I didn't deserve it."

Giving him a reassuring nuzzle, "You deserve it, Alden."

"What did you do while I was sleeping?" he asked.

"Lots of things, really. Whatever would pass the time. When Rueben showed me your hidden library—"

"—He showed you that? You…read those to me?"

"Yes," smiled Rebecca. She was waiting to have this conversation.

Alden turned away and gritted his teeth in a humiliated moan. *Rueben!*

"There's no need to be embarrassed!" Rebecca soothed.

"I'm not embarrassed—I'm grateful, only—"

"—Only what?"

Alden settled on his back. "I'm supposed to be masculine, not contemplating the mysteries of man or the universe."

She probably thought he was some sort of pantywaist now.

"Alden, you *are* masculine," Rebecca promised, shifting to give his hand a supportive pat. "Anything else I can pretend if you like."

"I would *never* ask you to pretend for me," Alden swore, suddenly serious, knowing what it meant to always be *on*. It would be cruel to assign to anyone such an expectation, especially her. He softened and held her hand against his chest.

"*My life has been the poem I could have writ,*
 But I could not both live and utter it."

"Thoreau!" Rebecca quietly exclaimed, pausing a moment to form her contribution.

"I'm Nobody! Who are you?
Are you Nobody, too?
Then there's a pair of us — don't tell!
They'd banish us, you know."

"That's Dickinson," noted Alden, using one arm to prop his head and the other to gesticulate.

"Come away, O human child!
To the waters and the wild,
With a faery, hand in hand,
For the world's more full of weeping than you can understand."

Together, they glowed. This was almost as good as honeysuckle. *Almost.*

"Yeats," Alden revealed. "He's one of my favorites. 'The Stolen Child.' It's about freedom and loss of innocence—"

"—Yes, he told me."

Alden's eyes widened, now starstruck. "*You* know William Butler Yeats?"

"We had a brief encounter a few years back while I was abroad."

"What was he like?"

"Warm and insightful."

Alden leaned back once more while Rebecca settled her head upon his shoulder.

"He was completely infatuated with a woman named Maud. It was all over him, poor man. There was a sadness there, too; something behind the eyes, something broken. Maybe it was his heart, though I suppose we're all a little broken in some way."

Alden nodded. *How right she was!* "Why were you there?"

"Doctors. For my—well, you know. I *need* it."

"I wish you wouldn't do that."

"What?"

"Tell yourself you should be *corrected*. Whatever it is you think you need, you don't." Alden was studying her now, strumming her side like a forbidden instrument.

"She walks in beauty, like the night
Of cloudless climes and starry skies;
And all that's best of dark and bright
Meet in her aspect and her eyes..."

Lord Byron's words never sounded so lovely, and the fact that Alden could recite them from memory took her breath away. For a moment, she wondered if he had ever used such an approach with other women, but, seeing as few knew of his love of poetry, Rebecca decided that would be improbable.

"And on that cheek, and o'er that brow,
So soft, so calm, yet eloquent,
The smiles that win, the tints that glow,
But tell of days in goodness spent,
A mind at peace with all below,
A heart whose love is innocent!"

Rebecca didn't ask but rather *pounced* Alden mid-sentence. A small *yelp* escaped him as he accepted her advance. Rebecca's kisses were loving, liquidly intimate, and seriously improper. Alden stifled a laugh and slid his arms around her slender waist. Kissing Rebecca was poetry, like the first sip of champagne, magically delicate with a hint of apple.

But no! They had settled this. It was over. This wouldn't happen again.

Gently lifting her away, "I told you not to do that!" Alden sharply whispered.

"You're reciting Lord Byron, and you expect me not to feel something?"

"*Feel* something, yes! Don't *act* on it! And keep your voice down!" Fighting his own arousal, Alden left the area, escaping further into a field.

"Where are you going?" Rebecca gasped, following him as she spoke.

"Away from you, Jezebel! And you call yourself a lady!"

"I *am* a lady!" she insisted. "I was merely overcome with emotion!" Rebecca had never instigated intimacy before, and while she could understand why it was viewed as dishonorable, it was absolutely worth it. *Perhaps Alice had the right idea after all!*

Alden gave a mighty exhalation. "Emotion? *That* was not emotion!"

"We could start the game again," she suggested cheekily.

"I don't want to play games!" he raved, his admission bringing him to a halt. "This is *serious*; we can't—it *can't* happen. I know you believe this is some sort of romance like in your storybooks and that somehow we could be together—"

"—You don't think we could?"

"No, I don't. For so many reasons, Becca. You're going to get hurt."

Rebecca moved closer, convinced Alden's bark was worse than his bite. Alden turned away. "If you had any idea how much danger—if you knew what *I* was capable of—"

"—I know what you're capable of," she pressed.

"Becca, you don't." He repeated himself to further illustrate his point. Only tall grass stood between them now, and her trusting eyes continued to beckon him.

It's happening already.

"You actually want this," he realized.

"Yes."

"Well, the answer is no." Rather than retreat, Alden planted himself in the middle of the field.

"How do you do that?" fumed Rebecca. "How do you *flip* like some sort of quick-break switch?"

"I don't even know what that is!"

"You *change*. You're pulling me close to you one minute, and the next, you're pushing me away. I'm not sure whether this is attributed to years of pretending or simply being a man!"

"Pick one!" Alden rubbed his face in his hands, much like a distressed little boy. Rebecca abandoned her romantic agenda to sit beside him. He always dismissed her when he was unsure of himself. What a nightmare to be constantly torn between who they wanted to be and who they were expected to be!

"Do you even like pretending?" she asked.

Alden lowered his hands to face her. "I used to."

He took a deep breath and paused momentarily, holding the air captive as he pondered. *How does one justify voluntary evil?* After releasing another explanatory sigh, Alden said simply, "It seemed fitting at the time, and it gave me an excuse not to think about the things that bothered me. I didn't have to deal with my troubles because they weren't mine anymore. I could leave them on somebody else's doorstep."

Alden took Rebecca's hands into his own, and they remained hidden by nature and nightfall. "My parents—the whole world changed when I lost them. I ran away with my brother, and we lied about our ages so we wouldn't be separated. He was only a kid. We *both* were. I never worked so hard to be so poor, and he died because I couldn't..." Alden shook his head, unable to finish the statement. "Then, the foreman fired me. I was eighteen years old and could have found work anywhere else, but I was so angry. I *hated* him. I *hated* that I was so easily replaced. I *hated* the world and that I'd lost everything that mattered. When you threaten to kill a man, make sure your affairs are in order, or you've at least got a sturdy alibi because two weeks later, when he was dead, I was the only person to be detained."

"Did you do it?"

"No," he disclosed solemnly. "I don't know what's more ironic, the fact that I didn't kill him, or now I'm hopelessly irreplaceable. I started this path, but a part of me always believed it was temporary, that I could turn around and go the other way..." Alden shook his head. "But you do business with the Devil, and you're bound to get burned. I thought all I had to do was pretend to be some guy's nephew for a while. It's been eighteen years."

Alden paused to let the silence fold into their conversation. He enjoyed being in this place with Rebecca, having quoted poetry to one another and escaping deeper into the field. This was Heaven, but he knew she sought to learn more about his time in Hell. "It wasn't a seamless transition," he admitted. "It took a while to get Julian just right."

"How do you mean?"

"Well, for example, Julian is right-handed, and I'm not. I am *now*, but I wasn't before."

Rebecca smiled. "*I knew it!* Did they tie your hand behind your back?"

She imagined a scenario not too different from Alexandre Dumas's *The Man in the Iron Mask*, with Alden as the young Phillippe, who learned the mannerisms of his horrible half-brother, King Louis XIV of France, to switch places with him.

"That would've been the savory way to do things..."

Alden massaged a phantom pain in his left palm. He could see how glamourous it may have sounded. The truth was that upon his arrival at camp after he initially refused them, the Disciples beat Alden within an inch of his life. Impairing his left hand was their first order of business. Alden flinched at the memory of them pinning him over the kitchen table. It was unfathomable how quickly the original group had broken his body, will, and spirit. And that was only the beginning.

"When we finally got started, it was easy to remove myself from all the terrible things I was doing because I never felt like it was me doing them," he explained. "I mean, it *was* me, but it wasn't the *real* me if that makes sense."

"It does." Rebecca ran her fingers through his hair, allowing him to rest his forehead against hers. "What would the *real* you do right now?"

Alden wanted to lay her down in the field and take her right there, but he abstained. Rising to dust off his trousers, "I'd tell you to go to Roger."

"Alden—"

"—Don't lay beside me again, Becca. Even if I ask you to."

He outstretched his hand to assist her, but Rebecca had already scrambled to her feet. "You've got that sickly look on your face," she said. "What are you not telling me?"

Alden sighed. It wasn't that he failed to share her affections; only outside factors were weighing in beyond his control, things she wouldn't understand. He framed her face with his hands. "Honestly, I wish things were different so that I could call on you."

"You do?"

Alden nodded. "I'd do it right. Proper, even." He gave her cheek a polite peck to prove such intent, to which Rebecca rolled her eyes.

"Well, that sounds *boring*!" With that, Rebecca started towards the campsite.

Alden reeled, "Now, wait a damn minute!"

"Since we're being honest," Rebecca confessed as she traveled, "You should know that I kissed you right before you woke up." She stopped, disappointed by her next statement. "But I won't pretend to assume it was as memorable for *you*."

The confession nearly brought Alden to his knees, overwhelmed at the realization that *she* had brought him back from the place between asleep and awake. It was *her* voice, *her* kiss, that pulled him out of the darkness. *Sonnet 47* rolled off his lips.

"So, either by thy picture or my love,
Thy self away, art present still with me;
For thou not farther than my thoughts canst move,
And I am still with them, and they with thee..."

Rebecca gasped. "You remember?"

"Yes." Alden brought Rebecca inward, trembling as he covered her in sweet, tender kisses, for in that moment, there were no words to describe his gratitude. He would give Rebecca what she wanted because he wanted it, too. They would be together. Anything else would have to wait.

CHAPTER THIRTY-SEVEN

That next morning, the group was welcomed by a magnificent sunrise that lined up to the sky like a great blue cloche, presenting a golden dessert. In typical Texas fashion, the storms subsided, making the weather conditions ideal for travel and promised more of the same agreeable elements, putting them ahead of schedule.

Rebecca hadn't meant to stare. "You're so young!" she sadly remarked to Simon, who was riding beside her.

"Don't let that fool you none. I've killed five men."

The other Disciples shook their heads at this and continued their journey.

"Five men," Alden began, fighting the instinct to pull Rebecca closer as her arms encircled him from behind. "What's that for you, Levi: a Tuesday?"

Despite the teasing, Levi smiled.

In time and with the proper guidance, Simon could be just as deadly as me.

"How far away is Brigham from here?" Simon asked.

Levi voiced a fatherly coo, "Not far at all. Why?"

"Oh, just something I heard from a couple of those Alexander boys while I was locked up."

Alden's eyes widened. "You were with them?"

"They were in a separate cell and weren't too happy that we didn't help them bust out," Simon explained.

Levi was the one to come to Simon's rescue. Clyde, Cecil, Clifford, and Creed Alexander belonged to a nasty brotherly quartet known for robbery, arson, pillage, and plunder. They foiled many Disciple missions in the past and planned to pay Brigham a social call. Roger frowned. Places like Brigham reminded him of his own hometown. Brigham didn't deserve another devastation, and the Alexander Brothers didn't deserve their time.

"That town already has one foot in the grave," Roger reasoned. "Anything worth looting has already been taken, and anyone worth robbing has already left."

"All the more reason," shrugged Levi.

Roger shook his head, "Vultures."

"Julian might appreciate the gesture," Manny offered, wishing not to have any discord within the troupe. Alden opened his mouth to speak, pausing to collect his thoughts.

"It's not part of the plan," he argued.

"Ah, yes. *The plan*," said Levi. "I know how eager you are to be rid of the girl."

Simon concurred, "They've got what's coming to them. It's five against two."

"You only count as half a person, Simon," Roger huffed in noticeable opposition.

"Still… Might be worth looking into," Simon said.

"It's your call, *leader*." Levi's coy compliance dripped with contempt.

Alden sighed. *This* was why he never wanted to be the gang's frontrunner. "We could check it out," he decided. "Simon, you'll snoop around while we sweep the area."

One hour and a leg-stretch later, Brigham presented itself to the ensemble: a handful of dismantled and dilapidated buildings stretched across a narrow strip of land. Time stood still in this place. Painted advertisements faded, gatehouses and barricades were set up to prevent unauthorized access, and the dusty windows that hadn't been knocked out were boarded up with a vow to return to them someday. The residents—what few remained—were out of sight. *This town was dying.*

"*That's* Brigham?" Manny asked in disbelief.

Levi sucked air through his nose and expelled a generous amount of phlegm. "Yep."

"That's not a *town*; that's a *street!*"

"You're right, Manny. See, *this* is what happens when wealthy businessmen and politicians make plans to create something and then change their minds." His eyes shot to Rebecca. Surely, it was understood by now that *he* wasn't the only evil in the world. She knew evil long before her capture. "Droves of people came here believing this could be the next Kansas City, yet all they got was a street before the funding got pulled."

Manny shook his head. "That's a shame."

"I'll say. It had potential, too. Look at this brilliant layout: a sundry at one end of the street and a saloon at the other." Levi's wingspan stretched an impressive amount. "No matter which way you're going, you'll leave with something you need."

Simon ran towards them, a scout slightly out of breath. "The Alexander Brothers already passed through. They're celebrating in the saloon at the end of the street."

"Of course they are," Alden fussed.

"What are you planning to do with *her*?" Levi asked, pointing to Rebecca. "Should we make it an even half-dozen? She knows how to use a gun now, thanks to you."

Drawing her gently by the hand, Alden answered, "I'll take her to the sundry."

The modest general store's walls and shelves told a dark story of invasion, a threatening use of force, and the struggle to balance both order and operation after several robberies. Horizontal slopes of inventory were picked over, destroyed, or abandoned. Rebecca scanned the showroom, squirming and arching her back in discomfort. Again, Alden was binding her hands together in both a technicality and a necessary precaution from an argument he didn't win. Manny, ever the peacekeeper, was the swing vote.

"I'm sorry about this," he said. "Is it too tight?"

Rebecca shook her head. "Where do you think the shop owner is?

Alden noticed blood spatter behind the counter, trailing into the back storeroom. "Don't worry about that." He continued his work. "Listen, I'm afraid I'm going to have to break our agreement. If you decide to run, you'd be well within your rights. I would advise against it, though. You're still quite a-ways from anyone who could help you. This is one instance where you *are* safer with me."

Rebecca shrugged at his suggestion of imminent danger. She hadn't felt endangered with Alden for many days now. "I suppose a man has the right to defend himself if they shoot first."

Alden's left eyebrow lifted. "A *loophole*? That's mighty generous of you. Do you still have that knife Manny gave you?"

"Yes." Rebecca had torn a thin strip of fabric from her skirt to fashion a thigh-holster that she could use to unravel and retrieve the weapon if necessary. Manny directed her to always give the pretense that she was unarmed, but she saw no harm in sharing this information with Alden since it was his idea to arm her.

"Good. If I don't come back, stay close to Roger and Manny, and if none of us—"

"—Who are these men?"

Alden paused before answering. "I'd say they were the competition, but no one truly wins doing what we do. They're bad men, Becca. That's all that matters."

Rebecca noted Alden's upset fingers as he completed her hand-holding harness. "You're shaking."

"I always shake a little right before…and sometimes during…" he confessed.

"Are you scared?"

"It's a mixture: part of me is scared, nervous, and excited, while the other part sort of slips away."

Rebecca's head turned slightly, having not understood what Alden had meant.

He would simply have to show her.

Alden promptly brought her face towards his own, his lips offering a hard, hearty kiss. Rebecca submitted and was soon hoisted onto the countertop in a connection that traveled like an electric current through their extremities. *Scared. Nervous. Excited.* An out-of-body experience that always left her wanting more. Alden slipped away, his ears reddened, and his hands now shaking for a new set of reasons. "It's like that."

Rebecca licked her lips, trembling and dizzy from having tasted unbridled passion. "I can see why you might enjoy it."

Grinning, Alden leaned forward to kiss her a second time as Simon's voice rang from outside the sundry. They were calling for him.

"That's my cue. Stay away from the window in case it moves to the street."

"Be careful." Rebecca couldn't believe she was telling a felon to use caution; only Alden's responsive smile made her weak in the knees.

He was a completely different person when he smiled.

"Don't worry; if they kill me, I'll just have to come back for you."

She returned his sentiment. "You would cheat Death for me?"

"He owes me a favor. And besides, you're the kind worth coming back for."

With a wink, Alden exited the storefront. Rebecca opted not to remove herself from atop the counter, for it provided a clearer vantage point of the street while adhering to Alden's warning. Trepidation soon filled the depot as Rebecca wished that somehow Alden could have taken her along. She played with the idea of having a life with him beyond the trip to Grady and wondered if he, too, imagined such things. Was there space for her in his mind while he performed those acts—any consideration for her at all—or would he check such thoughts at the door? Alden expressed anxiety in facing the Alexander Brothers yet walked into what he knew would be a stressful situation, possibly fatal. Rebecca's thoughts teetered; attempting to decode such a man was functional madness.

Still, there was something to be said about the benefits of their new relationship. Rebecca believed no woman was responsible for a man's happiness and vice versa, yet what she and Alden shared undoubtedly made them both happy. In addition to the romance and emotional growth, their heart-to-heart conversations about ego and will had created a bridge of trust between them. It was Mutualism at its finest.

Because the clock on the wall was long made inactive from gunfire and the fight hadn't moved into the street, with the saloon being at the road's end, there was no way for Rebecca to know how much time had passed.

Was there something specific she should listen for?

As she swayed, her elbow nudged a glass container filled with familiar stripes—*peppermint sticks.* There was only one left. Rebecca used her welded hands to remove the lid from the candy jar and carefully raised it to her face. The smell alone was enough to make her swoon.

She craved the taste but wanted it to come from him. Rebecca searched about nervously. There was an issue of money. If someone *were* watching her, she would ensure there was no misunderstanding.

"You'll send payment once you're back home," she told herself. "With interest."

Rebecca decided she would talk to her father about Brigham. It could just as easily be Rosewood falling between the cracks. She would tell him her first accounts of this broken promise of a town and demand that it be set right! Rebecca slid the sweet straw into her bodice, hoping it wouldn't melt, then tingled at the thought of what Alden could do if it did.

Sunlight poured in through the entryway as the front door swung open.

He's alive!

"You ready?"

Alden was visibly unkempt, dripping sweat from his brow and displaying blood from his open collar. They had acquired what they came for, albeit unfairly. Now, a hasty exit was in order!

Rebecca nodded and pointed to Alden's shirt. "You—you're—"

"Loophole," Alden panted as he severed her woven bracelets, lifting her off the counter merely to place her on another platform once they got outside.

Gambit held such a pleasant disposition for a horse. After spending so much time with the steed, Rebecca decided she, too, would bond with a horse once she returned to Windhaven Hall. Led by Roger, the procession continued southbound as the sun set around them, with Alden and Rebecca taking the rear. Rebecca preferred traveling in this formation because it allowed them to talk quasi-privately. Her arms wrapped around Alden during the ride, pressing the peppermint stick into her chest. She discreetly peeled the sugar baton from her flesh. It was slightly softened but still held its shape. Rebecca moved forward to wave the treat in front of him.

His jaw dropped, *"Did you steal that?"*

"The store clerk won't miss it."

Alden bounced in amusement. "We've ruined you, haven't we?"

"Not *ruined*, only *influenced*."

"Thank you," Alden accepted her gift. "Where have you been hiding this?"

"*Guess*."

Alden elevated and immediately positioned the sweet between his lips, convinced he'd never tasted anything so delicious. He wanted to kiss her again; he burned for it; his heart demanded it! Each beat held such longing that he felt thunder in his ears.

"Here I am, and I didn't get you anything," he said apologetically. "Wait—I *do* have something."

Alden reached into his vest pocket to produce a familiar family heirloom, her mother's silver brooch! Rebecca reached to retrieve the item from Alden's open hand. "You said it was important to you. I didn't have the heart to put it with the rest of the take from that night. And then, well, you know what happened… I apologize for not returning it sooner."

"Thank you," Rebecca whispered, touched. *He does care.*

"You might want to hide it," he advised.

Rebecca nodded and slid the accessory into her blouse just before Levi fell back in formation to address them.

"That was a fun little excursion," he said. "Though I do feel that shoving that kid in the street, Alden, was a tad uncalled for."

"He was in the way," Alden plainly replied.

Rebecca frowned at her partner's nonchalance. "Do you dislike children?" she asked, remembering his behavior is Discovery.

"Children make me nervous," Alden explained with a faltering timbre.

"Oh, but Alden, you have *such a way* with them!"

"Fuck you, Levi!"

Even Gambit seemed perturbed by Levi's effect on his master. With glee in knowing that he'd struck a nerve, Levi turned his attention to Rebecca, "Alden is a natural with children. Enormously paternal."

At this, Alden removed the sweet from his searing mouth with a trembling hand. "I swear to Christ if you don't—"

"*—Shut up! Both of you!*" Roger's command severed the tension.

Levi laughed to himself and returned to the front. "Now there's only one job left."

CHAPTER THIRTY-EIGHT

The city of Jardín was just beyond the main road, though its exterior resembled a *forest* more than a *garden*. Rebecca was uncertain of their exact location, but when setting up camp that evening, Levi mentioned numerous times the possibility of an early arrival at Grady. *They were close.* In the twilight hour, Alden led Rebecca away from the group's resting place. He told her very little, only that they needed to be alone.

Rebecca ducked under a branch. "Where are you taking me?"

"Not much further."

"Do you know where we are?"

"I know exactly where we are *and* how to get back."

An ambitious little creek traveled down the trail beside them, with muddy icing serving as partitions. It would be too easy for someone to lose footing and slip into the cloudy embankment. Rebecca looked at the fast-moving body of water.

"I hope you're not proposing that we *swim* to Grady," she teased. "The water looks filthy, and it hardly appears deep enough."

It was true; the water *was* murky, for the creek overflowed due to the generous amounts of rainfall.

"It's deep enough," he assured her, picking up the pace. Should they decide to wade through it, the top would undoubtedly skim Alden's waistline.

Rebecca fought to keep up with him. He seemed nervous all of a sudden, though Alden always seemed nervous when they were alone. Overeager branches reached for her arms and tugged at her hemline, nipping at the ankles. She slid, and before she knew it, Rebecca was caught wholly in their grasp. Each twisted movement added another tangle, but Rebecca dared not cry out. Luckily, Alden noticed that he lost a follower and, upon backtracking, began to peel away the plucky picklers. What should have been a tender rescue felt *awkward*, and the faint smile he offered once he took her by the hand suggested they might indeed be lost.

"Are you alright?" Rebecca asked.

"Of course," he responded, now concerned. "Are *you*?"

"Yes. Only, we're almost—"

"—We're almost to Grady, I know." With a sigh, Alden squeezed her hand. They had decided to be together, but they had yet to determine *how*. Both surrendered to the idea in haste. There was no long-term plan or understanding. They were simply avoiding their inevitable separation with each passing day.

Rebecca brushed off a stray twiglet that embedded itself in her blouse. "I've got about a million thoughts running through my mind, but right now, I only wish to know what you're thinking."

He led her to higher ground, up the hill with the free-flowing current churning beneath them. An assortment of trees horseshoed them between this space, promising they wouldn't be disturbed. Crickets, moving water, and other ambient noises joined in the flips and clicks of Alden opening his folding knife. Deep undertones resonated beneath it all, playing sociable sounds for a welcoming moon.

It sounded like a bass.

Or better yet, a band.

Alden abruptly snapped his weapon shut. "Listen! Do you hear that?"

"Hear what?"

"Music!" he stated. "There must be a party of some sort happening nearby."

They briefly stopped to listen for a title that tapped on the tips of their tongues. The folding knife made its way back into Alden's side pocket. Jardín was closer than he realized. Rebecca continued straining her ears to determine the name of the melody playing, yet all she could make out was a bassline.

"It sounds familiar, but I can't hear well enough to know what song is playing."

"Neither can I," he said. Alden moved his attention to marvel at a sky that hadn't been *that* clear in days, embroidered only by the stars. Rich blue light trimmed the treetops with glints of a silvery moon, shining in great contrast to the deep ambiance hidden in the forest, which possessed a more golden glow. *How could something so beautiful be so complex?* He looked to Rebecca, who was also admiring overhead.

She's like that, too.

"Is this why you brought me here?" Rebecca queried, nibbling at her bottom lip. "For the music?"

Giving a modest half-nod shrug, "Surprised?"

"Very."

Alden extended his hand, still fighting nerves, "Dance with me."

His request lacked formality and etiquette, but the magnetism of his invitation drew Rebecca right in. Gently, the pair glided over a patch of smooth and steady land. Alden delighted in how she fit right into him, like a dovetail, though she seemed to have her own preferences of how she wished to be held. A part of Rebecca calculated the steps and resisted his direction. She was as guilty of overthinking as he was.

"Are you going to let me lead?" he ribbed. "If we're going to be together, you have to trust me."

Rebecca's dance card was seldom claimed and never full, so it took a few sways for her to fully settle. Dancing wouldn't form any sort of strategy for them, but it was exactly what they needed.

"People should know your story, Alden."

Alden moaned. "No, Becca."

"They should know you exist."

"Julian would disagree with you wholeheartedly."

"I don't particularly care what Julian thinks."

Saying nothing, Alden stared ahead. Vernon instructed him and Julian to burn the jail in Nacogdoches. Any records of his incarceration were destroyed. As far as anyone knew, Alden never existed. Julian would be the one to leave a legacy, not him.

"Fine," said Rebecca. "I'll just have to tell your story for you."

Alden sent her out in a twirl, the sides of his mouth lifting slightly. "What sort of a story?"

"I'm not sure," she replied.

To Rebecca, Alden was David Copperfield, Dorian Gray, and Edmund Dantès, all simmering in the same spirited stew. He had compromised himself so fiercely, so significantly, but he housed the heart of a hero. He was set in his ways, yet capricious and broken, carrying a mighty shame. He struggled and lost much but remained strong, capable, and driven. Rebecca could easily identify themes, plot holes, and foreshadowing events within a narrative context. She often took pride in her ability to anticipate the ending of a novel before ever reaching its conclusion. By far, her favorite character, Alden, was a man filled with magic and mystery, yet he was stranger than fiction because she couldn't fully read him, nor could she guess how his story would end.

"Don't worry; I'll give you a pseudonym," she promised. "And, of course, I'll write you as an *interesting* man."

Alden laughed. "You'll have to if you want to make any kind of profit," he said, bringing her back to him. It seemed she could always make him laugh, even when he didn't feel like smiling.

"And I'll need to make him much more attractive."

"So you *do* find me attractive?"

Rebecca shied away, though she believed Alden was the kind of man who made stories worth telling. Neither noticed as the music began to fade, for they remained connected.

Alden nestled his face in the sweet spot along her neck. "Are you going to give him a girl?" he whispered. "Someone he can call 'sweetheart' or 'darlin'?"

"No."

His left eyebrow lifted, then settled. "He's better off that way. *Let him suffer.* It builds character." The back-and-forth continued. "Only if you change your mind will you make her like you?"

Rebecca concurred. "With improvements."

"No, no. Don't change a thing."

She felt Alden take a deep breath, his torso and back accordioning under her fingertips. He slowly withdrew from their embrace, holding her hands in a serious shift of emotions.

"That town isn't too far from here," he offered. "A short walking distance."

Though only the faint lights of Jardín were visible from their position, Rebecca knew he was right. Civilized folk were only a mile or so away. A town meant people, people meant the law, and the law would bring him in. She immediately sensed his uneasiness.

"I wouldn't worry about anyone coming out this far," she said. "We're safe."

"Do you feel safe?"

"With you? Yes."

Alden finally relaxed and pulled her close to him once more. He felt safe with her, too. A youthful enthusiasm settled in Alden's belly, a nostalgic feeling first experienced in his days of pulling on the braids of cute girls in the schoolhouse. His feet hadn't touched the ground from the time they started dancing. Something buried deep was taking over in an immersion comparable to the Holy Spirit. Wise, tall trees whispered the possibility of change, of *forever*, with the night holding a promise in its moon-shaped mittens. He could be baptized in this moment. He could give his heart away. He could rebuild and begin again. *What it would mean to have clean hands and a pure heart!*

"Becca, I need to tell you something."

"Yes?"

Rebecca waited patiently for an answer while Alden swayed her in the moonlight, his cheek pressed tightly to hers as he struggled to find the words. She heard him gulp and hesitate before finally stopping to face her straight-on.

"At no point," he started. "I need you to know that..."

Rebecca waited as Alden trailed off, pausing only to wipe his brow.

"Alden, what are you trying to say?"

He shook his head. Looking over his shoulder to the past would only make him a proverbial pillar of salt. And she warranted better. Alden's insides yo-yoed with the raw realization that he would never return to that place, but he could relish its familiarity. He could be present in *this* moment.

"It's nothing," he said. "Can I kiss you?"

"You've never asked before," replied Rebecca, puzzled.

"Well, I should have."

So she let him, but when he kissed her, it seemed he was saying goodbye. No one ever teaches you how to kiss goodbye; you just know. Before long, unapologetic swells of deep passion brought them both to the ground, where clever hands roamed freely until Alden ultimately had to stop himself.

"What is it?" Rebecca huffed as he caught her by the wrists.

With an affable smile, Alden equally huffed, "*Vigor.*"

A thoughtful Autumn Blaze dropped handfuls of dazzling red leaves down to them. Considerate constellations cheered on from the rafters while the sensible winds picked up, reminding them that fall would soon be upon them. Such a scene could beat candlelight on any occasion! *There wouldn't be another night like this.*

Alden trembled as he tucked that same stubborn strand of hair behind her ear. He was only a man, and every man had his limits. Rebecca was willing, showing him the desired response akin to a brandnew guitar eager to be strummed. The modest musician in Alden understood that each instrument required gentle adjustment before playing. He possessed the dexterity to tune her with balanced levels of intensity and care. All he had to do was ask. Yes, it would be incredible, but Rebecca deserved bells and bouquets from someone who would touch her after she wore the veil, after carrying her over the threshold, and only with her father's blessing. *He would never be that man.*

"Let me do right by you, Becca," he pleaded as he kissed her forehead. "*Please.*"

Disappointed, Rebecca nodded and sat upright.

"It's not that I don't want to," he explained.

Rebecca nodded again, embarrassedly smoothing over the wrinkles in her ruffled clothing. Her blouse had a grass stain on the back that would need explaining, and it would be a while before either of them were neutral enough to return to camp.

The pair leaned against the Blaze Maple for a while, letting the silence speak for them. They may not have used the evening as nature intended, but they wouldn't waste a single moment together. Alden permitted her to fall asleep on his chest. Being with Rebecca this way would have to be enough. He had no answers for her, no plans or knowledge of what the future held. There was only one thing he *could* give her.

Rebecca awoke to find an empty space beside her. "Alden?"

She arose to no response. Rebecca wasn't afraid of the darkness, only the disconcerting reason for Alden leaving her there. The nearby line of water could serve as a trail to lead her to a new destination, but a choice needed to be made. She could go in the direction that the music had played and locate the sheriff of Jardín.

Or she could follow the gunshots.

CHAPTER THIRTY-NINE

You did the right thing, Alden.

He took her; it only made sense for him to be the one to let her go. There was no way Rebecca would agree to leave on her own. He *had* to leave her there. A smart and resourceful girl like her would have no problems finding help in Jardín. As for her knowledge of Julian Crisp's secret decoy…

It doesn't matter anymore. I'm glad she knows.

Alden found the camp unchanged since venturing off to share a dance. How sweet it had been to slip away with Rebecca, to kiss her, and hold her one last time. He sighed, knowing it was really over. He could finally lay his head down and—

"—Git up, you jug of horse piss!"

Suddenly, the sharp pain of a boot clipped below Alden's ribcage. He raised his head to be greeted by the barrel of a lever-action shotgun. On the other side stood Clyde Alexander. *Shit.*

The Disciples resembled a highly-romanticized idea of outlaw. The Alexander Brothers were the harsh reality of what true crime existed in those parts. Shameless felons and grave robbers who—to quote Vernon—"couldn't tell dung from wild honey." But what they lacked in intelligence, they made up for in lethality. Something about their appearance reminded Alden of a grasshopper. They were byproducts of incestuous relations with tiny heads, tubular torsos, and elongated extremities bent in abominable fashions. There stood only a year between each of them. If positioned horizontally by age, the formation would appear much like a growth chart. Long, wispy black hair tapered over the collars of their heavily soiled clothing. It was anyone's guess as to whether they had ever *seen* a bar of soap. Either by the elements or pedigree, their skin held a yellowy-green hue. Their teeth had rotted out of their mouths, and if you dared to stand downwind of them, you'd be greeted by gnats and an unspeakable odor that seemed to follow them. Roger, caught sleeping on his stomach, faced Cecil's shotgun resting inches above his head. Creed's shotgun aimed at Levi's favorite body part. Clifford remained on his horse with both hands steering six-shooters, one pointed at Manny and the other poised for Simon. Alden slowly raised his hands above his head. He knew why they were there. *Everyone knew.*

The entire Brigham encounter played back in slow-motion. Alden remembered how the saloon doors flapped behind him like an angel's wings pushing in the outside air. At one time, that parlor would have been welcoming, but as with the rest of Brigham, the tavern was in ruins. Shards of glass sprinkled the floor, which was littered with cards, liquor bottles, and what remained of wooden tables. Cecil and Clifford stood at the bar, enjoying a bottle of whiskey. Little dialogue was exchanged. It was all too easy to relieve the brothers of their prize. Manny watched the exits while Simon grabbed the loot. Roughly ten minutes passed as Alden and Roger tag-teamed one sibling, and Levi apprehended the other. It was Cecil's blood that stained Alden's lapel. Cecil held a knife to his throat after the initial scuffle, so Alden stuck a broken shot glass into his shoulder, freeing him to let Roger give the knock-out punch. There were no fatalities; they merely roughed up the small-time duo.

"Fellas, I understand your frustration," said Alden. "But there's no need for hostility. Let's talk about this."

The Alexander Brothers maintained their aggressive stance. Alden would need to sweet-talk the miscreants to get them to stand down. Clyde was the eldest and, seeing as the others communicated in advanced gibberish, spoke for the group. Truthfully, understanding Clyde wasn't any easier.

"Boss, you can't reason with inbreeds," Roger whispered, raising his hands while resting on his stomach. His eyes scanned the surrounding area.

Where's Miss Rebecca? Perhaps she's hiding. Wise.

Clyde nudged the shotgun barrel into Alden's cheek. The firearm was in desperate need of cleaning, much like its owner. "Yew must think yer pretty slick! Personally, I think yer lower than a snake's belly in a wagon rut!"

"That's an ugly thing to say—" purred Alden, already in character.

"—But yew should've helped us back at Pearson Pointe!" Clyde continued.

Alden rolled onto his back. Most men had difficulty pulling the trigger if you looked them in the eye. "And why would I do that?" he asked.

"'Cause yew said we wus alleys!"

A confused expression swept across Manny's face. *"Allies?"*

"Yeah, that's whut I said. *Alleys!*" Clyde snapped to Manny before returning his attention to Alden. "*Yew* told us we both wanted the same things, and it would *be-hoof* us to team up."

"It would *what?*" Again, Manny tried to follow Clyde's backwoods drawl, posing the question with a thick accent of his own. He understood what it meant to struggle with English. Clyde looked down at Manny and, because he had to repeat himself, stamped his foot like a frustrated steer.

"Be-hoof. *Be-hoof!*"

"Do you mean, *behoove*?" Manny inquired.

"Quit fixin' my words! Yew ain't no better than me, yew filthy wetback!"

At this, Manny snarled. No one spoke to him like that and got away with it.

"Easy, Manny," Alden cooed.

Behoove. That sounds like the kind of word Julian would use.

Clyde shook his head. "We had buyers for them horses that little squirt stole at Pearson Pointe, but then he done git caught, and then *we* wus gotten caught, too!

Alden gritted his teeth. "Simon?"

Simon couldn't decide who he was more afraid of—the man pointing a gun at him or his true leader back at Sanctuary. If he failed on assignment, the real Julian would knock him senseless. "I didn't know, Julian! I swear!"

Alden faked annoyance. *Of course, you didn't. Because Julian doesn't tell anyone anything.* He understood the boy's bewilderment but maintained the arrogance of an aggravated superior.

Creed provided his account of Pearson Pointe, gesturing to Levi as he complained. "And *this* sorry sonofabitch got stingy with the dynamite, laughin' while me and Clyde wus in jail! Do yew know whut the punishment is for stealin' a horse in Putnam County? It ain't pretty!"

"Levi?" questioned Alden.

"My mistake, Boss," Levi shook. He'd rather be shot in the head than the groin.

Alden nestled on his elbows under Clyde's weapon and attempted to sit upright, slowly moving the barrel away from him. "It appears you fared well without our assistance."

"We decided we wus better off without yew chicken dicks! We got out all on our own!" boasted Creed.

Cecil Alexander planted a boot in Roger's back. "Whut I wanna know is why yew fellers come chargin' in like yew wus the cavalry when we wus in Brigham? If we's alleys like Clyde say we is, why'd you rob us? Whut the *Hell* is wrong with yew, Julian?"

Alden took a deep breath, attempting to negotiate peace. "It sounds like a misunderstanding."

"No she-it!"

Roger dipped his head in the grass to hide his amusement. Cecil sounded daft even when swearing. The other Disciples waited under gunpoint while Alden deescalated the situation.

"Obviously, there's been some miscommunication," Alden began as he signaled to the heavy arsenal aimed at them. "None of this is necessary."

Clyde spat in protest. "*Necessary*? Wus it *necessary* for yer boy over there to *brick* my brother's leg?"

Clifford Alexander's right leg hung over the side of his horse, a floppy, mangled appendage. No attempts were made to set the limb or even fashion it into a splint. Alden knew Levi had incapacitated him, but not to this extent. Clifford's siblings would fail to find the proper medical treatment. The poor fool would never walk right again.

"Christ, Levi!" scolded Alden.

Levi shrugged in sly satisfaction. When the fight started, Levi threw Clifford over his shoulder as though he were nothing more than a bag of feed. After sliding him down the bar, knocking over long-abandoned dishes and spittoons in the process, Levi seized Clifford's leg and twisted. The bandit's scream, mixed with how his tibia snapped under the weight of his body, was enough to satisfy Levi's bloodlust for many months.

Alden turned to Simon, who was responsible for carrying the loot. "Give them what they want."

Levi's head veered. "Julian—"

"—*Just do it!*"

Simon slowly sauntered to his resting place, having used the moneybag for a pillow. Once Clyde snatched the potato sack and lifted his shotgun away from Alden, the remaining Alexanders followed suit. Alden was the last to stand, believing it best to test the waters first.

"Can we call it square?" he asked. "Bury the hatchet once and for all?"

Clyde, with a spit, *"Fine."*

Alden dusted himself off as the men nervously dispersed, spreading like fallen marbles on a wooden floor. "So, what's next for you boys?" Making small-talk would buy Rebecca more time.

The second-eldest Alexander puffed out his chest. "We thought we'd mosey on over to Jardín and—"

"—Shut yer mouth, Cecil! They don't need to know our business!" barked Clyde.

Alden calmly processed this information. None of the others had mentioned Rebecca's absence. If he played his cards right, their untimely ambush from the Alexander Brothers might work to his advantage. "Just the four of you?"

"Yeah."

Alden crossed to Gambit, giving his steed a hearty pat. "Hmm…"

"Whut?" said Clyde.

"I'm curious about your strategy, that's all," Alden replied.

Levi folded his arms in suspicion, with Simon mirroring in parroted doubt. Roger and Manny turned to each other. If Alden was planning something, it was news to them.

Clyde looked to his brothers. *What did the Disciples know about Jardín that they didn't?* He turned back to Alden. "Yew fellers wanna help? Try to re-deem yourself?"

Alden nodded. "We could, but there's a problem."

"And whut's that?

"We work alone."

Alden kept a shotgun of his own stowed away on Gambit's back. The 1878 Hartford was outdated but proved reliable in the past, serving an impressive amount of damage when fired. The high velocity of the twenty-inch barrel made Clyde Alexander's torso pop like a bloody firecracker. There was no need to fire a second shot as, within seconds, a shower of projectile ammunition sprayed the camp. Levi's round entered under Clifford's pointed chin, rocketing straight out of his head and knocking him clean off his horse. Cecil wrestled Simon for his gun, only to find himself on the wrong side of Manny's smiling blade. Alden dodged Creed's final shot, letting it buzz past his ear to join the other bullets popping in the crossfire just before Roger emptied an entire chamber into Creed's chest. Soon, all that could be heard was the sound of men catching their breath and checking their persons for injuries.

"Well, *that* escalated quickly," huffed Levi.

"We'll take their guns and throw the bodies in the creek," Alden instructed. The men made fast work of dispatching the quarrelsome quartet.

"Did you have to do that?" Roger grumbled as he lifted Creed Alexander's lifeless body. Alden put his shotgun to rest and grabbed the lower half of the cadaver.

"Yes, I did." *He would explain to Roger later.*

Levi nodded in agreement. *No loose ends.* While he believed that Alden was inferior to Julian in every way, the man *could* think on his feet.

"They might have kept the law from following us," Manny reasoned as he wiped the blood from his knife onto the grass. He promised himself he would never use it again, but it slid across Cecil's throat with effortless familiarity.

"*Are* they following us?" asked Simon, sucking breaths through an invisible straw. His first gunfight was an adrenaline rush. "I can't go back to jail!"

"Nobody's following us!" Alden moaned.

"*Where's the girl?*" Levi had been temporarily detained after having a weapon aimed at his private parts but was the first to notice the missing party member. The group promptly paused the body disposal.

Alden scanned the area, surprisingly unalarmed. "She must have run off."

Roger's eyes searched Alden. *What have you done?*

"She's run off before," recalled Manny, pulling Clifford from the grassy knoll.

Alden gave a small, reassuring nod to Manny and Manny to Roger. Roger returned the gesture. *She's free.*

"Goddamnit! We have to find her!"

Levi was irate. If Rebecca somehow got to Jardín, there would be trouble.

"Should we look for her or dump the bodies?" Simon asked, letting Cecil's body bend in his arms.

Manny abandoned his corpse. "*Alden!*"

To his horror, a wounded Rebecca was slumped along a nearby tree trunk. The impact of the ricocheted bullet had stopped her in her tracks. It wasn't until she caught Alden's eye that she noticed the blood pouring out of her left shoulder. Manny's reach stopped Rebecca from hitting the ground, but only just. She was in shock, releasing a yelp when he began to apply pressure.

Alden dashed across the lawn, sliding to her side. "Levi!"

There was no choice but to refer her to Levi, whose medical expertise none of the others possessed. Levi crouched to examine the damage, and Rebecca flinched at his meticulous touch. "Not him!" she whimpered. "*Not him!*"

"He's the only one who knows what he's looking at," Alden reasoned. Her head lay cradled in his hands. They were the hands that took her, the same hands that fired the first shot. He might as well have shot her himself. "I promise I won't let him hurt you," he whispered. *Please, God. Don't let her die.*

Muddled conversations traveled across Rebecca in warbly waves, heavily and unfocused, until the Disciple's voices faded away with the world around her into the September night.

CHAPTER FORTY

"You're awake."

Alden's words held neither surprise nor relief. They merely escaped him. He sat in the chair at Rebecca's bedside, appearing sicklier and more fatigued than the night they met.

"You look awful," she said.

"I know," he replied, choosing not to tell Rebecca that she also wasn't sporting her best look.

Rebecca settled into the mattress and felt for the opening in her blouse. She would need a new shirt, for its collar was torn, and there was a large hole in the shoulder, stained with dried blood from where the bullet entered. Skin held together by light stitchwork slid beneath her fingertips.

"Levi did a good job," Alden stated. "You were bleeding... I didn't know what to do, but the bullet practically popped out of you once he started working. He said the wound was superficial."

"It didn't *feel* superficial."

Though stiff, Rebecca was relieved to find full rotation and use of her arm. She felt thankful for receiving medical care, yet she shuddered at the thought of Levi having his hands on her, probably smiling sadistically as he touched her. She didn't want to know how Levi restored her or where he found the materials to do so. All that mattered was that she was alive.

Alden's sad eyes studied her. "Are you in pain?"

"Mmm, no," she answered with a heavy yawn. "Just sore."

"You slept most of the day."

"I lost an entire day?" Rebecca believed their time together was sacred, so even sleeping felt wasteful.

He nodded. "Fortunately, we were ahead of schedule."

She attempted a slight stretch. "Have *you* slept at all?"

Alden shook his head. "No, and there's a few things I need to sort out before the morning, so—"

"—Will we still make the train?"

"Yes," he quickly replied.

Rebecca's sigh of relief permeated through the bedroom in Sanctuary, which suddenly seemed much smaller. "Where are the others?"

Running a shaky hand across his forehead, Alden explained. "I've locked us in. We won't be bothered."

"Did anyone else get hurt?"

"You don't need to worry about all that right now."

Rebecca then took greater notice of her surroundings. They were *not* back at Sanctuary as she had initially thought. Blank wooden slates stood before her in a half-empty bedroom, save for the furniture she and Alden were using and a small nightstand between them. A candle flickered in the windowsill across from the doorway, a second-string teammate to the moonlight that poured in. Alden's shadow loomed up the wall onto the ceiling, appearing nefariously monstrous and heavy overhead.

"Whose house is this?" asked Rebecca.

Alden shifted and cleared his throat. "It's vacant."

"Well, that's convenient."

He was fidgeting with his folding knife, a habit Rebecca knew he practiced when they were alone to suggest he had something on his mind. She recalled Alden's shock after discovering her by the tree trunk and his helpless expression while holding her injured frame. Alden had seen his share of bodies riddled with bullets. What made hers so traumatic?

"Alden, will you tell me something?"

With one knee bouncing and a face flushed with nervous sweat, "Hmm?"

Rebecca touched his hand. "Why did you take me that night— the night of the Rosewood Ball?"

Alden shifted a second time. He knew this was coming. She deserved to know the truth. She deserved to hear it from him. "I took you because...*I wanted you.*" Producing such words proved challenging. As if he were at confession, Alden bowed his head. "I watched you in the library with your father. You were...impressive. I was curious about you. You reminded me of me, but you were *good*. I know what it's like to have a proposition presented to you that compromises everything you ever pictured for yourself. But you didn't do what I did; you were stronger. You stood your ground."

"The wine glasses," Rebecca realized. "That was you."

"You kept standing there, staring at the clock; for a moment, I thought you'd spotted me. After you left, I followed you, but then I lost you sometime after you went into the garden with that fella. When the shooting started, I never imagined it would be *you* hidden in that carriage... You called me a coward," he shook. "You were so brave, Becca. I—I hadn't wanted anything for myself in such a long time, but I wanted you."

He stumbled over the fuzzy memories with broken speech and guilty sighs. Alden's simple answer held incredible weight. Rebecca was familiar with the concept of "love at first sight" but had yet to know of its practical existence outside the literary world. *Had he been silently suffering this whole time? Is that what he was saying?* No wonder he couldn't stomach the task of telling her the truth.

Alden stared ahead, opening and closing the knife in his hands absentmindedly while he continued, looking as though simply sitting next to Rebecca drained him of his life-source. "Who really knows why people want the things they want? Why do they fancy a particular hat over another or—I don't know, decide on which house they want to live in? What makes *that* house feel like home? *You just know.* I knew I wanted *you.* For whatever reason—not because I was drunk—it was like I'd wanted you my entire life. You felt like home. So, I selfishly took you. I didn't think about Julian or how it might jeopardize your life. I didn't think it through."

Turning on her good shoulder, Rebecca pushed down the bedcovers and slid closer to him. "It's alright. I'm not angry, Alden. I'm happy that we met. I forgive you."

Alden gulped painfully and set his jaw.

"What's wrong?" Rebecca asked. "You know you can tell me."

Alden placed his knife on the nightstand and sniffed. "Nothing."

Rebecca turned her attention to the nightstand, running her forefinger along the printed "J" inscribed on the blade's handle, tracing up, down, and across repeatedly while Alden attempted to steady himself. Whatever was bothering him seemed to have a tight grip on his heart. With his recent testimony, Rebecca imagined it must have been terrifying, the thought of losing her.

"Does Julian have one, too?" she asked, referring to the knife.

"No, I've had that since I was a young man."

The wooden grip was worn and desperately needed refinishing, yet the blade appeared sharp. If it weren't for the lighter tone of the tenth letter, Rebecca might have missed the tiny detail. "But it has a 'J' on it," she pointed out.

Alden shook his head, "It's not for 'Julian,' it's for 'John.' That was my daddy's name." Then, with a gaze that carved just as deep, Alden revealed, "It's *my* name. My *real* name."

Rebecca swelled as she processed the information, "It suits you."

"You think so?" For the first time since she awakened, Alden showed a glimmer of a smile. It was his most precious secret, his true identity, and he shared it with her.

"I do."

Alden brought her hand to his lips in a subtle gesture of affection.

Rebecca turned her hand to stroke the stubbled shadow across his cheek. "Do you still want me, Alden?"

He hesitated, then nodded. "Very much."

Rebecca sat upright and slowly smoothed the hair away from her face, tucking loose strands behind her ears. "Will you show me?"

"No. It's not right."

"It feels right." Rebecca leaned forward to kiss him, the way he taught her, the way she knew he enjoyed being kissed: thorough, heartfelt, and willing. She met equal parts resistance and reciprocation as Alden bent over the edge of the bed before forcing himself back into his seat.

"Becca, don't… you'll only make this more difficult."

She was injured and probably not fully aware of her request. Then again, she was also a woman who had endured kidnapping, fistfights, and explosions.

*Perhaps she **was** aware.*

Though she continued to beckon him, Alden would turn her down gently. This wasn't the first time he had broken a woman's heart. Many women swore their devotion to him—or *Julian*, rather—in the throes of midnight passion or the sweetness of a morning embrace. He did well to wipe their tears away before making his exodus, each time promising he would always think of them fondly. Those memories would casually fall away with each step, like dust from his boots.

But Alden would remember *this* moment. He took Rebecca's face in his hands, his thumb brushing away the teardrop that settled into a scar on her cheek. With each droplet he would clear, three more would take its place.

"You're so beautiful. Do you know that?" he said softly, thankful she couldn't see his heart breaking. Alden knew he was unworthy of such beauty, but that would never stop him from wanting it. The candle on the windowsill provided a spotlight as he moved forward to join her lips with his own, believing that if he closed his eyes tight enough, time would stop, and they could stay in this place forever.

But even forever wouldn't be long enough.

Alden rose to extinguish the candle. Now, only modest moonlight filled the space. "Rest now," he told her as he settled back into the chair. "I'll be right here when you wake up." But her hand soon found his, and Rebecca once again asked him to make love to her.

Beyond the traditional labels of family history or status, a name can influence power and alter perception. It might pave the way for future success and permanent significance. More than a mark of identity and a means of commanding attention, a name could invoke a spirit, strike fear in man's heart, or enhance his sense of belonging, validating his most innate human desires.

"Please..." Rebecca sighed in the darkness. "Please, *John*."

A name could also break down strongholds.

At long last, fingers feverishly fumbled over fabric and flesh accompanied by kisses, tears, and whisperings, which had been too long stifled until finally, *finally*, a connection. What began as two individual quests was now a paired expedition towards self-discovery, fully present and committed to the purpose of knowing something genuine. It was a place they would find together.

CHAPTER FORTY-ONE

The night was kind to them, elongating the hours and stretching its blanket of darkness well beyond the seams. Alden dozed on-and-off, but Rebecca slept soundly beside him. Though still dark outside, the morning was fast approaching. Gusts of wind danced on the rooftop while branches tapped at the bedroom window, imploring him to prepare for the imminent storm. Fingertips grazed Alden's side as Rebecca sleepily reached for him in response to nature's alarm clock.

Yes, Becca. I'm still here.

Smiling, Alden brought her closer to him. He could hold Rebecca this way if she rolled on her good side and left her wounded shoulder exposed. The makeshift stitches had held up better than he anticipated. Rebecca insisted that she was alright—that it wasn't too much for her to be with him, but even after being tender, Alden knew she would need to see a *real* doctor at some point.

"Becca?" he whispered.

"Mmm-hmm?"

"Run away with me."

He tried to ask before while they danced under the friendly moon, but this wasn't him talking with Julian's bravado, asking for a romantic rendezvous to which he always knew the answer. This was all him, and he was going all in. She could easily turn him down and have plenty of reason to do so.

Stirring, she answered, "I wish we could stay here."

"I do, too." And he meant it. If he could make it so, they would never leave that bed.

"Where would we go?" asked Rebecca, having yet to open her eyes. Alden's request was a well-known trope in the literary world. A forbidden romance between secret lovers who want desperately to be together, having no choice but to flee so they might find their own future happiness.

Alden paused a moment, still configuring the details. "Far from here."

They could go east or cross the border into Mexico.

"Away from the train?"

"Yes," he said, pressing a kiss against her temple.

Rebecca shifted, relishing the newness of waking up naked with a man. Her eyes practically glowed once she wiped the sleep away. "What's your last name?"

"What?"

She turned to face him. "I'll go with you—"

"—You will?"

"*If* you tell me your last name."

"Oh, what's in a name?" Alden posed, lowering his evasively cute gaze out of habit, though he knew quoting the Bard wouldn't avert her. She had explored him greatly, delighting that he was ticklish, and there wasn't a part of her body he hadn't claimed for himself. After being intimate, titles seemed trivial. She knew *him*; that was all that mattered.

"Well, I want it," Rebecca replied.

Alden gave a smiling stretch, pleased because he wanted Rebecca to have it, too. He already mentally hitched her full name to his convinced it flowed perfectly.

Alden was his middle name, and not even Roger knew of his ancestry—only Julian. It seemed enough time had passed to use his surname again, having saved it for the off-chance that he might one day start anew with someone he loved.

Love.

He loved her.

Turning his head, Alden whispered the long-lost family name into her ear. Rebecca grinned. *It did have a nice ring to it.*

"Now you'll go with me?" he asked. "You'll be mine?"

Rebecca drew him closer, having found a way to navigate him in the dark. "I thought I already was."

And just like that, he wanted her again.

After some time, Alden was dressed and on his feet. He would have to lead Gambit away from the farmhouse and sneak Rebecca down the stairs. Roger and Manny would need to know of their plan, though Alden was certain they would figure it out if he somehow missed the opportunity to tell them.

They would understand.

They would forgive him for not saying goodbye.

"If we're going to do this, it has to be now," he whispered to Rebecca. "The sun will be up soon. We have to be—"

"—Quiet?"

"*Silent.*"

Rebecca nodded and resisted the urge to pull him back into bed as Alden left her with only a kiss and a directive. *Wait for me. I'll tell you when it's time.* No longer a shadow but his own man, Alden was making plans for himself—for a *real* life—with *her*. They would be together, caring for each other for all their days as two people in love would unabashedly do. She beamed.

Love.

So, this is what it feels like.

The bedroom door soon clicked discreetly behind Alden, and he carefully crept to the stairwell. "Sinner," a voice scolded from around the corner. Alden froze.

Levi.

Levi was most dangerous when calmly observant. His pleasant tone and suggestive demeanor meant that his sinister wheels were spinning overtime. *He was onto them.* The bright orange glow of a cigarette surrendered his location. Alden would have tripped over him if he had moved any further.

"I'm messing with you," said the smoker. "It's too dark to tell if your expression is from surprise or exhausted satisfaction." Levi flicked stray ash into an empty tin cup. "I was going to check on our patient, but I suspect you've already thoroughly examined her. Took you long enough."

Alden swallowed back the sickening violation. "You were *listening*?" He and Rebecca tried to be subdued, but the thin walls of the farmhouse betrayed them.

Levi's smoke swirled in aggressive curlicues around him. "Bless your heart; you did try to be quiet. Don't worry; it was only me. I couldn't hear everything, but what I *did* hear I found to be wildly entertaining." He chuckled. "I bet you feel better now."

Knowing Levi's disgusting nature would surely press him for details, a now embarrassed Alden switched topics. They would talk business to deflect Levi's suspicion. Alden attempted to relax his body and joined Levi at the top of the stairs. "It looks like the rain has started again," he said. "We'll have to find a different route."

Levi grinned after Alden declined the drag he offered. For whatever reason, he had Alden shaking in his boots. "You should let me handle that. I know a detour."

"Roger knows the area," noted Alden.

"Not as well as I do."

Powerful winds clapped against the building's framework, causing both men to flinch. "Fucking shanty," Levi hissed. "This whole place is about to fall in on itself."

Alden nodded in nervous agreement. The two-story farmhouse had sounds and secrets that neither were familiar with. Levi took another heavy drag from his cigarette and continued the small-talk.

"This has been quite the eventful week."

"That it has."

The hallway window cast an interrogating spotlight on Alden. Levi shifted his bulky upper body to study his associate in what remained of the pale moonlight. *What was Alden hiding?* He'd been hasty in exiting the bedroom, and when they spoke, he seemed distracted. *Distracted.*

Sonofabitch, it happened right under his nose.

Levi hid his discovery, leaning in toward Alden to negate their tension. "But we're about done *here*, aren't we, Boss?"

Alden felt a drop of panicked sweat slide down his backbone. Levi's sudden sweetness made his stomach dip. He knew what Levi was alluding to. They would have to leave soon if they were going to catch that train. "Yeah," he nodded. "Almost."

"Well, if Roger's who you're after, don't let me stand in your way."

Levi extinguished his cigarette and hoisted himself using the handrail before slithering down the stairs. Alden followed suit, clutching the banister with a slippery hand. Levi's behavior suggested he'd be keeping a close watch on him and Becca. Getting to the horses undetected would be damned near impossible now.

"Alden, you've got to learn to control your impulses before you get us all killed!"

Roger's voice carried over the farmhouse's wraparound porch even in a whisper. Alden opposed leaving the home's interior if Rebecca needed him, or Levi continued snooping, but the three men needed a more private space to talk. The weather would mute their conversation, conveniently caught between blustery winds picking up at high speeds.

"¡Cállate!" Manny huffed. The winds were a *muffler*, not a *miracle*.

The breeze gave them a hefty preview of the nasty storm to follow and sprayed a mighty mist upon them. It felt as though God, Himself had blown a raspberry at their recklessness.

"We can't leave, can we?" Alden realized.

"You could, but it wouldn't be smart. I say we stick to the plan," Roger replied with a sigh.

"If we do this, I might never see her again." Alden felt the walls of remorse closing in with a new kind of fear. He should have slipped away the day before while Rebecca was unconscious, taking her with him. It would have been worth the risk, but he hadn't anticipated Rebecca living through the night, much less *sharing* it with her.

None had executed a hostage hand-off before, but even a successful delivery meant heightened security in the future. Alden couldn't return to Rosewood for some time—if ever. Roger slid down the support beam and began wringing his hands. This was exactly what he was afraid of.

"I still think it's worth a try." Manny nudged a stubborn raindrop off the edge of his nose, adding, "Roger's right. We should stick to the plan."

"I'm speechless," said Alden. "You actually *want* me to let Levi take the lead."

"Yes!" pressed Roger.

"You know where he'll take us," argued Alden in cyclical uneasiness.

"Yeah, *and*?"

"And I don't want to go back there, Rog."

With a shrug, Manny shook his head. "None of us do."

Alden continued. "If she knew what I did—"

"—What *we* did," Roger corrected.

"You have to trust that it won't matter," said Manny. "That place—what happened there—it's not who you are. You are not bound to this fate. You have the chance to start all over and be somebody else!"

"*I don't want to be somebody else!*" Alden raved with his hands now around Manny's collar in a hot-blooded retaliation. "I am *through* with being somebody else!"

"Then you know what you have to do!" Manny lessened as another showery mist scattered over them. He understood Alden's resistance. If they had another day or Levi was still unaware, Alden stood to have everything he wanted.

To be that close would scare anyone.

Roger nodded. "It's the only place that we—"

"—I know, Rog," Alden whispered.

The trio took a moment to consider what hung in the balance. Would a potentially happy future be worth revisiting the hellacious past? Alden lowered his head and moved his hands to Manny's shoulders, squeezing what words couldn't express. Scripture from the biblical book of Matthew echoed in his head:

If your right hand offends you, cut it off.

Severing ties with the criminal lifestyle and Julian's spirit would be difficult and dangerous. It might even kill him. This was much more than running away for love; it was separating himself from the things and people that no longer served him once and for all. Was it cowardice to admit that a part of him was afraid? Alden couldn't remember the last time he bet on *himself*. The heaviness of being Julian Crisp was all he'd known for nearly half his life.

"How do I do this, fellas?" he asked, finally looking at his friends. "There are no clear exits."

Roger straightened, blocking a gust of heavy wind from reaching the porch. "We'll make one for you."

Manny nodded in agreement. Despite the stormy weather approaching, the morning sun winked at them across the horizon as the rooster began to crow.

CHAPTER FORTY-TWO

The winds picked up with just enough rain to whip at their faces while riding, dampening their clothing and blurring their vision with each sprinkling swat. As mean-spirited as the weather was, Rebecca would have preferred the rain to the unsettling silence within their party. Alden had returned to the bedroom, disenchanted and stoic. With the directive he gave her, she expected a greater sense of urgency for their flight, but the further they traveled from the farmhouse, the more removed he became. The conversations Alden *did* have were with Roger and Manny, cryptic and soft-spoken.

"Pneumonia! Just what I always wanted," mumbled Simon as he wiped the rain from his face.

Rebecca gave a tiny smile, amused by the developing Disciple, who still possessed so many boyish attributes. She remembered that Alden was only a few years older than Simon when he started his life of crime. *An adolescent outlaw.* Sooner or later, corruption becomes commonplace. *When does one reach that point of no return?*

Roger's booming voice broke further contemplations.

"Levi, you piece of shit!"

The caravan reigned in abruptly near a small, secluded slice of land ironically named the *Newberry Farm.* Only, there was nothing *new* about this area, and no *berries* in sight.

"Why are we stopping *here*?" asked Manny.

Levi descended from his horse. "I thought *here* would be as good a place as any."

"No, not *here*. I don't want to do it *here*," said Alden.

"You've lost all jurisdiction, Aubrey," barked Levi. "You'll do it where I tell you."

Alden lowered Rebecca from Gambit, pulling her close enough to kiss her cheek tenderly. He'd lost the color in his face, and his hands trembled as Rebecca's eyes strained to meet him. *Something was very wrong.*

Levi snickered, swiping his hand across the thick leather seat while fat droplets of rain pelted his saddle, a *U-shaped* waterslide. "It's kinda poetic, come to think of it."

"I don't think he's got it in him," Simon offered as he propelled down his stallion.

Levi slapped his hand into a saddle puddle. "He was supposed to do it last night!"

"What is he talking about?" Rebecca whispered. She wouldn't take her eyes off Alden, whose breaths came short and thin. If it were possible, he was paler, and he wouldn't look at her.

"But then again, I can't say I wouldn't have done the same thing," poked Levi. "She *does* kinda grow on you."

Given how Levi spoke and the group's reaction, it seemed everyone knew they had spent the night together. Rebecca convinced herself that Alden wouldn't have shared such a private detail with anyone, especially *Levi*.

"Alden, I thought we were stopping at the train station," she said softly.

Levi chuckled, "Stupid woman…"

"There is no train!" Simon revealed with a swagger that made his mentor beam. His shotgun was readily armed and pointed at the back of Roger's head.

Levi had Manny under his own metallic intimidation. He turned to Rebecca. "Well, there *is* a train, sweetheart, but not for you."

Rebecca searched Alden again for answers. "I don't understand."

Looking away, Alden squared his shoulders. "I'll do it, Levi, just not *here*."

Simon rolled his eyes. "How many times have we heard that?"

It was then that Rebecca noticed Alden holding her by the wrist and not her hand. He hadn't held her this way since Sanctuary. His grasp was heavily stressed, tighter than she remembered.

"Alden," Rebecca wriggled her arm to get his attention. "Alden, you're hurting me." But Alden wouldn't look at her, nor would he loosen his grip.

Levi rested his arm on his saddle, still keeping Manny under a dangerously watchful eye. "What's the matter, Aubrey? You didn't tell her?"

Rebecca surveyed the burned-down farmhouse at the end of the hill. Thin sheets of rainfall framed the four graves planted adjacent to a homestead's remains, serving as an outline of the simple house that once stood. Charred and broken, the scaffold teetered on damaged land. "Tell me what?"

"Your boy's a kid-killer three times over," Levi declared. Adding with a smile, "Well, he didn't act alone. A little boy and two baby girls for what, thirty dollars?"

Manny spat in frustration. "We weren't after them! We were following orders!"

"Walter Newberry had what was coming to him," Roger interjected, slowly exiting his steed. "We didn't know he had kids! It was the middle of the night, for God's sake!"

Levi spun his weapon like a seasoned gunslinger, pointing at Alden, Manny, and Roger canonically. "You know what bothers me about comments like that? You stand there pretending to be repentant;

you're *reformed*, changed men. But you won't even own up to what you did. You make excuses for it!"

"We didn't have a choice!" Manny hollered. He had left Rico's support shortly after Roger dismounted, but Levi's gun held its target.

"There's another one!" scoffed Levi. "Bunch of hypocrites."

Roger's insides boiled as he contemplated his next move. Even with a gun, Simon was no threat. It was no more of a fair fight with Simon than for Manny to be with Levi. He could swat Simon's shotgun away, but that would end in a bloodbath.

"Would you mind getting that thing out of my face?" he growled. "We're on the same side!"

Simon leaned inward. "*Are we?*"

"So, what is this, a mutiny?" Manny called out.

Levi smirked. "Well, it ain't a prayer meeting!"

Alden endured the rain, wishing he, too, could dissolve into the earth. Having not yet drawn a weapon, he stood motionless, ashamed, cursing Julian and hating himself. Walter Newberry was originally Julian's mark, so he must have known Walter had children. Julian was aware of Alden's compassion for the innocent. He knew Alden was just impulsive enough to go back for them after the fire started.

Rebecca wavered in disbelief. Killing a grown man was one thing, but *children*? "Alden, you said your brother died in a fire."

As Alden stared through the blistered doorway of wet ash and soot, he was transported back to that critical moment. Walter Newberry had squelched on his debt. Roger and Manny secured the perimeter, but Alden struck the match. Such a minor act, so majorly destructive.

"I said there *was* a fire," he answered solemnly, the empty grey having returned to his eyes. Alden shifted to address Levi. "Let me take her down the hill," he pleaded. "I'll make it quick."

"You've had more than enough opportunities, Aubrey. *Now, get on with it!*"

Rebecca's rising anxiety peaked as Alden's grip tightened, and the four remaining men formed a circle around them, two of which moved under gunpoint. Now panicked, she turned to the others for an explanation.

"Manny?"

Manny sighed and folded his hands with the reverence of prayer.

"We tried to let you go so many times," he confessed.

She spun in the opposite direction. "Roger?"

Roger failed to look up from his shameful stance. "I'm real sorry, Miss Rebecca."

"That's why we let you walk around unfettered…" Manny continued. "You ran to that bounty hunter before we were ready for it. We had to get you further away from Sanctuary."

Together, the pair exchanged reasons for their deceit.

"But then Miss Alice saw you, so we had to change your appearance," said Roger. "After you kissed me in the street, we had to make sure you were hidden while we went after Simon."

"We even showed you how to defend yourself…"

"I couldn't do it."

"Nor could I."

Roger rubbed his forearms, feeling a chill, though he wasn't cold. "Every time we thought you'd run away, you didn't."

Rebecca's eyes widened as she again looked at Alden. "I promised I wouldn't."

After Roger and Manny both accepted their share of the blame, Alden finally faced her. "It wasn't their responsibility to dispose of you; it was mine." He resumed his explanation with a sullen, guilty countenance, allowing heavy raindrops to drip freely down his crestfallen face. "It's complicated."

There was a reason no one at camp was permitted to touch Rebecca but him. It was Julian's cruelest punishment yet. Alden had tried to warn Rebecca, to protect her, and spare her, but he could never get the timing right. His selfish actions sealed Rebecca's fate that very first evening. It would always end this way. *He never wanted to hurt her. He was simply following orders.* After all, Alden wasn't only responsible for himself. The rest of the Disciplines counted on Alden to follow through. Roger and Manny learned of his intentions in Discovery and were meant to assist, but equally struggled. Levi volunteered to complete the task, but Alden wouldn't allow it, for he knew what Levi would do. Upon leaving Discovery, those stolen moments that seemed so special were all shamelessly orchestrated. Almost every minute Alden spent alone with Rebecca was a premeditated setup, with him always leading her to a remote location where her body could easily be discarded. He *had* meant what he said about wanting her. Alden initially bartered for her safe return, but Julian convinced him it was a cheap infatuation and distraction. Julian used this vulnerability against Alden, promising that all would be forgiven once the job was done and that he would eventually forget about her. Alden never considered how strong his feelings were or the possibility that his affections might be reciprocated.

"I thought if I put it off for a while, it would be easier… But I couldn't do it," Alden confessed. "I even tried to turn you loose, and you came back. *Why did you come back?*"

"You *know* why." Rebecca shook as she attempted to free herself from the iron grip around her wrist, which shifted like a shackle but wouldn't break.

"A touching sentiment!" Levi applauded. "Personally, I don't give two shits about the reasoning, but I've been given strict instructions from Julian to make sure *this* happens so we can get back to work."

Manny growled. "I bet you *always* do what Julian says, don't you?"

Levi shrugged his brawny shoulders. "Look, no one *wants* to kill the disfigured girl, but it's got to be done." He stared down at Alden with a discriminating glare. "And if you don't do it, I will."

Roger was certain he heard Rebecca's heart break. She finally knew the truth, but nothing could right this wrong. He watched Alden respond to her queries mechanically with a stone-cold, shattered expression. All that progress made with him, all that time spent lifting Alden up in prayerful petition, defending him to Julian, and Manny giving counsel; it was all for naught.

Her tears soon united with the rain. "You're going to rob that train, aren't you? As Julian? That was the plan all along; only I was in the way."

Alden swallowed and sadly nodded.

"Was there ever a ransom?" she asked.

"Yes," he whispered.

"Yeah, but you were right about your daddy not giving a damn."

As Levi's taunts continued, Rebecca assessed Alden's earlier remarks regarding her worth; those kind words of encouragement and willingness to share so much of himself in a shy, subtle courtship were all a charade. He was Little Red's Wolf, a carpetbagger, a fraud. "Everything you've ever told me was a lie."

"Not everything," Alden reasoned, instinctually releasing Rebecca to reassure her, then reaching for her again. Rebecca batted his hands away, taking large steps to distance herself from him.

"*Don't touch me!* All those stories about your past with your brother and—" she retched at the words, "—those things you said you wanted for your life and—and how you felt about *me*—"

"—An impressive performance," Levi sang. "Though the 'bleeding heart' bit was a little much."

Rebecca spun to face Levi and acknowledge his recent medical treatment. "What about *this*? Why didn't you just leave me?"

Levi shook his head. "I knew you'd pull through. Alden was the skeptic."

It's only a flesh wound.

It's bleeding a lot for a flesh wound, Levi.

It's in a tricky spot.

Won't she bleed out if we don't do something?

Not necessarily.

How can you be sure?

Alden saw through Rebecca's memories of that fateful night. She'd heard what she wanted to hear. "We were too close to the main road into Jardín. I didn't think you'd survive, but we couldn't risk the owners of that farmhouse finding you if you did, so—"

"—*You told me that house was vacant!*" she cried.

Levi chuckled, "It is now."

Rebecca withered in disgust. "Alden, those people—you *didn't*?"

"*I* didn't," Alden affirmed. "I was with you."

"He never left you," Manny called from the other side of the circle. "He's telling the truth."

Levi clapped Manny on the back of the head to silence him. Manny was set on humanizing his friend, yet Alden knew nothing anyone said could atone for his deception. He and Rebecca were out of time. He'd finish this in a way that would honor Rebecca, but doing so would obliterate every remaining ounce of self-worth he had.

Manny watched as his friend struggled to summon strength.

Roger was right. This will kill him.

CHAPTER FORTY-THREE

You do business with the Devil, and you're bound to get burned.

Remembering Alden's words, Rebecca sobbed with blinding rage. More innocent lives were lost because of her. She should have alerted the lawman in Discovery when she had the chance, but Alden was so inviting with his verbal offer, so warm and charming. Rebecca knew she could never separate herself from the flesh he'd claimed—that she had so freely given to him, but she could claw and crunch at *his* flesh. She couldn't physically hurt him, but she would *try!* She could slap, scratch, and spit at him with newfound hatred. Her damaged shoulder would fail her, and Alden soon seized her by the wrists before bringing her into his chest. Rebecca wriggled in his grasp with mournful cries of his betrayal.

"You said you'd keep me safe! I didn't run! We had a deal!"

"None of us expected you to keep that promise," Roger proclaimed with guilty sorrow. If he were wiser, he could have prevented all this from happening. He could have stopped Alden from taking her to begin with or negotiated her release with Julian long before their journey began. He could have done *something.*

Exasperated, Rebecca leaned her head back into Alden's chest as she had done countless times before. "Of course! Because you're criminals! Cheats and liars, that's what you are!"

The group said nothing, and rain continued to fall gently on Rebecca's face in empathy, as though the sky had opened just for her. Alden's hands continued to shake, and she could feel his heartbeat pounding rapidly against her spine. She still carried the small blade Manny gave her, only it was just out of reach. Alden removed the folding knife from his gunbelt. He wanted to tell her he was sorry, that she had done well, and promise to use compassion as he silenced her.

"He ain't gonna do it," Levi teased.

Simon followed. "Where's your loyalty?"

"I am loyal!" Alden bellowed. His fingers searched for the tender spot on Rebecca's neck, making a mental blueprint as he slowly unfolded the knife with his thumb. She carried his scent mixed with something sweeter, something that was all her own, that he willed himself to always remember. Alden sighed and swallowed hard. The words were there; he knew what they tasted like because he whispered them to her while she was sleeping, yet he couldn't produce them.

"You look like you're about to be sick, Aubrey. Are you sure you can do this?"

"I told you I'll do it!" Alden roared, gnashing his teeth, knowing Levi wanted pain and blood. His hand crawled from Rebecca's neck to her mouth to keep her from screaming, but not before spreading his fingers to touch her soft face one last time.

He never cared about her scars.

He only cared about her.

Alden slid his foot between Rebecca's stance and swept her swiftly to the ground. *"Now! Do it now!"*

Rebecca felt the soiled soil rumble beneath her while Alden served as a human shield. He equipped the knife with his right hand while his left hand reached for his revolver. Along with Roger and Manny, Alden was poised to give his life. She buckled under the weight of his body, her face masked in mud while bullets buzzed around them. Grunts, groans, and gunshots grazed the grounds of the Newberry Farm until all that remained were the softened sounds of rain falling on failed agriculture.

A friendly voice called out to them. "Fellas? Miss Rebecca?"

It was Roger.

Rebecca held her breath as Alden rested heavily above her. He was still. *Too still.*

"We're here," Alden slowly answered.

Rebecca thrashed and kicked herself away from him. "Get off of me!" She rid her face of the wet earth as he withdrew, raising his hands in full surrender. He stayed on his knees, saying nothing, desperate for her mercy. His clothes were muddied, and stray bullets and debris had nicked him, but he was alive. Though furious, Rebecca understood that many of those bullets were meant for *her.*

"Simon's dead," said Roger, his face bloodied yet showing he would live to fight another day. "Poor kid."

Alden's eyes never left their focus on Rebecca, who slowly nodded with consent for him to stand. "What about Levi?"

Roger stopped to study Levi's injuries, noting the horses had skittered away in the scuffle. Levi was planted deeply into the ground, facedown, with a watered-down puddle of crimson forming around his ear. "Looks that way."

Roger's hefty footsteps squished in the distance. Alden rose to his feet and outstretched his hand. "Come on, Becca. We need to get out of here."

"*No!*" Rebecca cringed at the very idea of Alden touching her. She started to run but wouldn't get far, sliding forward as Alden wrapped himself around her in a strong-armed suspension. She could be angry and hysterical, just not *now.*

Struggling to suppress her, "Stop it! Stop fighting me! Listen! We *have* to go!"

"I'm not going anywhere with you—with *any* of you!"

"Becca, we can't stay here," Alden beseeched, rocking with her attempts to break free rather than resist them.

"*I trusted you!*"

"*I can still make this right,*" he implored with intense whisperings and eyes that performed a tearful duet. Promising not to raise his voice or his hands to her ever again, Alden lowered his volume to a calming voice of reason. "*Please let me make it right.*"

"Alden, those *children...*"

Alden felt Rebecca lessen in submission, and soon deep, gulping, raged sobs overwhelmed him, too, unearthing a droplet for every discretion, every lie, and every misdeed he performed as a Disciple.

"I tried," he shuddered. "When I heard them, I ran inside. I looked, but I couldn't—I couldn't get to them. Next thing I knew, the awning caved in, and I was trapped. Roger pulled me out before it all went down."

"Boss..." Roger's voice surged behind them.

But Alden continued to relive that moment. The farmhouse retaliated to the arson with profound rumblings and omissions of fiery cinder overhead. Alden would scream, and the house would swell inward to scream right back. *It went up in flames so quickly!* Smoke stuffed his lungs, stifling his throat in suffocation. He fought Roger in the doorway, with Manny beating down the flames that nearly consumed him. As they dragged him across the grass, Alden swung at his friends, cursing their names, kicking in response to the blinding physical pain with great anguish for what they had done.

"*I* should've died in that house, not them. There's not a night that goes by that I don't hear their screaming," he shivered. "Those kids—they were *good...* And *you* were good. *You're so good, Becca.* That's why I wanted you. I wanted to know goodness again—not because I thought it would help me—just to be near it for a while. These things—I've done horrible, unspeakable things, but they're not who I am, Becca. And they're not who I want to be."

"I know," she whispered. Suddenly, it all made sense to Rebecca: Roger's quest for salvation, Manny's desire for peace, Alden's instability; these men felt crippling remorse and carried the pain of unbelievably heavy guilt.

Alden buried his head into Rebecca's hair, silenced yet soothed in his submission. They said nothing for several minutes, choosing to simply hold each other and look away from the blackened house in the distance. They knew that staring at the absence of construction couldn't restore the wavering fixture any more than staring into a mirror would repair the integrity of her face, nor would it pardon the crimes he had committed.

"Boss…" Roger's calls expanded to a louder decibel.

Rebecca moved inward, reciprocating Alden's embrace. She heard him. He would have made a different choice for himself; only because of his genetic makeup, he was swindled. He was cheated out of it. Alden would try, but he would be haunted by his actions for the rest of his days, forever mourning a life he hadn't lived. Rebecca never considered herself a prize due to her own genetic disposition, yet Alden saw great value in her. *She* would be the one to save him because although she, too, was broken, she was good. Choosing *her* was validation, proving that Alden *was* capable of choosing good, even if he was unworthy of it. Rebecca remembered how Nicholas dismissed her worth and the value of their future together. In a way, Alden had shown her goodness, too.

"John!"

The couple broke apart to notice Roger, who fought for composure. He was the only other person standing in the wake of their dampened battlefield. At his feet lay their friend and peacekeeper.

The sky shrieked in dramatic despair. Manny had fallen.

CHAPTER FORTY-FOUR

They walked for hours, with Roger carrying Manny as the trio traveled through more rain until they found a suitable place to lay him to rest. Though there was a twinge of sympathy felt for Simon, it made sense only to take Manny.

Why would anyone want to bury a person who tried to kill them?

Rebecca never witnessed a man being put in the ground before, but Alden had undoubtedly dug a grave more times than he would have liked to admit. He and Roger were thankful for the remaining daylight that hung on long enough to complete their task. Fortunately, the Newberry Farm still had a shovel in the barn to bring with them; otherwise, they couldn't have buried him at all. A cozy grove with neighboring trees welcomed Manny into the afterlife.

He only wanted peace. He was at peace now.

Soft words were spoken as softer tears quietly escaped the mourning. Alden picked at the dirt under his fingernails, wishing they could have done more for their friend. Miguel Manuel Serrano had siblings back in Mexico but never shared how to contact them in the event of his death. They would need to find his family when this was all over. *And it would be over soon.*

In a surprising character swap, Roger chose to take Manny's blade while Alden donned the silver necklace of Manny's patron saint, *Michael.*

In the book of Revelations, Michael, the Archangel, fought and defeated Satan. In the Catholic faith, Saint Michael was a symbol of protection. Alden ran his fingers over the medallion in reverence. He never put much stock into cultivating the sacred into his own life, but his friend had.

How many prayers did Manny lift to Heaven on his behalf?

Alden's mother, Aubrey, prayed for him at the beginning of each day. She was always the first to rise and would regularly anoint the doorways of their home with oil. Alden could recall how she squeezed his hand at mealtimes in his youth before they said, "Amen."

*How many of **her** prayers had carried over, keeping Alden safe all these years?*

Much like a cat with nine lives, Alden considered how many possible prayers of protection he had remaining from those who went before him. They were all there: Benjamin and his parents, seated at a table in Paradise, waiting for him. He hoped Manny had made it into Heaven.

If Manny were there, maybe he could end up there, too.

A balmy smile spread across his face, spreading wider at the sight of Rebecca, who found solace in the surrounding countryside. Her entire universe was shaken after leaving Rosewood, but Rebecca somehow seemed more established and empowered. She'd since grown fond of the wilderness during her adventure, which was so majestically unapologetic for its faults. She passed by one tree that had been struck by lightning, appearing split clean down the middle, while another grew adamantly between two patches of rocky earth. No matter what the elements dished out, the world had a way of rebuilding.

Rebecca gradually worked her way to Alden, who sat quietly facing an open world on a nearby tree stump. She slipped behind him, sliding her good arm around his neck and nuzzling at his shoulders, resting her hands in front like a friendly scarf before bringing him in. "How are you?"

Dazed, Alden blinked slowly. His speech was sluggish and spattered with shock, but he raised a courting hand to join hers. "I am at capacity," he said, gently strumming her wrist and the invisible hairs that graced her forearm with his thumb. Even after so much time alongside him and the rest of the ragtag group, Rebecca was satin. He would miss her softness and how wonderful it felt to have her so near.

Rebecca drew closer. "Where's Roger?"

"He needed a minute."

They *all* needed a minute, but the steam engine was scheduled to arrive the next morning. As Alden looked at the stars, they reminded him of sands in a celestial hourglass. The little time they had left was precious. He nixed the idea of robbing the luxury railway. Returning Rebecca to Rosewood, where she would be safe among her kind, was now their main objective. It was the only way to protect her. It wasn't what he wanted, not even close. But as long as Julian Crisp lived, he was a threat. If they ran, he could find them. If he found them, he'd kill Rebecca and make him watch. If she died—

—*No, don't think about that.*

"What do *you* need?" Rebecca pressed as she accepted his redirection, leading her around to face him.

"I need you to know that at no point was I ever going to hurt you. All I've wanted since the night I took you was to get you home unharmed. Now, I realize how it must have looked, but I *never*—" he sighed. "I would have told you, but it had to be convincing."

Rebecca nodded, understanding that her genuine terror was required to execute his plan. Alden intended to take Rebecca down the hill away from the fight, stage a homicide, and return to the group where he, Roger, and Manny could overthrow the others. If it had worked, the couple would have gotten away. Had their foes been matched differently, had they been given more time, or had Alden somehow gained the upper hand, Manny might still be alive.

Alden's hands swept over and across her skirt, up to her waist, where they stayed. He nestled just below her navel and sighed in both comfort and determination. "I'm going to finish this, Becca." He lifted his head before gently bringing her hands to his own. With the way he was poised, it mirrored a proposal.

"I'd make you a promise if I thought I could keep it."

She pursed her lips. "Make it anyway."

They both knew what was going to happen. Even if he did kill Julian, Alden would have to disappear completely to survive. She was the daughter of a public figure, easily identifiable by her scars. He would forever be evading the law, which was making more and more advancements in criminal investigations daily. Asking Rebecca to wait or suggest that she accept the risks and disappear with him would be unfair.

But it would be nice to dream.

Alden positioned Rebecca onto his lap, letting one knee serve as an ottoman.

"When this is over, and we're together again, we'll cross the border into Mexico."

"What about Roger?" she asked.

"He'll be there, too," promised Alden. "We couldn't keep him away if we tried."

Roger was family, after all.

The image formed in their minds faster than expected, colorfully animated with possibility. Both could taste the enchanting territory, savoring its rich culture while creating a new life together.

"We can learn the Fandango," dreamed Rebecca.

Alden grinned. "Absolutely."

"We'd have a home together."

"Yes."

"And after some time, we could start a family."

With a gulp, Alden looked away. Facing her was too painful, and it blew his mind that anyone would want to create a family with him. He sighed. *This was why dreaming hurt.* He knew Rebecca *would* share his story with the world. She was resilient. She would live a long, happy life. At least for a moment, he had been a part of it.

Rebecca remembered how magical Manny made Mexico sound. "I still don't know Spanish."

"I'll teach you," he promised. "It's easier to practice when you live there."

She ran her fingers through his hair, "Cabello."

"Correct."

Playfully tapping his nose, "Nariz."

Alden smiled and raised his hand to thumb her bottom lip.

"Beso," she whispered, bringing her mouth to his before he could respond.

"There's lots of other words I wanted to teach you," his blue eyes sparkled. "That was the most appropriate one I could think of at the time. I guess you figured it out."

Rebecca shrugged, "Well, I had to. We never *did* get to finish our lesson."

"You're right; we didn't."

A breeze blew Rebecca's hair off her shoulders. All the remaining pins were lost in Newberry, yet she found she rather enjoyed the freedom of being caught in the wind. "Would you like to finish it?"

Alden lifted his eyes, turning to examine the surrounding area, having decoded her question not by what she asked but how she asked. The fact that Roger could return at any moment mattered little. *What was it about being in nature with her that felt so perfect, as though nothing could touch them?*

"*Here?*" he asked.

Rebecca nodded opposite where Roger had traveled to an assortment of trees that promised both privacy and shelter. "There."

"Now?"

"*Now.*"

And so, they ventured into the timberland. There were no secrets or hidden agendas within their nest, only an intimate exchange of ecstasy beautifully woven into a tantric tapestry.

CHAPTER FORTY-FIVE

The next morning, Rebecca titled on a stretch of land that towered over an open railroad track below. "Where's the Grady Train Station?"

"This *is* the station," replied Alden.

Puzzled, Rebecca looked to her partner for clarification. The lack of an actual building was a minor detail compared to what was to follow. "How do you expect me to board? Where will the train stop?"

"Well, unless you have a ticket somewhere I haven't seen—"

Rebecca blushed at Alden's comment.

"—This is how we do it," Roger concluded with an extended arm to gesticulate.

"We?"

"Outlaws," said Roger.

Alden stepped in. "It's not going that fast, and the rain has stopped, so you shouldn't have any trouble."

"You mean I have to jump?" she gasped.

The two men shrugged. Jumping on and off trains was as pedestrian for them as firing a gun.

Rebecca hugged her injured shoulder. "Will it hurt?"

Roger shifted. "It won't feel *good*."

Rebecca shook her head. "There's no way... What if I fall off?"

"Don't." Roger's warning was frank. A big man like him could survive such a rebound with the earth, but Rebecca wouldn't bounce back so easily.

"Try to land on this side," coached Alden, tenderly grazing her good shoulder. If the horses were still with them, it would've been a much easier transfer. "Climb down the ladder onto the car, find the conductor or luggage handlers—anyone, tell them who you are. They'll help you."

Roger added, "We'll watch for a few minutes and see you off."

Rebecca studied the approaching train. She was a *damsel*, not a *daredevil*! What if she missed the transport entirely? What if she was pulled down below the traveling cars and torn to shreds?

"You've survived more than most men we know," Roger joked. He gave her little time to worry further, bringing her inward. "Goodbye, Miss Rebecca."

"Goodbye, Roger," said Rebecca, wishing to take his voice with her whenever she needed warmth.

Alden ran a nervous hand across his face, having forgotten the feeling of an honest goodbye. Losing Manny or his loved ones in death was different, for none had much say in their departures. This was a bittersweet willingness to relinquish a part of himself, the part he never knew he needed. "Bye, sweetheart."

Rebecca smiled, surprised at her own lack of tears as Alden took her aside. He searched himself for the last kiss she would want: the heartbreaking release or an honorable receipt that concluded their romance. Their first kiss would always be memorable, but Alden also wanted this closing affection to leave an imprint. So, he held nothing back, hoping that Rebecca would be equally grateful for having loved and been loved.

There would be no regrets.

They warned Rebecca not to hesitate, stating that a running start would best guarantee an efficient landing. Alden and Roger gave her room, and soon Rebecca wooed gravity with lively legs rushing and a navy-blue skirt parachuting beneath. The impact of the railway carriage felt about as well as to be expected, rudely knocking the wind out of Rebecca in a forced salutation before she could claw her way to the edge of the steel shell.

Roger watched as she slowly panned to the side ladder before disappearing into the train's interior. "She made it!" he cheered.

"I knew she would," bowed Alden, his heartache palpable.

"You *had* to let her go," said Roger, sensing Alden's remorse. "It was the only way to save her."

Alden concurred. Rebecca was gone, so there was nothing more to say about the matter. He would use the journey home to clear his head and prepare for the ensuing confrontation with Julian.

"Are you sure you want to do this?" asked Roger.

"I'm sure."

"Then let's find some horses so we can get started."

Alden stared overhead, initially deciding *not* to watch the steam engine float away but giving in to temptation after a few minutes. He could swear the air around him held onto her scent in consolation. When an unusual train appendage caught his eye, Alden washed white in horror. Rebecca had successfully caught the locomotive, but what she failed to see was Edwin and Rueben scrambling over the steam engine's exterior, climbing atop two of the cars behind her.

Wait...that's not right.

They're not supposed to be on that train.

If Edwin and Rueben are there, who else is on board?

Alden and Roger landed right square in the middle of the train tops. As they instructed Rebecca to do, the men worked their way into the nearest car. The pair took an overview of the cabin, promptly pausing to assess any possible dangers. The luxury train provided a breathtaking view of beautiful landscapes from both sides. With this means of transport, one got what they paid for—a sophisticated way to travel, more pleasant than by carriage. During a routine heist, the transfer of authority would have been smooth for the Disciples, easy even—a brief introduction to those onboard followed by an instructional guide and a quick sweep down the line. There was no cause for alarm or reason to move from their seats. It would all be over soon, and if everyone cooperated, they'd "get along just fine."

But what happened here was pandemonium.

Scenes of ghosts and gunshots haunted the bar car with the screams of terrified travelers. Fear was the catalyst for much of the committed carnage. While not as fully packed as a commercially occupied train car, evidence of panicked passengers bunted the aisles through scattered luggage, hats, the occasional shoe, and discarded luxuries like books and backgammon. Shattered glass and puddles of brandy outlined the commuters' bodies strewn over the compartment's interior flooring. Those that had drawn attention to themselves or proven troublesome were gunned down instantly. Alden gasped. They boarded mere minutes after their colleagues.

How could so much damage be carried out in so little time?

Alden believed that stickups were executed quickly due to adrenaline and nerves, but the aftermath of his accomplices proved that in real-time, they *did* happen fast.

Becca.

She couldn't be more than a car or two away.

In the corner, near the next car's entryway, was a familiar friend's body.

Edwin.

It only took one bullet to bring him down. He was slumped in a corner, hatless, and hugging at the wound that had taken his life. Alden gave a heavy sigh as he crouched down to return Edwin's cap to its rightful place, shaken at the injustice of the brilliant mind in that pointed, little, balding head having gone to waste. As he stood, Alden and Roger noticed another associate, friendly and unthreatening.

"Rueben!"

After seeing two of their comrades dead, Alden and Roger went in for a full hug, which Rueben reciprocated.

"What happened here?" asked Alden.

"It's Julian. He's lost his damned mind. When he told us he was coming along, Edwin and I figured he was up to no good. I thought this was just a robbery at first, but…" Rueben continued catching his breath. "Me and Edwin—we *tried* to get away so that one of us could warn you. The three of us and Phillip—we were never more than a day or so behind y'all, but we lost you after Brigham."

Alden processed the information, recalling his final night at Sanctuary. The hostile exchange with Julian lasted over an hour with much gnawing and gnashing of teeth…

"What were you gonna do, huh? What was your plan? To play like she's your little woman, and that bedroom is your happy home?" Julian laughed. "Did you honestly believe that if you pretended, she'd somehow warm up to the idea?" He paused to light a cigarette. "I know what Vernon would say to all this. I don't think you've made your daddy too proud, either."

Alden clenched his fists. Julian knew that mentioning his father was a low blow.

*"You can stop acting like you've fucked her 'cause I know you haven't. You say you want her, but you won't take her." Flicking the ashes, "I know you, John; you'll be bored within a week, and then you'll be **begging** me to get rid of her. Although, it's funny—it's fitting, really—even though you've found a girl that's more pathetic than you, she'll never love you. People like us, we don't get love. At best, we get loyalty." Adding with a chuckle, "Tell you what, forget the girl. I'll buy you a puppy instead!"*

Julian continued to taunt his duplicate. After years of enduring his own psychological abuse from Vernon, it was second nature. "Let's say I **did** allow her to stay; even if you do manage to talk her into bed, she'll always resent you. 'Cause **I'll** have a go, and then **Phillip** and—ooh, maybe we could have a raffle!"

"Stop it, Julian," Alden shook in unbearable anger.

"When Levi breaks her in, my God, she'll **hate** you!"

Alden gritted his teeth. "I'm warning you."

"And if she doesn't then, once she finds out you barbequed some innocent—"

"**—Shut your goddamned mouth!**"

"It doesn't matter what you do; it'll never change what you did," purred Julian, "You know I'm right."

Alden's eyes watered, then squished at the pain spreading across his left hand. In frustration, he'd put his fist clean through the bedroom wall. **She can never know.** Julian took a judging look at Alden's bloody knuckles and shook his head. In their youth, Vernon used many tools to break them, but shame worked every time.

"Go in there and finish it, John."

"No."

"No?" Julian spat. "No?! **You've lost your mind!**"

"I won't do it," Alden calmly whispered.

"Yeah, I've heard that before."

Alden fought an urge to hit the wall again. Roger was right: he had to protect her, now. He couldn't let Julian goad him into foolishly losing his own life.

"You might be my boss, but you're not the boss of me."

"Where do you get off talking to me like that?" Julian's jaw dropped from shock. "**You are way out of line!**"

Still astonished, Julian extinguished his cigarette and started towards the door. He would remind Alden of the consequences of such *defiance. Alden wiped the blood from his knuckles and joined him, matching his pace, stride for stride.*

"Where are you going?"

"To get the others. They've waited for her long enough."

"No," said Alden, catching Julian's shoulder. "Do you hear me? I won't allow it!"

Julian flinched back as though Alden were a leper, unworthy of touching him. "It's over, John. This ends tonight." With that, the Disciple leader continued his exit.

"Julian, please!"

Julian stopped. The last time he heard Alden beg was as a teenager in the jailhouse. "I'm listening."

"I do want her," Alden confessed. "I just—I need more time."

"So, take her with you," Julian proposed with a shrug.

"To Grady?"

"Where you kill her once you've had her is immaterial." Julian turned. "Actually, why don't you take Roger and Manny with you? If you can't do it, I know they will. They're always volunteering to save your ass."

"I can do it, Julian."

"Like Aponi's sister?"

Alden took a deep inhalation through his nose to combat the sickening memory. When the massacre started, he had hesitated during their scuffle, and, at the last second, Catori broke free of him, making a mad dash to the woods. Alden helplessly watched as Levi silenced Aponi's older sister less than ten yards from her freedom. As he recalled Catori's final moments and envisioned Rebecca in that place, Alden turned away, only for Julian to pull him to the present.

"When you get back, I expect a full remission," he said, smiling. "And details." Peppermint-Tobacco clashed as the mirror images stood mere inches from each other. "How she smells, how she tastes, how you did it, how it felt… Everything."

"Fine."

"Everything, John."

"Alright! Fine!"

Alden nudged past him, knuckles bloodied, glass crunching with each footstep.

"Good. Now get out of here before I change my mind," Julian seethed, angry that he hadn't broken Alden completely. Then, exerting his dominance in one final threat. **"And if you pull another stunt like that, Alden, I'll kill you myself!"**

Saying nothing nor turning back to look at him, Alden left the bedroom...

Finally, it registered. Even if Alden had smothered her in Discovery, strangled her at Pearson Pointe, or drowned her in the creek near Jardín, ending Rebecca's life wasn't Alden's punishment. It was a means to an end.

"Julian wanted to make sure you got on the train," Rueben revealed. "He's planning to fake his own death, only—"

"—It'll be me instead of him," Alden realized.

"Exactly."

Roger shook his head. "We'd have never seen it coming. What's his move?"

"Dynamite," said Rueben. "He had Levi stash about ten or twelve sticks all over this thing while it was still in Rosewood before he headed to Discovery. That's why he left before y'all."

"Which was it? Ten or twelve?" pressed Roger.

"I don't know! Edwin and I got as many as we could before Phillip started shooting. I only pretended to be hit, but Edwin..." Rueben's countenance fell with the same sorrow as the card house they'd constructed in Sanctuary.

"How many would you say you found?" asked Alden.

"Five, maybe six each," Rueben replied. "We got rid of them; threw 'em out a window."

Roger watched the doors on either side of the compartment. "We need a plan. *Fast*."

Rueben agreed. "Phillip's making his way to the front. My guess is that's where most of the dynamite is hidden. I don't know where Julian went, but I heard him say they'd blast it from both ends."

Alden performed a quick maintenance check on his weapons. All firearms were in working order. "Jesus, isn't one explosion enough?"

Roger shrugged. "Well, you know Julian…"

Vernon's protégé was known for his dramatic flair.

Alden nodded. "We'll split up. Let's keep our eyes open for any nooks where one could hide something small. If either of you sees Becca—"

"*—I knew it! I knew it all along!*" Rueben burst.

"We can talk about that later, Rueben," Alden continued with a slight smile. "In the meantime, get as many people off this train as possible. I don't care if you have to push them out."

"I don't think there's many people left!"

"*We have to try!*"

As footsteps passed and the sound of doors closing faded in with the trolley's rocky rhythms, Rebecca let out a muffled whimper from behind the bar. Finding Levi alive and onboard the train initially made her freeze, unable to fight. He was no longer the polished man she'd grown accustomed to seeing, with dirt and mud caked all over his rumpled person, showing that no effort was made to wash the dried blood from his skull. He had kept her hidden, pinned to the floor, with one hand clamped tightly over her mouth and the other holding a hearty shard of glass against her throat.

"Don't you worry, sweetheart," he whispered, planting a sloppy-wet kiss against her temple. "Your boy's exactly where he needs to be."

Rueben and Edwin never saw Levi board the train, but Phillip and Julian had. Victory was in clear sight, and that made his trousers tighten. *Speaking of needs...* His weapon still in place, Levi lifted his other hand from Rebecca's mouth and began to roam down her front, pausing to stroke and squeeze each body part he had fantasized about. This time, no one would be around to stop him. Rebecca squirmed in the confinement of his arms, his heavy body forcing pops and pulls with each effort. The train's vibration resonated underneath, forcing them to bump against each other, making the pairing even more enjoyable for him and disgusting for her. He pulled up the skirted layers of her dress, exposing her bare legs. Rebecca swatted and kicked until the shard of glass gave a sharp reminder of its presence, her place, and who was in charge. If she screamed, it would be the last thing she ever did.

Rebecca permitted Levi to mount her and graze over the areas that would please him the most, the parts that would keep him distracted long enough for her to reach where she had secured *her* weapon. Alden must have known that Levi would try to violate her at some point, and Manny's modest blade was just discreet enough to preserve without detection. Once she obtained the dagger, Rebecca swiped up, stamped down, and twisted with a justified flourish of defense. Levi howled as the knife slashed across his right cheek and then into his shoulder, causing him to topple over while he clawed at his profile, the blood seeping in between his fingers. He rolled to his knees, resting on his laurels as Rebecca pushed herself upright.

"You bitch!" he snarled. "*This* will leave a scar!"

Channeling her inner lioness, Rebecca smiled with a raw yet womanly growl. "Now you look like *me!*"

At this, Levi lunged forward, but not before she would lift her knee to firmly meet him in the groin. Levi howled again and jabbed a thick thumb into the bullet wound he repaired only a day prior. Rebecca cried in twisted agony and quickly scrambled to the central aisle.

Which way did Alden go?

Knowing he instructed his men to split up, Rebecca wagged her head at both possible routes. Levi held himself in misery, groaning as he recovered while Rebecca made her exit, opting to head for the back of the train. Though it was his own, Levi relished in the fresh blood spilled, smearing it all over his face.

He *could* go after her…

But he had bigger fish to fry.

CHAPTER FORTY-SIX

Roger and Rueben were caught in a shoot-out with Phillip shortly after leaving the bar car. Pellets plinked and planked between them, creating a crossfire of ricocheted bullets. From behind a cabin door, the pair tag-teamed their opponent, who seemed to have a never-ending supply of ammunition.

"We've got to stop this train!" yelled Rueben beyond their barricade.

"I know!"

The duo proposed a truce between them, but there was no reasoning with the tertiary tribesman. Because he said nothing, Phillip had an additional level of stealth, and the increasing volume of his fired shots told both Disciples that Phillip was closing in on them.

"*Ah, shit!*" Roger exclaimed as a bullet grazed his knuckles. His firearm fell, giving a slight bounce into the middle of the aisle. Roger bent down to retrieve it, forcing himself into the covert horizontal position, knowing his hefty size would make him an easy target. Soon, the shiny hardware was within his reach, but a pair of shinier boots stopped him from stretching further. No shots were fired for several seconds. Roger gulped at the realization that Rueben had most likely been hit, and *he, too,* was about to die. Heavy wisps of unpitched humor traveled toward Roger, as they were the most vocalese Phillip could produce. Roger heard his assassin pull back the hammer moments before a shot from beyond knocked Phillip to the ground.

Rueben smiled and helped Roger to his feet.

"I told you I was a faster draw than—"

Rueben's chest suddenly contracted as a short, sharp shove sent him into the wall. When on the receiving side of a revolver, the *crack* of gunfire resonates differently, a surprise to them both. Roger quickly ducked at the incoming barrage of bullets. It wasn't until after he emptied his own weapon into Phillip that Roger knew Rueben was lung-shot. Roger promptly positioned his friend injured-side down, only to witness a wheezing protest as air and blood fought for seniority. Life slid through Rueben's lips in a steady stream, tapering into a bubbly foam. Within minutes, his lungs had collapsed. He was gone.

Heartbroken, Roger closed Rueben's eyes and took a moment to bid his friend farewell. "You and Manny—y'all were the best of us," he sniffed. "You deserved more."

Using Rueben's gun, Roger fired one last shot into Phillip's corpse to ensure he wouldn't rise again. With that, Roger pressed onward to the front of the train, climbing up and sliding down the pebbled path toward the unmistakably dirty smell of coal. Chalk-like and with a grainy residue, the fossil fuel left filthy fingerprints on Roger's back when he ventured into the train's front compartment.

The engine box stood 7 x 7 x 7, scarcely big enough to comfortably fit a normal-sized man, let alone *Roger*. Sweat dripped off his beard as he quickly studied the abundance of gauges and switches that accessorized the gaudy navigation panel. No dynamite was found, only the neighboring firebox that gave its friendly greeting. Roger swore at the incoming steam, squinting at the glaring heat and lifting his chin to assess the overhead mechanics. Running a hand through his messy mane, he revisited the main dashboard. Even the switches that *were* labeled proved confusing.

"Now, how do you stop this thing?"

"You don't."

When Levi attacked, Roger was ready for him. Roger quickly disarmed Levi with a headbutt, and soon, both men were throwing punches within the cramped quarters like twins feuding in the womb. Having secured him into a slippery chokehold, Roger repeatedly brought Levi's bloodied head down onto the window base, which was open by design. Levi's massive fists beat at Roger's lower half until striking a kidney, bringing Roger to his knees. Levi retrieved his weapon from its location, wading it sadistically like a baton.

"It's like my mother used to say, Rog: 'Spare the rod, spoil the child!'"

Levi kicked and struck his rival with such ferocity that he could no longer discern what blood was his own. Roger blocked as much of Levi's buffaloing as he could, using his forearms and hands to shield himself from the blunt force, breaking several fingers in the process yet miraculously maintaining consciousness.

Roger's eyes watered at the acrid heat that singed his beard while his hands strained towards a revolver just within reach. As Levi bared down to bring Roger's face into the fiery furnace, the revolver spat into Levi's belly, leaving a twisted expression on his face. Knowing he'd lost, Levi slid downward. Roger reveled in how close he had narrowly avoided expiration, giving himself several hearty huffs of relief and even a few nervous laughs. Then, he returned his attention to the steering column.

We all know it's gonna take more than a bullet to shut him up!

As Alden's words echoed in Roger's memory, so came Levi's resurrection. The red-faced strongman knocked Roger's firearm out the window in one fantastic blow, rendering Roger defenseless once again. Seeing double, Roger reached within the stacks of coal for something, *anything*, that could be used as a deterrent. Levi parted his lips, preparing to spew more wicked misrepresentations of the Gospel, but Roger silenced his sacrilege with a righteous rock. The holy pacifier wedged between Levi's teeth, scraping as Roger shoved the block further down his throat. Levi's eyes widened amongst gulped gurgles and choked objections; his hands clasped around Roger's forearms in vain as Roger pressed harder and harder until his efforts silenced the scoundrel once and for all.

Out of breath and wishing he had something epic to say, Roger dropped Levi's lifeless body to the ground, giving a gracious, smiling nod in reverence to the *true* champion. His enemy had been defeated, and yet Roger knew *this* victory wasn't his to claim. Without the assistance of a higher power, it could have just as easily been him.

"Thank you, Lord."

Meanwhile, further down the locomotive, Alden climbed onto the next-to-last car. After scouring the top of the train and coming across nothing, he passed through two connected compartments, quickly backtracking within the transport, hoping to find Rebecca somewhere in the middle. Blocking a center aisle was the train conductor's body alongside a bulky knapsack. *It was the loot.* Alden gave the crewman's corpse a brief pat-down, just in case, and quickly opened the bounty bag to search its contents. *No way was it left there by accident.* It made little sense to hide dynamite there, but Julian's plans seldom held logic. Alden lowered his head for only a moment when he heard a sweet voice call his name from the other side of the cabin.

Becca.

Her shoulder was bloodied again, and she trembled with frigidity, possibly from shock. When Rebecca made no effort to go to him, Alden dropped the bounty and started her direction.

"That's close enough," Julian warned as he stepped out from among the shadows with a barrel positioned between her shoulder blades. It turns out Rebecca was walking directly below Alden while he scaled the train's exterior. Alden skidded to a halt.

"Thanks for your help, darlin'," Julian purred, stroking the back of her head in the same fashion he had at Sanctuary before bringing the heavy butt of his revolver down. Instinctually, Alden went for his gun, but within an instant, Julian's aim was positioned right on him. "I don't think you want to do that, John."

"Oh, but I do."

Their individual draw times were nearly in sync, as they were conditioned to be so long ago, though Alden knew Julian's to be microseconds behind. Alden drew with his left hand as Julian quickly switched his target to an unconscious Rebecca, whom he dropped to the floor.

"As I was saying, you don't want to do that, John."

Alden's brave face broke. He *had* the shot. All he had to do was take it.

But would it be worth the risk?

In the face of death, Julian laughed.

"Ooh-hoo-hoo! This is going to be *fun!*"

CHAPTER FORTY-SEVEN

"Stay where you are!"

Alden raised his arms to follow Julian's directive under gunpoint. The Disciple leader had flung Rebecca to the floor, blocking the walkway, with a small stream of blood trickling down her forehead. Alden visually searched for signs of life. She was breathing but remained out of reach.

"Toss your weapons out the window," said Julian. "*Both* of them." He switched his aim back to Rebecca and pulled the hammer. "Do it, or I'll put a bullet in her."

Alden slid along a side panel wall to discard his firearms into the blurry landscape beyond a partially lowered passenger window. He quickly returned to the aisle, becoming Julian's target once more.

"Good," Julian smiled, pleased at Alden's cooperation. "Now, where's the take?"

Alden nodded in the direction of the abandoned bounty bag. Julian stepped over Rebecca, closing the gap between them, keeping the barrel pointed at Alden's head.

"Pick it up, turn around, and walk to the private car."

Shoot him or join him.

It seemed Alden was eighteen all over again.

He could attempt to disarm Julian, but the tight spacing of the traveling tin can might betray him, and he couldn't risk another stray bullet striking Rebecca. Alden sunk to recover the carpetbag as instructed and led Julian through several cars toward the back of the train, past the long corridor to the entrance of a tiny palace. They then approached the compartment door, whose lock was shot out, permitting it to applaud on the upbeat of the train's rhythm. A grand archway welcomed them into the sitting area that housed a fully stocked bar, a cold box, a piano, and furniture graced with diamond-shaped upholstery patterns of plush green and gold velvet.

Upon crossing the threshold, Alden hurled the bag of loot into the corner, twisting to jab Julian in the side with his elbow as the *crack* of a fiery discharge resounded along his temple. Alden's ringing ears compromised his equilibrium but not his ability to gain the upper hand. Shots two, three, four, and five sprayed the room, tossed like destructive confetti until Julian finally dropped the empty handgun.

Like most Disciples, Alden and Julian sparred playfully over the years to learn each other's fighting strategies. Hooks, jabs, and punches—both straight and overhand—flew through the air in an attempt to meet their destiny. Few swings made an impact, for both could anticipate their opponent's next move. Alden used the remaining unturned fixtures to his advantage, creating obstacles for Julian and putting the necessary space between them to prepare an attack. Then, going low, Alden crashed into his enemy, taking him to the ground, settling on both sides and double-dealing each repetitive blow. Julian used one hand to guard his face and reached for a broken chair leg to his right with the other. The blunt object forced Alden's dismount, highlighting his hair with streaks of blood. As both men jumped to their feet, Julian came in with a forward punch. Alden blocked his advance, ducking to slide into Julian's open chest space, wrapping one arm around his neck while the other fastened to form a triangle. Julian clawed for release within Alden's chokehold, but Alden steadied himself, keeping his head upright and squeezed tightly, huffing with gulps of pure adrenaline. When a hot stamp struck his side, just above his hip, Alden contracted, loosening his grip as he fell. He hadn't been *punched*; he'd been *stabbed*.

A mighty tide of crimson escaped Alden as he crunched, willing himself to stand; his pierced midsection seemingly fitted with an iron corset. Julian completed the reversal and staggered to him, rocking against the train's tempo, gasping for breath before digging his booted heel into Alden's shoulder, forcing him face-first into the floor. A great yelp filled the cabin as Julian drove the knife into Alden a second time, with the blade puncturing his upper back.

An out-of-breath Julian accessed his physical damage and crossed to a hanging oil lamp mounted on the wall. He removed the fixture from its installation point, releasing oily fumes to coagulate mid-air. Julian coughed and sniffed, parting the clouds with a wave of his hand.

"You're going to die on this train, John."

As Julian sprinkled oil along the cabin, he explained his original plan to blow the Grady train to Kingdom Come after the robbery. But, seeing that the explosives were discarded, he opted to set it ablaze instead. The passengers would all attest that they saw him—those still living, anyway. Levi was commissioned to kill Phillip, and vice versa, once they reached the rendezvous point. When the authorities found all the other outlaws dead in the wreckage, including Alden, the singular Disciple would be free.

It was the perfect getaway, with no loose ends.

After several attempts, Alden settled upright through the shaking, sweaty shock, struggling to apply pressure in two separate places. Though the blood wasn't in his lungs, a bright red river flowed into a blackish-purple puddle around him. No matter how grizzly a person's death could be, it never ceased to amaze Alden how much a person could bleed. Alden propped himself against the cabin wall.

"You stole...everything from me," he said.

"Bandit," shrugged Julian. "It's a shame, too; all that time and effort wasted on a couple of kids and a *Piece of Calico*! I hope she was worth it."

"You…and Vernon…you cheated me…"

"Out of what? Dying in that jail? Or did you *want* them to hang you?"

Alden swallowed hard. What had Vernon said about the foreman's death so many years ago? *Very messy.* He always figured it was Julian, but Alden had to be certain that his fate wasn't coincidental. "It was you… with the foreman. Wasn't it?"

Julian fought back a snicker. "It took you *this* long to figure that out?"

Settling his rage, Alden slowly unsheathed his last shiny line of defense. Though it felt pathetic due to its limited size, and he never *planned* on using it, Alden was glad for having taken the Derringer from Nicholas's body.

"Give me the matches, Julian."

This time, Julian *did* laugh. "What is that—*Oh, come on!* You're not about to shoot me with a mouse gun! I can't imagine it holds more than a couple of rounds."

Unwavering, Alden persisted. "One is all I need."

"Look at you, John! That thing's no bigger than a harmonica, and you can barely hold it up!"

"Give me the matches!"

"Fine," Julian shrugged, tossing the small brown box into Alden's lap. "I'll just wait until you pass out, which, from the looks of it, should be any minute now."

The Derringer then replied with a swift kick to Julian's chest, its crimson footprint leaving an outward trail. While it wasn't the hit he'd hoped for, Alden wounded Julian enough to incapacitate him.

"You son of a bitch!" gasped Julian. "I gave you what you wanted, and you *still* shot me!"

Alden smiled as he set the empty weapon aside and attempted a shrug. "Bandit."

Julian slid down the opposite wall, appalled by the turn of events. Alden gave a sigh of relief. *Justice.* Whether he lived or died, there would be justice.

"What about your girl, huh?" Julian snarled. "What do you think will happen to her if we're caught and marched to the gallows? You'll be dead, and she'll be ruined. Not that she wasn't already..."

Even as they fought to keep consciousness, Julian had to rub it in.

"My guess is you took every last bit of honor she had."

"I love her," Alden confessed.

"Do you? Do you *really*, John?" mocked Julian, seeming more annoyed than agonized by his injury. "If that's the case, you were better off letting one of us live. You might have given her some hope, something to hold onto, but you're such a selfish bastard. You always have been."

"Go to Hell."

Julian retched. "Oh, I'm gonna. But don't worry, I'll save you a seat."

Alden scanned the surrounding area for possible exits: the window beside him, the cupola above them, and the caboose's back door. He could *not* let Julian get away. Heartache seemed inevitable for Rebecca, no matter what he decided to do. The only thing that *would* make a difference was if Julian lived.

It has to be done.

The shortness of breath—that floating dysphoria—felt all too familiar. Alden could recall the dizziness he first experienced after abusing the laudanum at Sanctuary and how confusing it was to find his flesh resisting the dopamine rush. *It hurt.* Yes, it *was* possible to know pain while feeling nothing. Painful nothingness was his life for nearly twenty years. He had hoped it would be a smooth transition, but as he saw Rebecca sleeping on the bedroom floor, his body willed him to live. He even tried to call for her, that sweet name dripping off his lips, but his body wouldn't phonate, and soon he slipped away with Rebecca in that closing line of sight. That's how he would prefer to leave the world—with his eyes upon her. Dying now meant staring into a cruel mirror of irony, for Julian was the last and probably the first thing Alden would see as he transitioned into the afterlife.

"Come away, O Human Child..."

Suddenly, he was there, a young man sitting with family in his childhood home. The memories were much clearer now. Alden could hear them all laughing, loving. Benjamin told an original tall tale, a little boy embellishing in such a fantastical way that the outrageous story seemed plausible. Alden could smell his father's pipe and knew that his mother only winked at him because somehow, beyond the grave, she had seen him. His eyes widened.

"To the waters and the wild..."

He was then seated at a poker table with random players shape-shifting by the second. They were all dead men, most of them by his own hand. Their faces—he had long forgotten their names, but he remembered all of their faces. Those glassy stares remained fixated on him, along with Vernon and an ever-peaceful Manny, who waited for Alden to lay his cards on the table.

"With a faery, hand in hand..."

Roses and bluebonnets filled the library of Windhaven Hall, along with buzzworthy songs from friendly honeybees. Rebecca was reading by a window, wearing his cornflower blue shirt.

It looked better on her, anyway.

A tear slid down his cheek. The possibility of a different life with Rebecca had skimmed his fingertips in fiction-fringed *almost*. With a heavy heart, Alden whispered, "The world's more full of weeping than you can understand."

"What are you mumbling about?" snarled Julian, who was losing energy as quickly as he was color.

It took some doing to exercise his basic motor skills, yet Alden managed to retrieve one match from the tiny box. *Phosphoric salvation.* With the amount of oil Julian spilled, it would only take a minute or two for the compartment to be flooded in flames. Julian flinched in protest as a slight smile spread across Alden's lips. He knew what was coming and was prepared to let the inferno take him completely. But Julian was terrified, and it showed.

"Oh, you're tough, now!" Julian scoffed.

The objections continued, yet Alden concentrated on positioning his thumbnail along the tip of the match. Weeks ago, that nail would have been a nub, but there had been growth. And *he* had grown.

"You don't have it in you, John. You're not like me... You were *never* like me!"

Alden's eyes lifted to Julian, having completely lost their grey and were now a fully focused blue. "No," he said. "I was better."

CHAPTER FORTY-EIGHT

September 1898

"*Goddamnit*," Ranger Whatley muttered under his breath. It was uncharacteristic for him to swear in front of a woman, but he was no closer to apprehending Julian Crisp than before they started.

Rebecca shifted her weight, her story having reached its conclusion. Though it was always the same, each testimony seemed more exhausting than the one before.

"The pin was pulled to separate us from the cars that caught fire," she said.

"Any idea who did it?" asked Everett.

"No, I was unconscious. It wasn't until I reached the station in Grady that I woke up. That's where I first gave my statement."

Ranger Lawrence nodded. The line rider gave his report shortly after the investigation started. The train's last known check-in perfectly aligned with Rebecca's account of the robbery.

"Well, nothing about your story has changed," huffed Ranger Whatley in disappointment.

"There's nothing *to* change," she said. "I have nothing to gain from lying to you."

Before Horace could argue, Everett intervened. "Nobody said you were lying, Miss McNamara."

The trio stirred in their uneasiness, knowing Everett had just told a lie of his own. Rebecca smoothed her blouse, slightly adjusting the silver brooch on her right shoulder. Everett took to polishing his spectacles along his shirtsleeve, not because they were dirty, but because it was something to do. Whatley rubbed at his temples, taking in a breath so deep his nostrils flared. He would have to question Rebecca another way if she wouldn't tilt to their diplomacy.

Perhaps she's a pawn in Samuel McNamara's political game.

"Have there been any irregular visitors at Windhaven Hall? Any suspicious correspondence?"

Rebecca shrugged. "Not that I'm aware of. Why?"

"There's an important election coming up."

"Every election is important," she noted.

Whatley chuckled. "If you could vote, you might feel differently."

What did a woman know about politics?

"Do you know of any business your father may have had with the criminals in question?" he continued.

"Business?"

"Do you think your father might have arranged your abduction?" Everett secured the frames back over his face to make eye contact with his superior, but Whatley wouldn't be bothered. He was too busy locking in on Rebecca, whose sweet disposition soured quickly.

"What? No!"

"There's a host of folks all over the state that are counting on us to bring the Disciples to justice," Whatley offered. "The fact that we don't know if we're looking for one or two men puts us in quite a pickle. If I start a manhunt for this *Aubrey* character and it proves unfruitful, that would be a waste of precious hours and resources, not to mention an embarrassment to all parties involved."

The Ranger bent an elbow over his knee to lean in. He was close enough for Rebecca to smell his aftershave. *Masculine citrus with a soapy finish, smooth and refined.*

"You don't want to waste our time, do you? You don't want to tarnish our reputations? We're the ones trying to help you, after all. And think about your father. Hasn't he been through enough?"

Rebecca cradled her injured arm. She only wore the sling because her father told her to. Samuel McNamara appeared beside himself upon her homecoming, even going so far as to have a welcome party present, but once the guests of Windhaven Hall had left, so did his enthusiasm. Whatley sensed her withdrawal and maintained course.

"Why are you endorsing this theory that Crisp used a duplicate all these years?"

"It's not a theory, Ranger Whatley."

You must believe me.

When Rebecca looked to Everett for support, he faltered. Everett sighed.

Why is she making this so difficult?

Rebecca shook her head. "Gentlemen, what is it that you would like me to say? Might it be easier for you if there weren't a duplicate? I promised Alden that the world would know he exists."

"Even if it kills him? Because that's what will happen when we find him."

Lawrence beat Whatley to the punch, a fact that made Whatley's mustache twitch. *He* was supposed to be leading the questioning. Rather than scowl, Horace bit his tongue and allied with his apprentice.

Everett persisted, "You said you knew his surname, yet you never mentioned what it was."

"I don't remember," she lied. If Alden *were* alive, giving away his family name would be his undoing.

"Do you understand that men like him will say anything to save their own skin?" pressed Whatley.

Now facing intimidation from both sides, Rebecca began to fidget for the first time since the interview started. "Alden wouldn't—he wouldn't do that."

"No one would think any less of you for changing your story," Everett reasoned. "Tell us the truth."

"I *am* telling you the truth!"

"Then, where is he?" Whatley barked.

"I don't know!"

"Not even a *guess*?" The Ranger was insistent. "How do we know that you, a woman so fond of storytelling, aren't fully aware of Crisp's whereabouts and haven't manufactured this little narrative to protect him?"

Horace was standing now, berating Rebecca with the fervor of an angry mob. Rebecca clenched her fists. These men wouldn't break her; they wouldn't make her cry or surrender any more secrets.

"Am I looking for one man or two?"

Everett rose to meet his mentor. "Sir, with all due respect, I think we should—"

"—Am I looking for one man or two?" Whatley growled, his hands clasped over her shoulders, shaking Rebecca with obsessive urgency. It was inappropriate to handle a lady with such hostility, not to mention unprofessional.

Everett fought to break Whatley's hold, "Sir, that's enough!"

But Horace nudged his colleague aside. *"Am I looking for one man or two?"*

"Whatley!"

Rebecca went paper-white in Ranger Whatley's grasp, visibly alarmed but not shedding a tear. Whatley, realizing he had forgotten himself, exited the library in embarrassed haste. Rebecca took a moment to reclaim her composure, smoothing fallen strands of hair before settling onto the sofa.

"He doesn't believe me."

"You needn't concern yourself with what's believable," said Everett. "Let's focus on the facts."

Sitting alongside her, Everett placed a familiar object on the table before them. Rebecca gasped. Even without the fading "J" imprinted on the handle, she would know that folding knife anywhere.

"We found this in between some seats on the third car. The private car at the end was in ashes when we finally got to investigate. No bodies or human remains were found in that section of the transport or the surrounding area. The only leading information we have is this knife and what you've shared."

Rebecca shook with possibility. "So, there's a chance—"

"—*Yes*. That's why this is so important. Given the circumstances, it would be understandable if you were overwhelmed and got carried away when initially questioned."

"I did *not* get carried away," she sizzled.

He lessened. "You do realize that if what you say is true and there *are* two men, there's nothing you or anybody else can do to help him once he's caught. Not your father, not Ranger Whatley, not even me."

"I do."

Everett lifted his glasses to rub the ridge of his nose. "Why are you giving him up so easily?"

"I only wish to cooperate," said Rebecca.

Everett smiled slightly, "No, what you're playing is a parlay."

"Why would I do that?"

"You think we're withholding."

"Are you?"

The remaining lawman took to pushing the sofa's chocolatey fabric once more. He needed it to be over. He was in his prime; his talents could be best used elsewhere. The criminal justice system was evolving along with the rest of society. There were other wrongdoers to apprehend, ones that would be easier to catch. The Grady train fire had all but destroyed the last remaining band of outlaws in the territory. *And good riddance!* Yet Everett knew Ranger Whatley wouldn't rest until every Disciple was apprehended. He knew how the pursuit stole years of Whatley's life and impacted his career. The last thing Everett wanted was a wild goose chase.

He surrendered. "Like you, Miss McNamara, I love the written word. So, I know there's more than one way to tell a story..." His caramel eyes met hers. "We *do* have a surviving Disciple in custody. I can't say who—that's privileged information, but you should know that his account differs significantly from your testimony."

"I want to see him."

"You don't even know who it is. And a jailhouse is no place for a lady."

Rebecca batted her eyelashes to feign ignorance. All women kept this skill in their arsenal, but it was best used in moderation.

She was a weak, defenseless creature. Only a big, strong man would save her!

"It might help my memory. Come to think of it, maybe Ranger Whatley is right. Maybe I *am* confused."

Everett crossed his arms.

She's good.

She's very, very good.

He would have no choice but to indulge her.

The Rosewood Jail proved unimpressive, looking nothing more than a largely modeled outhouse. Rebecca pinched her nose. *It smelled the same, too.*

Then she saw him.

"Roger!"

Rebecca flew past the lawmen to Roger's holding area. Though imprisoned, Roger appeared unharmed. He wore the same clothes as the morning she last saw him and desperately needed a bath, but nevertheless, it was wonderful to see a friend.

For how long had he been confined mere miles from her home?

"Miss Rebecca."

It puzzled her as to how Roger became detained in the first place. She wondered if the structural integrity of the mediocre cell, whose ceiling was barely tall enough to graze the top of his head, could hold him. "You should've told me it was him!" she said, looking sternly at the Rangers, who both made a point to closely watch their exchange.

"Would that have changed your statement?" asked Whatley.

Rebecca returned to Roger, who rested his head between the bars like a bored, caged animal. He could easily break out of his chamber; she was sure of it.

What was keeping him there?

"I trust you've been treated fairly?" she asked.

"Not at all," he replied.

"Do you have a lawyer?"

"Nope, and I don't want one," he said. Roger reached through the barriers to tenderly touch her cheek, then stopped himself. "I'm glad you're alright."

There was a dullness to the sparkle in his eyes. He was acting strangely. He seemed…*different*. Rebecca couldn't place it, but she knew something had changed. She gave Roger another look-over. He wasn't as dirty as much as he was disheveled. Soot, sweat, and singed hairs framed his fuzzy face. His fingers were individually wrapped in gauze, with pus seeping through the bandages. He'd been burned, though his wounds were nowhere near as serious as those that Alden bore from Newberry.

"You pulled the pin," she realized. "You saved my life."

Roger shrugged. "Seemed like a good idea at the time. Anyway, it's the least I could do."

Rebecca's face fell. *He's never this distant.*

Was it his current surroundings, or was he genuinely unhappy to see her?

"Enough pleasantries," Ranger Whatley scolded. "Tell her what you told me."

A look of legitimate pain spread across Roger, his eyes deviating from their baseline as he searched for the gumption to speak.

"I don't think I can. I mean, *look at her.*"

Rebecca stifled her shock with a backward step. It was the first time Roger had ever spoken of her appearance in such a way. Whatley gently led her back to Roger's cell.

"We had a deal, Mister Mercer. I expect you to uphold your end. *Now, tell her.*"

Roger huffed and scratched his cheek. "These men said that you, uh, mentioned a fella who ran with us—that rode with us. You said he was identical to Julian. His name was Andrew?"

"*Alden*, Roger. You know his name," she protested. "You were there when he took me. You were there the whole time... You met him on the side of the road years ago. He was—you gave him your hat."

Roger swallowed hard and hung his head. *"Damn you, Julian. I didn't step in when I should have. The way Julian carried on, dangling you like a piece of meat to the others. He kept saying he had ungodly plans for you. And then he—"* Roger grimaced.

"Roger, what are you doing?" Rebecca stammered.

"We waited ten days for your father's reply. You were so brave, Miss Rebecca. I knew *Levi* would, but I never thought *Julian* would actually do it. I didn't think the others would, either. I just followed orders. It wasn't right. I *knew* it wasn't right."

"Stop it, Roger! *Just stop it!*"

Whatley lowered his gaze, and Everett watched in horror as truths were revealed.

"I'm thankful you've survived," said Roger. "Relieved even, but these men should know that this tale of nobility you've created on our behalf is a falsehood. I can't, in good conscience, let it continue. We *weren't* decent to you, not one bit, and as for this *Alden Aubrey*... He was never there."

Hot tears poured down Rebecca's cheeks. Suggesting that her testimony was a complete fabrication proved cruel and ridiculous. She slapped at the bars in hysterical justification.

"That's not what happened! I know what I saw! You—you're lying!"

Roger ran a hand through his hair, on the verge of a breakdown. "I wish I were. I wish I could be the man in your story. I'm real sorry, Miss Rebecca. For everything."

Soon, faces and conversations started to shift in Rebecca's memory. She was another Ophelia losing her mind. *Get thee to a nunnery!* Flashes of moments flowed in and out of her mental folds like a cross-stitch. Her eyes fluttered wildly as she attempted to process Roger's suggested revisions, but some changes simply couldn't compute. Rebecca screamed at his deception, and it took many efforts for Whatley to remove her from the room. Roger turned away, noticeably distressed, hiding in the darkest part of his cell. Everett shuddered in disbelief. He hoped Rebecca's account was factual, but her response to Roger's statement said it all.

After what they did, of course, she would make it all up.

"You just stood there and let it happen, didn't you?" Everett seethed. "You let those men—your *friends*—beat her, and then—"

"—Yes."

"I can't wait until we find Crisp because when we do—"

"—You're not gonna find him," pledged Roger. "You can't catch a shadow."

A cold sweat washed over Ranger Lawrence before evaporating into a steaming, righteous anger. He was fed up with despicable men and their selfishness. They had wreaked havoc on all that was good and pure in the world for long enough. The lawman retrieved a shotgun from the corner of the room. Even as he loaded and positioned the barrel between the metal bars, Roger remained facing the cell wall.

"Shooting an unarmed man in the back is beneath you, Lawrence."

"So, turn around and face me!" Everett demanded.

"I'm not worth it," mumbled Roger as he slowly complied. "So, save your bullets."

He's right. A quick death is too good for him.

Everett cursed the convict *and* himself as he begrudgingly lowered the weapon.

"I hope they hang you *twice*."

CHAPTER FORTY-NINE

Keeping Rebecca subdued enough to bring her home proved challenging for Ranger Whatley. His outburst earlier in the day kept him from passing judgment when Mister McNamara met them on the porch. Rebecca was weak from resisting the officer, crying with great travail, inconsolable in her shaken state. What began as shrieks and sobs soon turned into softened sighs of exhaustion, and a hefty steward named Stephen carried Rebecca to her room along with the assistance of Maya, the parlor maid. Whatley adjusted his sleeves.

I'm getting too old for this.

If Rebecca were *his* daughter, he would have sought psychiatric treatment, an exorcist, or any intervention to deliver her from devastation.

"Well, she's *not* your daughter, Whatley," said Samuel. "I appreciate your concern, but what Rebecca needs now is rest and time with family."

"Sir, if this continues, it won't be a suggestion."

Samuel stewed in his embarrassment. "I understand. Thank you, officer."

Once the ranger had left, Samuel called upon Doctor Fields, Rosewood's singular physician and long-time family friend. The extreme behaviors of women baffled them, but clinical trials suggested many advancements in such studies. There *were* options.

"I don't want her going to one of those places where she's strapped to a bed and poked like some sort of steed!" Samuel persisted. "She's never carried on like this. She doesn't even use smelling salts!"

Was Rebecca sensitive?

Sure, she's a woman.

Passionate?

She gets that from her mother.

Insane?

*Not **my** daughter.*

With a sigh, Samuel permitted Doctor Fields to administer the morphine, and within minutes, relief, along with an unsettling silence, filled Windhaven Hall for many hours.

When she awoke the next morning, Rebecca went downstairs to the home office. She tapped lightly on the door, waiting for admittance.

"Come in!"

Rebecca entered her father's study, stopping in the center of the room. A sophisticated base for administrative purposes, whether for work or remedial tasks; this was where decisions were made, where the flames of change could ignite! As a child, Rebecca loved musing about the space, filled with moody, masculine colors of earth and rich chocolates, joined by dark wood paneling on smooth oak walls, built-in shelves, and a fireplace. The scent of smoked cigars lingered above them, embedded into the plaster ceiling medallions and stenciled borders. It somehow seemed less extraordinary than she remembered. *Everything seemed duller now.*

Samuel welcomed his daughter with an artificial greeting that tested the waters for fear of setting her off again. "Good morning, darling. How was your…nap?"

"Well, I wasn't tired."

Not physically, anyway.

"But you are feeling better? Should I fetch Dr. Fields? He inquired about you not half an hour ago."

"No, thank you."

Samuel had yet to move from behind the custom-made partner's desk of Mahogany, brass fittings, and a green leather top. As Rebecca sat in an amber-colored armchair, Mister McNamara settled into his captain's chair.

"Why don't you go back to bed, and I'll have Beth or Maya bring you some tea?"

"Daddy, I'm fine. Really."

But her tone wasn't convincing. In truth, Rebecca could scarcely get her brain to stop flashing the memories of actions, faces, and words from weeks past. Additionally, a small part of her believed if she fell asleep for too long, she would awaken to find herself back at Sanctuary, or worse—that it was all a dream. The morphine only made it worse.

Samuel cleared his throat. His recommendation for a *siesta* had not been a request. *After that little display at the jailhouse, Rebecca would do as she was told.*

Still, he knew he needed to be gentle with his daughter. Anything less might sit poorly with the multitude of eyes and ears observing Windhaven Hall.

"You've been through a great ordeal," he said. "You need to rest."

His attention returned to the stacks of documents sprawled across his workstation. It must have been a productive morning, as tea dribble was already on his lapel. Rebecca scooted forward in her chair.

"Are you busy?" she asked.

"Ah, a little, but I can spare a minute or two." Samuel placed the papers aside. "What's on your mind?"

"I was hoping to speak with you about that town I saw during my time away."

"Yes, Brenham."

"*Brigham*, Daddy."

"What about it?"

Rebecca glared at her father. She had already told him about the tragic town's history and the fate of what was once such a promising settlement. If he would only consider the jobs it could create, of the opportunities for growth and expansion. It would definitely be an investment, but there was still time to act. Brigham wasn't dead yet.

Samuel deterred. "Brigham is in an entirely different county, Rebecca."

"Surely you know someone who could help. Think of all the good you could do!"

Samuel shook his head, knowing why it meant so much to her. *All criminals came from their own version of Brigham.* Management of such towns were financial matters—business affairs, not philanthropic endeavors. Leveling the place would be far more cost-efficient than trying to save it.

"Rosewood is my primary concern at the moment. Let's start with our own town before trying to help someone else's, alright?"

Her father then went back to work, scooping and sifting through stacks of parchment across his exquisite desk. Rebecca tilted her head. *There it was.* Julian's ransom note that possessed her signature alongside the strand of cinnamon hair Alden confiscated, tightly twisted into a single line of thought.

You were right about your daddy not giving a damn.

Levi's words felt even more painful the second time around. A shockwave of disbelief shot out from her fingertips, her eyes, her nose, and the points of her shoes. "You left me there."

Without lifting his head, "Hmm?"

The realization felt akin to taking another bullet. Sure, her father was a busy man. Rebecca's capture was on his list of things to do, but it wasn't a priority. His lack of urgency spoke volumes.

"You left me there?" Huffs of heartache heaved out of Rebecca's chest.

*Had he no concern for what happened to her? Of what **could** have happened?*

Samuel slowly redirected his gaze, first to Rebecca and then to the letter. "Listen—"

"—*You left me there! With murders and rapists!*"

"Sweetheart, there's no negotiating with men like that."

"You didn't even try! I thought that they were lying to me, that this never got to you, but it *did*! And you—*why would you do that?*"

The patriarch took a deep breath and prepared to console his daughter. Moving the evidence of his carelessness aside, Samuel stood to take Rebecca's hand. "All that matters is that you're home. Everything is going to be alright. You're safe now."

"For how long?"

"What?" He was patting her, much as he would a little girl disappointed over a broken toy. She reclaimed her hand with words as icy hot as her temperament.

"How long will I be safe? It's only a matter of time until you're pawning me off again to someone I hardly know."

"Rebecca—"

"—You knew I didn't want to marry Nicholas. You knew what kind of a man he was, what kind of life I would have with him, and you agreed to it, anyway."

"I did what I thought was best. Any other daughter would be grateful."

Both were traveling on a wiry, thin line. Was this tightrope-walking tradition or treason? Soon, one of them would say something they might regret.

Yes, this conversation would never be forgotten.

"I am not *any* daughter," Rebecca posed. "I'm *your* daughter!

Samuel ran both hands through his ever-graying hair, now in distressed disarray. "I understand you're upset because those low-lives were unfriendly to you."

"*Unfriendly?!* Is that what you believe? That I was somehow inconvenienced by all this as though it were mud on my shoe?"

Gritting his teeth, "I am aware of your personal accounts on the matter, and I would like to keep those *intimate* details private. The less attention we draw to ourselves during this time, the better. It would be best for all of us to move on with our lives and forget that it ever happened."

"But it *did* happen!

"What should I have done? What should I do now, Rebecca? Give me a solution!"

"Tell me *why*! I need to understand!"

Samuel McNamara crossed his arms, his eyes downcast and lacking the energy to argue. Rebecca continued to wait for his gaze to meet hers, for an answer he wouldn't produce.

He was ashamed.

Perhaps his hands were tied.

Or maybe he had selfishly hoped she would disappear.

That would have made things much easier and almost ensured a positive outcome in the election.

Their sighs broke the extended silence. Rebecca loved her father, even if he did have a motive, but he no longer had a hold over her. "I want my dowry and the additional funds you promised Nicholas."

Samuel leaned on his desk, giving a slight chuckle. "What would you even do with all that money?"

"I'd write."

He shook his head. "My dear, you ask too much. Even if I *wanted* to give—"

"—Are you saying you don't?"

"What I want is irrelevant. It doesn't work that way, Rebecca."

"Would it be different if I were a man?"

Generally, a child never prematurely inquired about their inheritance, but Rebecca would forgo etiquette's infrastructure. After what she experienced, Rebecca felt not only entitled but due. Stepping forward, Rebecca began.

"There's a great number of people who would pay to hear my story."

"Yet you will say nothing," sizzled Samuel with the familiar wave of a cautionary finger. "Not another word about this Alden-Crisp fellow or any other attachments."

"Why? Because it will hurt your campaign?"

The veins in his forehead bulging, "Because it's a family matter and family matters stay in the family! *And I because I said so!*"

"I made a promise, and I must keep it," she persisted. "The world *will* know the story of those men and what transpired while I was with them." Pausing, Rebecca straightened, bringing both hands up in front of her chest and pressing the tips of her fingers together. "But the way I remember *your* role depends entirely on you."

Samuel's eyes widened in disbelief. "You would blackmail your own father?"

"Call it what you like. After all, I *have* been in the company of criminals."

"Cowards!" Samuel spat.

Pointing back at her father, Rebecca engaged. "*You* decided to ignore the ransom demands! *You* were the coward! It's your choice, Daddy. If you choose not to give me what I want, everyone will know the truth. And if you send me away—if I mysteriously disappear—well, I can only guess how your supporters might react."

"You know *exactly* how they would react! I wouldn't get elected to do as much as judge a pie contest!"

He was right. The public would view him as a monster who exhibited the same cowardice he claimed outlaws possessed. Varying degrees of sensitivity kept Samuel and Rebecca at an impasse. *What had they become?* Both deserved peace and yet both would grieve, him the loss of a daughter and her a father.

Samuel submitted. "How much do you want?"

Rebecca considered the cost of discretion. Her father all but knew she was a "fallen woman"; he at least suspected as much, which would have social consequences, to be sure, but Rebecca no longer cared. She wasn't interested in protocol or propriety. She'd had honeysuckle, moonshine, and music. She faced dangers he would never know and had a love he would never understand. There was no need to explain herself to him or any man, yet Rebecca knew little about the cost of secrecy because she never shared her secrets with others before meeting the Disciples.

Should prudence have a price?

*Did **her** silence have any value at all?*

Smiling, she answered. "Stretch your mind for a ridiculous number. Add a dollar for every time you've offended, rejected, or forgotten about me. Then multiply it by the number of years you've done this and round it up. Once we have that number, we can negotiate."

Alden was correct about Rebecca having the prowess to fight for what she wanted. Delivering his words on personal worth added necessary force to that *bite* he encouraged her to save. With another sigh, Samuel McNamara scribbled a number onto a piece of parchment.

"Will this suffice? Or do you want more?"

A sum more generous than anticipated, it was an amount that communicated to Rebecca that she was being both *bought* out and encouraged to *stay* out. Rebecca understood that luxuries wouldn't be in her future. She would have to be smart with her money and budget.

Nevertheless, Rebecca remained determined and optimistic. More and more women were becoming independent, making way for themselves.

It could be done.

"No," she replied. "That's plenty."

Samuel nodded, now a businessman relieved at the completion of their transaction. He turned his back to her, allowing the forgiving sun to comfort him through a window. "Give me the afternoon."

"Very well."

"Where will you go?" he inquired, still sunbathing. "What are your plans?"

"Does it matter?"

"Let me arrange for an escort," pleaded Samuel.

"I don't need a man."

"Rebecca, you cannot possibly go alone!"

"So now you're suddenly concerned about my safety?"

Once again, they faced each other. Samuel's authoritative hand came down sharply on the desk to make his point. He expected his daughter to flinch, fearing his release of frustration, but Rebecca wouldn't be moved. His countenance fell, his eyes misted. "I'm your father."

"And that will never change."

Samuel kept a Smith and Wesson Russian .44 tucked away in a desk drawer. He retrieved the revolver and a box of bullets and placed them in front of her. Having a fine grip and nickel finish, the robust paperweight seemed fancier than the weapons she saw the Disciples carry. Heavier, too. Rebecca never considered the possibility of her father owning a gun, much less operating one.

"Should I show you how to use it?" he asked.

"That won't be necessary." Rebecca looked past the ransom note that continued to taunt her and slowly removed her father's sidearm from the desk. It *was* heavier.

"Everything I ever did for you was out of love," he gulped. "I loved you the best way I could."

The trembling in his voice was foreign to Rebecca. Rather than let her emotions get the best of her, Rebecca simply concurred and whispered, "I know."

There was no final embrace, merely an acknowledgment of the farewell. Upon her noble exit, Rebecca caught a glimpse of her reflection in the hallway mirror, a fixture she passed many times and, like all mirrors, tried to ignore. She stopped. Something was different about the woman in the looking glass. Rebecca was a new woman with a new life, illustrated by change and circumstance that wasn't decided for her.

She had taken ownership of her destiny.

She was equipped and fully prepared to protect that freedom at any cost.

She never felt more beautiful.

CHAPTER FIFTY

"Silly woman, you almost ruined the whole thing!"

At daybreak, Rebecca had barely begun her journey when Roger suddenly appeared in the stables. Experience taught her not to scream when startled and, much to her own amusement, not to be surprised by his arrival. She stomped her foot.

"I knew you could get out of that cell!"

"I was biding my time," he explained.

A locked door has never stopped me.

"And that was reason enough to make me appear as though I was delusional?"

Roger leaned over the stall housing. It was taller than he but reachable with the aid of an overturned wheelbarrow. "It had to be done. It had to be believable."

Rebecca's face reddened. *Another ruse!* "Just once, I would like someone to let me in on the plan!"

"Spoken like a true outlaw," smiled Roger.

Pausing their reunion, "Everett...Ranger Lawrence—you didn't—?" Rebecca bit her lip. She believed the lawman to be genuinely good. Whatley, on the other hand...

"—No, but he's going to have a mighty bad headache when he wakes up."

Horseback, they ventured out the back of the stables under the guise of pre-sunrise. Each explorer was searching for the same treasure, but Roger had his own itinerary and navigated with more reliable coordinates.

"You don't have to come along if you don't want to, Miss Rebecca. It's just that—"

"—Alden can't come here."

"I don't know if he's alive," Roger began. "I didn't see him after we split up, but *if* Alden's alive, I know where he'll be."

There was no need for persuading, for she had already made up her mind to leave. On a good day, the pair would cover twenty-five miles without exhausting the horses. Cooler weather nipped at their heels, yet the pair maintained a steady pace. They talked little of Alden or Manny on their journey—it hurt too much—choosing instead to compare experiences and turn away from their own understandings. Both had believed the world was definite and distinct. For Roger, purpose relied on what he could and couldn't control, whether by his faith or fists. For Rebecca, it was found in collections of printed black-and-white. But life's ever-changing complexities wouldn't be easily categorized for either of them: Truths were deemed subjective, and falsities were often necessary. If beauty could be corrupt, then unsightliness had the potential for nobility. Innocence was sometimes illusory, yet those who are worldly *might* be genuine. Good men are capable of wickedness. Bad men are capable of change. Nothing is binary; life exists as an assortment of exquisite greys.

It took thirty days, passing well into October, to reach Gallina, or *Candelaria*, as it was now known. The remote town sat ruggedly along the Chihuahuan Desert—on the elbow of West Texas—with the San Antonio del Bravo riverbed providing a simple path into Mexico. In many ways, the isolated area reminded Rebecca of Brigham, except there was something majestic about its division and lack of disturbance. Hot springs made exaltations in the distant foothills. The surrounding land revealed evidence of cotton farming along a slow-moving stream, and wild honeybees busily contributed to an already inspiring ecosystem. One would know solitude in this place. Stillness.

That's why he chose it.

Positioned along the "funny bone" of the elbow-town was a tiny pioneer house standing at 180 square feet. Roger explained that Alden won the property in a shooting competition twelve years prior and kept the residence registered under a *Joel Maddox*. Not that it mattered; there were less than sixty inhabitants in the town, and they generally kept to themselves. Rebecca scanned the hand-hewed homemade from cantilevered logs of untouched timber, with overhangs on its long, sloping roof fashioned above the horizontal rows of windows, a centered chimney, and a wraparound porch all positioned firmly on four flat rocks. Hitching posts were poised and ready for livestock, but the rustic tableau wouldn't be complete without an oak tree framing the yard, determined to thrive despite Candelaria's climate.

"He built it," Roger shared. "Not all at once, of course. I bet he hired someone to help him with the loft."

"This must have taken him ages..." marveled Rebecca.

Then again, as a Disciple, Alden had nothing but time on his hands.

The team entered the homestead together, with Roger needing to duck his head to fit. They were met with no salutations as they crossed the threshold, just an open layout design of planked flooring and sparse walls. Candlesticks, rugs, and a cast-iron stove were the only fixtures in an otherwise minimalistic—yet multifunctional—space, with a bed in the corner to accompany the neighboring necessities: a chest, table, and two chairs. A ladder in the middle of the room led to a modest loft, though neither felt compared to climbing it. There were books, too, stacks of them. Whitman, Melville, Thoreau, and even the philosophy books Rueben had mentioned. Aristotle, Machiavelli, Plato, and Dostoyevsky conversed friendly at the foot of the bed. Natural lighting had obtained its citizenship, now a permanent resident. It was hardly the fortress of Sanctuary, but the renovated cabin bore originality that was both charming and comfortable.

"Alden worked on this place for years, piece by piece, slipping away anytime he was on the job nearby. There was nobody around to disturb its construction. I only learned about it a few years back. He spent as much time here as he could. It seemed to restore him... Anyway, after Newberry, he stopped."

Roger skimmed through the pages of a Bible on the table, which wasn't as dusty as he thought it would be, considering how much time had passed. His family Bible was in The Colonel's saddlebag, leaving him when the horses fled Newberry. Though it held sentimental value, Roger knew it was only a book, a book he knew well and prayed would fall into the hands of a new owner who needed it more.

"He kept a journal," Roger added. "But my guess is it's hidden away somewhere at Sanctuary."

"I don't want to go back there," said Rebecca.

"Neither do I."

Rebecca opened a molded glass jar on the windowsill, revealing an assortment of sweets. She smiled and retrieved a peppermint stick. While a journal would have provided her with much-needed insight and closure, reading it would've been wrong. *Privacy is precious.*

"I'm sorry that he's not here. I honestly thought he would be. If I'd have seen where he went or..." Roger's voice trailed, replaying the same scenes of that fateful train ride over and over in his mind. As with Newberry, there were elements—details he had missed. He sighed. The finality of this house, of its vacancy, seemed irregular, unbelievable, like a bad dream.

Rebecca twirled the sweetened baton between her fingers, relishing in its escaping essence. What was this feeling of nothingness: bewilderment or denial? It wasn't easy to explain to Roger, who *had* displayed the something-ness she lacked, although he kept it hidden behind his masculinity. As he joined her at the window, Rebecca's eyes searched him. "What happens now?" she asked.

A mighty voice was calling Roger to serve, loud and clear, one that knew no geographical barriers. There were regions all over the state that were spiritually hungry and starving. Circuit riders were long phased out of the evangelical movement, but Roger believed he could still spread the truth—the beautiful, gospel truth, without association.

"The good thing is I can do it anywhere. Everywhere, really. You're welcome to join me, though I can't promise there'll be much to it. In fact, it probably won't be that different from what I did before…"

"You won't be robbing people."

"Yeah, there *is* that," Roger noted with a slight chuckle. Traveling clergymen routinely slept outside or in modest accommodations on routes ranging from six to eight weeks of travel. He would have to modify his appearance and definitely change his name, but as long as he stayed out of large cities and remained on the move, he could do the Lord's work. "We can stay here for a while if you like. If not, I'll take you wherever you want to go. When you're sick of me, just say so, and I'll be on my way."

"I could never be sick of you, Roger."

"Nor I of you," he replied. "I don't mean anything romantic by it, Miss Rebecca. Only—well, you're all I've got."

Rebecca nodded. After several seconds of awkwardness, Roger reached into his coat pocket. He had seen Ranger Everett store Alden's folding knife in a desk drawer before bringing Rebecca to see him. "John would want you to have it."

Trading the candy for the cutter, Rebecca crossed to the nearby table, absent-mindedly opening and closing the knife while she sat as its previous owner had done countless times before. *This was it. This was all that was left.* Memories and a blade, both destined to dull in time. Rebecca willed herself to remember the things she would miss most about Alden: his laugh, the way he would crook an eyebrow, the glint in his eye, the subtle upturn of his lips, and the way those below-the-surface dimples would appear when he tried to hide a smile. That dazzling smile, both gallant and gossamer. Rebecca traced the "J" with her thumb.

John...

She would miss his reckless love and tenderness. How he challenged her, both as the playful partner and a worthy opponent! Would there ever be anyone else?

I don't want anyone else.

Rebecca knew that it would burn, having welcomed the sensation once before, but none of the heroines from her novels had told her of how intense the pain would be—that it would linger. *This* was why Juliet, Isolde, and Cleopatra were desperate to leave this world after their lovers had gone.

When her tears came, Roger placed the peppermint stick on the table and crossed to Rebecca with an anguished expression. Soon, his own beard-staining tears came, "Please don't cry," he pleaded. His voice cracked a bit, having lost that mellifluous tone to grief. A fuzzy old bear on the inside, Roger's bottom lip trembled, and his tears became too much for him. He made no effort to wipe them away.

Rebecca rose to bury her head in Roger's chest. She *needed* to write while the feelings were fresh, while she could still remember how blue Alden's eyes were and how meaningful it had been to learn the stillness of surrender under a midnight sky. But how could she possibly create such prose with adequate meter and rhyme? There were no metaphors, no literary themes to personify her pain.

"I loved him," she whispered.

Roger, ever the protector, brought her in close. "I know. I did, too."

Brotherly love was both impractical and indicative. Even if they were at odds, those sentiments would always circle back to equality, goodwill, and respect. *Loyalty.* Self-sufficiency reigned supreme, but every man craved it. It was why soldiers kept such close interpersonal bonds. Combat forged those connections into the backbone of comradery. They were brothers in arms who bled together, laughed together, and died *together.* Because they had faith in each other, they had faith in themselves. Like Jonathan for his King David, it was the reason Roger went into the fire for Alden.

And I'd do it again.

"Why, Roger?" she sobbed. "Why do we love if it hurts this much?"

Composing himself, Roger collected his thoughts. If he had stopped Alden from taking Rebecca the night of the Rosewood Ball, Alden would have left this world a broken and miserable man. They and their friends would have perished on the train to Grady, and Rebecca forced into a loveless marriage. She already saw herself differently, stronger, and with more value. She'd grown and would continue to grow. Telling Alden's story gave him the freedom he never possessed while living. By sharing his life with others, Rebecca would change what her own life looked like.

"Because love helps us, heals us; it breaks the chains," said Roger as he took her face in his hands. "It won't ever make you less of who you are, only more. It'll make you the best you that you could possibly be. And it never fails. It can't." He then reached into his vest pocket to retrieve a handkerchief, which she graciously accepted. "I need to step out for a minute, Miss Rebecca. Will you be alright on your own?"

"Yes."

Rebecca wiped her eyes with the handkerchief before returning it to its owner, who also required maintenance. Upon his exit, a gust of wind pulled the front door closed behind Roger. Rebecca jumped at the entryway clap and moved to the corner of the room. The bed's soft feather pillow smelled like Alden, and the mattress's embrace felt warmer than she expected, familiar, safe.

Like a promise.